EVERY BEATEN PATH

A NOVEL

SARAH JENKINS

Copyright © 2020 by Sarah Jenkins

All rights reserved. Wayfaring Press LLC.

ISBN: 978-1-7350958-0-6 (hardcover), 978-1-7350958-1-3 (paperback), 978-1-7350958-2-0 (ebook), 978-1-7350958-3-7 (audio)

Scripture quotations from the American Standard Version. Public domain. And the New American Standard Bible®, Copyright © 1960, 1962, 1963, 1968, 1971, 1972, 1973, 1975, 1977, 1995 by The Lockman Foundation. Used by permission. (www.Lockman.org)

Cover design by Karen Fox: kfox@kfpimages.com. Original artwork by Eden LaRue

To my mother who always believed in me, my sweet Landon who taught me how to be a better person, and Jeff who cheered me on and enjoyed every story I wrote whether it was good or not. I miss you all.

Every tomorrow is another opportunity.

—JESS

1

MEMORIES

*T*here were at least one thousand five hundred seventy-two tiny holes in the ceiling tile above Nick Miller's hospital bed. He knew because he'd started counting them to avoid the nightmares that played on an endless loop every time he dozed off.

Nurses buzzed around him, checking vitals, asking questions, but it was all white noise. He only heard the screech of tires and twisting metal against wet asphalt, striking his memories like lightning every time he tried to focus on something else, even those hideous ceiling tiles. He hadn't even noticed the busty blonde from the night shift as she leaned across him to untangle his IV cord. He tried wishing it all away, as though nothing had happened. He cried angry tears when no one was in his room. He would have signed a pact with the devil had good ole Lucifer been able to erase the horror from days before.

He should be dead. It should be his body lying on cold steel in the morgue. Not Jack's. But he was still alive. He still had air going in and out of his lungs. A heart thumping inside his chest. Nick squeezed his eyes shut. *Just make it go away.* But it didn't, and memories flooded back as though pouring from a faucet that wouldn't shut off.

Another nurse barged in, same routine. Nick ignored her, pretending to sleep as she poked and prodded. Then he caught a waft of fragrance, a floral perfume as she changed his IV bag. The scent reminded him of the endless queue of starstruck young girls waiting backstage for autographs before Votive's home-coming show, their last show.

"You remind me of someone." Nick eyed her name badge.

She grinned. "I get that a lot."

He sighed, a kind of laughing sigh, breathy and rhythmic.

"Girlfriend?" she asked, pressing several buttons on the IV unit before turning her full attention to Nick.

"No. Just a girl. No one special . . ." His voice trailed off.

"Well, I hope she's pretty." She straightened the covers around him, tucking them close to his sides.

"Beautiful."

Ink stains were still visible on his fingers, fading into the grooves of his skin. He noticed them as she checked his pulse with a device that looked like a rat trap for his finger and recalled the large blue eyes of a stunning young blonde, flaunting her cleavage as she waited in line for an autograph backstage. Nick had grown accustomed to being propositioned and admired for his celebrity status and sultry voice. He could see her vivacious energy in the blue eyes of the nurse hovering over him, like an apparition of things better left in the past.

"Thinking about that *no one special?*" The nurse broke his concentration.

Nick shrugged.

"Whoever she is, I hope she knows she's got your attention." The nurse left almost as quickly as she had entered, leaving him alone with the blonde girl's image still bouncing around in his head.

I never even asked her name.

She was just another girl in a sea of giggling, screaming, female fans who wanted a chance to touch him, to tell him how much they loved him. He'd signed his name in black permanent marker, on the plunging neckline of her shirt as she'd directed, her intense gaze never diverting from his. This nameless blonde grabbed his hand, begging to be invited back. He'd grinned and tried to pull away as she tugged harder and leaned in to kiss his cheek, inciting jealous gasps from other girls in line. Nick had lingered for a moment, taking inventory of her tight figure, wishing he could stay longer as she pressed her warm body into his.

Now he wished he could go back and erase everything from that night. Well, not everything. It had been one of their best shows. He could still smell the bitter smoke and feel the blazing heat from stage lights and a packed audience thrashing about. He could still hear the screams and cheers rushing through open spaces in the crowd like jubilant waves, and the beautiful echo of die-hard fans singing the words to every song. Nothing compared to the rush of a sea of people shouting his name, glorifying his existence as he held their undivided attention with the sound of his voice and a few harmonious chords strummed wildly on his guitar. He lived for it. He craved it like a drug, and in those hypnotic moments, he was immortal, a Greek god soaring high above his subjects, bending them to his will with the charm of a magical lyre.

He also lived for the sweet taste of Jack Daniels, each gulp burning his throat, lighting a seductive fire inside his belly. He couldn't remember how many bottles they'd emptied that night. As soon as one was gone, a new one found its way into his hands. What he wanted, he got. In Nick's world, the word no was unacceptable.

The echo of silence outside his hospital room sent an eerie

chill through his limbs. He was used to beeping and footsteps, ambient chatter, the sound of rolling wheels against polished floors. His head ached, but every time he closed his eyes his mind raced back to the scene of the crash. So many hazy, fragmented memories, like shards of glass scattered inside his brain. He remembered hanging out with his bandmates after the show: bass player, Jack O'Malley, and drummer, Drew Hutch. He recalled Jack's short-man swagger, sauntering toward him with his usual "I know everything" grin and the bottle of white pills Jack shoved in his hands.

"Here," Jack had said.

"These aren't going to have me singing 'Free Bird' in a karaoke bar like last time, are they?" Nick looked around for a towel to wipe the sweat dripping from his face and neck.

Jack laughed. "I don't know, but I'd pay good money to see that again."

He stumbled, slapping Nick across the back, laughing as he made his way to a leather sofa in the middle of the room.

"Need a towel," Nick called out, waiting for a roadie to throw one in his direction. He was half drenched and still sweating, ready for a change of clothes and a bottle of vodka. He tossed two of Jack's pills down his throat as a white towel suddenly appeared in his other hand.

Nick buried his head in the rough cotton fibers. When he looked up, the beautiful blonde stood before him. Her top seemed lower, more open than it had in the packed hallway hours earlier. She'd been sitting with Jack on the sofa, but it was Nick she wanted. It was Nick she watched with unrelenting eyes. A different girl every night, chasing the lead singer like a prize to be won, but he gave them what they wanted . . . every time.

After that, Nick's memories were hazy, a fog of crew members hauling equipment, hormonal young girls throwing themselves at every man in the room, Drew's wife, Morgan, screaming threats at any tramp coming within two yards of her husband, and the blonde's passionate embrace that lingered until Jack motioned for him to go.

The harder his head pounded, the more his memories came flooding back, battering him on all sides like the beat of Drew's custom drum kit. Nick closed his eyes, recalling their last conversation in the parking lot behind Richland Arena.

"Let's hit Breezes," Jack announced.

"That's a strip club, man." Drew rolled his eyes.

"It's a high-class bar with beautiful ladies," Jack corrected.

"It's an overpriced gentleman's club with two-dollar hookers," Nick shot back.

"Never heard you complain before." Jack finished the last swig of his whiskey, cleared his throat, and spit on the pavement. "I say we cruise Lafayette Street and make the rounds. Best bar scene downtown."

"I'm with Nick," Drew said.

"My rental's all yours. Just return it in one piece." Their manager, Alan Worthing, tossed his keys toward Nick as he walked by with an energetic redhead clinging to his waist. "Leave me a full tank when you're done."

Drew caught the keys one-handed before Nick had a chance.

"Nice catch, man. Guess you have some skills after all," Jack teased.

"Drew's got mad skills. He can play the drums with his eyes closed." Nick grinned, half laughing as they all chuckled.

"I can out drum your hack guitar playing any day, my friend," Drew shot back, prompting loud coos from crew members and those hanging around.

"Burn, Nick!" Jack laughed so hard he nearly choked.

Nick couldn't remember the rest of their banter, the friendly chiding they'd always enjoyed, bandmates and brothers taking on the world. He didn't remember grabbing the keys from Drew or sliding into the driver's seat of Alan's black Mustang GT convertible. But he did remember Morgan's shrill voice screaming outside.

"You are not getting in the car with him!"

"It's fine. We'll just drive around a bit and meet up with you and the girls later. I'll text you." Drew attempted to calm her with his soft voice and steady demeanor.

"I mean it, Drew. He's drunk. He can barely walk. Did you see him? Take the keys. You drive." Morgan's green eyes raged.

"We'll be fine. He's fine. Stop worrying. Go have a good time. We'll meet up later."

"Drew!" She stomped her foot.

Drew kissed her forehead, meeting those angry eyes with a smile, and walked away. Nick remembered Drew squeezing into the back seat and Jack claiming shotgun as he peeled open a new pack of Camels. Morgan's eyes were still glaring when they drove away, music blasting, windows down, flying into the night without a care in the world.

Open lanes graced the interstate, little traffic under a darkened sky. Nick couldn't remember how fast he'd been driving. He barely remembered driving at all, but he could still hear Drew's chuckle and the blended aroma of Jack's cigarettes and Drew's weed filtering through stagnant air inside the car. Even the jumbled audio from blaring commercials and Billboard Top Ten was clearer than the crash itself.

A police officer told him he'd been going over a hundred miles per hour. He only recalled the flashing brake lights from the car in front of him, streaks of glaring red as he plunged his foot against the Mustang's brakes in a moment of incoherent frenzy and conscious panic. The loss of control surged his body into a weightless feeling, a sense of drowning then floating up on the surface of turbulent water.

He only knew what he was being told: their Mustang had

collided with the car in front of them, spun out of control, and crashed into the barrier wall. Had it flipped over? He remembered the sensation of being thrown, of flying through the air, twisting and turning. Random images flashed in and out of his mind, projecting scenes that conjured more agony than any physical injury he'd sustained.

Fighting with sheets and blankets, Nick struggled to find comfort. Every bone and muscle ached. No more jogs down memory lane. He needed sleep. Nick pushed his head deeper into the stacked pillows and looked down at the IV bulging from his arm, observing his limb as it lay motionless beside him, bruised and bandaged. He'd studied that arm before, when the world around him had turned cold and incomprehensible. The image of his bleeding arm nestled among shards of glass, his forehead plastered against the leather steering wheel, was the most coherent visual he'd retained from the accident.

He didn't know how long he'd been staring at his left arm that rainy night, examining every scrape and cut as though it were under a magnifying glass, but soon muffled voices and urgent pleas had encircled him.

"I need a stretcher over here," a female voice shouted.

"There's someone in the back! There's someone in the back!" Rescue workers gathered outside his shattered window.

Overlapping voices buzzed like a crowd of speakers blasting at once, asking questions, giving orders, talking on radios. He couldn't recall their faces, only their desperation.

"Dead on impact . . . Killed instantly." The most haunting words of all had resonated from a gruff baritone.

Nick didn't know until the day after the crash when he'd woken up, disoriented and face-to-face with nurses and hospital staff that Jack had been thrown from the car headfirst through the windshield, his body ejected several yards, landing in front of an onslaught of moving vehicles.

The once pristine Mustang had been cut apart to pull Nick and Drew to safety. He hadn't seen or heard from Drew since he'd woken up.

"He's alive and in ICU," the nurses had told him, but Nick didn't know anything else. He racked his brain imagining Drew's condition. Would he survive? Was he conscious?

Nick twisted the thin sheets of his hospital bed, gripping them until his hand turned bright red. He couldn't control the tears. He gritted his teeth, trying to weep quietly, wishing he'd been the one thrown from that car. Nick slammed his fist against the mattress and then against his thigh, harder and harder until his pleas were no longer silent. He needed physical pain to mask the agony crippling him from within.

He spent the next few days torturing himself and wishing it were all a bad dream, preparing for what would come next, even though he wasn't entirely sure what that would be.

He'd been lucky. His injuries were minor compared to the crash: a mild concussion, several stitches, deep bruising, and a chipped bone in his right leg that ached and throbbed with every movement. Now the catheter was gone. The rat trap removed. One moment he was weeping into a pillow and the next Nick was signing his discharge papers and half listening as a rather bloated nurse went over his home care instructions. They released him to his manager and the overpaid attorneys hired by his record label, who had arranged an apartment in Richland for Nick to recuperate while they sorted everything out.

He limped to the elevator wearing a new pair of jeans and an off-brand shirt Alan had brought to the hospital. He'd probably sent one of his errand boys to pick them out. The jeans were baggy and the shirt was a little shorter than Nick would have liked, but Drew wouldn't care.

Alan was against the idea of him visiting the ICU, but Nick needed to see for himself. He needed confirmation that Drew was still alive, that he hadn't stolen his life too. All he could think about were Jack's final moments, the horror he must have experienced, even if only for a split second.

It seemed like the longest lift he'd ever taken, but it still wasn't enough time to prepare his anxious mind to see Drew lying flaccid in his hospital bed and Morgan's red glare waiting for him outside the door.

"How dare you show your face here." Morgan had seen Nick coming as he rounded the nurse's station, catching him before he could enter her husband's room.

"I just came to see how he's doing," Nick said, peering behind her through the glass window of Drew's room.

Her scowl spoke before the words left her mouth. "How he's doing? You want to know how he's doing?" She slapped Nick across the face. "How are *you* doing? You look great. You look like you can walk right out of here."

Nick avoided her eyes. He pushed his hands inside his pockets to steady them.

"You know I never meant . . ." Nick stopped. He'd never liked Morgan, but seeing the helpless fear in her eyes, knowing Drew was fighting for his life, rendered him speechless.

"You always screw things up. You and Jack both."

"Will he be okay?" Nick mustered the courage to ask.

"Okay? Look at him, Nick!" Morgan pointed just beyond the large glass window of Drew's ICU room. "Does he look okay? He's paralyzed from the waist down! He's a freaking cripple, and it's all your fault!"

Nick said nothing.

"Do you understand what you've done?" Morgan's voice continued to rise, prompting nurses and other staff to intervene.

"I begged him not to get in that car with you! What were you thinking? You've ruined everything!"

A nurse approached, gently placing her arm around Morgan

and urging her into Drew's room. Nick watched them linger at
the foot of the bed. Morgan slumped forward, heaving as she
sobbed and wiped her face on the sleeve of her sweater. He
watched Drew's chest rise and fall with each breath and
wondered how bad his prognosis really was.

Nick should go, but his legs wouldn't guide him. Drew was
the only anchor he had to his life before the accident. If he left
the hospital, he'd be walking into a big unknown, a scary blank
page. He felt safer watching Drew, even with Morgan scowling at
him from the other side of the glass. There was comfort in
familiar things.

A sudden tap on his shoulder pulled Nick from deep thought.
It was Alan. Time to go, but not without one more menacing
glare from Morgan.

He turned to leave and followed Alan until they reached the
parking lot. Tiny drops of rain spit on him from thick, gray
clouds above. They married well with the tear drops Nick blinked
quickly from his eyes as he climbed into the back of Alan's chauf-
feured car. And then it was business as usual, Alan making
phone calls and giving orders while Nick rested his eyes and
murmured, "Wake me up when we get there."

2

GOING HOME

*I*n the months that followed, Nick paid little attention to theatrical ramblings and legal jargon spouted off in a courtroom full of curious citizens, angry family members, and hungry press. Paparazzi and news crews swarmed his every move. Headlines and newscasts boasted sensational reports of his public disaster: "Votive front man Nick Miller accepts plea bargain in DWI case." Ridicule and speculation plastered newsstands and TV broadcasts for weeks.

The final result: No jail time. One-year probation and revocation of his driver's license. That was it. His well-paid lawyers earned their fee, and cemented their own fame in the process.

The judge instructed him not to leave the state during his probation and ordered him to report weekly to his assigned probation officer, but other than that he was free to live his life, or what was left of it. He couldn't help feeling like he'd cheated the system, like he'd just won the biggest hand in the world poker championship by counting cards.

After sentencing, Nick wasted away in his apartment, peering through dusty blinds at press lingering outside, dying to land an interview. He had two items in his fridge, a box of baking soda that had been there when he moved in and a hunk of brisket growing white fuzz. His appetite for food dissipated. His thirst for liquor increased. Every drop of whiskey coated the knife-like pain twisting in his gut. He stood tall with a buzz, spread eagle wings and soared when his brain floated between this world and the next. His heavy heart raced every time he thought about Jack or heard his name on the news, banging against the wall of his chest like a landmine about to go off.

He lay awake at night while moonlit shadows traced pale lines across the wall. When he did sleep, nightmares would wake him, drenched in a cold sweat, reliving the accident over and over. In the deepest recesses of Nick's subconscious, Jack was still alive, laughing and dying all over again. He pointed a bloody finger, cursing Nick for sending him into the abyss. Then Nick would wake, reaching for the bottle on his nightstand, numbing sore muscles, an aching head, and his battered soul.

This vicious cycle became his existence in Richland, in the apartment he hated. He longed to go home, but LA was half a world away and unattainable to a man shackled with probation. He had to find a way to make this new situation work, but he only wanted to climb back in that Mustang and take Jack's place.

The silence of being alone enveloped him like a fierce ocean wave, pulling what little dignity he'd retained into a sea of regret. Walls closed in, narrowing around him. He couldn't go outside without being noticed, he had no one he trusted enough to confide in. Nick's entire existence had catapulted into something he didn't recognize. Anxious thoughts and desperate what-ifs trapped him like a prisoner inside his own mind, no escaping what he'd done, and no one to make it disappear. *Now what?*

He thought about his dad. Why hadn't he come to the hospital? Nick hadn't seen or talked to him since Nick left home nine years ago. Did he care enough to check on him? He would have seen the news. Perhaps too much time had passed. *Maybe I screwed that up too.*

A knock on the door jarred Nick from his thoughts. He glanced toward the window. Daylight. He wasn't sure what day of the week it was, or what time of day. Those details seemed to blend together like sand in a bucket, weighing him down.

Nick opened the door and Alan barged in sporting a designer suit and shoes that probably cost as much as Nick's last royalty check.

"Whoa, Nick. You look rough. Getting any sleep?"

"Not really."

"Let's talk."

Nick closed the door, following Alan into the living room with hesitating steps.

"Your lease is up soon. The label wants to move forward. It's time to start thinking about your future." Alan tapped the screen of his phone as he spoke, engaged in two conversations at once.

"What future, Alan?"

"Yours, Nick. Your career isn't finished just because you lost the band. You need to be writing more songs, get yourself in shape, start thinking about where you go from here." Alan pecked at his phone as though Nick were an afterthought.

"I didn't *lose* the band, Alan. You talk like we broke up. Are you even hearing yourself right now?"

Alan looked up. His receding hairline shimmered in the filtering light coming from each blind on the window.

"I'm not insensitive, Nick. I know what happened, but I'm a businessman. I have other bands to manage, artists to prep for success. You can keep going or quit. I don't coddle. You should know that by now."

Nick resisted an urge to lunge across the room and punch Alan in the throat.

"I don't need coddling. I'm still recovering. Cut me some slack."

"You're better, Nick. You need to get back in the game. Fish or cut bait. I'm here to make money."

"Is that all we were to you? Cash cows?"

Alan snorted and returned to his phone. Nick waited for an answer.

Alan looked up for a moment, then back at his screen. "I don't do charity work. It's a business. Everyone's here to make money. You've made quite a bit." He put down his phone. "You're one of the most talented musicians I've ever worked with. Your name will be in the Hall of Fame one day if you keep going. Are you ready to give that up?"

Nick paced the room. His stomach weighed heavy like it was full of bricks. He needed a drink. He stalled in front of Alan, a slight tremble in his hands, and faced him eye to eye.

"You can't just expect me to get back on stage like nothing happened."

Alan placed a firm hand on Nick's shoulder. "You can't expect your record label to wait around forever."

Nick continued pacing back and forth around the room while Alan rummaged through his kitchen cabinets. Alan found a bottle of Nick's favorite whiskey and poured a generous glass, handing it to Nick with a pat on the back.

"You need to have a plan. Label execs are meeting with us tomorrow."

"Tomorrow?" Nick asked.

"I'll pick you up at nine."

Nick chugged the amber liquid in two large gulps.

"You need a shower, a shave, and some fresh clothes. Get it together, Nick. Big things are coming."

Alan walked toward the door, answering his vibrating phone as he looked back in Nick's direction and nodded.

Nick searched his glass for residual drops of alcohol he might have missed, gazing deeper as though it might offer some mystical powers, a make-shift crystal ball. He didn't want to meet with execs. His heart started pounding again. He could feel the breath being squeezed from his lungs. *I'm not ready for this.*

"Nine o'clock," Alan said, closing the door behind him.

Nick meandered through the apartment, running scenarios through his head like bouncing balls on a roulette wheel. Then he picked up his phone and called his dad. It rang. He hung up. *What am I doing?*

He plunged his body onto the slick cushions of a leather sofa, sliding back to rest his head. He picked up the phone and dialed again. This time he let it ring twice. He hung up again.

Up and down, he paced the floor. He wrestled with himself, unlocking the screen of his phone, then turning it off, over and over, until he gave up and dialed again.

"Hello?" His father's voice echoed in Nick's ear, a forgotten phantom.

He opened his mouth to speak, but nothing came out. What could he possibly say after nine years? He hung up and tossed his phone on the table in front of him. Hearing that voice was strangely comforting, but it also scared him. He wanted to go home. He'd thought about it many times, but pride won out and fear held the upper hand. Going home would mean facing the reasons he'd left.

Nick finished the bottle of whiskey Alan had rescued from his cabinets and fell asleep on his sofa until a sharp knock on his door at nine the next morning.

Alan's long face hovering over him reminded Nick of the look he'd given them the morning they'd showed up late for an interview at an LA radio station. Nick and Jack had been hungover then as well. They'd stayed out too late, playing poker with friends, and Drew had practically dragged them downtown the next morning. Alan's menacing glare that day was nothing compared to the squinty-eyed stare and head shaking he was giving Nick now as he prodded him off the couch, glancing at his watch every two seconds.

"Get up. Get your crap together," Alan chided. "Way to impress, Nick. You look like you've been on a three-day bender."

He forced Nick into a hot shower, a clean T-shirt and jeans, and a quick brush of his teeth before rushing him out to the shiny black Mercedes and driver waiting in the parking lot. They didn't speak much on the way. Alan had both his laptop and his phone out, punching at keys until the tapping noises drove Nick insane. He'd give a kidney for a pair of earbuds and a flask of vodka. They pulled into the garage of a luxury hotel downtown, and Alan escorted him inside to one of the smaller conference rooms.

Nick made eye contact with each of the four stuffy suits seated around a long table in blue chairs, chatting over coffee, their gold Rolex watches reflecting harsh fluorescent light from the ceiling. He knew two of them. They halted their chatter and greetings began. It was all noise to Nick. He'd been in meetings like this before, where guys in suits said grandiose things they didn't really mean. Their fake white smiles and golden spray-tanned skin reminded him how phony this business could be.

"When you're ready, we'd like to back your solo career," one of the execs told him.

"It's time you made an album. It'll be a hit, Nick. The fans love you. It's you they want," another continued.

Nick wasn't ready to hear that. He certainly wasn't ready for the piece of paper they slid across the table in front of him. Too many zeros behind an inflated dollar sign. The number didn't seem real. Too many changes at once. Thoughts were spinning in his head.

"It's a sad thing that happened to your bandmates. We're all sorry to see Votive dissolve this way, but this isn't the end. You still have a lucrative career ahead. We can have you set for a European tour when your probation ends, release your solo album before that if you want. What do you say?"

What could he say? He'd just been offered eight figures to launch himself into a greater pool of fame while his best friend lay buried in the ground and Drew would never walk again.

Nick rubbed a thumb over the glossy paper, staring at numbers that didn't add up. "I can't make a decision like this right now. I need some time." This was a lie. He knew his answer. He couldn't perform, not now, probably never again, but he didn't want them to know that. At least not yet.

"Of course, Nick. We understand you need some time to sort this out. We're prepared to give you that time. You're an asset to this business. I hope you know that."

He was an asset to their wallets. In the seven years since they'd signed with Break Voice Entertainment, Votive had been awarded four multiplatinum albums and had sold out three world tours. *Rolling Stone* listed them number four in the top ten most influential up-and-coming rock bands of the twenty-first century. Nick's gifted song writing, earthy voice, and skilled guitar work had made most of that possible.

"Just don't take too much time. We need to know you're on board, Nick. We need to know we're investing in someone who's going to be a team player," an exec who looked about the same age as him added.

The execs shook hands with Alan, shooting the breeze and babbling about things Nick didn't have any interest in. He continued to stare at the proposal in his hands, the most money he'd ever been offered in one contract. The numbers stared back, reminding him of all the pieces of himself he'd be giving up if he took it.

"Why don't you take some time off, write some new songs,"

Alan said, turning to Nick as the men began to disperse. "We'll schedule another meeting soon."

"I've got nowhere to go."

"I'll ask them to extend the lease."

"No. I hate that place. I'm not going back there." Nick folded his arms across his chest.

"Where do you want to go?"

"You know where I want to go," Nick said.

"LA is off the table as long as you're on probation. You backed yourself into a corner. What do you want me to do?"

Nick considered his options, heart racing again, breath leaving his body faster than he could control it.

"My dad lives in Bridgetown," he blurted out before thinking.

"Sounds charming," Alan said. "Go lay low for a while. Probably less press to hound you there than in the city."

"I'm not sure—"

"I'll arrange for a car to drive you," Alan cut him off. "Stick to your probation meetings. Keep writing songs. I'll be in touch, Nick. Things are looking up."

Easy for you to say.

Nick sat outside his apartment door after Alan dropped him off. He'd had his fill of being alone. Sharing an apartment with his conscience was more excruciating than a conversation with Alan. He didn't like himself enough to be his only companion. Going home would be uncomfortable, painful, but staying in Richland, where he'd killed his best friend, would haunt him until he couldn't take it anymore. He had nowhere else to turn. *I guess it's time to go home.*

3

TUESDAY MORNING COFFEE

*J*ess focused all her attention outside the coffee shop window, refusing to look Mark in his all-knowing eyes.

"You need to talk about it, Jess." Mark sipped his latte, waiting for a response.

Her gaze remained fixed on the woman across the street placing a tiny baby inside a stroller. "Is that why you invite me for coffee each week? You think you're going to open some magic window into my soul?"

"Don't be cynical. I'm concerned. We both are."

"You can tell Elise I'm fine."

Mark released a long, strained sigh. "Am I not supposed to care about your struggles? Look out for you? Protect you? I'm your brother, Jess."

She turned to face him. "You can't save me. I'm not some lost puppy with a wounded paw."

"I never said you were."

"No, but you treat me like a wilted flower about to fall apart any moment. At least trust me to heal on my own terms."

"Hoarding sixty boxes of Pop-Tarts and cases of Abby's favorite snacks isn't normal, Jess."

"What gave you the right to go through my pantry in the first place? It's *my* house, Mark. What makes you an expert on normal?"

"You're not eating, I know you're not sleeping, and I can't remember the last time I heard you laugh."

"Ha, ha, ha. There. Happy? I laughed."

"Cut it out, Jess."

"You can't tell me how to grieve. You can't coach me through it like one of your church members."

"You used to be one of those members." He slid his hand across the table to touch hers.

"That was before my daughter died." She jerked her hand back, returning her gaze to the mother across the street.

"Surely you don't blame God for that?"

"You have your faith, Mark, and I have the lack of mine. Can't we agree to accept each other and move on?"

"It's been a year. You haven't moved on. That's the problem. You need to start living again."

"When I'm ready, okay? It hurts. Is that what you want me to tell you? Every night I lie awake with a gnawing pain in my gut, like I'm being ripped open. There's a giant hole in my heart. It aches, and I don't know if I will ever be myself again. Is that good enough for you?"

He sighed. "It's a start."

"It's garbage. She was too young to die, and I blame *him* for it. He was the one texting another woman while driving our daughter to ballet class. I never should have let her get in that car with him. I should have taken her myself. I'm surrounded by memories and regret and I'm stuck."

"You need to snap out of it."

"Snap out of it? You're telling me to snap out of it?"

Mark leaned forward. "That's not what I meant. I just feel like we keep having the same conversation and I'm tired of going in circles with you."

She withered, slumping farther in her seat as teardrops dotted the front of her cream-colored blouse.

"Jess . . ."

"Forget it, Mark. Just forget it, okay? I tried. I met you for coffee, like I do every Tuesday, and I have tried to be cordial, but you are going to have to accept the fact that your sister is broken. I'm empty without her. She was all I had. I want to hold her again, see those big blue eyes and those sweet, pouty lips. I want to brush her hair, snuggle her into bed. I want to *hold* her."

The floodgates opened and she was powerless to stop each choking sob from coming faster and louder, no matter how hard she pressed her hands to her face.

Mark slid onto the bench next to her, pulling her small frame against his broad shoulders. He held her close, letting her dry her tears on his sleeve, like she had so many times after their parents passed, when she was young and vulnerable and he was the only one around to protect her. Her agony hacked into weaker portions of his heart, becoming his own agony and leaving him defenseless and scared, feelings he couldn't shake no matter how much alpha male bravado he rallied to the surface.

"I'm not the enemy, Jess. You can talk to me. And if you don't feel like talking, you can cry, scream, kick, whatever makes you feel better. I just want to know that you're okay."

"I know," she said between sobs. Jess glanced around the room. A few meddlesome onlookers stared in her direction. Others read books and newspapers, drinking their coffee, ignoring the situation entirely. She pushed away from Mark, salvaging what little dignity she had left after leaving herself so open and exposed in a room full of strangers.

"Let me take you home," he whispered.

She nodded. They drove home in silence. Tree-lined streets signaled the older, historical neighborhoods in Bridgetown before Mark pulled into Jess's driveway.

An elderly woman struggled to carry a large black trash bag toward Jess's bin. She could barely lift it off the ground, but relentlessly tugged and pulled at it, cursing under her breath.

"Looks like Mrs. Timmons is at it again," Mark said.

"That old bat always thinks her trash is mine." Jess opened the car door, glaring back at Mrs. Timmons, whose hands were now firmly planted against her lumpy hips.

Mark pulled his key from the ignition and jumped out to mediate.

"Mrs. Timmons, we've been over this. The newspapers are yours. They deliver them to your address, not mine." Jess snatched the bag from the old woman, stuffing it into her trash bin. She was in no mood to argue with her crazy neighbor who treated possums as if they were pets and had once called the cops on their mailman because she thought he looked like a rapist.

"It's not just the newspapers. It's the trash blowing over from your yard into mine. Don't deny it. I've called the city and reported everything," Mrs. Timmons shook her head and scrunched her lips upward until they nearly reached her nose.

"Look here, old woman. There isn't any trash in my yard to blow over. It's probably from the garbage bags you leave sitting out. I've told you stray dogs will tear into them."

"All right, ladies, I'm sure we can work something out that's acceptable to both parties." Mark stood between them.

"She plays her music too loud at night. Keeps me awake. I can't sleep with that noise," Mrs. Timmons growled.

"I don't play music at night, or at all for that matter. You have completely lost your mind. Alzheimer's, dementia, brain-eating amoeba . . ." Jess crossed her arms in front of her chest.

"Jess, really? This isn't helpful." Mark lifted his brow.

"I know what I hear, loud music every night. It's dreadful."

"Perhaps it's ringing in your ears!" Jess snapped.

"Enough!" Mark demanded.

"You haven't dealt with this for months and months like I have. She's crazy. You're a hateful, old woman and you seriously grate my nerves."

"You grate mine!" Mrs. Timmons balled a fist in front of her face and shook it in Jess's direction.

"Mrs. Timmons, has it ever occurred to you the music might be coming from a different house? And, Jess, perhaps you could help Mrs. Timmons with her trash, even take it to her receptacle for her."

They looked at each other, then back at Mark.

"Maybe. I guess I can keep an eye out for straying trash if she'll agree to stop calling the city on me," Jess replied.

Mrs. Timmons cleared her throat. "All right. Deal. But I know that music is coming from somewhere, and if I find out it's coming from your place, I'll—"

"I assure you it's not! Why would I blast music late at night? It makes no sense."

"You're young. All young people make no sense." Mrs. Timmons shook her fist one last time and wobbled away toward her back yard, mumbling under her breath with each step.

Jess stomped all the way to her front porch, lingering outside the door as Mark followed.

"No invite inside?" he asked.

"I'm tired, Mark. I need a nap. You're welcome to stop by later if you're so inclined, and I'm sure you will be."

"It's ten o'clock in the morning, Jess. Hardly time for a nap."

"If you're wondering why I'm so snippy all the time, it's comments like that."

"I'm con—"

"If you say the word *concerned* one more time . . ."

"*Concerned.* There. Now tell me I'm overly concerned. Tell me I'm taking the big brother routine too far. Jess, everyone goes through trials. Everyone suffers loss at some point in their life. It's not your grief I'm concerned about. It's the way you're handling it."

"Exactly! You don't get to tell me how to handle *my* grief. I'm working it out, but it's on *my* terms, okay?"

He paused. "Okay."

"I know you're trying to help, but you're not."

"I counsel people, remember? I know a thing or two about loss. Don't act like I can't understand what you're going through on some level."

She looked away, blinking tears. "I close my eyes, and I see her playing, laughing, talking to herself like five-year-olds do. I open them and she's gone, vanished, but I can still hear her voice like she's right here with me, like she never left."

"I'm sorry, Jess."

They stood silent on her porch for several moments, neither knowing what to say next.

"If I ask a question, will you not bite my head off for asking it?" Mark said.

"Depends on the question."

"I knew you'd say that. It's the same question I always ask. Will you come to church with us on Sunday?"

Jess resisted rolling her eyes. "If I say maybe and I'll think about it, will you take that as an answer?"

He grinned. "I'll take it."

"I'm happy you're a preacher, Mark, but I don't share your faith."

"You did once," he replied.

"A lot has happened since then."

"So, you'll think about Sunday, and maybe eat a real meal, at least one, for me?"

She rolled her eyes, no resisting this time. "Does spaghetti from a can count?"

"No, it absolutely does not. Come over to the house tomorrow night. Elise is making pork chops. I'm sure there will be pie."

"She always makes a pie," they said in unison.

Jess chuckled, catching herself quickly.

"There's that famous giggle." Mark smiled, big and round like a Cheshire cat.

"Savor it. It's not likely to return anytime soon," she smirked.

"Dinner tomorrow?" he asked again.

"Maybe," she replied.

"Six o'clock." He headed down the steps.

"Maybe," she called out.

"Bring some whipped cream for the pie," he said, smiling back at her before plopping into his car.

Jess watched him drive away. Maybe she would show up for Elise's famous pork chops. Maybe she would stay home and watch videos of Abby's first steps. Maybe she would fall asleep on the couch and dream about braiding that thick brunette hair. Maybe she would wake up and find it had all been a terrible dream.

Maybes were dangerous. Maybes gave hope, and hope was a precious commodity.

4

PRODIGAL SON

The drive from Richland to Bridgetown took about an hour, half of that on a two-lane highway where the speed limit was only fifty, though his driver was doing sixty, maybe seventy. Nick rested his head against the window, keeping low in the back seat, hoping to avoid conversation with the pudgy man who smelled like old aftershave and black jellybeans.

Familiar scenery unfolded as they neared Bridgetown, passing weathered landmarks, faded by time and age. A mix of houses and brick buildings dating back to the Civil War, with modern storefronts and family-owned businesses sprinkled in between. A memory was attached to almost every corner they passed on the way to his childhood home. The library where his mom bounced him on her lap at story time, the ball field where his dad dragged him to watch the Lupton Tire Factory's softball team lose half their games, and the schools where he and Jack walked the halls of their youth all passed by in a flurry before they reached Mozier Boulevard and his father's single-story brick home.

Pulling into the driveway was easy. The idea of seeing his father for the first time in almost a decade twisted Nick's stomach into a hundred knots. He stepped out of the cushy sedan into the hedge-lined yard of his past and tried to breathe through the weight pressing harder in his chest.

Dale Miller stood beside his 1960 Ford pickup, cleaning heavy tools with grease-soaked rags. That old blue truck, parked in the yard, hood open, motor parts scattered in the grass beside it, reminded Nick of every project he'd competed with for his father's attention.

No words passed between them as Nick slung his belongings over both shoulders, making a beeline toward the front door. The driver sped off before Nick was within a yard of Dale. Two dissident glances passed between them, neither willing to make the first move.

You're back, Dale's green eyes whispered. He sighed, watching Nick cross in front of him.

I'd rather be anywhere but here. Nick's glare shouted, avoiding direct eye contact. He hurried into the house before Dale had a chance to say anything.

Inside, heavy air and rotting fruit hit him like a forcefield. Tiny insects circled a bowl of brown bananas on the kitchen table as he passed by, dragging his heavy bags down the hallway to his old room. He opened the door and stepped back in time. Nothing had changed. High school band posters still hung on gloomy walls, and his shabby gray quilt still covered the worn-out twin bed he'd slept on since elementary school. He stood in the doorway, soaking it all in, nostalgia and fear consuming him at once.

A museum of memories had been waiting for his return. His old guitars, the two he'd left behind, collected layers of dust in a corner. He'd brought his favorite acoustic with him, a 1959 Gibson J-45 Sunburst, once owned by Eric Clapton. His girl. His go-to instrument. He'd paid an entire advance for her at auction and she'd been with him during the high points of his career.

Dropping onto the lumpy mattress, Nick removed his Gibson

from her case and strummed a few chords. He held her close, guiding each string like a musical shepherd, humming each note in unison as he slid calloused fingers across her mahogany neck. When he closed his eyes, he pictured Jack sitting on the bed with him, devouring a bag of chips, leaving grease stains on the quilt. Some of those old stains were probably still there. He strummed a little faster, pressing each string a little harder, leaning his body into the moment, caught between memories and a strange new reality he wasn't prepared for.

Music healed him. He found peace in melody, strength in harmony. When life assaulted him from the outside, music defended him like a fortress within. He'd built walls around himself after his mother's death, but music touched a deeper part of his soul no person had ever accessed. He transformed when playing his guitar, a lost wanderer brought home.

Creaking door hinges startled Nick, bringing his music to a halt. Dale stood between wooden frames, watching, waiting for Nick to acknowledge his presence.

"How long are you staying?" he asked.

"Kicking me out already?" Nick replied.

"Wondering what your plans are."

"Yeah, well, I can leave if I'm not welcome."

Nick strummed again softly, closing his eyes to avoid his father.

"You could have called."

He stopped and met Dale's eyes with confidence. "Most people are welcome in their own homes."

"I haven't seen you in nine years," Dale reminded him.

"Whose fault is that?" Nick snapped.

"I'm the one to blame?"

"You weren't much of a father." He continued his strumming.

"Then why are you here?"

Nick lifted his chin high. "I didn't have anywhere else to go."

"So I'm supposed to foot the bill for your bad decisions?"

"Give me a break, Dad. I've got more money than you'll make in a lifetime. I don't need your support. I just need a place to crash."

"They make hotels for that. Apartments, condos . . ."

"Look, I had an apartment in Richland. I just . . . I just need . . ."

"You can't stand being alone." Dale said.

"You think you know me?" Nick's voice rose. "You think raising me for eighteen years, if that's what you want to call it, gives you a clue about who I am and what I need?"

"I never asked you to leave."

"Yeah? Well, I never wanted to stay."

"And yet, here you are."

"If that's a problem I'll go. I'll leave right now. Say it. Make it official, Dad. I'll never come back."

"Where will you go? I saw the news reports. The press won't leave you alone. Maybe you don't deserve to be left alone, but you're not using my house as an escape. If you stay, you pitch in. You carry your weight or you hit the road. Got it?"

Nick's eyes cut like daggers. Resentment swelled inside him, boiling at the edge of his resolve. "I got it."

Dale sighed. He stood there, looking at his son, half inquisitive boy he once knew, half miserable man he'd become. There were so many things he wanted to say, but he didn't know where to begin. He wasn't sure Nick would even listen.

"You hungry?"

Nick snorted. "I know where the kitchen is. I can feed myself."

Nick attacked the strings of his J-45, desperate for distraction, strumming loud enough to drown out Dale's voice, should it resume. He focused all his energy on a song he'd started composing before the crash, when Votive had been working on their fifth album, scheduled to begin recording at the end of their tour. The tour was over. So was Votive.

Stabbing pain burned his chest, his gut churned in agony. Guilt strangled him each time he played one of *their* songs. Jack's face hovered in front of him, smiling prankster, teasing Nick with that know-it-all grin he missed more than their late-night sessions composing songs together.

He reverted to songs of his youth, the core inspiration he'd clung to all those years. He didn't notice when his dad left the room, slipping away unwanted. He kept playing, releasing painful memories with every note.

Nick had blamed his dad when things got heated after his mom's death. He blamed his manager every time something went wrong on tour. Now he blamed himself for everything falling apart. Blame had been a constant in Nick's life, a skill he'd mastered well. He wanted forgiveness, but forgiveness meant forgetting, and there were things he didn't want to forget. He clung to his memories of the past so much sometimes that he failed to participate in the present.

Jack's memory surrounded him like a shadow. Everything Nick touched reminded him of all the years spent in creative harmony with his best friend, long nights, wild parties, their bond with Drew senior year, and the three of them deciding to leave town after high school. He'd met Jack in fourth grade, the year after his mom died. Their friendship had taught him how to laugh and lighten up, to approach the world with confidence. The only confidence he had now was in his ability to screw up.

He locked the door to his room, withdrawing from everything outside. Hating himself and everything, except music. Music held a power over him he had never been able to explain. The only productive thing in his life. The one thing he knew he'd actually done right. Now he needed it more than ever, a lifeline to pull him away from the avalanche swallowing him whole. He buried his head in his hands, searching for some small spark of hope. *I need a reason to keep going.*

5
_____

THE OTHER SIDE

*M*ark had been trying to breech the surface of Jess's grief for almost a year after the brutal accident that killed her husband and five-year-old daughter. Abby had been a ray of hope for him and his wife as they struggled to have a child of their own. He'd cherished every moment with his niece, and the day of the accident had been the most devastating of his life, worse than when his parents died.

His wife, Elise, had knitted sweaters and crocheted socks for Abby. They'd taken her to her first movie, on day trips to the zoo, to visit the airfield to watch single-engine planes take off. Abby was the closest they had ever come to having a daughter of their own.

Mark exhausted all his energy trying to force Jess to open up. Their Tuesday morning coffee dates were becoming more and more frustrating. He'd almost given up inviting her to church, knowing it angered her, but he couldn't seem to help himself from extending just one more invitation. Her trust in him was dissolving and that scared him most. Everything he did caused her to shut down more. He was losing her, and he didn't know how to stop it.

Elise entered the living room of their fully restored, Victorian house, noticing Mark's faraway stare and his size twelve loafers propped on her freshly polished coffee table.

"How'd it go with Jess?"

"How do you think it went?" Mark's broad shoulders sank into the cushions behind him.

"She needs more time."

"How much time? She's wasting away. She barely eats. She only leaves the house when we manage to drag her out to dinner. Her pantry is filled with foods she used to buy for Abby. I'm hanging on by a limb trying to figure out how much time it's actually safe to give her." Mark sat up and leaned forward, resting his arms across his sturdy legs. He thumbed through a stack of home décor magazines on the coffee table, then swiped at the top layer in a burst of irritation.

"What's the alternative?" Elise asked as she bent down to pick up the magazines that had fallen to the floor.

He pondered, admiring her figure as she tidied up. "I don't know."

"You shouldn't. You're not supposed to have all the answers."

"Oh no, here we go. Is this the 'just love her and be patient with her' speech? I could do without that one today." He half grinned, touching the side of her face where loose, honey-colored curls rested against her temples.

"No, it's the 'stop pushing so hard, and let your sister's grief take its natural course' speech." She smiled and put her hand to his.

"That's pretty close to the spiel she gave me."

"She's right. Grief is as individual as the people who suffer it. Everyone approaches it differently. You know that."

"I wish she'd talk to me. I've been the closest person in her life since we were kids. She needs to confide in someone."

Elise sat next to him on the sofa. "And what about you?"

"What about me?"

"You bury your own pain. Perhaps it's a family trait."

"I talk about Abby. I've opened up to you, and others."

"It's not Abby I'm talking about, Mark." She placed a hand on his leg.

Mark looked away. He leaned forward, resting his elbows against his knees. "I talk to God about *that*."

"Good. I wish you would talk to me." Her honest eyes penetrated his resolve.

He looked away and then back again, finally turning his body to face her better, meeting her eyes with sorrow.

"I really thought we had it this time. I really thought this baby was going to be ours."

"It's the birth mother's right to change her mind. A woman should never be forced to give up her child, especially if she can provide a good home." She placed a hand on his back, tracing his shoulder blades gently with her fingers.

"*We* could have given him a good home. We were so close. Four miscarriages, three failed adoptions, and still no closer to having a child than the day we got married."

"Perhaps we aren't meant to be parents." She folded her hands in her lap.

He faced her with bewilderment. "Elise, you've wanted to be a mother as long as I've known you"

"We don't get everything we want." She touched the side of his face, watching flecks of light dance in his hazelnut eyes.

"Preaching to the preacher? Your strength amazes me. I believe you could stare down the barrel of a gun and still form a smile."

"I'm not always as strong as I seem, but I'm realistic. I can't worry about things I have no power to change."

He took her hands into his and hung his head, unable to meet her eyes. "I blame myself sometimes."

"Why?"

"It may sound ridiculous, but I'm your husband. I'm supposed to give you a child. I feel like I've failed in my duty, like I've failed us both."

Tears formed in the corners of her eyes, seeing the pain in Mark's and the burden he must have carried in silence this whole time.

"Your duty is to love me, not give me children. As much as I want to hear incessant crying at three a.m. and have a waste basket full of tiny diapers, God is the one who gives children, and I'm content just living my life with you."

"If everyone shared your faith . . ." He met her eyes again, touching his forehead to hers. "If I'd been given the moon and the stars, it wouldn't compare in any form to the gift I was given when I found you."

She smiled. "Always the poet. We'll get through this together. Please don't blame yourself. Every hardship gives us reasons to hope."

She believed that. Elise had muddled through each excruciating loss with the notion that hope would bring her through. She kept hoping, kept believing, and even when she wanted to break down and cry, she forced on her bravest, strongest face and kept going because the alternative, to her, was as painful as the loss itself.

He kissed her forehead. "There's a sermon in there somewhere."

She laughed. "Don't start telling people I write your sermons for you."

"Only the really good ones." He grinned, squeezing her hand.

They held each other for several moments, comforting each other without words.

"Back to the other thing. Mark, I do think you're pushing Jess too hard. Pull back a little. Let her breathe. Maybe she'll come to you."

Mark nodded. He knew Jess needed time to heal on her own, without her overprotective big brother getting in the way, but he didn't know how to be anything else. When their mother died of breast cancer, he'd held the family together. When their father died a couple years later from a heart attack, he stepped up and became a father figure to his teenaged sister, balancing college classes and home life. He'd always looked out for her. But maybe watching from a distance, letting her take care of herself, was the best thing he could do right now. It might teach him how to love without taking over, without always being the one in control.

6

A QUIET WALK

*N*ick wiped saliva from the corners of his mouth, waking with a familiar hangover banging against his head. He fumbled for a pack of cigarettes on the floor, lighting one quickly, sucking warm smoke inside his lungs. A swig of whiskey floated in an overturned bottle next to his bed. He gulped it, savoring the burning sensation as it glided down his parched throat.

Lying in bed, staring at the half-lit ceiling, Nick pictured the blonde he'd kissed the night of their last show. He hadn't thought much of her since leaving the hospital, but memories of his last night with Jack and Drew circled his mind. He recalled Jack snuggling next to her, his arm around her shoulders, grinning with wide eyes, Jack's best impression of flirting, something he'd always been terrible at. The memory of the look on Jack's face stung Nick to his core, all smiles and joking. That playful gleam reminded Nick of their days off, trips to Lake Tahoe, hikes in Yosemite, beach house dinners with friends, and every moment they'd been free to be themselves, no pretense or show, no need to play the big musician roles they often tired of.

Watching Jack's hopeful countenance hover above him like a ghost, Nick was jolted back to reality by the careless creak of door hinges a few feet away.

Dale stood in the doorway, gripping a coffee mug in his right hand as he observed the piles of trash accumulating in Nick's room and the burnt haze clouding the air around them. "You're not smoking in my house."

Nick rolled over, flicking ash onto the floor. "It's my room."

"I own this house and everything in it. If you don't like the rules, you can leave."

"Give me a break," Nick huffed.

"You can smoke outside. Clean up your liquor bottles while you're at it."

"I'm a grown man. I don't take orders from you."

"Then start acting like one." Dale walked off, down the hall and back to the kitchen toward the smell of eggs and sausage.

Mumbling and cursing, Nick carried his empty bottles to the trash bin out front, more annoyed at being awake before noon than having to smoke outside. He rested on the crooked steps. Loose pieces of concrete wiggled underneath him as he lit another cigarette, watching heavy clouds drift in an overcast sky. Tiny raindrops splattered his skin. He closed his eyes, opening his ears to the sounds of dogs barking, children playing, and the rush of warm air barreling toward him.

"Drink this." Dale appeared as if from nowhere, thrusting a mug of hot coffee in Nick's direction.

He hesitated before taking it. "Thanks."

Dale sat next to him on the top step. They sipped their coffee in silence. The sprinkling rain passed, leaving behind sticky air that smelled like wet dirt. Nick wiped his face and gulped another mouthful of hot, bitter liquid.

"I'm glad you're back." Dale broke the silence.

"Yeah, right," Nick snorted.

"Maybe that's not what you want to hear, but it's the truth."

"Whatever. Nine years, not one phone call, not even a visit. You don't care. You never did."

"It's a two-way street, Nicholas. How many times did you call home? I don't remember any visits. You know what I do remember? How angry you were the day you left, storming out of here like a spoiled brat. I never cared? That's the story you're going with?"

Nick remained silent.

"Still that same selfish kid. I worked my bones to the ground trying to provide a good life for you. You think it was easy raising you alone after your mother died? I worked fourteen-hour shifts at the tire factory to put a roof over your head and food on the table. Maybe that wasn't enough. I did more for you than your mother ever did."

"Spare me your father-of-the-year speech. Things were better when Mom was around."

"Which part, exactly? The days when she was too drunk to get off the couch, or the nights I paced back and forth waiting for her to come home, afraid she'd driven herself into a ditch?"

"I don't need a tour down memory lane," Nick said.

"Probably not. You're doing a great job drowning your memories inside a bottle. Pretty soon you won't have any left." Dale stood up. He took one more sip of coffee and a deep breath before returning inside, letting the storm door slam behind him.

Nick's mind went in hyperdrive. Fuzzy images flashed behind his eyes, scattered memories from the accident still trying to make their way through, bullying him into remembering pieces he wanted to forget. He needed to punch a wall, scream out loud until his lungs hurt. He'd light himself on fire if he thought it might quench the torment swallowing him whole.

He fetched his guitar, strapped it across his chest like an anchor, and went for a walk. Nick strolled the tree-lined streets of nearby neighborhoods, strumming his J-45 and lingering in the fleeting moments of sunshine between drifting clouds. Each path he took opened a different portal to the past. He and Jack had raced their bikes down many of these streets, darting back and forth from road to sidewalk as cars drove by. He passed a spot where Jack had lost control in a moment of distraction and fallen to the ground, scraping a layer of skin from his knee. Jack had pretended it didn't hurt, but Nick had seen the pools of water in his eyes and knew he was just trying to be brave. He recalled the look of fear on Jack's face when he told his dad his new bike needed repairs. Mrs. O'Malley gave them extra brownies that day.

He charted no specific course, only walked forward, playing favorite riffs and pieces of unfinished melodies he hadn't yet written down. The world around him disappeared, blanketed by the remotest corners of his subconscious as he lost himself in the melody of open chords and the ghosts of Bridgetown's past, his past.

Suddenly, a burst of rain showers poured like a fountain, threatening Nick's prized Gibson. He ran for the nearest shelter, a large covered porch of a two-story plantation-style house, like some he'd seen in Charleston on their last tour. He watched streams of rain soak the concrete sidewalk near the house, high-lighting parked cars and darkening the asphalt beside them, then wiped the mahogany with his shirt, examining every inch of his J-45 for damage.

Nick breathed a heavy sigh of relief and caught a glimpse of movement out of the corner of his eye. A slender woman, nestled in an Adirondack chair at the other side of the porch, wrapped tightly in a red crotchet blanket, eyed him with intense curiosity. He stood motionless for a blundering moment that seemed like eternity.

"Sorry. I know I'm trespassing, but I got caught in the rain.

Couldn't let it damage my girl. She's worth a lot of money." He held up his guitar.

Nick waited for a reply, wondering if he should be worried. She didn't respond.

"I'm sure you're not used to random strangers invading your front porch when it rains." He half smiled, nervous and unsure what to do. Rain continued to pour, a death trap to any acoustic guitar. *Should've stayed home.*

"You can play if you want," she spoke.

"You sure? I feel kind of strange, like a criminal or something." He chuckled.

"Are you?"

"What?"

"A criminal?" she said.

"Uh, no."

"Then I'm sure. Doesn't look like the rain will let up for at least a few minutes. You might as well play while you're waiting."

"Um, thank you. I'm Nick, by the way."

"Jess," she replied.

"Short for Jessica?"

"Nope, just Jess."

"Well, Jess, got any requests?" He leaned against the railing.

"My musical tastes are a bit eclectic. I don't really know a lot of new stuff."

"Try me. There's not a whole lot I can't play. I might surprise you."

"Okay. Bob Dylan."

He laughed.

"Why is that funny?" she asked.

He shook his head. "It's not. You just don't look like a Bob Dylan kind of girl."

She arched her right eyebrow, squinting her eyes a little. "What *do* I look like?"

"I guess I had you pegged for a country girl. Carrie Underwood or Miranda Lambert, maybe. I don't know." He fumbled his words.

"I may need to change my look." Jess pulled her blanket tight. Even though it was seventy degrees outside, she stayed cold, chilled from the inside out.

Nick didn't think she needed to change her look. Brunette, fair complexion, hair that fell just above her shoulders in loose waves. She was quite pleasing to look at, and something about her drew him in.

"What do I know? I'm just a guy with a guitar, right?"

"Who isn't playing," she reminded.

"Right, Bob Dylan. Um, okay. How's this one?"

His fingers slid across the bridge, strumming and picking a few strings over the sound hole. Then bursting, as though from an explosion, he broke into full strum, playing Dylan's "Like a Rolling Stone." His body swayed, eyes closed, head bobbing gently to the rhythm of the song. Jess watched him play his girl, intrigued by the melodious courtship he seemed to have with the instrument.

He sang the only words he knew, the chorus. Probably the only words most people knew to that song. What he didn't know, he just made up, amusing himself a little too much in the process.

She smiled, barely, but warm and inviting, a gentle glimmer of contentment in her usually somber countenance.

His singing continued, belting a few scattered verse lyrics out of order and in no way resembling Bob Dylan's masterpiece.

Her smile turned into soft laughter. Then she caught herself, clamping a hand over her mouth. Laughing hurt. It had become a foreign expression, something awkward and uncomfortable that felt wrong and ugly.

He came to a stopping point, strumming a shortened version to the ending.

"You know that song is over six minutes long. I gave you the sample version. It's probably the most famous Dylan song there is. A true classic."

"Impressive. Where'd you learn to play like that?" she asked.

He shrugged. "I grew up playing. Took lessons when I was a kid. Played every day. Just found some proficiency, I guess."

"You have a beautiful voice. Vocal lessons?"

"Not growing up. A few instructors here and there in the studio, but nothing really formal."

"Studio?"

"Uh, yeah, recording studio," he said.

"You've made recordings?"

He chuckled in disbelief. "Don't you know who I am?"

She twisted her face. "Should I?"

"Well, I kind of thought I was a household name."

What had he just said? Nick's ears turned red with embarrassment. If making a fool of oneself were an art form, Nick had mastered it.

"That came out wrong. I'm sorry. I have no idea why I said that. I mean, I, um, a lot of people know who I am, and sometimes I just assume . . . but I shouldn't assume, and obviously I came off like a pretentious snob just then . . ." He trailed off, not knowing what to say next.

Jess buried her face in her knees, trying to hide her amusement.

"Can I start over?" he asked.

She giggled. "Please do."

He walked toward her, holding out his hand. "Hi, I'm Nick Miller. Lead singer and guitarist in a band called Votive." He

stopped. "Well, I was . . . I mean we're not a band anymore, but .
. ."

She shook his hand. "I told you, I don't know any of the
newer stuff. I grew up on big band and Bob Dylan, a little Sinatra
thrown into the mix every once in a while, and a lot of blues."

He backed away. Hearing himself say the words *We're not a*
band anymore tugged at a tender place in his heart. "Sinatra? I
can't help you there." He returned to his guitar, noticing the rain
beginning to clear, but still too wet to leave the dry safety of
Jess's porch.

"Do you know any other Bob Dylan songs?" she asked.

"A few. Got a particular one you'd like to hear?" He couldn't
shake the anger and guilt assaulting him like needles in his chest.
Images of Jack and Drew flooded his mind and he could feel tears
brimming just behind his eyes. The concrete floor of her porch
grew cold with moisture, reminding him of the chilled pavement
the night of the crash. He was instantly drawn back to the shattered Mustang, his skin pressed into a bed of glass with screams
of horror all around him. In that moment, he knew what he had
to play.

"I've got one you'll like. Everyone's favorite. It's been covered
a hundred times."

Sitting back down, right arm draped over his guitar, Nick
proceeded to create the most harmonious sound Jess had ever
heard on an instrument in person. His fingers, gliding effortlessly
across well-worn frets, pressed each string with intended preci-
sion as he sang the poignant words to "Knocking on Heaven's
Door."

She watched Nick play one of the most soulful renditions
she'd ever heard of a song she'd sang with her parents dozens of
times as a child. She noticed the heavy pain behind his eyes, deep
faraway stares, as he crooned each note in perfect key. He sang
with so much intensity, like the words held a hidden meaning,

something painfully familiar. Jess thought of Abby. There was a sad aura in that song, a soul-tugging hook. Tears trickled from her eyes, running a liquid race down flushed cheeks. She hid her weakness, shielding her face against the blanket.

Anguish emanated from every note as he sang. Lyrics of darkness and death, mirrored decisions he'd been making in his own life, wandering so far off the trail he didn't recognize where he was. Didn't recognize himself.

When his playing slowed and the song came to an end, they sat in silence. Jess didn't know what to say. Her chest felt heavy. She didn't want to cry in front of a stranger.

Nick had disappeared in a memory of Jack signing autographs outside a TV interview when they released their second album. A nervous fan had dropped her bag. Jack retrieved it for her, making extra small talk to calm her nerves. He was the guy who made everyone feel important, even Nick when he was plagued with self-doubts.

Rain showers had passed. Rays of sun peaked over Jess's house, reviving streaks of midday light. He feared facing her with watery eyes, showing his vulnerability to a woman he'd just met, but when he did, he saw that hers were the same.

"Did I upset you?"

"No, I'm fine. I'm going inside now. Thank you for playing." She headed for the front door.

"Thank you for letting me." His legs refused to move, forcing him to stand motionless, unsure what to do next.

Just inside the door, holding it partially open, Jess faced him halfway, but she didn't meet his eyes. "You should stop by again sometime. I really enjoyed your music." She disappeared inside the house.

Nick stared at her door for several seconds, a rich shade of cerulean blue with a bronze knocker below three-square panes of glass. That had been one of Jack's favorite colors. He'd ordered a custom bass in a similar shade, one he played often and never let anyone else touch except for Nick. He wished he had that bass with him. Then he wondered what became of Jack's other belongings. They were probably turned over to his parents. Or perhaps they were still at his house in LA, two doors down from Nick's lonely beachfront condo he wished he could go back to.

He wrapped the guitar strap over his shoulder and bolted down the steps, strumming old favorites as he walked. He would take the long way home and clear his head, explore other familiar places from his childhood. He was in no hurry to get home and brush shoulders with his dad again.

7

THE PAST RETURNS

*D*ale rested rough elbows against the kitchen table, feasting on a dinner of baked chicken, mashed potatoes, and sautéed green beans. There had been mushrooms, but scorched fungi don't make for good eats. He could still smell them wafting from the trash can. The chicken needed more salt, but it wasn't bad for a new recipe.

The front door opened and closed. Footsteps grew closer, and Dale never looked up as Nick passed by the kitchen on the way to his bedroom.

"Saved you a plate."

Nick eyed the dish of steaming food next to his father. "Thanks, I'm not hungry."

"A belly full of liquor won't keep you full, son," Dale called toward the hallway as Nick disappeared into his room.

He reappeared seconds later, hovering in the doorway with sour eyes and gritted teeth. "I haven't had a drink today. Not that I need to report to you. Why don't you think of me as a tenant? I'll even pay rent if that's an issue."

"I'm not a landlord. I didn't ask for a tenant. Sit down and eat this food so it doesn't go to waste."

Nick couldn't think of any quippy remarks. He shuffled toward the table, shaking his head, and kicked out a chair, dropping down in a huff.

"If it's cold, there's a microwave behind you," Dale said.

Nick picked at the mass of food on his plate. "I know where everything is."

"Salt?" Dale held out a shaker.

"Enough with the small talk. Can we not pretend everything is okay between us?"

"Who's pretending? I offered salt," Dale said.

"I don't want any salt!"

Dale inhaled slowly and exhaled out. "Why are you here, Nicholas?"

"Didn't we already have this discussion? And don't call me Nicholas. I haven't been called that since I left home."

"That *is* your name. Am I supposed to call you Nick?"

"Just forget it!" Nick shoved his chair away from the table, standing up in a fury.

"Sit down." Dale grabbed his arm.

Nick dropped onto the chair. He'd do anything not to have this conversation.

"What's happened to you?" Dale asked.

"I'm not doing this with you. I'm not." He jumped up, almost knocking his chair over, jarring the table enough to spill Dale's tea and turn over the saltshaker.

"I want to help, Nicholas."

"Why? Why the sudden concern? What is it you think you can possibly do for me? What makes you think I even need help?"

"I watch the news. You were driving a hundred and twenty

miles an hour down the interstate. Your blood alcohol level was point one five. Do you have any idea how dangerous that is?"

"Do you? You don't even have a beer in your fridge. Have you even been drunk?"

"We aren't talking about me," Dale answered.

"Why not? Let's talk about you. Let's talk about all the nights I spent alone. You worked all the time, and when you weren't working at that godforsaken factory, you were tinkering with one of your stupid projects, an old vehicle, a motorcycle, anything but checking in on me."

"I did the best I could after your mother died. You can't possibly blame me for your screw-ups. You've made your choices. You have no one to blame but yourself. You're just like your mother." He pointed a sharp finger in Nick's direction.

"Good. I'll take that as a compliment. I'd rather be like her than you!"

"Would you?" Dale stood up, shoving his chair under the table. He wanted to shove Nick, hold him by his collarbone and shake him. "You want to be just like her? So wasted you can't stand up on your own? Falling down so much that people mistake your bruises for abuse? Unable to form a coherent thought or speak a clear sentence? That's what you want to be? Having everyone who loves you scared to death they'll get a phone call saying you've been in an accident, and then, God forbid, it actually happens and that phone call comes at three in the morning . . ." His voice shook. His chest rose and fell with every quickened breath. He would not lose his son like he had Lenore.

Nick paced the floor, kicking at things, looking for something to hit, to punish as much as he was being punished. "She was a good mother. She was kind, and funny, and smart. I remember her, Dad. She made people laugh. She grew vegetables in the backyard—"

"You don't remember everything."

"I remember the crash," Nick replied.

"Do you? I know I do. That phone call changed my life forever. I jumped up, frantically throwing clothes on to wake my eight-year-old son and get to the hospital as quick as I could, but you weren't in your room. You were supposed to be sleeping. It was the middle of the night."

"She woke me up." Nick stared at the floor, recalling scenes he'd tried to bury, scenes that often found their way into his dreams and at moments when he was alone with nothing to distract him. "She said we needed to go for ice cream. I remember her laughing, wearing only a long shirt, no pants, no shoes."

"She was drunk, Nicholas. She was always drunk."

"I was on the floorboard of her car. Paramedics pulled me out. I never saw her."

"It's better that you didn't. It was bad. It's a miracle you survived." Dale paused. "If you'd been anywhere else in that vehicle . . ."

Nick looked up and saw the bitter gloom behind his father's eyes. He didn't know what to say. It didn't change the loneliness, the distance between them. They viewed those years quite differently, as though each lived a parallel story in the same house.

"Nicholas . . . Nick . . ." Dale broke the silence. "There were a lot of things you didn't see as a kid. Things I shielded you from. Your mother was sick for a long time. There were nights I didn't sleep, holding her head in my lap on the bathroom floor so she wouldn't choke on her vomit. She had violent outbursts, some of which she tried to take out on you, but I always stood in the way. I bore whatever I could to protect you. When she died, I did everything I could to hold it all together. You'd think things would have gotten easier, but they didn't. The older you got, the more resentful you became."

"I missed her. I needed *you*. You weren't here! Even when you were physically here, you never wanted to talk about it. You were too busy with other things, hanging out with your car buddies, working insanely long hours. I grew up alone."

Dale waited, searching for the right words. He couldn't express the desperation he'd felt then and now. He rubbed his neatly trimmed, graying beard and gave up. "I'm sorry you felt that way. I don't know what to say. I was here. I took you with me to car shows. I had you work alongside me under the hood of every restoration project. I took you to fairs and carnivals, and came to every pageant you had at school. If you don't remember me being there for you, then I'm at a loss for words. I've always been here . . . as much as I could be."

Nick stared at a rip in the old linoleum floor, rubbing and picking at it with his shoe. His shoulders drooped, hanging lower and lower. "You weren't at the hospital."

Dale turned away. He leaned against the sink, hanging his head.

"I was there for almost a week. You said you watched the news, but you didn't care enough to see if I was okay?"

Dale opened his mouth to speak, but he didn't trust the right words to come out. Everything he'd said seemed to be wrong, seemed to make Nick angrier.

"What if I had died? Would you have even held a funeral?"

Dale couldn't hide his watery eyes. He looked up, weary and ashamed. "I was there. I did come."

"When?"

"First I heard of it, I went straight to the hospital. I stood outside your room and . . ."

"And what? Didn't have the courage to come in and face me like a man?"

"You weren't behaving like a man!" He slammed his hand

against the counter. "You were angry and bitter, arguing with a police officer . . ." Dale's voice trailed off. "You were . . ."

"I was what?"

Dale took a deep breath. "You were okay." He exhaled. "You were going to live and I tried to step inside that room, but what was I going to say?" He shook his head. "You just chewed my head off for offering you salt. What would you have said if I'd been brave enough to walk in that hospital room?"

Nick tried to make sense of this revelation. He didn't understand how they'd gotten to this point, two strangers who knew each other so well, yet hardly at all. He stood there, moving his head back and forth, searching for some great comeback, a wise Shakespearean insult to rail at his father. He came up empty. They'd run out of words to hurl at each other.

"I'm here now," Dale said.

Nick met his eyes with scorn. "So what? Is that my consolation prize? No thank you." He walked out, huffing and muttering under his breath.

Dale flinched as the door to Nick's bedroom slammed behind him. Such a familiar, haunting sound. He lamented all the things he could have done differently, should have done differently. *Am I a coward?* He should have been by Nick's side at the hospital. Guilty or not, he needed someone there with him. Dale had failed him in that moment. It was too painful. He was too scared and stubborn.

Dale cleaned up the spilled tea and salt and sat down to a plate of cold food. He stared at Nick's plate across from him. They were strangers. Two cold plates on the same table with nothing more in common than genetics.

8

NEW FRIENDS

*C*hurch was fine for some people, but Jess resisted it, uncomfortable no matter which pew she sat in. She had believed in God at one point. Mark had convinced her of his all-knowing hero after he became a believer in college. Now she partially blamed this God for the painful things beyond her control, the lives he could have saved if he wanted to. First her parents, now her daughter. This all-powerful being had failed to protect the people she cared about most.

Mark stood at the pulpit, motioning with his hands. His words didn't register. She didn't want to hear them. She'd only agreed to be there so Mark and Elise would stop hounding her. Elise didn't hound so much as quietly goad. Still, they had both been unwavering in their attempts to encourage her church attendance.

Mark read from John chapter four, delivering a sermon about worship. "God is spirit, and those who worship him must worship in spirit and truth."

Jess heard only muddled words, focusing her attention on tiny dust particles highlighted by rays of light streaming through the windows of the small auditorium. *What if your spirit is broken or unwilling?* she thought to herself. *What if you aren't sure what truth really is?*

She waited patiently as Mark went on and on, commentating and cross-referencing scriptures. She wanted to go home, curl up on the sofa, and fall asleep. Sleep had become her closest ally. The iPad she carried from room to room, played home videos of Abby on continuous loop until the battery died. One short charging session later, and the cycle resumed all over again. Repetition had served her well the last several months.

The service ended before she realized the final song had been sung. Well-dressed bodies emerged from wooden pews, gabbing and gawking. Jess remained seated, watching the sea of people maneuver back and forth, their conversations nothing more than a jumbled mass of random phrases and sounds floating in and out of her ears.

"Don't you look lovely today, dear." An older woman leaned toward her, smiling with crooked teeth.

Jess smiled back, feigning amiable when she'd rather display her biggest sneer.

"We're so glad you came this morning," the woman continued.

Jess looked around for Mark and Elise, finding them engaged in conversation with a young couple across the room. She brushed past the old woman and slinked into the foyer, away from unwanted pleasantries, where she waited by an exit, wringing her hands and focusing all her energy on controlling her breath to avoid a panic attack. The rhythm of her heart pounded each time someone approached her. Social graces had not been a strong suit since the accident. Once full of bubbly life and humor, Jess now vacillated between empty shell and bitter cynic.

"I hope you'll let us take you to lunch." Elise appeared beside her, resting a hand on Jess's back.

"I'm not hungry," Jess replied.

"You could keep us company while we eat. We just want to spend time with you, Jess."

"Of course you do." She didn't look Elise in the eye. Instead, she folded her arms in front of her chest, focusing her attention on a rather odd-looking plant stuffed into a brass pot across the narrow foyer.

"Ready?" Mark said, breezing up beside them moments later.

The short ride to Sauer's Family Restaurant seemed to last forever. Jess counted every car and building they passed along the way, dreading the crowded dining room full of smiling families dressed in their Sunday best, sharing food, and laughing at each other's jokes.

The waitress seated them in a back corner, between two windows, affording Jess an unhindered view of everyone and everything in the restaurant.

"Two sweet teas," Mark told the waitress. "Jess?"

She looked up, eyeing the curly headed woman. "Water."

The waitress slipped away and Mark began probing his sister. "How was service?"

"Fine." She sighed.

"Did you speak to anyone? I saw Mrs. Grainger talking to you."

"Can we not do this?" Jess angled her tense body, shielding herself from as much human contact as possible.

"Thank you for coming with us, Jess. It means a lot." Elise smiled, trying her best to break the tension between the two of them.

"I'm tired of walking on eggshells around you. Nothing I say is good enough. Stop shutting us out," Mark snapped.

The waitress returned with tall glasses, already wet with condensation.

"You think I'm trying to shut you out? I'm just trying to make it through the day without falling apart. Death doesn't come with an instruction manual, Mark."

"That's not what he meant." Elise inserted.

"You can't mope around, giving up on life," Mark continued.

"I can do whatever I want. You can't just corner people all the time, forcing your little grief counseling intervention sessions on them." She folded her arms across her chest. "Take me home."

"No," Mark said.

"No?" Jess replied.

"This isn't you. You were never like this. I can't . . . *we* can't stand to see you this way."

"It's not a choice," Jess said.

The waitress reappeared to take their orders, but Jess didn't want anything. Mark ordered for her. She could eat it or take it home to rot in her fridge. He didn't care which.

The room buzzed with laughter, clinking dishes, and lively conversations. Jess eyed a clear path to the nearest exit, estimating how many steps it would take to make it out the door.

"Jess, we love you. We have good intentions." Elise took a sip of her tea, attempting to remain as neutral as she could.

"She knows that," Mark huffed, throwing his hands in the air.

"Can we please stop talking about this? I'm tired, I'm frustrated, and I'm sitting in a room full of happy people. I just want to be left alone."

"That's not what you need," Mark snapped.

"Mark . . .," Elise cautioned, placing her hand on Mark's arm. The veins on his temples were swelling.

"She can't cut herself off from the world."

"You don't get to decide this for me." Jess's breathing quickened, becoming shallow and frantic.

"We understand what you're going through," Elise whispered.

Jess met her eyes with a sharp glare. "How could you possibly understand? You've never lost a child. You have no idea what I'm going through."

No sooner had those harmful words left her mouth than Jess realized what she'd said. Too late to take it back, Jess clenched her jaw, slinking farther in her seat, coiling into an imaginary ball and closing herself off from everyone and everything around her.

"How could you say that? How dare you say that to her." Mark pounded the table with an open hand.

"It's okay," Elise said.

"No, it's not," Mark huffed.

No one spoke a word until the waitress returned with their plates. Jess picked and jabbed at the breaded chicken smothered in gravy that looked like a gelatinous river oozing over the deep-fried edges. She tried to eat but the thought of food made her queasy. She ate random meals here and there, but even her favorite foods tasted like cardboard.

Mark paid the bill while Jess and Elise walked out to the car. Jess needed this day to be over. She climbed in the back seat, reluctant and resentful. She could hear Mark's quiet exasperation on the ride home; his deep breaths and occasional head shaking only fueled her resentment more. He seemed to be holding back a multitude of comments and observations he'd like to unleash at her, but his stiff silence said enough. When they pulled into Jess's driveway, Elise opted to wait in the car. Mark walked her to the door and Jess kept two steps ahead, hoping to barricade herself inside the house before he had a chance to say anything else.

The beautiful hum of guitar strings carried by a light breeze gripped her as they neared her porch. Nick sat in the same place he had before, strumming his J-45 with such intensity he didn't seem to notice them approaching.

A faint glimmer appeared in Jess's eyes, a softness in her cheeks and posture when she saw him, and Mark noticed. "Who are you?" Mark said, stopping near the top step.

Nick looked up, about to speak, but Jess beat him to it. "His name is Nick. This is my brother, Mark."

Nick stood up, holding out a hand. "Nick Miller."

Mark glanced at the hand before him, offering his own while he looked the younger man over; blond hair, blue eyes, unshaven face, thin T-shirt, faded jeans. "What are you doing on my sister's porch?"

"She told me I could come by and play again, so—"

"Again?"

Jess turned toward the door. "I invited him." She disappeared inside the house, leaving Nick to fend for himself.

"I know who you are. You're Dale Miller's son," Mark said.

Nick shrugged. "Yeah, everyone knows Dale."

Mark studied him, scrutinizing every gesture. "Quite a mess you've gotten yourself into."

Nick was silent, searching for a safe response.

"I'm an evening news with dinner kind of guy. Morning news with breakfast," Mark said, tilting his head slightly forward.

There it was. His past would follow him no matter where he went or who he met. Plastered over every media outlet in the world, his face had become synonymous with bad decision making, a poster boy for how not to live your life.

"Yeah, well, I guess I'm going to go." Nick moved forward.

"How did you two meet?"

Should he answer that question? Mark had the menacing presence of a mountain lion guarding its cubs. Nick tensed his shoulders. He had to say something.

"It was raining. I took shelter to protect my guitar. Accidental trespassing turned into a solo concert." He laughed, nervous and awkward.

"She doesn't need any trouble," Mark said.

Nick inched his foot closer to the edge of the steps. "I don't plan on causing any."

"She doesn't need any complications either," Mark asserted.

Nick faced the mountain lion. "Well then, we might have a bit of an issue because complications tend to follow me around."

Jess returned, sitting down in her favorite chair, red blanket swaddling her thin frame. Both men looked in her direction, then back at each other.

"I'm sure Elise appreciates waiting alone in the car," Jess said.

Mark wondered how he'd come to this moment, an inconvenience to his only remaining blood relative.

"I'll pick you up. Tuesday. Same time." He eyed Nick once more, conjuring his best scary big brother grimace and headed toward the car.

"Of course you will," Jess said under her breath.

"What happens Tuesday?" Nick asked, watching the car pull out of the driveway. He turned back around. "That's none of my business."

"It's okay. Mark takes me out for coffee on Tuesday mornings."

"That's nice," he said.

"Not really, but it's a compromise."

"Ah, compromises—gotta love 'em. My biggest compromise right now is living back home with my dad. I can think of a million places I'd rather be, but it's complicated, and in a hurried moment it seemed like the only place to go. So I'm twenty-seven and I sleep in a room with all my high school band posters taped to the wall. How's that for compromise? More like pathetic."

She watched him tune his guitar, using his ears to test the sound.

"Doesn't seem so bad," she said.

"It would if you knew my dad." He paused. "No, that's not true. He's not so bad, I guess. It's me really. I'm a big disappointment. Coming home has reminded both of us how much we've lost."

He finished tuning the last two strings. Glancing up, he caught her watching him, curious and patient. He was different with her. She didn't seem to care about his fame. She seemed genuinely interested in what he was doing and what he had to say. He was suddenly more aware of himself, his real self. He'd only let his guard down like that with Jack and Drew.

"Look at me spilling my guts to a stranger. Do you have this effect on everyone?"

"What effect?" she asked.

"I don't know. That disarming quality that makes people comfortable enough to talk about anything even though they don't know you. Like a bartender."

She chuckled. "I'm not sure I've ever been compared to a bartender. My brother accuses me of not opening up, keeping everything bottled. He doesn't find me so easy to talk to."

Nick joined her, sitting in the chair next to hers. He strummed a few random chords, checking the key.

"How do you do that?"

"What?" he asked

"Tune your guitar without some high-tech device."

He smiled. "I've been doing this a long time. I don't know, you just get a feel for it, an ear for it. You know?"

"I don't have a musical bone in my body."

"Everyone has some form of musical ability, even if it's just appreciation for the sound. Playing an instrument is as much about feeling as it is theory and technique. It's an instinct. Like the guitar has a soul, there's a connection, and we feed off each other." He laughed. "I mean, not really, of course. Guitars and instruments don't have souls, but metaphorically speaking, if they did, that's as close as I can describe what it's like."

She watched him with continued curiosity.

"You think I'm crazy," he said.

"No, just listening. I think it's incredible how you can play like you do, or any musician can, for that matter. I've never had the discipline or the inclination."

He met her eyes, trying to decide if they were green or blue. A little of both, he thought.

"Music is my life. It keeps me sane. Helps me cope. When I'm playing, everything feels right. Pain is easier to handle. It's thera-peutic." He swallowed hard, thinking about Jack and Drew. He thought about his entire life thus far, it's lack of meaning or having any significance. He'd stamped his mark on the world, but he had nothing to show for it except a bank account full of money and a laundry list of regret.

"Pain is such a relative term," her voice drifted.

Nick noted the sound of sadness she seemed to echo, the quiet solitude of her composure. He didn't ask questions. He had no right, no place, but he wondered if she'd been through some-thing terrible. He wondered if maybe he'd found someone who might understand what he was going through, but he dismissed that notion. No one could understand what he had done.

"They say it's all about how you deal with it, right?" he said.

"How do you deal with it?" she asked.

He thought about his answer before replying. "Bottle of Jack, a few shots of vodka, sleep till noon. Probably not the answer you wanted to hear. I'm not the best example for coping with life. I certainly haven't done a very good job of it."

"You're still young," she said.

He laughed. "Not that young. Nearly thirty. Close enough anyway. How old are you?"

"Thirty-four," she replied.

"Guess I shouldn't have asked you that."

She shook her head. "I don't think it's rude to ask a woman her age. Her weight is another matter."

"I might be stupid about some things, but I know better than to ask a woman how much she weighs." He chuckled and noticed a warm smile growing across her face. He could sit there all day, staring at her, lost in the charm of her simple beauty, a girl next door with haunting eyes. Then he realized he really had been staring, a bit too long, and looked away quickly, trying to save face.

"So, thirty-four, huh?"

"Yep."

"Teenager in the nineties?"

She arched an eyebrow, pulling her blanket closer. "I'm scared to ask where this is going."

He laughed again. "I was just thinking you were old enough to really enjoy one of the defining decades of rock music. So many great influences that have shaped everything since. I was too young to appreciate the artistry, the sheer mastery of that era."

Her eyebrow remained arched, mouth curled at one corner. "I have no idea what you're referring to."

"Ah, come on. Nineties alternative rock? Grunge rock? Pearl Jam, Nirvana, Alice in Chains, STP?"

She concealed a grin, shaking her head.

"Nothing?" He searched for any hint of recognition.

"I told you I don't know new music."

"Compared to Bob Dylan, I guess you could call this new, but we're talking classics here. *Ten*, the greatest album of Pearl Jam's career, the one that paved the way for practically every alternative rock album after it. Okay, that's opinion, but it's a valid opinion."

"Like I told you before, my musical knowledge is very limited.

I'll admit it. I'm a musical bore, an ignoramus of tunes." Jess shrugged.

"I'm sure you're anything but boring." He met her eyes and didn't look away.

"So, what am I missing? Show me this defining decade I apparently slept through."

"Brace yourself. You're in for something truly fantastic. Not that I had anything to do with it." He lowered his head, strumming a few chords, picking at single strings in melodic patterns.

His fingers formed what seemed like random shapes. Jess watched each fingertip slide and move onto different strings and frets as he struck a pick up and down across the sound hole, vibrant tones emerging. He bobbed his head, rocking his body back and forth. His foot tapped the concrete floor of the porch. Each movement natural, yet so perfectly timed to the music and echo of each chord.

When he opened his mouth, words escaped. Passion fueled the melody. His body swayed faster, sharp jerks bending to the rhythm. Jess studied his demeanor, his pursed lips and closed eyes, examining his intensity, like he owned each note. His touch seemed to enchant each string, bending them to his will, each sound his own mystical conjuring.

He sang louder as the song progressed, each word wrapped in deeper meaning. When he finished playing, with one final strum, he took a deep breath, looked up, and smiled. "'Alive,' by Pearl Jam. Released in 1991, but that was the acoustic version from their 1992 Unplugged concert."

Jess marveled. "You play with such spirit, like you're a part of the music."

"I connected with music at a very young age. My mom had me taking piano lessons when I was five or six, convinced I'd be the next Chopin. It was the guitar I connected with most.

Snagged up my first beaten-up acoustic at a thrift store when I was eight."

"I envy that. Being able to pick up an instrument and play it. I can't even carry a tune," she said.

"My mom died when I was eight, and my dad worked a lot. We handled that loss in very different ways. It was pretty much my guitar that kept me company. Then I discovered all this amazing music that really spoke to me and I couldn't stop playing. I think I wore my dad out, disappointed him a little."

"How so?" she asked.

"He's a big Eric Clapton fan. Raised me to be one, and I am, but I kind of pushed Clapton aside for Eddie Vedder. The song I just played for you, Vedder wrote it about himself, about the moment his mom told him his dad wasn't really his dad after all and that his real father had passed away."

"That's terrible. I can't imagine not being given the opportunity to know one of my parents. It must have been devastating to lose your mom when you were so young. What happened?"

"Car accident. She'd been drinking. Wrapped her car around a tree."

Jess didn't know what to say. The mention of car accidents always sent chills down her spine.

"I survived," he said.

"You were in the car?" A look of horror crossed her face.

"Yeah."

The porch became silent. Jess closed her eyes, breathing in warm air. She focused her mind on anything but Patrick and Abby.

"Play something else," she said, eyes still closed.

"Okay." Nick pulled his guitar closer to his chest. "How about Nirvana?"

She shrugged. "Sure. I wouldn't know it anyway."

"We're going to change that. Your music catalogue is about to expand. This one is called 'All Apologies.'"

He played with the same intensity he had before, this time gentler. His presence relaxed to match the tone of the music. His vocals bellowed the urgency of the lyrics.

Jess leaned against the back of her chair, straightening sore muscles. In that moment she had peace. The deep vibration of tightened strings lulled her thoughts away from the endless cycle of grieving. For the first time in months she enjoyed the summer breeze sweeping across her skin and the sound of branches swaying on the old magnolia tree near the porch. An escaping tear didn't bother her. It rolled away, disappearing into the fibers of her blanket.

They sat together, musician and audience, until Nick stopped playing. He'd run the gamut of nineties rock culture. In a matter of minutes, he'd served as tour guide for every musically inspired moment of his life. Locked inside every note, a little piece of himself emerged, puzzle fragments of the broken man he'd become.

Strumming the final chords of his last song, "Glycerine," by Bush, Nick poured his heart into each word. The music moved him to deeper feelings than words could express.

"That's a beautiful song," she said.

"Jack used to make fun of me when I played it. Called me a big teddy bear, a softy." He laughed under his breath.

"Who's Jack?"

Nick looked up. Lost in the moment, he'd forgotten he was speaking to someone who didn't even know who Jack was. "A friend. Bandmate. A really good guy." He pushed the guitar away from his body and propped it against the porch rail beside him.

"What instrument does he play?" she asked.

"Can I use your bathroom?"

Nick avoided the question. Though he really did have to go.

The beers from earlier were kicking in and it seemed the perfect escape from having to talk about Jack.

"Um, sure. I guess." She motioned him inside, guiding him to a bathroom near the stairs.

It seemed such a large house for one person. The small half-bath showed no evidence of use. Dust collected in corners. Sink dry. Hand soap unopened. Toilet paper still in its package.

When he walked out, he noticed a family portrait hanging in the foyer above an antique buffet table. In it, Jess sat next to a dark-haired man, both smiling, leaning against each other in what looked like an open field. A little girl, probably two, with thick brown hair curled at the ends, sat in front of them, propping one arm against Jess's knee. Her tiny smile lit up the entire picture, causing Nick to smile too.

Footsteps shuffled nearby. He glanced to his right. Jess stood near the stairs, watching him.

"Is this your family?" he asked.

Her eyes glazed with tears and she turned away.

"Is that that your daughter? She's beautiful," he said, wondering why she didn't answer. "She has your eyes, and your smile."

"You should go." Jess held her breath, hoping he would walk out. No goodbyes, just leave, and leave quickly.

Instead, Nick walked right up to her, trying his best to make eye contact. "Did I say something wrong?"

"I'm tired. You need to go . . ." Jess avoided his compassionate gaze. Her voice trailed off, waning under strangled breath.

"Okay. Thank you for, um, I guess I'll see you soon, maybe?" Nick stammered for the right words, but he didn't know what had caused this sudden shift in mood.

"Maybe," Jess replied. "Now please go."

He walked out, hearing the door close behind him. His guitar waited for him against the rail, having witnessed the strange incident. The red blanket lay coiled in Jess's now empty chair, personless. Something had transpired in the house just then. He couldn't tell what, but he knew he'd said or done something he shouldn't have. Just when he thought he might have found a friend, someone to talk to about all the screwed-up things in his life, a door had closed in his face.

He couldn't bear the thought of going home, so he walked until he found a liquor store and purchased a bottle of Jack's favorite, Crown Royal. *Here's to you, old friend. One more bottle down.*

9

BLUES

A man of few words, Dale Miller maintained a quiet composure. He'd worked at the tire factory for almost thirty years, moved up in rank, and had been a supervisor for nearly a decade. He lived a plain life, no frills, spending his weekends under the hood of his blue-and-white 1960 Ford pickup truck. *Old Blue.* He ogled old vehicles the way Nick ogled guitars.

Nick watched from the front door, beer in hand, eyeing his father's dedication. Dale connected with greasy car parts like Nick's fingers did with the strings of his Gibson. Dale's aging hands, covered in grime, twisted and tinkered with metal chunks and gadgets Nick knew very little about. A small boom box blared familiar tunes from a cinderblock behind the truck. Nick couldn't deny the subtle comfort in this nostalgic scene. *Home.*

"Still listening to Clapton? Haven't you tired of this CD yet?" Nick said, approaching Dale and startling him from concentration.

"One never tires of Clapton, son." He wiped a round object with a grease-soaked cloth that smelled like burnt oil.

"At least get a Bluetooth speaker. This old boom box is outdated."

"I like it. If it's not broken . . ."

"Yeah, yeah, stop trying to fix it. You've said that a thousand times." Nick shook his head.

"It's truth. I like older things, classics. All this new technology isn't for me. I surround myself with things I can tear apart and fix, rewire, tighten down, replace parts. You get the picture."

"Spoken like an old timer," Nick teased.

"I'll take that as a compliment. Why don't you put that beer down and help me?"

Nick debated. He placed his beer next to the boombox and stood beside his father, staring blank faced into a sea of machinery.

"I have no idea what I'm looking at," he said.

Dale grinned. "Well, son, this is a truck. It drives on wheels."

"Yeah, I got that much." Nick rolled his eyes. "You haven't changed a bit."

"Change is for the birds. Hand me that crescent wrench. These old trucks are a bit sensitive sometimes. I'm replacing the engine. I hope you know what an engine looks like."

Nick lifted his head to the sky and let out a pronounced sigh. "Yeah, I got that too."

"Good. I'd hate to think I'd failed to at least teach you that much." He nudged Nick's arm.

Nick could identify a few items under that rusty old hood. He'd picked up a few things growing up under the watchful eye of such a fastidious mechanic.

"I'm installing a 292 Y-Block in this baby. She'll roar like a lion when I'm done."

"How long have you had her?"

"A few months. Bought her off a guy at the plant for next to nothing."

"What happened to the old Plymouth?"

"Sold her. Doubled my money."

"You loved that car," Nick said.

"I did. Then I fell in love with this one. She's just like the one my dad had when I was a boy. All right, less talk, more work." Dale rubbed the back of his wrist against his forehead, wiping beads of sweat as they rolled into his eyes.

The sudden crunching sound of gravel alerted both men to footsteps in the driveway. Dale bumped his head on the truck's hood, looking up to see who was approaching. Jess stopped a few yards from them, hands in pockets, shoulders drawn up as though she were seeking approval. Nick took a small step back. He was speechless and suddenly nervous. He hadn't expected to see her again so soon.

Her skin glowed under rays of heavy sun, eyes gleaming. She seemed to hold a trance-like power over his resolve. Then he realized he was staring with his jaw slightly dropped. He smiled, swallowed hard, and tried to think of something clever to say.

"Hey." Nick handed Dale the crescent wrench and went to meet Jess.

"Hi," she said softly.

Dale watched with curiosity. He hadn't noticed this softer side of his son before. He grinned and continued working, but watched them, periodically glancing up. It comforted him to see Nick with a smile on his face. He'd missed that.

"You walked?" Nick asked.

"It's not far. You walked it. And I don't drive anymore." She glanced at Dale, then back at Nick. "Are you busy? You look busy." Part of her hoped he was so she'd have a reason to go back home, but she'd already come this far.

Nick glanced back at his father. "No, not really. I don't know squat about cars."

"I feel bad about the other day. I was rude. I didn't mean to be." Her blueish-green eyes twinkled in the bright summer sun, complimenting her pale complexion.

Nick shrugged. "It's okay. I probably overstayed my welcome. I asked too many questions."

She grinned, an awkward feeling. Her facial muscles barely remembered how to form that steep curvy thing at the ends of her mouth, but they seemed to be relearning every time she was with him. "You were fine. It's me. It's all me." She looked away. "My life is really complicated and I'm not used to discussing it with people."

"We all have baggage. Some of us more than others. I doubt your life is as complicated as mine. I mean, it can't be worse. I don't mean that what you're going through isn't as bad. I'm not trying to make less of it. This is coming out all wrong." He breathed a heavy sigh and looked around for some sort of lifeline, but he was on his own and failing miserably. He took a deep breath and wondered why this woman had such an effect on him.

"It's all right. I know what you meant." His stammering amused her, sweet in an adorable sort of way. He seemed as nervous as she was and that eased her mind a bit.

"I don't even know your situation. I shouldn't say things like that. I just meant that my life is pretty complicated too, and I understand on some level, I guess." He went in for the save.

Nick suddenly realized he didn't have much experience talking to women. As absurd as it seemed, there hadn't been much opportunity. He'd only had a few female friends, and every woman he'd been romantically involved with had either been a one-night stand or a short-lived fling, with an emphasis on flinging—not conversation. He'd made *People Magazine*'s list of sexiest men. Every woman he encountered made it so easy for him to get what he needed and get out. A sad existence, but one he couldn't deny.

Jess was different from those girls. She was quiet, thoughtful, not self-absorbed. She made him want to stick around and have a conversation, get to know her. She wasn't throwing herself at him or obsessing over his celebrity status. For the first time, he didn't feel obligated to orchestrate a meaningless seduction.

"I was wondering if I could make it up to you." She broke his concentration.

"You don't have to . . ."

"I really don't want to go alone," she said.

"Go where?"

"It's a jam session—"

"I'll get my guitar," he blurted out before she could finish.

"It's blues. My brother will be there, and I can't go by myself, I just . . . can't. I don't have to go at all, but he invited me and you play and I thought maybe . . ."

"Sounds like fun. I don't know a lot of blues tunes, but the riffs are easy."

He hesitated. How would they get there? He could ask his dad for a ride, but that would be pathetic, and no way would his dad let him break probation in one of his prized vehicles. He'd have to tell her his story at some point, but he hoped he could avoid it for a little while longer.

"Can we walk there? I, um, can't drive . . . right now." Shame coated his voice.

"It's several blocks away, but I'm up for a walk."

Helpless was what Nick had felt when his rights were stripped away. Remorse was what stung him now.

"Let me grab my guitar and we'll head out." Nick jogged toward the house, eager to be off the hook with his dad.

Jess kicked at pebbles in the driveway while she waited,

shifting them with the tip of her shoes, her hands still in the pockets of her tapered denim capris. She kept her head down, watching the ground as though it had something important to say.

A grimy hand appeared in front of her. "I'm Dale."

She looked up, forging her best impression of a smile. "Jess." She shook his hand, noticing the overwhelming aroma of motor oil.

"I didn't realize Nicholas had made any friends since he's been home. It's good to see him getting out." He noted her awkward stance and bent posture.

"We sort of met by accident. He's a talented musician."

"I wish I could say I knew that from experience, but I've never seen him perform, not really, only listened from another room."

Jess looked up, eyes opening wide. "You really should see him play. His passion is impressive."

Nick reappeared, guitar in hand. "Ready?"

Jess nodded.

"Have fun," Dale called out as Nick led her away. He watched them walk off, happy his son had found a reason to get out of the house that didn't involve a longneck bottle. He had a day's worth of work ahead of him on Old Blue, but he couldn't help wishing he could tag along.

Silence shrouded their stroll down peaceful neighborhood streets. The quiet calm of Bridgetown hadn't changed much, it was still sleepy and mellow. Nick could feel the drip of perspiration sliding down his temples and the back of his neck, definitely not the season to be walking across town. He glanced at her every few minutes and occasionally caught her glancing back.

Neither knew what to say, but both had questions they were dying to ask.

"So, where are we going exactly?" Nick broke the silence.

"My brother's friend, Monty, holds backyard barbeques for their musician friends. It's a small group of amateur players and singers, local boys who have been playing together for decades."

"Does your brother play?"

Jess laughed, catching herself off guard. "No, he lacks the necessary coordination. It must run in the family. He does sing though."

"I have a question," Nick said, coming to a halt. "How did you know where I live?"

She blushed. The subtle hint of rose in her cheeks became her, lending radiance to her pale complexion and adding more depth to her delicate features. "I think you mentioned it."

He smiled. "No, I don't think I did."

"Mark may have mentioned it. He knows your dad, I think." She tried to save face, but knew he wasn't buying it. She had called Mark to ask, but she didn't want Nick to know that.

Nick eyed her with fascination. "I guess it's fair then. I know where you live."

"You think I'm stalking you?"

He chuckled. "Are you?"

"No."

"Too bad. I might actually like that."

She shook her head, ignoring his flirtatious humor. She did admire his smile though. It wasn't just warm, it was genuine. He had an easygoing manner about him that reminded her of what she used to be like before the accident, the part of her Mark was always hinting at that she'd lost. There was something about Nick that made her miss her old self and realize how different she'd become.

They walked a few blocks more before Jess finally gave in,

asking the burning question on her mind. "Why don't you drive?"

And there it was. The inevitable moment that would force him to confess his heinous misdeeds.

She waited for a response, wondering what he might be hiding.

"You don't beat around the bush, do you?"

"We are walking halfway across town in summer heat. Seemed fitting to ask."

He couldn't blame her. What kind of man doesn't drive?

"You must not watch the news. Or read the paper. Or get out much." He kept his eyes focused straight ahead as they continued walking, afraid to look in her direction.

"That bad?" she asked.

"Yeah."

"Well, I don't get out much. I don't watch the news, and I generally don't talk to many people. So if you're looking for an unbiased person to tell your story to, you've got one right here."

Easier said than done. Nick hadn't met many unbiased people in his life. He'd only known a handful of trustworthy individuals, and the best one of those was gone.

"No offense, but it's not really a story I'd like to tell. It's the kind of story one tries to forget. Only there's not enough liquor in the world to make me forget."

She didn't say anything. They walked a few more steps, and he began to lose his patience. What was she thinking? Her expression was blank, impossible to read. He had to tell her something or she might think the worst.

"I guess I should explain," Nick said, watching the amber hues of her hair change between bouncing light under a row of trees.

"You don't have to."

He wanted to tell her, but choosing the right words didn't

come easy. He should just be honest and say *the thing*, but he could hardly say the thing to himself. How was he supposed to tell a stranger?

"Court took away my license."

There. He did it. The proverbial can of worms had been opened. He quickened his pace, waiting for them to spill out all over his mangled carcass.

"Why?" she asked.

Now he couldn't face her. He focused his attention on two Yorkies fighting over a frisbee in a nearby yard and vowed to say as little as possible. "I wrecked a car."

She knew he was being intentionally vague. "Must have been quite a wreck." She pushed away images of Patrick behind a steering wheel and his car rolling over with their daughter in the back seat.

"They don't revoke your license for nothing." He took a deep breath. "Seriously, though, it's all over every media outlet. You could easily search it online, get all the gory details."

Her heart plummeted and the sinking feeling in her stomach made her queasy and uncomfortable. "I don't want gory details. Sensational gossip doesn't interest me. I hate the news. I hate reporters and the way personal information spreads when something tragic happens. People should mind their own business."

He halted, turned to face her, and studied her expression. Her eyes gleamed full of passion and pain, a sad countenance held together with bravery and stubborn fury. There was a story behind those piercing eyes. Perhaps as tragic as his own. But he wouldn't ask about it, not yet.

"You might be the only person on earth who feels that way," he said.

"I shouldn't have asked. It's none of my business why you don't drive. I guess we both have our reasons."

"It's a fair question," Nick replied.

They walked on, stopping in a newer subdivision with modern two-story, brick homes and well-manicured lawns that looked too pristine not to be artificial.

"This is it." She pointed to a large brick house with a wisteria wreath hanging on the front door.

Nick followed close behind. When she rang the bell, a tall, bearded man answered the door with a toothy grin that overwhelmed his somewhat smaller features.

"Jess! Come on in. Everyone's outside. It's great to see you again. You look good." Monty gave her a big hug.

"This is Nick," she said.

"Pleasure, Nick. I see you brought a guitar. Going to play with us?" Monty held out his hand.

Nick shrugged and shook Monty's hand. "I'd like to."

They followed Monty through an open floor plan to the backyard where a cozy group was gathered, eating grilled meat and homemade side dishes. Mark caught sight of Jess immediately.

"Here comes trouble," Jess said in a low voice to Nick as Mark approached.

Nick stiffened, seeing the mountain lion once more. But the look in his eyes seemed more approving this time, relaxed and subdued compared to their previous encounter.

"You came," Mark said, relieved to see her standing before him.

"Yeah," she answered.

"Hello, Nick."

"Hey."

The small talk and pleasantries were enough to make Jess gag. This was why she preferred the comfort of home. The fortitude it took to be gracious amid shallow human interaction drained the life from her. She used to be better at this. *Before.* That seemed like such a long time ago, like years had passed and no one had changed but her.

Elise joined them, and Jess rolled her eyes, forcing a long, dramatic sigh from her lungs as she folded her arms across her chest. She was trapped, swallowed whole, suffocated.

Jess still harbored guilt for the careless words she'd spoken in anger at the restaurant, and the silence lingering between them was sharp enough to cut through glass. Ambient noise from nearby conversations grew louder, diverting their attention to the laughter and merriment in Monty's well-manicured backyard, much to her relief.

"Mark! Get over here. This fool wants to start with Stevie Ray Vaughan," Monty called out.

Nick observed as a lively group of men took seats in lawn chairs, tuning an array of instruments as they chattered. Mark joined them, jumping into the conversation, cracking jokes, and patting a couple of the guys on the back. He motioned Nick to follow, and Jess backed away, joining the other women standing near the food table.

"Nothing wrong with a little Stevie," a dark-haired man wearing a blue silk shirt called out.

"Sure ain't, if you like them juiced-up covers of other men's work," a large black man holding a harmonica teased, receiving chuckles and laughter from the others.

"Aw, come on. Stevie had some good stuff. The man could play," the blue shirt replied.

"If I want to hear rock and roll, I'll listen to rock and roll. Blues is something different. It's from the soul. You don't just play the blues, you feel the blues," the black man said.

"Gentlemen, we have a visitor," Mark spoke. "This is Nick Miller. I think he'd like to join us. Nick, meet the boys."

Mark introduced Nick to Seymour Rutledge, the large black man holding a polished harmonica, making sure to add he'd been a former roadie for blues legend B. B. King. Then Jake Langston, wearer of the blue silk shirt, a music teacher and proud collector of vintage Fender Stratocasters. Greg Oppman, on bass, had long, stringy gray hair and wore a fedora. Greg's beard hung down in a point to his chest, reminding Nick of ZZ Top.

Then Mark introduced Nick to Copper Jackson, the other black man seated next to Monty, a thin, aging man wearing a bright-orange shirt and gambler straw hat.

"Copper is a Bridgetown icon. He has written songs for the some of the greats and played in blues clubs across the country. He's a legend." Mark patted Copper's shoulder.

"Seventy-four years old, and still going strong," Copper added.

"Our illustrious host, boasting that rather sharp-looking mandolin, is Monty Grey. We went to school together, but he's a couple years older than me, hence all the gray hair." Mark grinned.

"Don't worry. You'll catch up with me soon enough, old man," Monty teased.

"Welcome to the group, Nick. I see you've got a vintage J-45 over there. That's a mighty fine instrument, a work horse. Looks like it's in good shape too," Seymour noted.

Nick smiled. "She has a history."

"Does she now? We like instruments that tell a story. Whatcha got?" Seymour asked.

"She belonged to Eric Clapton. Made three tours with him in the eighties. I bought her at an auction and she's been my muse ever since." Nick beamed with pride.

"That must have set you back quite a sum," Jake said.

"She was an investment," Nick replied.

"Now, there's your Stevie Ray Vaughan song." Greg started humming.

"'Pride and Joy.'" Copper's smoky voice spoke in rhythm. "Stevie wasn't bad. Left his mark in his time, in his way," he said, picking at a twelve-string guitar.

Jake joined in on his Fender. "'Little Wing.' You guys can't tell me this song doesn't have heart and soul."

"It's got heart, I'll give you that," Seymour said.

Jake's Fender and Greg's bass, plugged into practice amps, produced electrifying sounds, egging on the group's musical pride. Copper's twelve string and Monty's mandolin held their own, adding depth to the sounds bouncing around Monty's fenced yard.

"Now, y'all know I want to hear some Muddy Waters, 'Mississippi Delta Blues.'" Seymour closed his eyes and bobbed his head as though they were already playing it.

"Yes, now." Copper nodded.

"You know it, Nick?" Monty asked.

Nick squinted, positioning himself on the edge of his seat, guitar nestled on his lap. "No, but you guys start playing and I'll jump in."

"Let's do it, boys," Monty said.

Nick had never listened to Muddy Waters or heard the raw, emotional bellow of "Mississippi Delta Blues." He liked it. It had old-school heart, the stuff of real musicians, ones who played on street corners and in basement clubs, decades before Nick was even a possibility. Copper's smokey voice added depth as he sang along.

They changed it up a bit, put their own style to it, but every note held that same hungry sound, filling the humid summer air around them. Muddy Waters would have appreciated their rendition had he still been alive. They did him justice . . . always did.

Nick watched closely, listened with keen ears. He joined in, picking up the song and style as though he'd played it a dozen times before. He surprised himself a little, feeling almost as natural as he did with his own music.

"I thought you didn't know Muddy Waters?" Seymour asked when they finished the song.

Nicked laughed. "I don't."

"You don't play like someone who don't know," Copper chimed in.

"I'm a quick learner."

"You don't say." Seymour smiled, eyeing Nick with a baiting look. "Let's see what else you *don't* know."

Jake strummed a few random melodies while the other men chatted, calling out song titles and blurting out opinions. Nick soaked it all in, rejuvenated by playing with such a talented group. He missed this, playing for the love of music instead of a record label's purse strings. Free to express his craft, not entangled in a world of superficial motives and greedy contracts. He also reveled in this newfound anonymity. Maybe they knew who he was, maybe they didn't, but they treated him like a human being, not someone on display. It was nice to blend in, to feel like one of the guys.

Copper began picking and strumming while the others shot back and forth, still deciding what to play. His rugged voice, raspy and aged, droned through a whistling summer breeze that rustled leaves in a nearby hedge. "Blues Before Sunrise," a Johnny Lee Hooker favorite. His body swayed. His face contorted with each strum on that scratched-up, worn-out, twelve-string that still played as well as it had shiny and new.

Nick remembered something his dad had told him years ago when he questioned Dale for adding extra verses to some of Eric Clapton's songs. *If you don't know the words to a blues song, you can easily make them up. Blues is that angsty feeling you get way down inside. Emotion expressed through song.* He was right.

They ran through a list of favorites, all the legends, all the greats. Jimmy Reed, Buddy Guy, Little Milton, Elmore James, Lonnie Johnson, T-Bone Walker, Howlin' Wolf, and Otis Rush. They didn't forget the legend himself, B. B. King, Seymour's number one choice. Mark swayed along to the rhythms and belted out lyrics with his deep, booming vocals.

Jess watched from the sidelines, comforted by childhood memories. Her parents' music had become her brother's, and then hers, passed down one family music day at a time. She may not have known anything on the Billboard Top 100, but her blues catalogue surpassed the basic knowledge of most. There was a strange comfort in those somber notes. Her body bent to the rhythmic sway of each chord, and soon she caught glimpses of Nick's wandering gaze, searching for her figure in the huddle of women. His tender, blue eyes suppressed deep emotion. She looked away, not daring to meet him with a smile. Smiles were few and she wasn't going to waste one on a guitar-wielding stranger.

"All right. Let me try one on you guys. You might actually know it." Nick changed his tuning and plucked a few strings to test it.

"Lay it on us, man. If it's old-school, I can guarantee you we know it." Seymour oozed confidence.

"This is a twist on an old classic, Nirvana style. Kurt Cobain nailed it. Hopefully I won't screw it up."

When he began playing the whole yard fell silent. Nick closed his eyes. Tones deep within rose to the surface, erupting from urgent vocal cords. Beads of sweat rolled down his forehead. Each strum executed an emotional attack across six strings. His body jerked and rocked at the mercy of the song's passionate climax. Eyes squinted, he belted out the harsher vocals similar to Cobain's version but with his own signature croon, the sultry, soothing voice that had made him famous.

Nick recalled with crystal clarity the last time he played that song. Jack's twenty-seventh birthday. Rowdy bars, cheap women, enough alcohol to drown a goat, and Jack's all-request guitar serenade courtesy of his best mate, Nick. An entire set of old

Nirvana songs later, Nick played one more, his favorite. He played until he nearly passed out. He did pass out that night, on top of Jack. It was the only thing either remembered the next day, and they laughed until they both threw up in Morgan's new car. She had never forgiven them for that. She rarely forgave them for anything.

When he finished playing, Nick leaned back, letting his guitar rest on the ground against his knee. His onlookers were speechless. The admiration in their eyes gave him a rush of confidence.

"Leadbelly. 'Where Did You Sleep Last Night.' Recorded in 1944 for Musicraft Records, but he titled it 'Black Girl,'" Copper called out, shaming Seymour, who was at a loss for words.

"How did you know that?" Seymour snapped.

"How did you not?" Monty asked.

"You're losing it, Seymour. That magic touch is fading," they teased and hounded.

"Ain't nothin' fading. I know who Leadbelly is. Huddie Ledbetter. You know they sent him to prison for killin' a man. He sang a song to the governor asking for a pardon and they granted it."

"That's right," Copper said.

"Is he the one who first recorded 'Midnight Special'?" Jake asked.

"That's the one, and one mighty fine version of 'House of the Rising Sun,'" Monty added.

"You guys know a lot more than I do about this music. What I usually play is a bit different. I like this, though. It's heavy. It's real. Cuts you like a knife," Nick said.

"You said it right there. That's the Blues. Most people play music that makes them feel. Blues is a feeling that moves you to make music." Copper nodded, reaching for a bag of peanuts near his feet. He crushed each shell open, popping peanuts into his mouth a few at a time.

"I like that." Nick smiled, glancing back at Jess. She didn't notice. She was distant, her eyes distressed and weary.

"You should join us again sometime," Mark said to Nick.

"I'd be happy to," Nick replied.

"Only if you let me take that J-45 for a spin." Seymour grinned.

"We'll see if she's in a good mood that day," Nick chuckled.

The men laughed, joking and carrying on in that back-slapping, guy-conversation way that women find amusing.

Jess stepped away, toward the house. Music resumed as she entered through the tall sliding glass doors into Monty's kitchen. She'd brought Abby here several times. A spot near the television, where Abby had once played with her dolls, targeted Jess's heart like a blazing arrow. She could almost hear the delicate sounds of Abby's voice, whispering pretend conversation. She closed her eyes, picturing that round cherub face with big blue irises, the most beautiful child she'd ever seen. There were days when time stood still, as though gut-wrenching events had never taken place. Times when Jess could picture herself still living in that world. Patrick drinking his morning coffee. Abby watching cartoons.

She didn't want to open her eyes, knowing it would all disappear and reality would be screaming at her again.

"Jess."

A wisp of air startled her from morbid concentration. Jess turned around to see Elise standing beside her.

"I was hoping we could talk." Elise had always been straightforward, no nonsense.

"I'm sorry for what I said at lunch the other day. It was cruel and harsh and I wasn't thinking." Jess emptied her thoughts before Elise could finish her own.

"I know that. I'm not angry with you."

"You're hurt."

"A little. But hurt goes away. Time heals all wounds. I just wanted to make sure—"

"Will you quit it with your quote of the month crap! Time does *not* heal all wounds. Some wounds fester. They sit there and ooze and blacken until they eat away like the plague. It doesn't just go away! How can you say that to me?" Jess snapped. "You're just a spoiled preacher's wife who has never had a family of her own and probably never will!"

Even as the words left her mouth Jess regretted them, but there was no taking them back. Emotional triggers won that round, unleashing like a box of demons that couldn't be contained. She was tired of trying to please everyone. Jess folded her arms high on her chest, releasing a low-pitched growl.

Mark barreled into the kitchen, shutting the door behind him so quickly they both jumped at the booming thud. "Is everything all right? We can hear you outside."

"It's my fault. I should have chosen my words more carefully," Elise said.

Mark lunged at Jess. "We are sick and tired of having to tiptoe around you. When are you going to snap out of this and realize you aren't the only one who lost something? You don't own the patent on suffering. Get over yourself."

"Mark." Elise raised her voice just enough to warn him.

Jess had nothing to say. This was the same conversation they'd had countless times with no progress. She stared him down like she had when they were younger and he wouldn't let her get her way. Only this time a steady stream of tears rushed down her face, dripping from her jaw onto the floor.

"What I don't understand is how you can befriend a total stranger and barely talk to me. Me, Jess. Your own brother. I'm the one who has always been here for you. I'm the one who took care of you, got you through school, kept a roof over your head after Mom and Dad passed away. I'm the one who stood up for you every time Patrick ran out. I've always been here, but it's like you don't see me, like I don't have a place in your world anymore."

She still had no words. It wasn't for lack of trying. She searched her mind, her heart, objects in the room, anything to break her silence. All she could do was stand there, glaring, shaking her head and trying her best to stop the tears from flowing, but they only ran faster down her cheeks. She wiped at her face and turned away. She couldn't look him the eyes.

Mark threw up his hands and stepped back. "I don't want to fight." His voice broke. Liquid pooled in the corners of his eyes. "I don't want to do this with you anymore." He walked off. Jess turned to Elise, the last person she wanted to see in that moment. Everything was spinning out of control. She didn't feel like herself anymore. She needed to get out of there. It had been a mistake to come.

Mark retreated to a guest bathroom, shaken and angry, but mostly just hurt. The cold tap water against the skin of his face didn't wash away the sting of defeat grinding his insides. *Get a grip.* He rested both hands firmly on the vanity, watching an aging version of himself stare back in the mirror, lines beginning to deepen on his forehead and around his ears. He'd never wanted to take the place of their father, or be anything other than what a brother should be to a sister, but things happened the way they did and he felt responsible for her. He was all she had left. She was the quiet girl in school, few friends, no serious boyfriends until Patrick. It had been her decision not to go to college and he didn't argue. He supported her working at a local clothing store, barely making minimum wage. When she married, she no longer needed to work, and he supported that too. Patrick was in finance and made plenty of money to give her the life she deserved.

Mark took a deep breath, watching his reflection change in

the mirror from anger to fear, wondering if he'd done everything wrong in his attempt to do it all right.

Across the hall, a spare bedroom offered Mark a quiet refuge to reflect on the unraveling threads of his tiny family. Perhaps he'd poured too much into Jess. He hadn't been prepared to raise a teenager. He'd barely been an adult himself back then. If he and Elise were able to have children of their own, he wondered what kind of father he would be. *What if I don't have what it takes? What if I'm the reason Jess is struggling so much?*

He buried his head in his hands, rubbing his face over and over, finally resting them on the back of his head, elbows propped against his knees. Monty's cat, Hermes, appeared from under the bed and paraded in front of him. He'd disturbed her from an epic cat nap and she made sure he knew his blunder. Mark ran his fingers through her long, silky white hair, feeling the subtle vibration of an approving purr. Life was easier with cats.

"Good girl," he whispered as she rubbed her body against his leg, smearing white hairs around the hemline of his jeans. "Time to go back out and join the crowd." Hermes pranced toward the door and gave an expecting nod. "Okay, okay. I'll let you out." He opened the door for Hermes to escape, but closed it behind her. He wasn't quite ready for music and laughter. He needed a few more minutes of solitude, a moment to pull himself together, a space to make sense of this emotional roller coaster.

Nick edged inside the glass doors to the kitchen, looking for Jess.

"She's outside." Elise pointed toward the front door.

"Is she okay?"

Elise shrugged and shook her head. Her expression gave little consolation. Nick retrieved his guitar and found Jess sitting on the small step-up to the front porch, holding her arms as though it were cold on the hottest day of the year.

"Hey."

She looked up at him with confused eyes.

"Thought maybe you'd left me."

She didn't say anything, so he joined her on the flat concrete.

She stared at an odd-looking patch of grass, partially green, partially yellow and fading as though that one spot was wilting away while the grass around it flourished and thrived. She could sympathize with that uneven patch. Life seemed to go on for everyone else, but her world had stopped and she couldn't seem to switch it back on.

"We can sit here all day. I'm game. It's sweltering. I'm kind of hungry. But sitting on cemented surfaces is good. It's like a workout for your knees, a wakeup call for your butt." He peered in her direction, searching for any hint of a smile. Nothing.

She glanced at him for a second, the saddest puppy eyes Nick had ever seen. They were also the most beautiful eyes he'd ever seen. Each time he saw her, they seemed to reflect different shades of green and blue. Whatever her story was, it didn't matter. She was the first person he'd felt like talking to since the accident. A small piece of himself seemed to reemerge every time he was with her.

"I'm not one of those drama queens." She finally spoke.

"Didn't think you were."

"I used to be a better version of myself."

He nodded. "Me too."

She turned to him. The sun reflected lighter portions of blond in his hair, contrasting darker shades, pleasingly woven through-out. He was a nice-looking man. He was rather more than nice-looking, but so different from Patrick. Patrick had a confident air about him, a fearless repose that made others concede to his superiority. Jess had never felt equal to her partner. She languished in the shadows behind him. Looking at Nick, she saw a man who held no overwhelming presumptions, no grandiose gestures to dangle in her face. He possessed a soft, welcoming smile that soothed her with its promise of security.

"Will you walk me home?"

He stood and held out a hand. She accepted it, allowing him to help her up. He squeezed her fingers between his for only a moment, one of those passing seconds that seemed to last for minutes, and wished he could hold her longer. Her fingers fit perfectly inside his grip, like they were meant to be there. She seemed so delicate, yet so full of stubborn passion and life not fully realized.

"Lead the way," he said as he let go and reached for his guitar.

They didn't speak much on the way home. Occasional remarks about the history of certain landmarks and houses, a few memories they'd experienced as children growing up in that quiet town, but no deep revelations. Not yet.

When they arrived on her porch, Nick lingered for a moment, about to say goodbye. He wasn't sure how to end their outing, and he wished he had some clever suggestion to initiate another meeting. Instead, he hovered awkwardly while she unlocked her front door.

"Do you like damsons?" she asked, stepping halfway into the house.

"What are damsons?"

"Those round, purple things that look like giant grapes."

"Are you making this up?" he asked.

She laughed, catching herself quickly. "No. You've never heard of a damson tree?"

He scratched his head. "Um, no, not that I recall. Is it like an apple?"

"No, it's not like an apple. I think it's a plum or something.

For Pete's sake, this was supposed to be a simple question," she huffed, suppressing a grin.

"Damsons."

"Yes, damsons," she replied.

"What about them?" He suppressed his own grin.

"I have some, and I have my grandmother's recipe for damson preserves . . ."

"Like grape jelly?"

"No, not exactly, but for the sake of this conversation, sure. I might make some tomorrow. Do you want to come?"

"You're inviting me to make jelly?"

"Preserves," she corrected.

"What's the difference?" he asked.

"Do you need to know the difference to accept the invitation?"

He smiled, baring all his teeth. "No."

She waited. "Well, so what is it?"

"I'll think about it," he said, backing away. "And I'll see you tomorrow."

Jess shook her head, frustrated yet amused.

Making jam from what sounded like a made-up fruit. That was an invitation he'd never had before. He chuckled under his breath as he walked home. *Damsons. Maybe I should look that up.*

10

TIES THAT BIND

*T*he next morning Dale was at it early, scrubbing the kitchen sink, mopping floors, doing laundry. He'd become quite the efficient houseman living on his own for so long. Just off the night shift and three coffees later, his determination bubbled over.

"Didn't you work last night?" Nick grumbled, stumbling into the kitchen with one eye open, rubbing at the other eye with clumsy fingers.

"Watch your step. Just mopped that spot." Dale nodded to the section of linoleum in front of Nick.

"I need a beer," Nick barked.

"You don't need a beer. You need a goal. Something to work toward."

"I'll work toward that fridge and get a beer. There's a goal," Nick snapped. He sauntered around slick spots, pushing past his hunched-over father, only to find he'd already consumed his last bottle...facepalm. He'd broken Jack's most essential rule: *never run out of beer*. The second most essential was *never tell a woman you love her until you've seen how she spends her money.* Jack had a rule for everything.

"Looks like you have a choice to make?" Dale hovered beside him.

"Yeah, go to the store or go back to bed."

"Or have a hearty breakfast and accompany me to the hardware store to pick up a few materials for a little project I'm working on."

"What project? You turning into Martha Stewart all of a sudden?" Nick yawned.

"Bathroom sink isn't draining."

Nick shook his head. "Great. This old house is falling apart. Since when do you know anything about plumbing?"

"Son, I know a little about most everything, especially when it comes to fixing stuff. Are you coming with or not?"

"Don't you sleep?" Nick asked, releasing another yawn.

"Occasionally." He bumped his son on the shoulder. "Take a shower. I'm leaving in thirty minutes."

"What about that hearty breakfast you promised?"

Dale glanced back as he exited the room. "There's a frying pan on the counter and eggs in the fridge. Have at it."

Nick shook his head again. *Of course.*

"I like mine over easy," Dale called out from the hallway

"From rock star to short-order cook. Who wouldn't want to be me?" Nick mumbled, starting breakfast while his father hummed seventies rock songs from another room.

They returned from the store with a bag of tools and parts. Nick knew nothing about drains or plumbing. He could turn the water on and off, but that was it.

"Hand me that wrench, son."

Nick handed Dale the only tool he recognized. "Are you sure you know what you're doing?"

"I'm going to loosen the slip nuts. Do you know what slip nuts are?"

Nick stared at the exposed pipe below the sink. All he saw was pipe. So maybe his dad knew a *few* things about plumbing . . . "Go ahead. Let's get this over."

Dale loosened the slip nuts and removed the pipe, pouring settled water into a bucket below. He felt around inside the p-trap with his fingers, pulling black gunk and debris in large clumps.

"Ugh, how does that even accumulate inside such a small space?" Nick asked.

"Years of use," Dale replied. "These washers are bad. That's what we bought at the store. Watch and learn."

Nick's eye roll did not go unnoticed, but Dale chose to ignore his son's charming cynicism and continued with enthusiasm. "You have a meeting with your probation officer tomorrow."

"Yeah, I know. Don't remind me. These weekly visits are pointless."

Dale wanted to say that drinking and getting behind the wheel of a car was pointless, but he restrained himself.

"We need some music," Nick said.

"You sing for a living, go ahead," Dale replied.

"What, just serenade you while you fix a pipe? That's a little weird, don't you think?"

"What's weird? You want some music so you sing a little song. Unless you can't sing without your guitar . . ."

"I can sing without my guitar. I can sing circles around that tone-deaf voice of yours any day."

Dale laughed. "Okay, then do it."

Nick settled against the wall, thinking of what he could sing on the spot, something his dad would appreciate. Clapton. It had to be Clapton. Then he remembered the night he and Jack were sitting together on the bathroom floor of a hotel in San Jose, nursing busted lips and black eyes over a bottle of gin and Crown Royal. He'd almost forgotten that crazy night, the bar room brawl, twelve stitches, and drunken laughter as they propped their bruised bodies against the toilet, recounting every second of the fight. They'd known it would make headlines, and it had, but it blew over quickly. Two weeks later no one even remembered.

"Are you going to sing?" Dale asked.

Nick cleared his throat. There was only one Clapton song he could think of in that moment. He opened his mouth. Shaky notes at first, turning into a delicate a cappella.

A song written for a film about drug addicts but composed while Clapton was grieving the tragic loss of his son, Conor, "Tears in Heaven" had been one of Nick's favorites, reminding him of his mom, and now Jack. He continued singing, eyes focused on the tiled wall in front of him, until he realized his dad was almost finished with the job.

Dale kept silent, relishing his son's gift, a passionate, emotional voice that reminded him of Lenore singing to Nick before he'd fall asleep at night. She had the most beautiful alto Dale had ever heard.

"I met him once," Nick said when he finished. His eyes were still focused on the outdated subway tile, its dings and cracks and discolored grout.

"Who?"

Nick cocked a half grin. "Eric Clapton." He turned to face his father.

Dale was stunned. "You met Eric Clapton?"

"Yeah, well, briefly, but we did speak."

"Where? When?" Dale put his tools down and gave Nick his undivided attention.

"Backstage at a music festival in Toronto a couple years ago."

"What was he like?"

Nick smiled. "Very cool. I'd forgotten something and was headed back to grab it, and there he was. He'd just come off stage, still holding his guitar. I thought of you in that moment."

"What did you say to him?"

"He asked me if I was Votive's front man and I just stood there like an idiot and said yeah. He told me he enjoyed my work and that we should play a set together some day."

"Wow, that's incredible, Nicholas."

"I told him my dad was a huge fan. He said to tell you hello."

Dale smiled, letting Nick's story sink in. "What do you know? Eric Clapton said hi to me."

"Don't let it go to your head," Nick teased. "You know, that festival is on YouTube. You could watch it on your laptop."

"Would I get to see you play?" Dale asked.

"Yeah, we're on it."

Dale's eyes lit up. "Let's clean up this mess and watch it."

It only took a couple moments to pull up an amateur video of the music festival and Clapton's performance. They watched together, commenting and having a somewhat civil conversation. Nick tried to revive the rapport they'd had when he was younger, but it felt off, tense, awkward. A distance he couldn't navigate lodged between them like an uncomfortable silence neither could shake. But Nick was determined to try.

"I had a really good time at that jam session yesterday."

"I was wondering about that," Dale said.

"I learned some new stuff."

"Did you play any Clapton?"

Nick laughed. "It was old-school blues, Dad. Johnny Lee Hooker, B. B. King. Classics."

"Clapton is blues the right way."

"You're so biased," Nick said.

"I'm a fan."

"There *are* other musicians out there. You know that, right?"

Dale curled his mouth at one side, a teasing half grin "Of course I know that. But there is only one Eric Clapton."

"True."

"Let's watch your band play," Dale said.

Nick hesitated. *Too soon. It's too soon.* His instinct urged him to walk away, but he couldn't disappoint his father. He had an inner need to please Dale, to know that he was proud of Nick's accomplishments.

A few clicks later, Votive took the stage on Dale's laptop screen. It was a show they'd played in Seattle, one of Nick's favorites. He remembered the trouble they'd had during sound-check. Some technical difficulties with a monitor, a guitar tech who got sick, and Jack had disappeared for hours, only to be found moments before they were scheduled to play. He'd met someone, a woman, and that was a big deal for Jack, who refused to settle, preferring his wild rock 'n' roll lifestyle to anything conventional. He'd poured his heart out to Nick after the show while Drew and the others weren't around. It was a moment that stuck out to Nick. He wasn't sure why it seemed so significant now, but he held on to it, anchoring himself to the past.

"Is it raining?" Dale asked.

"Seattle. It always rains."

"Won't it mess up your instruments?"

"It can, but the stage is covered. It's mostly the audience getting wet."

"You look drenched," Dale said.

"We were covered in sweat. It was ninety degrees."

"In Seattle?"

"Summer heat wave."

"Looks like it."

Nick hated watching himself on stage, but seeing pride in his father's eyes as they shared a piece of Nick's history filled a tiny void he didn't know was there. A comforting warmth washed over him, an isolated bubble of happiness.

Nick's eyes focused on Jack. He hadn't seen him since their last night together. There he stood, bouncing around onstage, shoulder-length brown hair, barely visible goatee, and short, stocky body. He held his bass close, bending at the waist as he thrashed his head back and forth. Drew sat at his Ludwig kit, lime-green mohawk held perfectly in place with enough gel to cement a driveway. The two closest friends he'd ever had. Friends he didn't have to pretend with. Friends who understood him from the inside out.

"You guys sound really good. I'm impressed, Nicholas."

Nick wasn't impressed, not with himself. He stared at Dale's laptop, into the eyes of the man whose life he'd cut short. His trusted advisor and confidant. The one person who knew his moods and triggers, his struggles, and the way he reacted when he wanted something more from a girl than just a one-night stand. He was the person who had Nick's back in every argument, backed him up amid any criticism. They had been more like twin brothers than best friends.

Dale noticed the tension in Nick's legs and shoulders as his body stiffened, his painful grimace and faraway stare. "Is this hard to watch?"

Is he serious? "What do you think?" Nick snapped.

"Don't take it out on me, son."

"What kind of question is that? You haven't asked me about him since I've been here." Nick tried to bury the painful stings gnawing away at his resolve. So much guilt and remorse, it was overwhelming.

"I assumed you didn't want me to."

"You assume a lot of things."

Dale touched his son's knee, but Nick jerked away.

"Don't do that. Don't start being all fatherly now just because you see I'm upset. Let's just keep things real here, okay?"

"So we're back to this? I've always been here for you, Nicholas."

"Yeah. Says the man with the broken son."

He couldn't take it anymore. Nicked stormed off, stopping just outside the door to his room. He almost went back, to have one more word, one more jab to make his dad hurt as much as he was, but he resisted. What good would it do? He disappeared inside his room, locking the door, and flopped across his bed facedown. He wrestled with tears until fighting seemed worse than the tears themselves. He sobbed quietly into faded sheets, tears of guilt and loathing. He hated himself for letting Jack down, the friend who had trusted him with his life. Even when they were kids doing idiotic things like climbing the school roof and shooting armadillos with BB guns, Jack had let Nick lead. He'd blamed Nick later when they got in trouble, but he'd trusted him to call the shots and Nick had never let Jack down, until now.

11

REVELATIONS

*H*e woke smothered in wet bedding with swollen eyes and salty cheeks. No desire to leave the house, but Jess expected him. The damsons would be waiting. As lovely as she was, Nick's heavy limbs and weary mind preferred the containment of his bedroom walls. Yet some unseen force goaded, propelling him from the bed and into the bathroom to wash cold water over his parched skin.

He should feel safe here. The home where his mother read stories to him in the rocking chair his father built while she was pregnant. Where he learned to throw a ball, ride a bike, play tag. In a world of monsters he'd created for himself, this house was the one place safety should abound, but it crowded him like everything else, a trap waiting to swallow him whole.

After changing his shirt and lacing up a pair of heavy, black boots, Nick slipped out of the house unnoticed. He walked his usual path a couple blocks away to the Bridgetown historical district, with its aging magnolia trees and perfectly situated antebellum-style and Victorian homes. Jess occupied her usual nest on the porch, covered in the same red blanket. Predictable. Comfortable.

She watched him approach, a barely-there smile growing in her somber expression.

"You're late," she said.

"Fashionably?" Nick asked, brow arched.

She eyed his wardrobe. "If you call jeans and a T-shirt fashionable."

He enjoyed the warmth of an impossible smile forming in the muscles of his jaw. The same warmth that impelled him to keep going, to find a reason to be happy. She had a way of making him forget who he was and what he'd been through, like he had a clean slate.

"This is as fashionable as I get."

"I guess it will do." She smiled, and her eyes glowed greener than they had the day before.

She led him into the house, passing by the same family portrait now watching him with warning eyes. He guarded his words and followed her into a kitchen that seemed too small for a house that large. It wasn't tiny, but it felt more like a pass-through than a kitchen, an oddly shaped square with too many counters and barely enough room for a table.

"These are damsons." She pointed to a colander full of purplish-blue fruit that did, indeed, resemble large grapes.

"That's a lot of fruit," he said.

"My neighbor has a damson tree. She gives me the extras." Jess pointed toward the window. "*That* neighbor. My other neighbor is a stubborn old bat who drives me crazy."

Nick watched her shake excess water from the colander and glide about the room, gathering utensils and ingredients. She moved like his mom had, busy in the kitchen on cookie baking days, something he remembered fondly from childhood. There was something about this woman that made it hard to look away. He could stand there all day admiring her delicate features and her wavy hair brushing against the soft skin of her face each time she turned around. But more than that. She made him want to learn new things and see the world from a different perspective. *What is it about her?*

"This was my grandmother's recipe, but my mom perfected it after she passed." Jess broke his concentrated stare.

"What can I do to help?"

"Wash your hands and then dry these off before putting them into the pot."

He'd never been one to try domesticated things, but he had to admit this was kind of exciting. He made a mean grilled cheese, but he'd never attempted anything that went into a jar and could be stored in a cool, dry place for several years. Jack would tease if he were there now.

Jess looked around with her hands on her hips. "I thought I set out the sugar."

Nick looked around as well, searching for anything that resembled sugar. The door to a large, walk-in pantry was cracked open so he stepped inside to look. A ceramic cannister labeled *Sugar* sat on a narrow ledge near the doorway.

"Is this it?" Nick asked, reaching for the cannister. He glanced around at the collection of food stacked on every shelf. There were dozens of boxes of strawberry Pop-Tarts, snack-sized applesauce cups, and kid's cereals, organized alphabetically.

"Big fan of Pop-tarts?" Nick asked, turning toward Jess, now standing directly in front of him.

"I didn't want you to see that," she said.

"Saving up for hard times?" he joked.

"No." She hesitated. Heart beating quickly, eardrums pounding, Jess's fingers began to tingle. It was a compulsive habit she didn't want anyone to know about, this oddity that somehow kept Abby with her, still alive in familiar items and daily routines. Mark had nearly flipped out when he discovered her excessive hoarding, snooping around like the house was still his. Now Nick had seen it too, and she was scared he might think she was crazy. Sometimes she wondered if she was crazy, or just pitiful.

Color drained from her face. Her hands began to tremble. Nick searched his repertoire of small talk for something pleasant to say, coming up empty and defeated. Uncomfortable moments were not his forte. He'd always waited for Jack to lighten the mood with inappropriate humor or obscure words of wisdom from Drew. Now he was on his own.

"I'm sorry." Her eyes filled with tears. "I'm so embarrassed." She looked down and away, anywhere but at him.

"It's okay," he said

"No, it's not. Nothing is okay." Jess turned away from him. She tried to regain her composure, but the more she fought it, the faster tears streamed down her cheeks.

She hurried to get out of the room, leaving Nick alone, holding the sugar.

Nick waited, unsure if he should go after her or head for the door. He placed the sugar near the sink and inched step by step out of the kitchen, peering around corners until he found her huddled on the couch in her living room.

He lingered just outside the room, one foot in the foyer, one pointed toward where she was sitting. "Are you okay?"

"Does it look like I'm okay?"

"What can I do?" he asked.

"Nothing. You can't do anything. Mark can't do anything. Elise can't do anything. There's just . . . nothing." Tears rolled faster down her soggy cheeks. She wouldn't look at him. She held a square pillow against her body, picking at frayed edges.

Nick considered going home, giving her privacy, escaping for dignity's sake. He knew what it was like to need solitude, fearing an emotional breakdown in front of others, but there wasn't anything he wanted to go home to. Watching her fall apart in front of him, still barely knowing her, made him nervous and uncomfortable. Yet her pain seemed as heavy as his own, and there was a strange comfort in that. He wanted to know more.

"I can listen," he offered.

"You don't want to hear my sob story. I'm a complete mess." She struggled to get each word out between choking breaths.

"Whatever it is, you shouldn't have to bear it alone." Nick walked closer, debating whether he should take a seat next to her on the sofa or remain standing, hovering like a vulture.

She kept her body angled away from him, trying to sob quietly, but failing with every muffled gasp.

He sat down near her, keeping several inches of space between them.

Jess turned her head just enough to meet his eyes, as sad as her own. They seemed to understand, to comprehend the misery that consumed her. She glanced past him to a picture of Abby and Patrick collecting dust on a nearby table. Patrick was holding Abby on his shoulders. Abby's smile was as big and round as her cherub face, her widened eyes dancing with glee. *Play with me, Daddy*, Jess could hear the adoration in her little voice. *Daddy's princess.*

"I lost someone. Two someones."

"The picture in the hallway?" he asked.

"Yes."

A huge boulder settled in Nick's stomach. "What happened?"

She hesitated. Talking about it made it real. It couldn't be real. She wasn't ready for reality to take up permanent residence. His warm hand rested on her shoulder, pressing down with the gentlest squeeze. His touch was comforting, yet alarming. She took a deep breath, releasing the air slowly, preparing herself to reveal the most tender place in her heart for the first time since the accident had happened.

"I don't know where to begin. Patrick came home late. Typical. We argued. There was always someone else, some other woman. He wanted an open marriage. I didn't. I was fed up with the lies, with everything, and he just kept apologizing. He offered to take Abby to her ballet class. She looked like an angel in her bright pink tutu, her satin ballet slippers with bows on the ends that Mark had bought for her. Of course she wanted to ride with her daddy. He was her knight in shining armor. So, I let him take her. I kissed her goodbye, barely, on the forehead. I should have held her tighter, for longer. I just let her go. I stood on the porch, watching them pull out of the driveway in that overpriced BMW he always drove too fast. That was the last time I saw her." She paused. "Mark drove by the accident on his way home. Police cars everywhere, pieces of metal and debris scattered across the road. He knew it was them." Her voice stalled. She couldn't say anymore.

Nick sat back, picturing what the Mustang he had been driving must have looked like, the debris and shattered glass spread across multiple lanes. Her vulnerability was raw and consuming. He wanted to console her, but he didn't know how. He said nothing and waited for her to continue.

"The police report stated he was on the phone when it happened, texting a woman. He lost control when he veered into the other lane and swerved to miss an oncoming truck."

"That's horrible," he whispered, barely audible, but Jess heard it clearly, like a bullhorn.

"That's not the worst." She jumped up and fled to a window across the room. "The car was so compressed, so mangled, they had to . . . It took hours. I can't even think about what she must have gone through in those final moments. What was the last thing she saw? What did she hear? Did she call for me?" Her voice faded as if into her distant thoughts as she stared outside the window.

"Did he hit something?" Nick asked, scooting to the edge of the couch.

"Telephone pole," Jess answered. "Bridgetown's worst wreck in twenty years, according to the papers. 'Cheating husband dies in crash, killing five-year-old daughter.' That's when I stopped watching the news."

"I get it," he said.

She whirled around to face him. "You can't get it. You may have been in an accident with your mom and I'm sure that was horrible, but not like this. You haven't been through *this*." Her voice shook with anger. "Everyone thinks they understand, thinks they can put themselves in my place, but you can't know what I'm going through. Patrick killed my daughter. It was his fault. He was careless and reckless and stupid." She tried to compose herself as her chest rose and fell with each labored breath. "I hate him and everything he put me through. I was alone in my marriage. She was all I had, and he took her from me!" Jess turned back to the window, her cheeks flushing red with embarrassment at her outburst. She couldn't control her flooding emotions. She clenched her eyes shut and wished she was alone.

Nick thought about what he should say, knowing he needed to be careful with his words. Her revelation made him question himself even more. "I can't put myself in your place, but I know the agony of losing someone you care about. I know tragedy. I know remorse. I know the guilt that keeps a person awake at night, eating away at what little pride they have left. It's not the same, maybe, but I live with regret every day."

She turned to face him again. "What do you regret?"

He met her eyes, trying hard not to look away. He needed someone to confide in so much it scared him, but how could he tell her this after what she'd just told him? Knowing what she'd been through made him feel as guilty as Patrick. She would hate him if she knew.

"It's not a story you'd want to hear. I shouldn't have said anything."

"I just turned myself inside out in front of you. You don't think I'd want to hear your story? Are you being presumptuous or just arrogant?"

Nick wished he would learn to keep his mouth shut. Jack used to say he could dig a hole deeper than any shovel. Now he felt like he'd backhoed a ditch around himself. He wanted to tell her everything, but once he told her, he wouldn't be able to take it back. He'd never been more unsure of himself than in that moment. Chills ran the length of his body and he looked for an excuse to back away.

"You went through something horrible, but I caused something horrible. Trust me, you really don't want to hear this."

"Do I at least get the opportunity to judge that for myself?"

"Why? Why do you want to?"

"You brought it up. Plus I'm standing here all vulnerable and open, with you knowing more about me than I do you. At least tell me something."

He took a deep breath. His hands were sweating. His voice was shaky. Never nervous on a stage facing thousands of people, yet afraid of his own shadow in a room with one other person. The irony almost made him laugh.

"Don't say I didn't warn you." He sat on the edge of the sofa, rubbing his palms against his legs as though he might get up and pace the room, but he stayed on the couch and took another deep breath before finally telling her what happened. "A few months ago we played our big homecoming show in Richland. Just off a world tour, it was our first show back home in three years. A big deal. We played an amazing set. I think it was one of our best shows. I know it was." He stopped. Looked up. Met her eyes with intention. "I'm not a saint. We drank a lot, every night. Whiskey, bourbon, beer, vodka, whatever was around, we chugged it like water and we did a lot of stupid things."

She noticed his leg shaking as he lightly tapped his heel against the floor.

"Life was a big party." He laughed. "That's what we told ourselves, you only live once or some nonsense. Jack had a bottle of pills. I know I took some. Most of that night is a mass of puzzle pieces I'm still trying to put together, but some things I remember. I was driving too fast. It was raining. I didn't see the car braking in front of us until it was too late."

He didn't want to continue. Nick eyed the nearest path toward the front door. The easiest way out had always been more appealing than facing responsibility, but Jess was the first person he'd even come close to confiding in and he needed to get this out. He'd come this far. He had to finish no matter what happened after.

"We hit the barrier wall on the interstate. Drew was in the back. Somehow he survived, but he's never going to walk again. And Jack . . . well, Jack is the worst part of it."

He had to stop. He couldn't go there, to that place where he knew he wouldn't have control, laid bare and defenseless. Control was the only thing he had left, and it was running in the other direction.

Jess stayed by the window. "It's okay," she said. "You don't have to say anymore."

Nick focused on her sobering eyes. Honest, compassionate eyes. A single teardrop slipped down his cheek.

"Jack went through the windshield. They had to use dental

records to identify his body. I killed my best friend, Jess. I'm a murderer."

She took several moments to process this new information.

"Say something."

"You're not a murderer. You didn't do it on purpose."

"I chose to get behind the wheel of that car, and Jack paid the price. He's dead because of me."

"True, but . . ."

"But what?"

"I don't see a murderer when I look at you."

"Why not? You said Patrick had been careless and reckless and stupid. That pretty much sums up what I did. I've been struggling with so much guilt since the accident, and hearing your story has made me see just how guilty I really am." She hesitated. Nick *had* been reckless. He had been responsible for his friend's death. She should be disgusted, horrified, angry. But she wasn't, not with him.

She joined him on the couch. "You aren't Patrick."

"You don't know me well enough to make that call."

"I knew him well enough. He was selfish and arrogant, boastful and pompous at times. He ruined my life long before he killed our daughter. Being married to him was like living in a prison. I don't know why I stayed, really. Abby was the one thing that kept me going. She was my whole world. And then she was gone."

"So how am I not just like him? I can be selfish and arrogant."

"I don't know. It's hard to look at you and see him. You didn't know him. You didn't see the way he laughed at me, embarrassed me, the way he scolded me for not giving him what he wanted. He could be the coolest, most charming guy in the room and then a split second later the most bitter and scornful person you ever met. I don't see that in you."

"What do you see?"

Jess looked into his piercing blue eyes, followed the broad lines of his nose and chin, the lines around his cheeks and mouth. She gazed deeper into his eyes, full of pain and uncertainty. There was a softer side to this unpolished musician. He cared about more than just himself. He seemed to care deeply about his friend.

He didn't wait for a response. "I should have died that night. It should have been me, not him."

"It could have been all three of you," she said.

"So why wasn't it? Why am I still here?"

"I don't have answers to those questions. My brother might say that it's God's will. He would tell you that God has a purpose for you or something."

"Is that what you believe?"

She sighed. "I struggle to make sense why it would be God's purpose to take my child away. Why would a loving God allow an innocent little girl to suffer like that? Why would he allow me to suffer? Why not take Patrick and punish him? Why Abby? She didn't do anything wrong."

"Do you believe in God?" Nick turned to face her better.

"I used to. Now I don't know. I'm just angry and hurt, and I don't understand." She looked away.

"I never thought about God in all of this. Maybe your brother is right. Maybe there's some hidden reason why things happen to us. Maybe we're supposed to learn something."

"What could I possibly learn from having my heart ripped out of my chest?" she asked.

"Good question. If I knew the answer I probably wouldn't be so lost."

"I guess we're lost together then."

"Just two lost souls swimming in a fishbowl."

"Huh?" Jess shot him a puzzled look.

Nick laughed. "It's a Pink Floyd song."

"Who?"

He grinned. "They were a popular band in the seventies. Never mind."

She shook her head and concealed the tiniest hint of a grin. "Is it always about music?"

"For me, yeah. Music keeps me sane."

"You didn't bring your guitar today."

"I figured I didn't need it if I was making jam."

"Preserves," she corrected.

Nick smiled. "Damson preserves."

"Which we haven't made."

"Kind of seems pointless now, huh?"

"Maybe."

They both looked away.

Jess was embarrassed for having revealed so much to someone she knew so little.

Nick wondered if she would even want to see him again after she'd had time to really think about it. "I get it. The stuff in your pantry. It's your way of keeping her here with you."

She took a sharp breath. "You're the first person who has understood that." Tears made a grand reentrance. "I'm not trying to pretend she isn't gone. Some days I do, but I'm not delusional."

"You're trying to hold on to all the little things that remind you of her."

She nodded.

"There's nothing delusional about that."

"Tell that to my brother."

"Everyone has an opinion, rarely a solution."

The room filled with silence, a warm peacefulness that didn't need any extra words. Nick wished he'd brought his guitar. Moments like that were more satisfying with a melody in the air.

"I guess we can try making jam another time?" she said.

"Preserves," he corrected.

They both grinned.

"I don't think we'll ever get this right," she said.

"I'll have fun trying," he said.

She smiled again. Jess could get used to that. Smiling. She used to be good at it. Nick gave her a reason to try it again.

12

A LITTLE HOPE

"Mark? Mark!" Elise cried, bursting into his office.

He looked up from the power point presentation on his computer. "What's going on?"

"Martin Strombridge and his wife have been holding Bible studies at the women's prison in Richland," she said, walking over to him and leaning against his desk.

"Yeah. I gave him the contact info to get that going."

"Well, last night they met a young woman who's been sentenced to twenty years for armed robbery and aggravated assault. She's only nineteen, and she's pregnant. She has no family, no ties, and the father is also incarcerated."

Mark knew where this was going. He removed his reading glasses and let out a long, breathy sigh.

"Mark, she's willing to terminate her rights. She wants to give up the child for adoption."

He sighed again. "We've been over this. It's too soon. I'm not ready."

"Well, I am and this is could be the one. She has no one to

give the baby to. When she gives birth, the state will place the child in the foster care system."

"Elise, it could end up being like every other time. We don't know this woman. We don't know her history, her background. What if she changes her mind?"

"What if she doesn't?" Elise persisted.

"What about the father?"

"He's never asserted his rights, and he has agreed to sign the papers." She stared him down with determined eyes.

"Elise, I don't want to go through this again. I know this is important to you. I know how badly you want this, but I just can't."

"So you want to give up? Is it not important to you too?" Her shoulders tensed as she edged closer to him.

"I'm not saying that."

"What are you saying?"

"I'm saying cool it for a while. Put the brakes on. Stop looking at every pregnant woman as a potential birthmother." He shuffled papers, taking in long breaths as he tried to shift his focus to something else.

"Words of wisdom from the preacher? Mark, I know this is hard, but what if this is God's gift to us? What if this time is *the* time?"

"And how much torment do we put ourselves through testing what may or may not be His timing?"

"This child needs a loving home, and we're able to provide one. Why are you being so negative?" Her eyes pleaded with him.

"I'm being realistic. Sometimes I think you are too optimistic. I admire your faith and your enthusiasm, Elise. It's one of the things I love most about you, but every story doesn't have a fairy-tale ending. God's people endure hardships. Some things just don't work out like we want them to."

"I know that, Mark. I of all people know that. But should we stop trying? There's a child coming into the world in a few months, whether we take it or not. This baby needs a home. I want to offer it one."

He rubbed his face with his hands and leaned back in his chair. "When Abby died I watched Jess go through agonizing pain. I've watched you suffer over and over again. There's something deeper in a mother's loss that I can't grasp. But when I see that torment in your eyes, it breaks my heart into pieces. I don't want to lose another child, and I can't watch you go through that again."

She sat on his leg and leaned against him, her tiny frame nestling perfectly within his broad, muscular physique. They were at two ends of a spectrum, trying to meet in a middle that didn't seem to exist.

"I don't want to lose another child, but I'm not ready to stop trying. I still believe this is going to happen. I wish you were on the same page." She reached for his hand, lacing her fingers between his.

"Where does all your strength come from?" he asked.

She smiled, breathing in the manly scent of deodorant wafting from the warmth of his shirt as she took comfort in his embrace. "You of all people should know the answer to that."

He did, and she had a way of reminding him where his focus should be. He glanced at his Bible lying on the desk, partially sticking out from a stack of sermon notes, its leather binding worn and fading around the edges. She'd given it to him in college, their first Christmas as a couple. It was the first Bible he'd ever owned and his most cherished copy.

He sighed long and hard. "Okay."

She pulled back, meeting his eyes. "Okay?"

He hesitated. "One more time. That's it, Elise. I mean it."

She kissed him, so many emotions emerging at once, and faced him with watery eyes. "Faith, remember?"

He caressed her arm, resting his head against hers. She was the glue holding him together, the calming influence to his strong-willed nature.

"I have faith, Elise, but even the strongest faith doesn't ensure everything will work out the way we want it to. Through faith comes many trials."

"Trials produce patience."

She astounded him. He often thought he'd learned more from her than anyone had ever learned from him.

"The waiting is what kills me." He stroked her short wavy hair.

"I know. Me too."

Elise came home alone after visiting the prison with Mark. He'd gone to the church building to finish his PowerPoint. She walked upstairs, consumed by thoughts of their meeting with Shandra, a scared young girl, determined her child would not go into the foster care system. They'd met many scared women in the search for a child to call their own. Often they were very young, goaded by their families to give up the baby in hopes for a better life.

Shandra had practically raised herself, living on the street since her mother overdosed when she was fourteen. Her boyfriend, Dominic, a drug dealer, had taken her in when she was sixteen. Shandra was a failed child of the system, one who had fallen through the cracks and managed to make a life for herself, however misshapen and pitiful that life had become.

Elise turned the knob of a door near the top of the stairs. The nursery. She lingered just inside, hesitating for a moment. She seldom walked into this room. After each miscarriage the door had been closed, only to be opened again during each adoption process as Elise collected diapers and clothing, adding little touches to the room to personalize it for each child. Each child who never was. Walking into this room roused an ache in her heart, feelings of loss and dread, fear and anxiety. She wanted a child, and she wasn't going to stop trying.

Stepping farther inside, the neatly kept room jarred her. Memories and painful events flooded her at once. The sound of Mark's voice whispering in her ear at the hospital the day they'd lost their first child, a little girl, echoed in her head as if she were reliving it all over again. *It's okay. It's going to be okay.* She remembered the wetness of his tears smeared against her cheek as he repeated those same words over and over, trying to convince himself as much as her. So many times they had cried together, holding each other, absorbing the strength of the other person.

Elise sat down in the wooden rocker. She imagined what it would be like to hold a baby in this room, to hear those tiny cries in the wee hours of the night. All the things mothers probably took for granted. Poopy diapers, spit-up, fussy days, colic, waiting in the doctor's office with a tantrum-throwing toddler, everything and anything that meant she was a mother.

She'd rocked her niece to sleep many times, but nieces and daughters were two different things. Abby had been the closest thing to a child of their own she and Mark had ever had. That was why he'd spoiled Abby so much. Jess's disapproving glares every time he brought Abby home with ice cream and candy never deterred him from treating her to their special "Uncle Mark and Abby Days." She died three days after their second failed adoption. Their toughest year.

Elise didn't wallow. She didn't commit herself to drowning in sorrow like Jess had. The only way she'd ever dealt with struggles was looking forward. Glancing back never made it better. Fear was easy. Bravery was something she had to muster.

Elise prided herself on having it all pulled together, neatly wrapped with a bow on top, even if lava was brewing under the surface. Her heart ached, but she wasn't going to show that to other people. She put her best face on for the world to see and pushed the ugly stuff into a far corner where she could deal with it later.

She heard a shuffle downstairs. Footsteps thumped closer until Mark appeared in the doorway, watching her with an expression she couldn't read.

"Let's leave the door open this time." She smiled.

"A little risky, don't you think?" he said.

"What's risky about confidence? You don't believe in luck. Letting the light into this room is like a gesture of good faith. I'm tired of doubts and fear."

He stepped inside, looking around the museum of defeat, so much hope compiled into one room that had never served its purpose. "I'm still full of doubts."

She walked over to him and placed a hand on his shoulder. He picked up a rubber duck from the top of a basket full of bath toys and squeaked it a few times.

"I need to know that you want this as much as I do," she said.

He pulled her close. She stood five feet, 2 inches against his six feet, two-inch stature. "I do," he whispered.

"Let's go shopping for baby clothes." Elise looked up at him with a wide-eyed grin.

"Don't you think that's jumping the gun?" He took a step back.

"If it doesn't work out we'll donate them to someone in need. Please?"

He didn't want to go shopping. He looked around at the room that already had plenty to begin with and wondered what else they could possibly need. He couldn't say no to the beautiful eyes of the woman he loved so dearly. She completed his shortcomings and enhanced his strengths. He was willing to do just about anything for her. He prayed it would work out this time.

"Just a few items. We already have so much."

She grinned. "Deal."

He held her a little while longer, wishing he could be as optimistic as she was. He wanted to be happy and joyful, but caution seemed more logical. He needed to protect her from heartbreak, protect himself from reaching a place he feared he might not come back from.

13

CLARITY

*B*ridgetown's annual charity drive brought hundreds of people to the middle school gym. Eager volunteers showed up to collect, sort, and box clothing, food, and other necessities the city's food pantry would distribute to underprivileged families in Bridgetown and surrounding communities. Mark and Elise were the first to arrive, early that morning. They had served on the oversight committee for six years and were expecting their biggest turnout since the event began.

Jess agreed to come. She wasn't sure why exactly, but she hadn't been able to come up with an excuse that didn't make her look selfish. Mark hadn't been the one to call her. Elise had extended the invitation, and that had surprised Jess. She'd been expecting a guilt trip from her pesky big brother about getting out of the house and doing something positive in the community, blah, blah, blah. Not hearing from him for a few days wasn't the sigh of relief she'd thought it would be. Jess thought about calling him, but she couldn't bring herself to make the first move. She had as much pride as he did, both too stubborn and reluctant to admit their shortcomings. A Stuart family trait.

Mark kept his distance, learning new boundaries with Jess. As unnatural as it felt, he had stepped back, giving her as much breathing room as he could stand without feeling like he'd abandoned her completely. It was torment. He hated his need to be in control even more than she did. They exchanged welcoming glances from across the room. Jess even returned his smile, something she hadn't done in a long time.

Long tables, assembled in row after row across a glossy gymnasium floor, held piles of donations ranging from clothing to toys and an array of household goods people needed to get rid of that were still in good condition. Boxes and crates were stacked around the room, some empty, some spilling over with shoes, nonperishable foods, and a vast assortment of toiletry products. Elise directed volunteers to their tasks as more items were being dropped off throughout the morning. Everything needed to be sorted, boxed, and labeled, then stacked according to category for loading into moving vans waiting outside. From there it would all be taken to a distribution center to disperse among those seeking assistance.

Jess had donated Patrick's clothes at the last drive. She wanted to bring some of Abby's, but the simple act of walking in Abby's room was unbearable. That morning she'd tried her best to go through Abby's clothes, knowing they would benefit another little girl, someone who needed them, but she couldn't. Giving away Abby's belongings was like losing her all over again. They were just things, but they were *her* things, and to Jess they were part of Abby, the last piece of her that still existed in a tangible state she could smell and touch. She wasn't ready to let go. Maybe next year. Yes, she would try again next year. And the year after that. And any time she was given opportunity. Jess wanted to be over it, done with the wasting away and skewed sense of reality, but it was like being trapped at the bottom of a well with no way to climb out.

The gym buzzed with activity, people passing back and forth, occupied with the many tasks needed to make everything run like clockwork. Jess watched as boxes were emptied out for better sorting. She folded T-shirts by size in a cozy corner no one else wanted to work. Fine by her. Staying out of the way and keeping to herself was all she could stomach. Too many people, too much noise. Jess longed for her peaceful nest on the porch.

Nick showed up late, lost in a sea of strangers. Elise, who had been the one to invite him, put him to work stacking books and shoes at a table with two other guys who seemed as clueless as he was. Several yards away he caught Jess's eye, two awkward glances meeting in silent conversation. They hadn't seen or spoken to each other since the failed attempt at damson something or other in a jar. He wondered what she thought about him now that she knew. He wondered what he should say to her after having revealed so much, so soon.

He wanted to approach her, say hello, hear the soft tones in her voice, but hesitation paralyzed him, and he waited for her to make the first move. Nick watched her fold shirts, glancing up from shoe wrangling every few minutes, occasionally meeting her own long-distance stares. Silent camaraderie. He smiled. She grinned. He did his best silent infomercial showcase of a rather snazzy pair of red-and-white running shoes. She returned his display with a two-for-one deal on screen print Tees, modeling them playfully. *Sold.*

Mark noticed their exchange from his corner of half-stacked boxes. He knew they had made a connection. He couldn't ignore it. Knowing someone else had succeeded in penetrating Jess's defensive walls when he had been trying for months with little success was a painful jab to his ego and his heart. *I'm supposed to be the one she turns to for help.* Yet watching them, seeing the gleam in her eyes that had been vacant for so long, made him wonder if he was trying too hard to fit inside a role he wasn't designed for.

Maybe she didn't need him to protect her. Maybe what she needed, he wasn't able to give. If someone else could get through to her, help her find her way back, he should be thankful.

"What are you looking at?" Elise snuck up beside him.

"A spark of hope." Mark lifted the stack of boxes in front of him and carried them outside, leaving Elise to guess his meaning.

The room overflowed as the number of drop-offs increased and more volunteers showed up. Jess had been standing so long her back twisted in a dull, radiating pain. She rubbed her spine, stretching stiff muscles, and continued packing boxes by T-shirt size.

Nick cleaned scuff marks from a pair of soccer shoes. He had an entire table of boy's athletic wear in front of him, and even more boxes of footwear stacked around him, but he couldn't stop thinking about Jess. She intrigued him. Most of all she seemed to see right through him. He didn't need to pretend with her. He didn't want to pretend when he was with her. He could open up, be himself, like he always had with Jack, though she was much prettier. Nick laughed at the thought. Jack would approve of her. He'd probably be flirting with her, asking for her number. They'd probably end up arguing over who had seen her first.

Caught in the act of staring again, Nick shrugged and glanced at a stack of boxes ready to go. He needed to get out of that room, clear his head. He carried them outside, thankful for sunshine and fresh air, and helped load them into an empty van. He watched the loading efforts and counted the number of men supervising the vehicles. He'd played for charity events, auctioned off memorabilia for worthy causes, but he'd never been a part of something like this, where community came together like family. None of these people were promoting albums or movies, or perfecting a persona for the world to idolize. He realized how long he'd been away and how much he'd missed the simplicity of his former life.

Nick startled at the pat of a large hand against his back. He turned around and Mark motioned him to follow. They walked away from the commotion of the school, to the calming atmosphere of a neighboring park. Mark sat down on a weathered, gray picnic table and waited for Nick to join him. Neither spoke for several moments. Every bird chirp and rustling tree branch became more amplified the longer their silence continued.

"What are your intentions with my sister?" Mark finally spoke.

"Intentions?" Nick asked.

"Yeah."

Nick rubbed his arm. "I don't think I have any."

"She's fragile."

"Yeah, I know."

"She's been through a lot."

Nick agreed.

"How much has she told you?" Mark asked.

"Enough."

Mark nodded.

"I know she's in a lot of pain."

Mark inhaled slowly, releasing it in one long, quiet sigh. "When our parents passed, she was still a teenager. I was in college. It wasn't easy but I took care of her."

"What happened?" Nick asked.

"Our mom developed an aggressive form of breast cancer. She died before Jess's sixteenth birthday."

"I'm sorry."

"Our dad died a couple years later from a heart attack. Grief does terrible things to people."

"Yeah." Nick looked away.

"You've had your share of grief," Mark said.

He had. Nick couldn't help thinking how much he and Jess had in common. He didn't mind that Mark knew so much about him, but he did worry what opinions he'd formed as a result.

"Are we here to talk about me or Jess?" Nick asked.

"Both," Mark replied.

"I know your opinion of me is really low. You read the head-lines. You see a man who's reckless and out of control and you want to protect your sister. I get that."

"But?" Mark inserted.

"I don't know. What do you want me to say? I'm not trying to hurt anyone. I'm just trying to survive one day to the next. Keep my head above water."

"She's sinking too."

"I know," Nick replied.

"Two drowning people can't save each other," Mark said.

"I'm not looking for a savior."

"Maybe you should be."

"Is that church talk? Save your preaching for Sunday."

"Preacher or not, I know a thing or two about loss. I counsel people in all kinds of situations. You have to be able to stand on your own two feet before you can take on someone else's problems."

"I'm not trying to take on anyone's problems."

"When you get close to someone, when you start to care, their life becomes part of yours, problems and all, whether you want it to or not."

"Who said anything about caring?"

"If you don't care then why are you here?" Mark asked.

"I don't know. I used to think I had an answer for everything. I thought I could take on the whole world. I don't have any more answers."

"If you don't care then you should walk away because—"

"Look, I care. I care about a lot of things. Caring isn't the problem. I don't know what you want me to say. Why are we here?"

Mark looked him in the eyes. "I want you to be careful. Jess doesn't need another reason to hurt. She doesn't need anyone destructive in her life."

"You think I'm destructive? Maybe I am. I know a few people who think so."

"I think you need help. I think you need the kind of healing you aren't going to get until you're willing to admit you need it."

"There isn't any help for someone like me. I'm a wasted cause."

"If you really believe that, then it's true," Mark said.

Nick huffed. "Is this where you tell me about hope and believing in myself and all that crap?"

"No. You haven't asked for my help."

"And if I did?"

Mark eyed him sharply. "I'd tell you to man up. Stop feeling sorry for yourself and try to see the blessings in your life. You think it's all over? You walked away from that wreck. Don't tell me there isn't meaning in that."

"I killed a man," Nick snapped. "His life was worth more than mine."

"Would it have been better if you had died in that crash?"

"Yeah. If anyone deserved to live, it was him."

"But he didn't. You did."

Nick scowled.

"You can't change what happened. Life would be easier if we could take things back, but then we wouldn't learn anything. The fact that you're still here gives you a pretty big opportunity to make things right, to examine your character and figure out what kind of person you want to be. If you can't see that you'll never get beyond all of this."

Nick listened, allowing Mark's words to sink in. Then he looked up and saw Jess in the distance, handing boxes to one of the men working on the moving trucks.

"Think about what I said. Call me if you want to talk." Mark left him alone, joining his sister outside the school.

Nick watched them disappear inside the gym. Mark's wisdom made perfect sense, but Nick wasn't looking for unsolicited wisdom. He didn't know what he was looking for. His own words were sinking in harder than ever before. *I killed a man.* How do you come back from that?

His heavy heart beat faster. Nick could feel the suffocating strangle of frustration choking his resolve as he swallowed hard and clenched his fists to tame his brooding emotions.

I don't want to feel like this anymore. Walking home, he did the only thing he knew to make it better. Nick stopped at a liquor store and purchased two bottles of Jack Daniels. He didn't mind the thought of drinking himself to death. Sleep sounded fine too. Never waking up sounded even better.

14

TIME

*D*ale waited up, worried and irritated. The analog clock by his mantle ticked away, counting down each second his son was unaccounted for. *Tick. Tick. Tick.* Familiar sounds, reminiscent of time spent in that very chair waiting up for his wife, Lenore. He sat in darkness, watching moonbeams dot the living room wall. *Where is that boy?* His thoughts became a jumbled mess, but he refused to panic. Nicholas had a good head on his shoulders, at least he used to, *maybe*. Sadness crept in. He mourned the child he'd once held in his arms, the boy he'd taught to read and played catch with in the backyard. He regretted every day he'd spent apart from Nicholas. He rejected this pompous man his son had become.

He thought of Lenore, her long, sand-colored hair pressed against the sides of her face the day Nicholas was born. They'd held him together, crowded onto a hospital bed barely made for one person. She was covered in perspiration and exhausted. He'd worked a double shift and was running on fumes and remnants of a stale candy bar from the waiting room vending machine. Yet they'd laid so peacefully, watching Nicholas, staring at his tiny features and limbs, counting every finger and toe until Lenore fell asleep and Dale was left holding his son alone, the little being that had made him a father.

Twenty-seven years later, he now sat alone, empty arms, waiting for his son to walk through the door. Nick's drinking had increased since his arrival. In so many ways he resembled his mother. They had the same jawline, hair color, and skin tone. His laugh even sounded like hers. The way he gestured with his hands, the perceptive looks that could penetrate a person's resolve; they were all Lenore. Dale saw few things of himself in Nick. He had Dale's eyes, blue and brooding. They both ate their cereal the same way, chocolate milk, never white. Nick also had an impressive memory like Dale's, instant recall of facts and figures, colors and sounds. Everything else seemed to come from Lenore, and Dale didn't mind. He'd loved her since the first week he'd met her. Still loved her.

How do you save someone who doesn't want to be saved? He questioned himself over and over, searching for reason and logic. Nick's words looped in his head, *Says the man with the broken son.* He couldn't stop thinking about it. How had he managed to raise a broken shell of a man? What had he done wrong? What could he have done differently? Doubts weighed heavy, clouding his perception of the past.

They'd been close for many years, even after Lenore's death. They'd maintained a strong bond until Nick entered high school, when Dale first noticed him slipping away. It couldn't have come out of nowhere, but raging teen hormones and Dale's promotion at the factory might have played a role in it. He'd been working longer hours. Nick refused to spend time with him, choosing his friends over Dale's automotive passions and the boring old men he ate Sunday brunch with. He should have gotten to the bottom of things back then. Now it seemed too late.

Turning on the lamp beside him, Dale took out the leather-bound photo album he kept on a shelf underneath the small end table and thumbed through page after page of family photos, stopping at one of the three of them visiting Marmont Plantation, a nearby historical attraction. Nick was grasping both parents' hands, legs pointed outward as they swung him back and forth between them. Dale rubbed a finger over their faces in the photograph, same smile, same fiery passion for life in their eyes.

He flipped a few pages, turning over time-lapsed fragments of a thirty-year history. Lenore had always been a drinker. When they first met she had a beer with every meal, but it wasn't until Nick turned two that she started drinking heavily. By the time Nick turned five, she was wasted by lunchtime every day.

One picture stopped Dale dead in his tracks. Christmas. Nick was six years old. Lenore held his small head between her hands, tilting her forehead to his. The purest look of love and admiration emanated from their expressions. Nick had been her shadow, Mommy's little helper. Even in her darkest hours, Lenore had managed to make him feel safe and loved. Nick hadn't known the raging demons that plagued her until after her death, when he was old enough to understand. Dale had struggled to discuss her illness with him. How do you tell your only child his mother destroyed everything good in their lives?

The front door swung open, banging against the wall behind it. Dale glanced at the clock. Two thirty-two.

Nick staggered inside the house, leaning on solid structures for support. Dale stood up, and Nick recognized his figure in the shadows. "Still up?" Nick slurred.

"Do you have any idea what time it is?" Dale asked, turning on more lights.

"Do you have any idea that I don't care?" Nick laughed. "Who made you warden?"

"Get to bed, Nicholas. We'll talk in the morning."

"Get to bed?" Nick's laughter became hysterical. "I'm a grown man, old man." His speech was so slurred he repeated syllables.

"You're drunk."

A devilish grin formed on Nick's face, curling up sharply at each corner of his mouth. "Ding, ding, ding! He wins the prize. Rocket science."

"Nicholas."

"That's me. Maybe *you* should go to bed. On second thought, why don't *you* get drunk? We could have a father/son bonding moment. I bet you don't even know what drunk is."

Nick laughed so hard he nearly doubled over. Dale reached out, grabbing him by the arms, pulling him up to steady him against his own stocky frame.

"Come on, son. Let's get you in the bed." Dale tugged Nick forward.

"I don't want to go to bed. I'm not done yet. I still have a bottle of . . . Wait. I left them on the . . ." Nick turned toward the door.

"You can get it in the morning. You've had enough to drink, Nicholas."

Nick's countenance changed. "Didn't I tell you not to call me that?"

Dale held him by one arm. "All right, son. We'll talk about it in the morning. Now get to—"

"No! I'm talking now! Get your hands off me!" Nick shoved his father away, staggering back. He lost his balance quickly, dropping to the floor with a loud thud.

Dale remained calm. He reached down to help Nick off the floor, but his hands were slapped away.

"Don't touch me!" His unsteady movements made it impossible to stand on his own again.

"Nicholas, let me help you." Dale pulled him hard, bringing him to a standing position.

"I told you not to call me that!" Nick swung at Dale, missing him completely and forcing himself into a wall. The crash jarred him, but he was so numb from the liquor he barely felt the impact.

Dale saw Lenore against that wall, the way she used to lunge at him, hit and swing at him until she passed out. She would pick up whatever object was closest and hurl it in his direction.

"Please, son . . ."

"Pleeeeease, son," Nick mocked him. "You whine too much. You're pathetic."

Dale said nothing. He watched Nick slide across the wall trying to hold himself up, then took a few steps back to give him space.

"I learned something today. I learned that I'm a worthless piece of sh—"

"Watch your mouth," Dale snapped.

"Or what?" He laughed again. "What are you going to do? Haven't you learned by now that you can't control me?"

"It's not about control."

Nick snorted. "Everything in life is about control." He collapsed to the ground. "Your rules are about control. My drinking is about control."

"You're *out* of control," Dale muttered under his breath.

Nick sat on the floor staring up at his father. The sullen gaze of hazy blue eyes pierced Dale's heart. Teardrops escaped and he wiped them quickly, grabbing every ounce of strength he could muster. They remained silent for moments that hung like a thick, eerie, fog swallowing the room whole. Nick's slack frame crumpled farther against the floor.

"How did I get here?" Nick asked.

"The floor or the house?" Dale replied.

Nick's eyes were distant, fading into the abyss of intoxication.

"This place in my life. I'm famous. I have it all. I'm a rock star." He huffed.

Dale couldn't tell if he was being serious. He squatted in front of Nick.

"I want to help you, son, but you have to let me."

Nick looked his father directly in the eyes, breath reeking of whiskey. "You can't help me. You never could." A trail of tears ran down the left side of his face.

"Tell me what to do. Tell me how to fix this," Dale pleaded in a soft whisper.

"I'm not an old car or some equipment at your factory. I can't be fixed."

"That's not true, Nicholas."

"I should have died in that car with Mom."

Dale's legs gave way and he plopped to the floor. Chills ran through him like ice in his veins. "What are you talking about?"

Nick slumped over sideways, collecting in a heap on the floor. He studied the ceiling above him, spinning violently like strobe lights at a club. "I was in the seat next to her. She kept yelling and saying things that didn't make sense. She was slapping the wheel, slapping me, swerving and cursing. I was scared so I got on the floor and scooted as far back as I could, where she couldn't reach me. Then the car started spinning and I felt this powerful force against my back. I closed my eyes, and when I looked up her face was covered in blood, eyes wide open, watching me."

Dale squeezed his jaw, rubbing his beard and gritting his teeth to hold in the anger and confusion rushing over him. "You never told me that. You said you didn't see her."

"I tried to tell you."

"When?" Dale asked.

Nick rolled over, eyes full of tears, silently pleading for the pain to end. "Every time I wanted to talk about her, you changed the subject. Eventually I just gave up."

Dale closed his eyes, weighing this revelation. He had failed as a father, failed to search deeper, to know the extent his son had suffered. He'd failed to protect him from someone they both loved dearly. A rush of anger washed over him, wishing he could go back and fix it. He needed Nicholas to know how hard he'd tried as a parent. That he would burn the whole world down to save him from whatever pain he was going through. There were so many things he wanted Nicholas to know, but he couldn't form the words. He didn't know where to begin.

Nick finally passed out, dead weight against the hardwood floor. He seemed as delicate and vulnerable as the day he'd been born. Dale watched his son sleep, monitored his breathing, checked his pulse rate. He touched his hand to Nick's forehead. *How did we get here?* It was a question that needed to be answered, but even more than that was the question, *where do we go from here?*

15

REGRET

*D*ry mouth, pounding head, the feeling of a twenty-ton truck pinning him down. Nick woke the next day late in the afternoon, aching from head to toe. Barely able to open his eyes, he squinted, straining to see where he was. Once, after a long night of strip clubs with Jack and some guys from another band, he'd woken up in an alley behind a Chinese restaurant with a bottle of Jim Beam in his hands and a gang of cats licking his clothes. The harder Nick partied, the more disconnected from himself and the world he became.

He recognized his bedroom and the quilt draped loosely over his street clothes, sticky with sweat. He didn't remember coming home. He didn't remember getting into bed. He barely remembered walking into the liquor store the day before, but he could recall with clarity the sweet taste of Jack Daniels burning his throat gulp after gulp.

The bedroom door creaked open. Squinting again, he watched his dad enter slowly. Then he remembered. Fragments of conversation from the night before and what a jerk he'd been. Nick wasn't ready for confrontation. He needed some water, a couple of beers, and five more hours of sleep.

"You're awake," Dale said.

"Barely," Nick replied.

"Can I get you anything?"

"No." In that moment Nick wanted to say more. He wanted to apologize for lashing out, tell his dad how badly his body ached, how much he was hurting on the inside and needed Dale's help. He wanted to apologize for being such a lousy son. But he didn't. He just laid there, ignoring his dad and the situation. If he pretended it never happened, maybe it would go away.

Dale closed the door.

Nick fumbled through the pile of trash accumulating next to his bed. He found a half-empty water bottle and two bottles of beer with at least a swig still in them. The taste was rancid. He downed it all anyway, tossing the bottles across the room.

He stretched and twisted, an attempt to revive himself from his half-dead state. Flopping and tossing, staring at random objects, and watching sunlight filter in through partially open blinds made him more restless. His stomach turned somersaults, churning in agony.

The urge to jump up and run down the hall to the bathroom struck so suddenly he barely made it in time. Vomit ejected from his throat as he hung his head halfway in the toilet, clinging to the rim. Green bile and chunks of who knows what floated in the cloudy water, a smell so foul it made him throw up again. Every time he thought he was finished another wave coursed through his body, burning his throat and sending sharp pains to his abdomen.

A light tap rattled the door.

"You all right?" Dale asked.

Nick panted. "Yeah." He hadn't been this sick since Jack's last birthday.

"I took the day off work. If you need anything let me know."

Nick didn't respond. He hugged the toilet bowl, hoping it would end. Eventually he sprawled across the chilled tile floor, relishing its cool relief against his hot skin.

When he finally made it back to his room, he sank into his bed, keeping as still as possible. The ceiling fan whirled above him. His heart pounded through his chest with every inhale and exhale. *Just a few more hours of sleep.*

A hard object pressed into his left hip from under the covers. He dug through layers of blanket and sheets and pulled out his cellphone. He'd kept it turned off since the accident, only using it to contact his probation officer and check his voicemails from Alan, avoiding social media. The home screen displayed a back-stage picture of him and the guys goofing off after a show. This time he focused on Drew. He'd wondered about him so many times, too cowardly to reach out and get answers. *Should I call him?* The question traveled circles in his head until he finally watched his finger tap the call button in his contact list.

The phone rang several times. Maybe he had a new number. Maybe he saw it was Nick calling and didn't want to answer. Morgan was probably screening his calls. Then a familiar voice startled him.

"Hey, man," Drew's raspy voice croaked on the other end as though he'd just woken up.

"Drew?"

"Yeah, man. Don't you know who you called?"

He laughed. "Yeah, just making sure."

"How you been?"

He should have been asking Drew that question. "I'm staying at my dad's."

"Back home in good ole, small-town America. Bet you're loving that."

"It is what it is."

"How's probation?"

"Sucks. The guy is nice, but he whistles through his nose when he talks. I hate having to check in like I'm some sort of criminal." Nick paused, remembering he was a criminal.

"Better than getting some arrogant prick who wants to make your life miserable."

"Yeah, I guess."

"You don't sound good."

Nick hated emotions he couldn't control. He clenched his fist and slammed it against the mattress.

"I'm good, man. Should be asking about you." His voice rose and fell. He struggled to hold back the eruption of guilt threatening his composure.

"I'm adjusting. I stay in bed a lot, which means I'm completely caught up on all the latest TV shows. Morgan waits on me hand and foot. I don't know how I got so lucky with her. They're making a wheelchair for me . . . custom fit, all the bells and whistles. I'll be riding in style."

Nick tried to hold it together.

"You there?"

He couldn't stop it. Nick broke down. He sobbed as quietly as he could through clenched teeth and tightened fists.

"I screwed up everything. You, Jack, Votive . . . You should hate me, Drew." Nick breathed deeply between sobs.

"Nick." Drew hesitated. "You've got to stop blaming yourself. All three of us were responsible for what happened. I'm not your victim, man. Neither was Jack."

"I was driving the car, Drew."

"Yeah. And how many times did I get behind the wheel after a night of drinking, or Jack for that matter? Think of all the stupid, irresponsible crap we got away with over the years? We're lucky it didn't happen sooner. Wallow in that for a while."

"I killed him."

"Did you wreck the car on purpose?"

"Does it matter?" Nick sat on the edge of his bed. "I'm tired of everyone minimizing what happened, as though an accidental death is somehow better than if I'd held a gun to his head."

"Okay, you killed him. You're going to have to find a way to live with that."

"And if I can't?"

"What's the alternative?"

Nick was silent.

"Nick. We chose to get in the car with you. Jack and I own just as much responsibility."

"Doesn't feel that way."

Drew was quiet.

"Morgan hates me."

Drew chuckled. "You know how she is. She hates everybody. Mostly you. Morgan's a strong woman, strong-willed and hot-tempered. You guys never really liked each other anyway."

Nick smiled. "Did she tell you I tried to visit you in the hospital?"

"Yeah. Said she gave you a piece of her mind. Bet that was fun."

Nick laughed. "Like always."

"Have you seen Jack's parents yet?" Drew asked.

"I can't go over there. What would I say?"

"Might be a nice gesture. You were like a second son to them."

"Was," Nick replied.

"Might give you closure, all that psychobabble stuff."

"Drew?"

"Yeah."

Nick hesitated. He wanted to tell Drew that he was drowning, suffocating, falling apart from the inside out, but he chickened out.

"Never mind."

"You sure?"

"Yeah."

"Do me a favor, Nick. Forgive yourself. 'Cause I know you, man. You'll hate yourself into the grave, and that's not going to fix any of this."

Nick didn't say anything.

"And don't go so long without calling next time. I miss you, man."

Nick teared up again. "Yeah."

"I've got to go. Morgan's home. She'll flip out if she knows I'm talking to you."

"Okay, later." Nick hung up.

The silence of his room offered no comfort. He burrowed his head against a misshapen pillow and went back to sleep.

16

CONFRONTATION

*N*ick walked down Aubrey Lane two days after his conversation with Drew, having finally worked up enough courage to see Jack's parents. He stopped outside their small, one-story house, reliving scenes from his childhood, two young boys building forts and playing pranks on unsuspecting neighbors. He'd met Jack in fourth grade when the O'Malleys moved to Bridgetown from Portland. Jack was the new kid, and Nick was the loner who sat by himself at lunch. They bonded quickly, and by middle school they'd been inseparable, each spending as much time at the other's house as they did their own. Nick remembered Mrs. O'Malley's home-cooked meals waiting for them on the table and their favorite caramel popcorn she kept on hand from the family grocer down the street.

After making his way up the cracked steps toward their front door, Nick almost turned around. *What am I doing here?* He rang the doorbell with a shaky finger, palms sweating, nervous rhythm of his heartbeat bouncing inside his chest. They were definitely home. He'd seen both cars parked in the driveway. It was nearly dinnertime. He hoped they weren't sitting down to eat. Nick's attention zeroed in on a large dent in the siding, pieces of house chipping away next to a window in need of several coats of paint. He startled when Patricia O'Malley opened the door. Her eyes grew wide, and she took a sudden breath at the sight of him.

Neither knew what to say. Their last meeting had been in the courtroom at sentencing, they'd only seen each other at a distance, with no words exchanged between them, only short glances of remorse and disapproval. Nick cleared his throat. Ordinary conversation wouldn't do, but anything would be better than silence. His tongue refused to cooperate, sticking to the inside of his mouth like glue.

"What do you want?" she finally asked.

Nick stammered. "It's been a while." *Idiot.*

"Yes," she acknowledged.

"I thought I'd . . . I came to . . . I know I . . ." No matter how he tried, the words wouldn't come out right.

"Why are you here?" she asked.

"I don't really know. Maybe we can talk?"

She hesitated on the other side of the glass door for a moment, scrutinizing him. When she finally motioned him inside, Nick stepped lightly into the outdated living room, a familiar atmosphere enveloping his senses and transporting him into the past. It hadn't changed a bit since he and Jack were in school. Same furniture, same décor, same pictures displayed on tables and walls. It was like entering a time machine.

"Have a seat," she said.

Nick sat down on the threadbare couch opposite her armchair, the same couch he'd plopped onto so many times growing up. He and Jack had made the decision to move to Richland while sitting on that couch, three months before graduation. He couldn't help recalling many moments spent on that old, gold sofa as he situated himself near the edge, trying not to get too comfortable. He waited as she lit a cigarette, the last one in her pack.

"I don't really know why I came. I guess I needed to pay my respects."

"Respect?" She shifted her bony frame, smoothing creases in the skirt of her brown polyester dress. "What do you know of respect?" Smoke billowed around her auburn hair.

"I know I hurt you."

"You don't know anything." Her raspy voice crackled. "You boys flew out of here with wild dreams, never paying any mind to the families you left behind or how your decisions might affect your future. Jack could have gone to college. He could have found a trade, really made something of himself."

"Jack didn't want to go to college."

"Don't you tell me what my boy wanted. I knew him better than anyone. I carried him, raised him, gave him everything he needed. I know what he was capable of, and it was a lot more than guitars and concerts."

"He did everything he ever wanted to do. Being a successful musician was Jack's dream, and he accomplished that. He was good at it."

"I don't care about that music nonsense. I care about my son. We hadn't seen him in six years. Couldn't see him when he died because of the closed casket . . ."

Nick watched thin, wet lines stream across deep wrinkles in her face. She sniffled, taking another puff of the nearly finished cigarette. He shouldn't have come. He considered running for the door, but his legs were locked. He sat frozen on the couch with no idea what to say next.

Heavy footsteps bellowed from the kitchen as the back door closed with a loud clap. Nick recognized the sound of those steel-toed boots. He remembered them well.

"Patti," a gruff voice called out from the kitchen. "Did you know Wes Thompson sold his house to a contractor? Manny Whitehall says they're going to build some sort of—"

The weighted footsteps stopped abruptly as Ben O'Malley entered the living room, seeing Nick on his sofa. His jaw quivered. Nick had never seen him that angry.

"What in devil's name are you doing in my house?"

"Sir—" Nick started.

"Don't sir me. There aren't enough formalities in the world to put you right with this family, boy." Ben stood just behind his wife. "You've got nerve showing up here."

"Mr. O'Malley—"

"I'm not finished." Ben pointed a finger in Nick's direction. "We don't want you here. It's all I can do to be cordial to your father when I see him at Waffle House on Sundays. You won't ever be welcome in this house again. You got that?"

Patti remained silent. She reached for a new pack of cigarettes, lighting another one while Ben ranted.

"I didn't come here to upset you—"

"It ain't your coming here that's upsetting. It's the fact you killed our son. Encouraging him to run off and chase some pipe dream. We hardly saw him. He seldom called. I know you did your daddy like that too. Ungrateful piece of white trash—"

"Ben," Patti warned. "Don't get riled up. Your heart."

"I'll get riled up if I want to. My heart stopped beating the day they brought my son to the city morgue and told me I couldn't see him because his body was so mangled. We had to wait three days for the dental records to verify it was him! How'd you walk away from that? Why are you sitting here on my couch and not him?"

Silence penetrated the room like a knife. Patti looked away while Ben stared Nick in the eyes, nostrils flared, breathing hard.

Nick couldn't argue. They couldn't possibly hate him more than he hated himself.

"If I could trade places, I would. Jack was my best friend. I'd give my life for him."

Ben snarled. "But you didn't! You didn't give anything, you selfish son of a—"

"Ben!" Patti scolded. "This isn't helpful. You know what Dr. Billings said."

"Drinking, drugs, getting behind the wheel of a sports car with a dad-blamed blood alcohol content that would kill a bull. You want to act like your mama? Do it without someone else's son in the car!"

Nick didn't want to think about repeating history. He didn't want to connect his mother to what had happened with Jack. Keeping her tightly sealed in his past, where he could view her the way and when he wanted to, was comfortable and reassuring. He couldn't bring himself to look in the mirror and admit he was choosing the same path, that he had been as reckless as his mother.

Nick stood up, pointing his finger directly at Ben. "You didn't know my mother. Don't bring her into this." His voice shook.

"You brought *my* son into that stupid band of yours! Brought him into that car *you* wrecked! I'll tell it like it is in my own house. You got that? Your mother was a slosh-faced drunk. Everybody knows it. All the guys down at the plant used to talk behind your daddy's back, how she went whoring around. You're just like her, you piece of trash."

"Ben, please!" Patti pleaded. She stood up, placing a hand on her husband's shoulder.

"You shut your mouth! My mother was a good woman! She was a good mother!" Nick jabbed his finger in Ben's direction, ready to explode.

"She was a drunk who nearly killed her own son! And now you've killed ours. Only child we had! There ain't nothing you can ever do to right that. Nothing."

Nick sat back down, soaking in the truth. Patti's soft whimpers echoed in the stillness of the room. Ben said nothing. He stood like a statue, gritting his teeth hard enough that Nick could hear them grinding.

"I came here to apologize, but you don't want my apology."

"You're dang straight I don't want an apology from you. I don't need, nor do I ever want anything from you. It's bad enough I have to live in the same town, but I'll be hanged if I'm going to see you in my house another moment. Now either you get out on your own, or I've got a shotgun in the other room with your name all over it." Ben's eyes raged like a madman.

"Benjamin O'Malley!" Patti looked from her husband to Nick, eyes pleading with Nick to leave.

Nick complied and walked toward the door. He passed by a picture of Jack taken at their high school graduation. Jack smiled, young and proud, long dark hair pulled back in a ponytail. There were no pictures of Nick sitting out in his father's house. None of his mother. There were twelve pictures of Jack scattered about that old, shabby living room. Twelve memories Ben and Patti chose to relive each time they sat down on their worn-out sofas.

On the porch, Nick felt the reverberating bang of the door slamming behind him, jarring his bones. He closed his eyes. An evening breeze rolled over him, warm with summer heat, but his skin was cold, chilled like an eerie presence trying to possess him. He wished it would all go away.

Angry blood coursed through his veins as he picked up a small flowerpot and threw it, growling and panting like an animal. Patti watched from the window. If Ben showed his face, he'd give him the finger and tell him to go to hell, but Patti didn't deserve that. He shook his head and left quickly, marching down the sidewalk, head high, feigning pride for the world to see. But he'd rather crush himself into a million pieces. Human shrapnel. Make the outside match the inside.

He spent hours walking around town, unwilling to go home. The rowdy aura and smoke-laced scent of booze from Joe's Place pulled Nick into the crowded corner pub, in a questionable section of town. Raucous conversations and drunken laughter attacked his ears. He took comfort in the familiarity of wafting smoke and the pungent aroma of body odor and cheap whiskey.

"Bottle of vodka," Nick ordered the bartender.

"Whole bottle? This isn't a liquor store."

"Just hand me a shot glass and a bottle. I'll tip you well and I'm not driving." Nick slumped onto a barstool, leaning over the counter.

"It's your dime, buddy." The bartender placed a bottle of Absolute in front of Nick and returned to a group of women at the other end of the counter.

Several shots later, the events unfolding became hazy. Had a large man with a bushy beard, wearing a bandana thrown a beer bottle at him, or had Nick picked up an empty bottle from the counter and thrown it at the man? He wasn't quite sure. The words *pretty boy* and *boy band convict* were vaguely present in Nick's mind, insults made by a table of hysterical bikers across the room. His own comebacks were even foggier, "bloated tub of lard," and "nice bike, did your mama buy it for you?" Had he really said such ridiculous things? It didn't matter who said what. Faster than the bottle had been thrown in either direction, Nick and the scruffy biker were throwing punches like school-yard children.

Nick ended up with a bloody nose, a gash in his left leg, and a giant knot on the back of his head. He estimated there had been about six people in the brawl, but the vodka was playing dirty tricks on his brain, so it might have been three. Hard to tell.

Nick sustained the most damage, but he thought he'd managed to inflict a couple of black eyes and some bruised ribs in the process. Sitting on the side of the road a couple blocks away, his busted head and bruised ego did nothing to feed his dwindling high. He'd been thrown out by the bartender. His brawl-mates had dispersed, leaving him alone, resting against a street sign, hugging his vodka bottle tight.

Blue lights flashed beside him. *Great. Just what I need.*

"Can you stand up, sir?" an officer said as he approached.

"I'm leaving, okay?" Nick attempted to get on his feet.

"How much have you had to drink tonight?" another officer asked.

"Not enough that I need any help." Nick succeeded in standing.

"We got a call about a fight at Joe's Place. Were you involved in that?"

"Maybe. Am I under arrest? If not, I'm going home."

The officers blocked Nick's attempt to walk forward. "Are you aware that public intoxication is against the law?"

Nick shrugged. The two officers engaged in private conversation and then Nick heard his father's name mentioned.

"Are you Dale Miller's son?"

"Oh great. Really? Yeah, I'm Dale's son. Does that give me special privileges or something? I don't need any favors," Nick huffed.

"Why don't you come with us and we'll take you home."

"I don't need a ride." Nick stood as tall as he could in his condition and stared back with glazed eyes, his best attempt at defiance.

"Look, we can take you home or we can take you to the station. Which is it going to be? We can't leave you here like this. We've received some complaints."

Nick weighed his odds. A warm bed sounded better than the drunk tank.

"Fine."

They ushered him into the squad car, calling Dale on their

way to his house. Dale met them outside, arms folded, eyes bitter.

"Thanks, Scott. I've got it from here." Dale took over, dismissing the officers as he urged Nick into the house.

"Get your hands off me!" Nick snapped, just inside the door.

"Nicholas, get to your room, now."

"Don't order me around. I'm not a child!"

"You're behaving like one. Go sleep this off before you do or say something we'll both regret."

"Oh, I'd hate to cause you any regret, *Dad*. Disappoint you yet again. Hate to bring embarrassment to your fine name!" Nick screamed a slew of expletives at Dale.

Dale had never seen his son *that* angry. Something about Nick's demeanor chilled him, scared him.

"Nicholas, calm down."

In the spin of a single second, Nick unleashed a fury he didn't know he was capable of. Without warning he punched his father in the face, causing Dale to stumble backward.

Nick walked down the hall, into his room, and sat on the bed. Drunk or not, he knew what he had done.

Dale followed after him, stopping outside the open doorway.

"Pack a bag," Dale spoke, calm and steady.

"What for?" Nick swallowed a giant lump in his throat.

"You're not staying here."

He watched his father's nose begin to swell.

"Look, Dad—"

"Pack a bag, Nicholas. Now."

"Where am I supposed to go?"

"I don't know. That's your problem. I told you when you got here, my house, my rules."

Nick didn't argue. He was too far gone. He'd crossed the line. He was tired, his head hurt, and he was ready to pass out.

Nothing mattered anymore. He was drifting in a sea of pointlessness.

Dale stood in the doorway while Nick collected his things, then followed him to the front door, shutting his only son out of his house. He didn't know what else to do. There had to be boundaries. He'd never done any good enabling that sort of behavior. Nick needed a wake-up call. He locked the door and turned off the porch light.

Nick sat on the front steps, against the door, not knowing his father sat on the other side, crying silently, having just done one of the hardest things a father could ever do.

17

MORNING AFTER

*N*ick woke, midday, sprawled out on a narrow sofa, arm hanging over the side, hand resting against a carpeted floor. His tongue stuck to the roof of his mouth, lips glued together. His head pounded like a bass drum, pushing agony behind tired eyes, barely able to open them.

Stirring in the room with him, a shuffling of feet, captured his attention, but he couldn't move his body. His limbs were heavy, his torso weighted down like a pallet of bricks.

"Well now, look who's up," a familiar voice buzzed over him.

Nick strained his neck to see who it was. He recognized a dark figure, medium height, large build. Blinking and squinting, he focused his eyes enough to see Seymour Rutledge standing beside the couch, grinning ear to ear.

"You sure did a number on yourself," Seymour said. "Thought for sure you'd be sleeping all day."

Nick struggled to sit up, body aching and throbbing all over, head dizzy with pain. Seymour sat down next to him and held out a glass of water.

"You need to hydrate. Hangover like that could kill a skinny white boy like you." Seymour laughed.

Nick grinned as much as his aching facial muscles would allow and reached out to take the glass from Seymour's hand. He nodded, hoping that would suffice for a thank-you.

"Drink it all, man. I'll get you another. We gotta fix you up right. Don't want to waste a good musician now."

Nick cleared his throat. The sounds that emerged were as raspy as a bull frog, but he tried to speak anyway.

"Where am I?"

"My place. Mark brought you over last night."

Mark? Nick furrowed his brow. "Mark?"

Seymour chuckled. "You don't remember much. Mark found you on his sister's steps. Said he was driving through, saw you passed out halfway up the front porch. He checks on her a lot. He's got his own issues."

Nick said nothing. Embarrassment strangled any words he might have managed to grunt.

"Jess didn't see you, if you're worried about that. Might serve you right if she had."

"Don't joke like that, man," Nick croaked.

Seymour laughed. "You sound worse than my cat coughing up a hair ball."

"I feel like a freight train hit me," Nick barked.

"I think it did."

Nick drank the water, thankful for some cool relief to his sandpaper throat. He leaned back, resting his head against fluffy cushions.

"You know, I used to party a bit myself," Seymour told him.

Nick squinted, peering at Seymour through one eye. "So did I, but I wouldn't call this partying." A ceiling fan whirred above his head, wafting cold air against Nick's sweaty skin. Small comforts.

"What would you call it then?" Seymour pried.

"Drowning my sorrows."

"Been there too, my friend. Takes more than a bottle to do that job."

Nick shifted, stretching stiff back muscles. "Not enough bottles in the world."

"My point exactly."

Nick opened his eyes, turning his head to meet Seymour's exacting stare. "What do you know about it?"

"I've lived longer than you. Been around the block a few times. I know this business you're in. Lived in that world a long time. Saw a lot of things when I was a roadie. Nothing like a backstage party. I drank with some legendary musicians, got drunk with them, high with them. Did a few other things I'm not proud of."

"What does this have to do with me?" Nick snapped.

"You got demons, Nick. Don't let them control you."

Nick closed his eyes again. "It's just guilt. I deserve what I get."

"So that's it? Just giving up? Drink yourself to death? Or maybe you want to do something reckless and end up in prison, where you think you should be anyway."

Nick hissed through his teeth and jerked forward, fumbling through his pockets for a pack of cigarettes."

"I've spent a few nights in jail. Ain't a place you want to go."

Nick eyed Seymour sharply. "What were you in jail for?"

"Armed robbery. Eighteen years old, hanging with the wrong people. Did eleven months the first time."

"First time?" Nick questioned.

"Got out and went right back to the same shady group. Did eighteen months on the next stint for breaking and entering, and aggravated assault."

"After that?" Nick sucked a warm pocket of tobacco smoke inside his lungs.

"Wised up a little. Focused on my music. Landed my first gig as a roadie, which later led me to the best job in the world working for B. B. King. I learned a lot from him, but not before I spent years binge drinking, always on the edge of that cliff."

Nick huffed. "Is this where you tell me your redemption story? Encourage me with the epic tale of how you got your life together and how I should too?"

Seymour laughed. "I was cynical like you. Hated people talking to me about what they thought were my faults."

"But you had a big turn-around, and now you try to help others pull their life together. Whatever, man. I don't need an intervention."

Seymour nodded. "I don't give interventions. You got to intervene in your own life. Ain't nobody out there can do it for you."

Nick exhaled, releasing a long trail of smoke. "That's a load of bull."

"Is it?"

"Yeah," Nick snorted.

"I watched a girl die. Overdosed on heroin. Room full of people and we just sat there watching her convulse on the floor until she choked on her own vomit."

Nick looked away.

"You remind me of her."

"Why?"

"Got the same sad look behind your eyes."

"Grief?"

"No. Pity."

Nick scoffed. "I'm not an addict."

"She felt sorry for herself."

"You think you know me? You think you have me figured out? You couldn't save her, so now you're trying to save me? I get it, but no thanks."

Seymour laughed. "I'm not trying to save you, man. You can't save a man who's drowning himself. I've got insight, that's all. Acquired wisdom."

"I didn't ask for your wisdom."

"No, but you slept on my couch. You're puffing smoke into my air. I have the right to speak my mind, same as you."

Nick stared at the circular patterns of wood grain in Seymour's coffee table. A million thoughts engaged his mind, but he couldn't articulate a single one.

Seymour smiled. "Stay here as long as you need to."

"Might be a while. My dad kicked me out. How pathetic does that make me?"

"Can you blame him?"

"No. I lost it last night. Punched him in the face. I've never hit him before."

"Booze makes us different people. He's showing tough love. Maybe that's what you need."

"Maybe. Look, can we change the subject?"

Seymour smiled again. "I'm heading over to Copper's place to work on some old riffs. Wanna tag along?"

"Sure. Can I shower first? I feel like a corpse in summer."

Seymour laughed. "That's pretty bad. Yeah, it's down the hall. Let's get you some more water first. Kitchen's this way."

Nick gulped down nearly half a gallon of water and a handful of aspirin, seeking relief from his grueling hangover. He winced at Seymour's turkey sandwich.

"I don't think I'll be eating anything for a while."

Seymour chuckled. "I'll refrain from pulling out the chips and salsa then."

"Ugh. Please." Nick rubbed his abdomen.

It wasn't the worst hangover he'd experienced, but the events leading to this one churned his stomach more than the lingering vodka. He was crossing lines, making a mess of everything, but he didn't know how to get his footing back.

18

CHANCE MEETINGS

*J*ess stood in the produce section of a local market, bagging apples and oranges, pears and nectarines. She savored the fragrance of real food, fresh and crisp. Determined to reform her grief-stricken buying tendencies, she explored the array of food choices, bypassing anything she'd once purchased for Abby.

The kiwis seemed mushier than she remembered, lumpy and easily punctured. Perhaps these were too ripe. She poked and prodded a few more before placing them back in the pile. No kiwi this round.

Chills enveloped her arms as a wave of icy air permeated the store. She rubbed her skin, wishing she'd worn a sweater. Then she remembered ice cream. It had been a long time since she'd indulged in a bowl of cookies and cream with hot fudge syrup. She made a mental note to buy some next time. Baby steps.

The alarming feeling of being watched caught her off guard. Jess looked up, surprised to see Nick standing behind a display of grapefruit. He smiled. An awkward, nervous smile. She recognized sadness behind his pale blue eyes and smiled back, happy to see his familiar grin.

He strolled toward her, feeling like an idiot for passing out on her steps, even if she didn't know about it. *I hope she doesn't know.*

"How have you been?" Jess asked.

"Good," he lied.

"How's your father?"

"Working as usual." The small talk was killing him, but her voice was soothing to his frayed nerves.

"That's nice." She wanted to ask him where he'd been lately, but it wasn't any of her business.

"How's your brother?" *Enough. Say something real.*

"Mark is . . . Mark."

"Still not getting along?"

"Things are better, maybe. I don't know. It's just weird between us. So much has happened the last couple of years. It's complicated."

"I get it," Nick said.

"They're adopting a child."

"Really? That's great."

"Yeah. It's been a long time coming. It's still early though. The birth mother could change her mind."

"I never understood how all that works." Nick picked up a lemon from the pile next to him, rolling it around in his hands, occasionally tossing it into the air.

"It's as complicated as anything else," she said.

"Sums up life in general."

"Sometimes."

Nick eyed her cart, the fresh produce, lean meats, and variety of baked goods and cheeses.

"No Pop-Tarts?" he asked.

Jess looked down. "No, I'm trying to give that up." She

looked at him with a half-curved smile, tilting her head and shrugging her shoulders.

"You look really good. Happy, I mean. Content."

She smiled, barely meeting his deep gaze.

"Hey, Jess! How are you?" Seymour appeared as if from nowhere, grinning ear to ear.

"Hi."

"Grillin' out tonight. Want to join us?"

"I can't. I'm supposed to meet Mark and Elise."

"Maybe next time." Seymour patted Nick on the back and returned to his shopping.

Jess turned back to Nick. "Spending time with Seymour?"

"Yeah, I'm kind of living with him right now."

"Oh?"

"Yeah, it's . . ."

"Complicated?" Jess finished his sentence.

He laughed. "Yeah."

She got him, he thought. She could relate to him, and he needed that kind of camaraderie now that Jack was gone.

"I need to get home," she said.

"Can I walk with you?"

She nodded. He waited outside while she checked out, watching her through the glass doors, thinking of things he could say that were more meaningful than the weather.

"I'll carry those." Nick pointed to her bags when she came out.

"Thank you."

They walked for two blocks without saying a word. Someone needed to break the silence.

"You haven't been around much since the charity drive. Actually, you haven't been around at all."

Nick shrugged.

"Not that it matters. Not that you're obligated. I'm just curious. You seem distant."

Nick thought of all the things he wanted to say and all the things he couldn't. "I . . ."

"Why are you staying with Seymour?" she asked, shocked by her own boldness.

"I got into it with my dad."

"About what?"

He couldn't tell her the whole truth. He was too ashamed. He was becoming the ugliest version of himself and he didn't want her to see it.

"I don't know. I was drunk. I reacted. I told you I'm not a saint."

"What did you do?"

He stopped and faced her. "You really want to know all of this?"

She stared back, trying to read him. "If I'm asking too many questions . . ."

"I hit him," Nick blurted out before she could finish.

"Why?"

"I was drunk, Jess. Drunk people do stupid things."

She could see his agitation. "You were angry?"

"I'm always angry when I'm with him."

"Why?"

"I don't know." He regretted taking this walk.

She took two of her bags from his hands, lifting a tiny burden. "I'm sorry you're not getting along with your dad."

And just like that, her soft voice, gentle and pure, lulled him back to safety. Simple words offering so much comfort. She was breaching a deeper part of him he'd never been fully aware of.

"I'll figure it out," he said.

They continued walking, not saying much, a cooler breeze

easing the heat. Her perfume caught his attention as they walked side by side, occasionally colliding shopping bags. He inched closer, taking comfort in her presence, wanting to say more, but holding back. They reached her house faster than he anticipated. He would spend all day with her, even if they had nothing to say. The sound of her breath was better than the madness unfolding in his own head.

Jess turned her key in the lock, taking the rest of her groceries from Nick. She placed them inside on the floor and lingered on the porch for an excuse to continue the conversation.

Nick felt a sudden need to defend himself. "I don't have to stay with Seymour. I have plenty of money. I can buy my own place, live my own life. I can take care of myself."

"I never said you couldn't. I didn't assume it either." She arched her brow.

Nick stood directly in front of her, hands tucked in jean pockets. He gazed into her eyes, standing a few inches taller, bending his head toward hers. Her sweet, fruity fragrance, surrounded him, calming his senses. *Is it perfume?*

"People assume a lot of things about me."

"Why?" she asked, noticing him moving closer.

"They think they have me pegged. Think they know everything. Maybe I fit the cliché. There are so many things I don't want to be, but I can't seem to get it right. Not sure how to fix all the things I've messed up along the way."

She touched his arm lightly, a reassuring gesture that opened a flood of emotions inside him.

"Maybe you don't have to fix everything all at once. Maybe you start with one problem and go from there."

Her touch was heaven against his skin, humanity, simple affection. She offered compassion and kindness, something he knew he didn't deserve, yet needed more than anything.

"How do I do that?" he asked.

"I'm like you. I don't have all the answers. I'm still trying to sort out my own problems. Maybe talk to your father. Tell him what you just told me."

He wished he could.

"I'd rather stand here and tell it to you." He took a step closer, breathing deeper, watching her.

Jess took a step back, locked in his penetrating stare.

"That's a heavy burden to place on one person," she said.

He moved close enough that Jess could feel the heat from his body and hear the gentle rhythm of his breathing. She took another step back, but he grabbed her hand, pulling her toward him.

"Not when it's the right person." He leaned in, bringing his face close to hers.

It was only a moment, a fleeting second. His mouth neared hers. He could smell the fruity scent of her clean, silky hair. *Not perfume. Shampoo.* She smelled wonderful, exciting his senses. He moved in to kiss her, but Jess turned her head and pulled away. She entered the house, glancing at him from behind the glass door. Nick hung his head. *Why did I just do that?*

"Bye, Nick," she said, closing the main door, leaving him alone on her front porch.

He stood there for a moment. It might have actually been the first time a woman had ever refused him. He couldn't blame her. Who would want him in this condition?

Turning to leave, he noticed an old woman standing in the yard of the house next door, arms folded across her chest. She watched him with contempt. Nick stared back, wondering what this old woman thought, what she had seen. He'd had his share of gawking neighbors, but the last thing he wanted was to embarrass Jess.

He strolled back to Seymour's, taking his time, soaking in memories of his hometown. This aging city with so much history had a charm he was only beginning to recognize. He'd stayed away too long, and now he feared there might not be anything left for him to hold on to.

19

GRAVESIDE

*H*e didn't know why he went to the cemetery that day. He'd woken up with Jack on his mind, dreamed of Jack the night before. His plate full of cheesy eggs ala Seymour reminded him of room service on tour, Jack's favorite. He knew he should have stayed away. His gut chided him the whole walk there, begging him to turn around. He wasn't ready to face a headstone. He could barely stomach Jack's absence.

The graveyard seemed deserted, a ghost town of granite markers and fresh mounds of dirt. Nick wandered the neatly kept rows and paths. It was the oldest cemetery in Bridgetown. In its far corners the remains of many Civil War soldiers found their final resting places. He hadn't been there since his mother died, but an eerie calm of sorrow still resided, a thick cloud looming over green grass and tall trees.

He found it. A dark gray marker bearing the inscription *Jackson Brian O'Malley, Loving son of Benjamin and Patricia O'Malley*. Nick knelt on the ground, directly in front of the glossy head-stone. He stared long and hard at its morbid etching. Seeing the actuality in writing sent a shiver through his body, pounding his already weak resolve. For the first time it was real. It was absolute.

Why? he asked himself, punching the ground. *Why did I take those keys?*

Wind caressed his face, brushing teardrops from the corners of his eyes. Guilt overwhelmed him. Shadows of his past enveloped him. He was losing control, and fighting became fruitless.

You idiot. Why did you get in the car with me?

His voice trembled as he cursed the empty space around him, ripping up grass in a fit of rage. "You idiot, Jack! You stupid idiot! Why did you let me take those keys? Screw you!" Nick's voice echoed across rows of silent markers.

He bowed his head. Sorrow filled his senses. All was still, calm . . . dead. There wasn't any life in that place, just a lonely field of bodies. What had these forgotten souls done with their lives? No doubt many had lived longer than Jack. No doubt many had lived better.

"I need you, man." Nick couldn't stop the flow of tears, isolated in a prison with walls closing fast around him. "I can't do this without you. We've always done the hard times together."

He laid down lengthwise on Jack's grave, imagining what it would be like to sink into that soft earth, drift slowly underground, and share the bitter end with his best friend. He could almost feel loosening dirt cover his skin, blanketing him in earthy slumber. *I need this pain to go away. I can't live with this guilt anymore.*

"Jack?" he whispered. "I'm drowning. I can't feel myself anymore."

He stood up. In a fit of rage and tears he kicked at the ground, panting and screaming. "It should've been me! It should've been me!"

He continued yelling. Deep, guttural sounds replaced words. Passersby stopped with flowers in hand, watching him unravel in a spectacle of frenzy. He dropped back down, resting his arms against bent knees. Rocking back and forth, his body swayed to the rhythm of his tears, pain too heavy to suppress. *Someone help me.*

"Tell me what to do, Jack. Tell me what to do." Nick grabbed handfuls of hair, standing back up, pacing back and forth.

Time drifted. The sun dipped lower in the horizon, tinting clouds with mixed shades of orange and pink. His head ached. It throbbed and pulsed, but the pain meant nothing. His heart ached more. He felt every worthless deed hanging in front of him, urging him to give up. He'd made a mess of too many things.

Bending lower, Nick placed a salty hand against Jack's tombstone, tightening his grip until his fingers turned white and tingly.

"You didn't deserve this."

When he stood up his body faced Jack's grave, but his feet carried him backward toward the cemetery gate. He watched Jack's marker grow smaller in the distance, haunting the landscape. He could almost see Jack standing there, nodding at him, that classic smug grin teasing and taunting, baiting him with a witty jab and a great comeback.

He took heavy steps on his way out, reflecting on a broken life. Trying to piece things together left him struggling to make sense of where he'd gone wrong. A million mistakes swarming him, causing regret to swell and seethe inside him until he couldn't breathe.

Nick did the only thing he knew to do, the only thing he'd taught himself to do when the pain was too much to bear. He walked into the closest liquor store and purchased a bottle of high-priced vodka, a brand of whiskey he'd never seen before, and a pack of cigarettes.

He had nowhere to go. Drinking himself into oblivion didn't actually help, but in the moment he felt better, numb and weightless. His burdens drowned in a sea of alcohol. Nick sipped from each bottle, then guzzled, humming incoherent tunes as he numbed his mind, letting everything wash away. Who needs reality when drunken illusions beckon you to a new type of existence where nothing is wrong and you're on top of the world. Suddenly he had a renewed sense of power and control in his life. Nothing was wrong. Everything was right.

He thought of Jess in that moment. Sweet-smelling brown hair, rosy lips, fair skin, and those passionate, sorrowful eyes. He wondered what those lips tasted like. He wondered if her skin smelled as wonderful as her hair. The vision of her carried him away, down dark roads, under streetlamps and the pale glow of moonlight. He found himself on a sidewalk staring at her house, no lights on. He stood there, chugging the last few ounces from the bottle in his hand, tossing the empty glass aside. He wiped his wet mouth across his arm.

Nick staggered across the yard, stumbling into shrubs, barely making his way to the back side of her house. He rested his forehead against her back door, swaying side to side in a failing sense of equilibrium. The glass was cold against his skin. Locked. He pounded against metal, laughing under his breath.

"Jess! Open up!" his voice echoed. "Open the door, Jess!"

His pounding continued, fist to metal frame.

"Don't leave me out here, Jess. You in there? Hello?"

Footsteps preceded a turning knob on the old wooden door and Jess's tired eyes peeking through a crack. She opened it, standing in front of the glass, wrapped in a satin robe over white cotton pajamas.

"Nick? What's going on?"

He smiled, a curious grin, taking inventory of her figure.

"Hey, Jess." He laughed. "Just out for a stroll. Can I come in?"

She noticed his slur. "It's 2:00 a.m. I'm sleeping. Trying to."

"Come on, Jess. Let me in." Nick focused his attention on the outline of her breasts.

Jess moved back, clutching her robe tighter with one hand and the door handle with the other. "Probably not the best idea."

"Come on. Just for a little while." Nicked pressed his body against the glass. "Man, you're beautiful."

Jess froze. She'd never seen him like this and it scared her. "I think you should leave."

"I just wanna talk. I don't bite . . . unless you want me to." He grinned like he had the devil inside him. This wasn't the Nick she knew.

"You need to go."

"Let me stay a while. Don't you want me to stay?"

"Go home, Nick." Jess closed the door, locking it securely.

His temper flared. "Jess! Open the door!"

She stood on the other side, listening, waiting for him to leave.

"Jess! Open the door, now!" His banging resumed. "Why are you doing this? Let me in. I just need to talk."

She flinched every time his fist hit the door. *Bang!* Her body shook. *Bang, bang, bang!* She jumped and backed into a storage tote, knocking over several boxes. For a moment she froze, searching for something she could use to defend herself in case he managed to break in. Then she ran upstairs to get her cell-phone and called Mark.

"Let me in, Jess!" he continued, screaming profanity.

He pounded harder, beating the glass with urgency until his fist broke through, scattering shards across the steps and ground below. He panted, giving in, giving up. Succumbing to whatever was ready to swallow him whole. Then he lost his balance and

sat down, paying no attention to the pile of slivers beneath him.
He held his right hand in his lap, squeezing it in the palm of the
other. Blood seeped from his wrist. He couldn't tell how deep it
was and he didn't really care.

He waivered back and forth, cursing under his breath, in and
out of reality, when a shadow appeared a few feet in front of him.
Nick looked up, squinting to see more clearly. Jess's backyard
was spinning, but he recognized a pair of brown eyes, wide with
concern. *Mark. Of course.*

"What do *you* want?" Nick asked.

"I might ask you the same question. Is everything okay?"
Mark proceeded with caution.

"Looks fine to me." Nick sneered.

Mark eyed the dark stain spreading across Nick's jeans.
Under the floodlight it looked black, but Nick's hands were
covered in red liquid. A quick glance around and Mark assessed
the situation.

"I'm not quite sure about that. A bleeding man doesn't seem
fine to me."

Nick squeezed his injured wrist harder. "I'm fine."

"Yeah, you said that. Can I take a look at it?"

"You a doctor now? No. You're a church man. I don't need
any sermons tonight."

"You could just consider me a friend and let me help you."

"I don't need your help."

Mark rested his hands on his hips. "Jess might appreciate you
not bleeding to death on her steps. Can I at least give you a ride a
home?"

"Where is that?"

Mark paused. He didn't have an answer. "Where would you
like to go?"

"You really want me to answer that? I'll tell you where I'd like
you to go."

"That's it. You're leaving now." Mark stepped forward, attempting to grab Nick by the arm.

"Get your hands off me!" Nick jerked away.

Mark struggled to keep his temper at bay. "Listen here. You're going to leave. You can accept my help and let me drive you somewhere, or I'll call the police and let them handle it."

"Who put you in charge? She's a grown woman. You're her brother not her husband." His slur worsened. His body swayed as though he might collapse at any moment.

"Is this what you want, Nick? Is this how you're going to spend your life?"

"How I spend my life is none of your business, preacher man. Go back to church."

Mark frowned. Sadness filled his heart for the empty shell of a man before him. Nick was hitting rock bottom. Mark didn't know why, but he could see this talented young man on the verge of sinking.

"Yeah, it's your life. Do what you want, but not here. You owe Jess that much respect. Whatever this is, she's not part of it. Don't drag her into your mess."

Nick huffed. "I haven't done anything to Jess." He stood up and tried banging again, his bleeding hand slipping through open pane, hitting the solid door behind it. "Jess, open the door!"

Mark placed a firm hand on Nick's shoulder. "Come on, it's time to go."

"I told you to get your hands off me!" Nick swung around, slapping Mark across the face and losing his balance in the process. He fell face-first onto the ground, a pitiful slump in freshly mowed grass.

Nick moaned as he fumbled to get back on his feet. Mark stooped down to help him, pulling hard on the heavy man no longer in full control of his body. Nick struggled, fighting to maintain his independence, but Mark continued the tug of war until he was confident Nick could remain on both feet without assistance.

"Why can't everyone just leave me alone? I don't need this. I don't—"

"What do you think you need?" Mark faced him eye to eye, keeping his body directly in front of Nick's. Where Nick moved he moved.

Nick glared back, glassy blue eyes fading. "A means to an end."

"The end of what?"

Nick swallowed hard, averting his eyes, now glossy with tears. "Suffering."

"Pain doesn't disappear in bottle."

"No, it doesn't," Nick agreed.

"I'd like to help you, but you have to meet me in the middle. You have to want my help, and I don't think you do."

"I don't want anyone's help."

"Well, go on then. Fix it yourself. Go make an even bigger mess than you already have. Nothing you do is going to bring your friend back. You can't undo what's already been done."

"You don't know me. You don't know what I'm going through. You don't know anything about me! You think watching the news gives you insight into my life? That friend had a name!"

Lights appeared in neighboring windows. Jess watched from her own window, seeing him unravel with no way to help him.

"What was it?" Mark asked.

Nick swayed side to side and back and forth, unable to focus.

"Your friend's name. What was it?"

Nick released a burdened sigh. "Jack."

Mark stepped closer. "I know his parents."

"Two accidents, two deaths, but I'm still here. They die, but I don't." Nick turned around, kicking random objects, whatever he could find to inflict his frustration on.

His words chilled Mark's center. He knew what Nick meant. He'd lived in Bridgetown his whole life, knew Dale, remembered what happened to Lenore. Mark watched him make a fool of himself, but he saw something bigger: a man who'd been given opportunity, a man with second chances.

"'And inasmuch as it is appointed unto men once to die, and after this cometh judgment.'" Mark's voice softened.

Nick laughed. "What kind of nonsense is that?"

"The Bible."

"Figures."

"Your life isn't finished. You can change the path you're on. But I wouldn't expect you to understand that when you're so drunk you can't even stand without falling over. Let me take you home. Sleep this off. Let Jess get back to bed. You've caused enough trouble for one night."

Nick staggered toward the house, gazing at Jess's silhouette, then back at Mark, angel versus demon. Gravity seemed to disappear, like floating clouds, feet lifting from the ground.

"Am I flying?" he muttered.

"Come on." Mark held out a hand, guiding and coaxing him to the front of the house.

Nick agreed, stumbling and bending in multiple directions. Mark held on to him, helping him walk, stabilizing him as best he could to maneuver him to his car.

Nick fell asleep on the drive to Dale's, his head slumped against the window, wrestling with strobe light dreams, body limp and shapeless.

Mark pulled into the driveway and turned off his lights. He sat in the car for a few minutes, listening to Nick snore, debating if he should ring the bell or take him back to his house. He hated waking a man in the middle of the night, especially like this, but it wasn't his place to get that involved. He hadn't been asked to intervene. Whatever the outcome, Dale needed to be with his son, and Nick needed to talk to his father.

Dale answered the door in pajama pants and an oversized T-shirt, heavy bags and dark circles under his eyes. Mark recognized several nights of broken sleep when he saw it. It had been his own battle in recent months. Mark relayed the briefest version of events he could, apologizing in the process, but Dale walked past him. He was nervous and angry, but also relieved. He opened the passenger side door, catching his son's body as it poured out sideways.

"Wake up, son." Dale shook him.

Nick muttered and moaned, finally reviving enough to stumble toward the house with the help of both men. The more his mind woke, the more belligerent he became, pushing and shoving, cursing at Dale and Mark.

"Nicholas, that's enough!" Dale grabbed Nick's arm, veins swelling on his forehead.

"Leave me alone!" Nick staggered away, panting and flailing about.

Mark tried to help, but Dale refused.

"I'll take it from here. Thank you for bringing him. I'm sorry you had to deal with this."

Mark nodded. "If there's anything I can do . . ."

"Thank you."

Nick doubled over the bushes, heaving and puking. Dale stepped forward with caution as the engine of Mark's car started behind them. He reached out to place a hand on Nick's shoulder.

"Go away!" Nick shouted, heaving again.

"Son, let's go inside. We'll get you cleaned up and bandaged."

"Always telling me what to do. You never said anything when Mom died. You never said anything about Jack. You don't care!"

He sounded like an angry eight-year-old. Dale aided him

toward the steps, but he broke free of his father's grip, shouting more profanity until he was out of breath.

"You're dead to me! I hate you!"

Nick collapsed just inside the front door, banging his head on a side table. Blackness swept over him. Covered in a blanket of deep sleep, veins still coursing with liquor.

Dale carried his son to his room, the way he had when Nick was a boy and he'd fallen asleep on the sofa. Only this time it was more of a struggle, a slower pace, a bit of dragging. Dale cleaned him up, cared for his wounds, watched him sleep.

Silence echoed in every corner of Dale's house that night. He slept on the floor outside Nick's bedroom, propped against the wall, listening through a crack in the doorway, hoping his son would live to see morning, and worried he might end up like Lenore.

20

FATE

*W*aking up to the smell of fried eggs and bacon when he had the worst hangover in the history of hangovers was more than miserable. It was cruel. Nick's stomach turned and flipped, doing somersaults beneath his abdomen as he wrestled with a headache that struck like a nuclear weapon behind his eyes. His mouth was dryer than cotton, sticky and rough. His breath was another matter altogether, offending even his own senses.

He couldn't sleep. His body wanted to, but his mind was awake, not fully, but enough to pull him out of bed in search of relief. He wandered into the kitchen, retching at the greasy aroma induced by Dale's late breakfast.

"Ugh, that smell. Don't you know how to make a bowl of cereal?" Nick complained, shuffling into the kitchen still wearing his blood-stained jeans and dirty T-shirt from the night before.

"Good morning," Dale replied.

Nick scratched his head and rubbed at his face. "I need a beer."

"Coffee would be better. I can make you a fresh pot."

"I want a beer." Nick opened the fridge, but no alcohol.

"There's orange juice," Dale said.

Nick slammed the fridge door. "Would it kill you to keep a few beers in your house?"

"I don't drink."

"Yeah, I noticed."

"Would it kill you to go one day without it?" Dale interrupted.

His head was still spinning, aching more the louder his voice rose. "Just stay out of my business."

"You're in my house. That makes you my business."

"Yeah, well, how did that happen? I thought I was banished. Remember?"

"You had a little incident last night. *Remember?*" Dale spoke calm and steady.

"What incident?" Nick dismissed his father's comment, filling a glass with tap water to relieve his parched tongue.

"That's what happens when you drink too much, son. You don't remember anything."

"Whatever. So I was drunk and you picked me up somewhere. Sorry to burden you, *Dad.* I'll head back to Seymour's ASAP."

It broke Dale's heart to see his son miserable and clueless. Lenore had been the same way. She'd make a complete fool of herself in a room full of friends and then play it off the next day, no memory of what happened.

"I didn't pick you up, son. Mark Stuart brought you home."

An icy chill rose from the base of Nick's spine. "Again? Does this guy just follow me around?"

"You really don't remember?" Dale asked.

Nick ignored him. Then a sharp, stabbing pain in his wrist directed his attention to the bandage on his hand. "What the—"

"That's what happens when you put your hand through a plate glass door."

"What?" Nick searched his mind for clues.

"When is it going to be enough? When will you learn to face your problems like a man and stop hiding behind a bottle? You're taking the coward's way out. This is not how I raised you."

"How did you raise me? Tell me that! You want me to face this like a man? Where were your words of wisdom when Mom died? When I was crying myself to sleep every night?"

"I was crying too, son."

"All those years I blamed myself for her death. I carried a burden you can't possibly understand."

"Her death was not your fault, Nicholas."

"I'm not discussing this with you. I don't care if I ever discuss anything with you ever again. I was doing okay until I walked back into this house. I was fine until I had to face the reminders of why I left this forsaken dump in the first place."

"Okay? I don't call crashing a Mustang and killing your best friend *okay*."

"Shut your mouth!"

Dale shook his head back and forth. He had nothing left to say that would make any difference.

In the heat of the moment, Nick picked up a drinking glass and hurled it across the room. It hit the wall behind Dale, crashing into several pieces.

"You're not fine, Nicholas."

Nick slammed his fist against the counter.

"I want to help you, son. I just don't know how."

"Everyone wants to help me. Everyone wants to make it all better. I just want to be left alone. I want this nagging, ripping pain inside my gut to go away. You can't help that. You can't *fix* what I'm going through." Blind anger turned into watery eyes. He struggled to hold back a breakdown bursting from within.

Dale had no answers. He had no wisdom or insight. He had no clue what he should do. He felt completely helpless.

"Tell me what happened last night," Nick asked, his voice shaking.

"I wasn't there, but it seems you went to your friend Jess's house and pounded on her back door hard enough to break the glass. Scared her quite a bit, I think. You cut your hand. Mark brought you home."

Nick scoured his mind, piecing together fragments until whole memories finally surfaced. He remembered talking to Jess. He remembered busting the glass door. He remembered his conversation with Mark, not everything, but enough to realize what a complete fool he'd been. He also remembered Jess watching from the window, the intensity behind her eyes. He'd struck fear into the one person who'd actually brought a little light into his life. *What have I done?*

"I have to apologize."

"I don't think that's the best idea. I think you should stay away—"

"I can't leave it like this. I can't have her think . . ."

"You've done enough damage. Let it go."

"I can't let it go. She's the one good thing in my life right now. I have nothing else to hold on to. Do you understand that? Do you even get that I don't want to be here? I can't find one single reason to be on this miserable earth." Tears streamed down Nick's face.

Dale shed his own tears. "Your life has more worth than you know, Nicholas."

"I'm just an overpaid musician. There's nothing valuable in that." He left the room.

Dale wept quietly. His body shook as he tried to stifle the sobs forcing their way out. Then he let go and allowed his emotions to take over. He was tired of fighting, tired of holding it all in. The man who had always been able to fix anything couldn't repair the damage in his own son.

Nick didn't bother changing clothes. The only thing on his mind was getting to Jess as quickly as possible. He had to show her how sorry he was, convince her it would never happen again. She had to know he never intended to hurt her. He hoped it wasn't too late to salvage the friendship they had formed.

Her porch was quiet, a still life portrait with a lonely red blanket in an empty white chair. His hands trembled as he rang the bell. He waited, but no answer. He hoped she was home. She had to be home. He rang again. Then he knocked, lightly at first, but soon turning into frantic beatings against her front door, though not like his possessed banging the previous night.

"Jess, are you home? It's Nick. I need to talk to you." He continued knocking and ringing the bell.

Jess was home. She was sitting just inside the entryway at the bottom of the staircase, listening.

"Jess, are you in there? Please let me explain. I just want to apologize. I'm sorry about last night. I wasn't myself. Please come to the door, Jess."

She didn't move.

His knocking grew more and more frantic. Shallow breathing turned into desperation. "Jess, if you can hear me, I'm sorry. Please know that. I didn't mean to hurt you, or scare you, or . . . Jess, please just come to the door. I'm sorry. You have to know that. Jess . . ."

No sound. No answer. Silence behind the door.

Jess hugged her knees, wondering if she should go to him, but she couldn't. She just listened, waiting for him to leave. She didn't have the strength for apologies and excuses. Her entire marriage had been a mantra of apologies and excuses, each one carefully crafted by Patrick with his charming ego. *Not today, Nick. I just can't.*

"Jess, you're the only person I can talk to. The only person who understands. Please don't shut me out. If you're in there, please just let me talk to you. Let me see you. Don't leave me out here alone." His voice broke, full of desperation. But she wasn't coming.

Nick turned to leave, but instead he slid down until he was nothing more than a lump against the door, pleading for an end to his pain, to cut out his suffering heart. *What am I supposed to do?*

When he finally returned home, he thought he might talk to his dad. Maybe he could find a way to confide to him, but Dale wasn't home. He'd gone to work. The house was as vacant and lifeless as Jess's front porch. Every room whispered insults, confirming his worst fears and doubts. *Wouldn't it just be better if I wasn't here anymore?*

He sat for over an hour at the kitchen table, crying with his head on his arms, rehashing and reliving every painful moment he'd ever experienced. He imagined Jack sitting across from him, staring at him with a look of sadness, judge and jury, convicting him of his wrongs.

He could hear Dale's voice in his head, right as always. He *was* a coward. No man would put the people he loved through so much torment. A real man wouldn't hide. He would face his problems, take responsibility, find a way to make things better. But he didn't want to make it better. He wanted to erase it, destroy it, send it all away. He realized he wasn't a man at all. The world was better off without him.

Nick emerged from the table with a new sense of purpose. He glided down the hallway to his father's bedroom, tearing through items in Dale's closet until he held the thick black box of a .40 caliber Smith and Wesson. He sat on the bed and opened it slowly, pulling the shiny gray firearm from its protective foam. He gripped the gun in his right hand, staring at it, contemplating.

One hard shove and the loaded magazine was locked in place, ready to go. Safety off. Finger to trigger. Nick held the cold metal against the skin of his temple, closing his eyes. Cold as ice, it numbed the side of his head. He readied his mind, applied light pressure against the trigger, eager for the pain to be over.

He dropped the gun to his lap, short breaths, heart pounding in his chest. *I can't do this sober.*

Nick jumped up, running to his bedroom. He tore the room apart looking for alcohol, something to dull his senses and found a half-empty bottle of Crown under his nightstand. Fitting that Jack's favorite liquor would be Nick's final send-off to meet him. Gone with two huge gulps. It wasn't enough. He needed more.

Nick retrieved the gun from Dale's room, forcing it into his back pocket. His dad had the only running vehicle . . . *or did he?* Rushing outside, Nick lifted the old, roll-back garage door and pulled the tarp off his father's 1982 Harley Davidson Shovelhead motorcycle. He knew it would run. Dale kept everything in running condition.

It purred like a kitten. He shot off, not caring about his probation, or anything else. He only had one vision.

One stop at the liquor store and then he took off like a flying dagger, speeding through town, heading toward Valley Bend State Park. His intention was simple: find a quiet spot and do it. Just do it. No thinking. No hesitating. Just pull the trigger.

Dale left work early that afternoon to check on Nick. He'd been worried all day. He couldn't function well, couldn't do his job.

Something in his gut didn't feel right. He had no appetite and all he could think about was getting home to Nick.

A frightening aura swallowed him as he entered the house, a strange, sick feeling that something was terribly wrong. He searched every room of his twelve-hundred-square-foot home, no sign of his son. He sat down on his bed, then noticed the Smith and Wesson box lying open near his feet. Empty. He reached for it with trembling hands, body cold with dread. Nick was gone. His gun was gone. *Oh Lord. Where's my son?*

Dale shot up. He drove to Jess's house, hands still shaking, blood draining from his face. He hoped Nick was there. *Please be here.*

Jess answered the door.

"Have you seen Nick?"

Her jaw dropped. He looked like he'd seen a ghost.

"He was here earlier, but I didn't answer the door. What's going on?"

Dale hung his head. "He's gone. I went home to check on him, but he's not there, and my gun is missing. I'm worried what he might do."

"We should talk to Mark. He has a close friend in the police department. If Nick's on foot he should be easy to—"

"He took my motorcycle."

She let out a gasp. "Let's go. We're wasting time."

Dale drove his old blue truck, barely managing to keep the wheel steady. He played every worst-case scenario he could think of over and over in his mind. When they pulled into Mark's driveway, Elise was sweeping the front porch. He parked and got out, but waited for Jess to do the talking.

"Hi, Jess. What's going on?"

"Get Mark out here now." She had no time for pleasantries.

"He's working in his study."

"Fine. I'll get him."

Jess started up the steps, but Elise called for Mark, and in seconds he appeared on the porch.

"What's going on?" Mark looked back and forth between Dale and his sister.

"Nick is gone. I think he might try to hurt himself. Will you help us?"

"He has my Harley and my gun." Dale added with struggling breath.

Mark nodded. "We'll take my car."

Jess rode in front with Dale on the edge of the middle seat in the back.

"Where do you think he would go?" Mark asked.

"I don't know. This morning he was talking about his life having no value, and when I got home he'd taken my gun. No note. Nothing."

They drove through Bridgetown, searching any place he might be, liquor stores, Seymour's apartment, local bars. Mark phoned his friend at the police station, who assured him he'd call if he heard anything. They were trying to pull a needle from a haystack. Nick could have been anywhere.

"We'll find him." Mark placed a steady hand on Jess's quivering leg.

"I shouldn't have left. I shouldn't have gone to work today," Dale murmured from the back seat.

"We're going to find him," Mark assured.

Jess nodded, closing her eyes. *Please let him be okay.*

It took moments to speed through Valley Bend. Nick rode that Harley as fast as it would go, taking sharp turns with reckless abandon, hitting bumps in the uneven pavement with racking force. It took moments to speed through the state park, and only a second to feel the ground lift beneath him and black shadows to envelope him.

Crashing a car was like a slow-motion video played backward. Crashing a motorcycle was like turning off a light switch. It was over before he realized anything had happened. He wasn't conscious. There would be nothing to remember.

A glimmer of promise illuminated the hopeless car ride when Mark's phone rang. It was Phil, a Bridgetown detective. Neither Jess nor Dale could gauge what was being said on the other end. Mark tossed his phone in Jess's lap, speeding up as he turned the car sharply and headed in a different direction.

"What did he say?" Jess asked.

"There's been a reported motorcycle crash at Valley Bend. Units are there. Life Flight has been called. That's all he knows."

"Oh, dear God, help him." Dale's voice seemed to crumble. "I'm not a religious man, Mr. Stuart, but I need to ask you to pray for my son."

Mark swallowed a giant mound in his throat. "I'll pray for you both." He looked at Jess.

"I haven't prayed in a long time. Not sure I'd know where to begin." She wanted to tell Mark to pray to his God and leave her out of it, but she wanted Nick to be okay. Someone needed to pray; it just couldn't be her. She didn't think God would want to hear anything she had to say.

They arrived at Valley Bend, maneuvering its twists and turns, up and down hills, past playgrounds and ball fields, picnic areas, and even an eighteen-hole golf course. Through a long stretch of tree-lined road, thick, green forest, with a few picnic shelters here and there, they saw a sea of flashing lights, blinding reds and blues. Chaos and commotion enveloped an entire portion of road, blocked off on both sides.

Mark pulled over. Dale jumped out first, leaving his door open. He ran, pushed through gathering onlookers, searching for a visual to confirm or deny it was Nick.

Jess followed with Mark close behind. He spotted an officer he knew.

"Over here." He tugged Jess, pulling her with him to question the officer.

Dale broke through tape and lines of people to get closer to bustling rescue workers and a large congregation of police giving and receiving orders.

"Sir, you need get back. You can't be here," a short, heavyset officer warned him.

Dale glanced at the paramedics climbing uphill. They were in a ravine. Scraps of twisted metal and debris littered the embankment, but no sign of a recognizable motorcycle.

"Sir, I'm not asking you again. You have to move back and let us do our job," the officer repeated.

"My son. I think it may be my son."

"Sir, if you step over there someone will talk to you in a moment, but you have to move back."

Dale stumbled backward, still watching the commotion in horror. He could barely breathe.

Mark grabbed Dale's arm and pulled him away from the scene.

"I spoke to an officer who said two hikers called 911 after witnessing a black motorcycle flip over the ravine. They couldn't make any other identifications."

The three of them watched in suspense as police and a host of emergency workers ran back and forth, working the accident scene like a Hollywood movie. All they could do was stand there, watch, and wait. Dale could barely hold still.

Jess chewed her nails, fidgeting and bouncing from tiptoe to heel. Mark put his arm around her. He was feeling the anxiety too, wondering what more he could have done to help this young man, wishing he'd tried harder.

Then suddenly a stretcher emerged, paramedics crowding around it, lifting it up and securing it on the road near the ambulance.

"Everyone stay back, make room, please," an officer called out.

They couldn't see much and Dale couldn't stay away. He lunged forward, catching glimpses between gloved rescue workers in white shirts. A face on the stretcher became visible. Bruised and bloody, hard to recognize, he knew it was Nick. He just knew. Dale pushed closer, as close as he could get until an officer blocked him.

"Sir, if you don't get back we'll have to remove you by force."

"That's my son. Please. That's my son. Nicholas Miller. I'm his father, Dale Miller. Please," Dale pleaded. "I have identification. I can show you . . ." Dale fumbled in his back pocket.

Another officer nodded. 'Okay, sir. They're loading him now. Life Flight is waiting at the golf course to transport him to Richland. Would you like to ride along?"

"Yes, please." Dale waited until they motioned him to climb aboard.

Jess ran forward. She stopped just before they closed the ambulance doors. Tears in her eyes, she stared long and hard at Dale, his eyes even sadder. He nodded his head, mouthing the words *thank you* until the doors were closed and the ambulance took off.

She stood motionless, Mark's hands resting on her shoulders. Would he live? Would he die? Would they even be standing there if she had opened the door when he came to apologize? She knew that life could change in the blink of an eye, that every decision leads to another.

"Everything is connected, for good and bad," she said.

Mark turned to her.

"That's the true definition of fate. It's not some cosmic force in the universe deciding everything for us. It's the breadcrumbs we leave on every path we take, the outcome of our choices."

He held her close as they walked back to the car.

"Providence, Jess. Free will and Providence." he said.

"That's church talk," she said, leaning into him for comfort.

"That's faith," he said, opening her door.

She turned to him. "The assurance of things hoped for, the conviction of things not seen?"

Mark softened. "You remember."

She smiled. "I never forgot. I'm just not sure what I believe."

He wasn't about to lecture her in that moment. He wouldn't dare ruin their cordial exchange. Instead, he would savor the hope that maybe they'd soon see eye to eye, or at least be on the same side.

21

LIFE AND DEATH

*J*ess hadn't been to Richland Memorial Hospital since her mother passed. The sounds and smells were the same, triggering pockets of grief she hadn't fully processed. She detested the sight of nurses and doctors, sterile environments, the incessant beeping of monitors, that cold atmosphere she'd come to know too well over the years. "Please let him be okay," she whispered.

When they were finally allowed inside Nick's ICU room, they saw his body, pale and swollen, hooked to a myriad of cords and equipment. She cringed at the sight of a ventilator tube in his mouth. His face was deeply bruised, and he was covered in casts and bandages. She'd never seen a human look more damaged.

Mark stood next to Dale in the doorway discussing Nick's condition, but Jess walked past, creeping closer to his bed. She stood beside him, watching, taking his hand in hers. Teardrops rolled down her cheeks as she caressed his clammy skin, glancing occasionally at the high-tech equipment crowded around the bed.

"We're here for you," she whispered.

Mark appeared at her side, wrapping his sturdy arm around

her for support.

"Is he going to be okay?" she asked.

Mark shrugged, shaking his head. For the first time, he didn't know what to say.

Dale watched from the end of Nick's bed, squeezing his left foot, hoping to get a response, but Nick's body remained still, an inanimate lump of battered flesh under white sheets.

"They said surgery went well, but they don't know when he'll wake up," Dale said.

"How bad is it?" Jess asked.

"All I know is what they told me downstairs, internal bleeding, swelling on the brain, multiple fractures. I'm still waiting to hear from the surgeon."

Jess winced. The thought of how much pain Nick's shattered body must be going through made her insides churn. Her heart hurt for him.

"I keep blaming myself. So many things I could have done differently, should have done differently. Why do we realize our mistakes when it's too late?" Dale lamented.

Mark moved closer, placing a hand on Dale's shoulder. "You can't do that to yourself. Blame is a natural part of grief, but we aren't the ones in control."

Dale met Mark's big brown eyes. "All I know how to do is fix things. I can't fix this."

"No," Mark replied.

"I shouldn't have left the house. I should have stayed. I should have checked on him, locked up the gun." Dale balled up his fist.

"Every day we make a thousand decisions. We don't know where each one will lead us, and we aren't supposed to."

"I knew how much pain he was in. I went to work anyway. I abandoned him when he needed me most." Dale's voice broke.

"You didn't know he would take your gun. You can't claim

responsibility for a grown man's actions, even if he is your son. A parent's job is to prepare their children to stand on their own. What they do after that is up to them."

"What if I didn't do my job right? What if he wasn't prepared?"

Mark didn't have an answer, at least not one he thought Dale would want to hear. He didn't have an easy fix or a profound epiphany that would solve Nick's situation. Mark knew from his experience with Jess that it was impossible to do everything right, and that even if he had, he never could have prepared Jess for all the loss and hardship she experienced.

"That's why I pray."

Dale nodded. He understood. He wasn't a religious man, but in that moment, he needed something to believe in.

Jess took Nick's hand into hers, squeezing, holding tight. Her tear-filled eyes pleaded for him to wake up. She hadn't prayed in so long. Her faith had drifted to some faraway shore, buried underneath dead parents, a husband, and a child. She hadn't felt the urge to pray since Abby's death, but something now sparked longing in her soul. She wanted Nick to have one more chance. Maybe he didn't deserve it, perhaps he'd make the same mistakes again, but she couldn't stand to see him fighting for life when he had so much life left in him. She recalled his beautiful melodies, the passion behind his eyes, the sincerity in his voice. If God would listen, maybe she could say a prayer. She would plead for his life. Then she remembered this God her brother prayed to was the same God who let her child slip away. Why would he listen now?

A tall, lanky man appeared inside the doorway of Nick's cramped ICU room. "Mr. Miller?"

"Yes," Dale replied.

"I'm Dr. Hammond."

Mark motioned to Jess for them to leave, but Dale stopped

them. "No. Please, stay."

"Are you sure?" Mark asked.

"I don't want to hear this alone."

Dr. Hammond didn't waste any time. He rattled off Nick's injuries and prognosis like he was reciting a textbook. "As you know he has multiple cuts and abrasions, a fractured left arm and collarbone. These are minor in comparison and should heal well. His right leg sustained multiple fractures. We repaired blood vessels to stop internal bleeding in his thigh and attached a rod to his femur. His internal bleeding was quite severe. He sustained damage to his spleen, which we repaired, as well as several torn and crushed blood vessels. The swelling on his brain isn't bad enough to need surgery, but we are monitoring it closely. Only time will tell how much damage he sustained to his brain. We can't assess that until he wakes up. He also had some bleeding around his lungs. We repaired as much as we could. He's got a long road ahead of him."

Dale just stood there. It took every ounce of strength he had to maintain composure.

"What's his prognosis? Where do we go from here?" Mark asked for him.

"We wait. Right now we're doing everything we possibly can. He's got to wake up, and there's no timetable I can put on that. We'll monitor him for any signs of danger. If he pulls through, he's looking at months of therapy. To be frank, he shouldn't be alive. I've been a trauma surgeon for eighteen years. Most cases like his don't make it off the table. Many don't even make it into the OR."

"Is my son going to live?" Dale's voice trembled.

Dr. Hammond glanced at Nick. "I don't have that answer. All I can tell you is that he has a steady heartbeat, his blood pressure is improving, and his oxygen levels look okay. Beyond that it's a waiting game. I wish I could tell you more."

Dale backed away, shuffling toward the head of Nick's bed, touching his hand and squeezing his fingers.

"How long will he have the ventilator?" Jess asked.

"Until he wakes up and is breathing on his own. Sit tight. It's going to be a long haul."

"Thank you," Mark added.

Dr. Hammond nodded. As quickly as he'd entered, he disappeared down the silent ICU corridor.

"Help me understand. Help me make sense of this." Dale pleaded, his eyes weary and bloodshot.

"Sometimes there isn't any sense in the things that happen to us," Mark said.

"I know he did this to himself. I know that. I just wish I could have been there to stop it. He's so young. His future so bright. I blame myself. I want to blame him, but then I see him lying here helpless, and . . . I can't . . . I can't blame him. He was just a scared little boy forced to witness too many things. I could have shielded him better."

Mark stepped closer. "A lot of people have bad childhoods or become screwed-up adults. Not all of them end up like Nick. He chose a path. That's the burden of loving others. We endure the pain right along with them."

"He's a broken man," Dale said.

"Broken men can heal," Mark replied.

"Do you really believe that?"

"Yes."

Eventually Mark and Jess left the hospital, returning to their own homes, leaving Dale to contemplate his son's prognosis. The evening wore into an overcast night outside the quiet ICU. Dale kept a steady vigil by Nick's bedside, refusing to leave unless they made him. He promised his unconscious son he'd do everything he could to make him whole again. He meant it.

22

AWAKENINGS

*P*anic struck as Nick woke to bizarre noises, his body freezing, a large object lodged in his throat. He couldn't breathe. More panic. Struggling for relief, he shoved and pushed at any cord or wire grazing his hand. Nurses scurried in, and a flash of events unfolded without full awareness on his part. Blurry vision made it hard to comprehend the erratic movements around him. It was like being trapped in a glass coffin, underwater, peering up into the world, but unable to speak or communicate.

Moments, maybe hours, passed. He opened his eyes again. This time he could breathe, no foreign object violating his windpipe. Strange noises still echoed, but he was able to recognize them. He realized he was lying in a hospital bed. The ceiling tiles looked the same. He'd counted their grooves and holes before. Smells jogged memories he'd tried to forget. All his senses were on overload, battered by the aftermath of a near-fatal experience.

Throat scratchy and sore, he could barely speak. He barked, sounding more like an injured seal than a man. Searing pain melted his nerves. The morphine drip wasn't dripping nearly enough, and there weren't any nurses in the room. He ached everywhere, barely able to move. Then everything seemed to spin. Dizziness took over, and his eyes closed once more.

Each time he woke, the same old ceiling tiles stared back at him, boring and dull. His head hurt. His leg itched. Vision still blurry. An intense throbbing in his shoulder radiated around the front of his neck, sending sharp jolts of pain into his chest. Unable to raise himself up, or even turn over, he waited. Nick waited every time he opened his eyes.

An audible sound shuffled somewhere in front of the bed. He listened. Watched. Then the most angelic face appeared. Jess.

"You're awake." Her eyes lit up.

He nodded.

She noticed him looking past her. "Your dad went downstairs for coffee. They told us you had woken up, but every time we're in here you're sound asleep. They took you off the ventilator yesterday."

Nick moved his right hand, resisting a painful pull in his chest. He managed to find hers, nudging his fingers against her cold knuckles. He needed human contact, needed to know this was real, that he was okay. She took hold of his hand, squeezing gently.

"We're all here for you. Your dad hasn't left the hospital. Mark and I come every day. Monty and Seymour were here yesterday. A lot of people are pulling for you."

He tried to speak but coughed loudly instead.

"Take your time. No rush."

Seeing her gave him strength. He dared not look away or she might disappear. He had so many questions, but they could wait. His throbbing head begged his eyes to close. Sleep returned. This time he dreamed, random visions that made no sense, but more comforting than the nightmares he was used to.

The next time Nick opened his eyes, his dad was sitting next to him, reading the paper. *No one reads the paper anymore*, he thought. Dale did. He always had.

Nick moaned and grunted under strained breath. Disorientation clouded his thoughts, jumbled and confused.

Dale tossed his paper aside and moved closer. "Hey, son." He touched Nick's hand.

"Hey," Nick managed to mutter, barely a whisper. His eyes dimmed, fading in and out as Dale called for one of the nurses.

They seemed to pour in around him along with a tall, bearded man wearing a white coat. Nick was so tired. His body didn't want to cooperate. He couldn't move like he wanted to, and that frustrated him, but the large doses of narcotics coursing through his system made his pain somewhat manageable.

Dr. Weisman identified himself, then conferred quietly with a nurse before asking a round of questions. "Can you tell me your name?"

Nick looked from person to person, his eyes weary from bright lights and too much stimuli. He moaned, opening his mouth, and breathing heavily. "Nicholas."

A surge of emotion overwhelmed Dale's composure, and for a brief moment he thought he might breakdown, but he held steady. Hearing Nicholas say his name out loud, his full, given name, was the first sign of hope since he'd come home. Dale blinked away tears of joy as Dr. Weisman continued his test.

"What is your last name?" Dr. Weisman asked.

Nick thought for a moment, groaning more, his throat raw and painful with each sound he attempted. "Mi . . . Minner."

"Minner?" Dr. Weisman asked.

Nick closed his eyes. "Micker."

Dr. Weisman whispered to a nurse, who sat quietly typing notes on a laptop.

"Miller," Nick mumbled, then said more loudly with a hoarse voice. "Miller. Nick Miller."

Dr. Weisman smiled. "Do you know where you are, Mr. Miller?"

Nick's gaze drifted toward his father's pleading eyes. "Richland. Jack."

Disappointment showed on Dr. Weisman's face. "Where did you say you are?"

"Richland. Jack died."

Dr. Weisman gave more instructions to the nurse.

"Excuse me, Dr. Weisman. I think he's trying to tell you he's in the same hospital he was in when his friend Jack was killed earlier this year," Dale said.

Dr. Weisman returned to face Nick. "Mr. Miller, are you at home?"

Nick fumbled his hand along the sheets, finding his father's thick fingers.

"Hospital. Memorial. Richland." His breath grew faster, grunting and grimacing with each painful jolt to his body.

"Very good, Mr. Miller." Dr. Weisman made eye contact with Dale, nodding. "Can you tell me today's date?"

Nick shook his head. He was tired of answering questions. "Summer. Hot."

"That's good enough for me." Dr. Weisman grinned. "Next I'd like you to poke your tongue out. Can you do that?"

Nick did. His reactions were much slower than usual, but he understood and was able to respond correctly.

Dr. Weisman performed a pressure test on Nick's fingernails, measuring his reaction to pain. He also shined his very annoying light into Nick's eyes, examining his pupil size and shape and their reaction to light. He conferred with a nurse in the hallway while another checked Nick's vitals and increased his pain meds.

Nick drifted in and out of sleep again, mind exhausted and scattered. When he remained conscious long enough, he remembered holding Dale's gun, its cold steel against his skin. He remembered rolling the garage door back and starting his dad's bike, but the rest was blank, wiped away, and he wondered what had happened after.

Dr. Weisman returned. He addressed Dale, but looked at Nick periodically during the conversation.

"I'm giving him a thirteen on the Glasgow Coma Scale. This is good news. It means the traumatic brain injury he suffered is mild. There may still be some swelling, but it should continue to go down with time. Mild TBI means he stands a very good chance of regaining anything he's lost and returning to his previous life. He'll need physical therapy for his leg. The fractures were bad enough that it may be months before he can actually walk again. Most likely he'll need occupational therapy for any fine-motor skill delays. Only time will tell the long-term extent to his functions, but he's the most promising TBI case I've had in a while. His speech is good. I doubt he'll have much trouble there."

"Will he come out of ICU?" Dale asked.

"We need to monitor him a little while longer, make sure he's out of the woods, that his vitals stay strong. If he keeps this up I see no reason he won't be moved to a regular room by the end of the week."

A deep sigh of relief washed over Dale. He'd experienced many moments of joy and elation in his life, but never quite like this one. "Thank you. That's the best news you could have given me."

Dr. Weisman nodded. "Please understand that he has a long road ahead. We still have more evaluations to make and tests to run, but it does look good. His body is going to need a long time to heal."

"I understand." Dale clasped his hand around Nick's.

Dr. Weisman turned to leave, but stopped. "Also, please understand this. Your son is very fortunate to be alive. Most people in his situation don't make it to the emergency room. I don't know him, but if he didn't have a reason for living before, he certainly should have one now."

Dale pondered those words the rest of the day as he held vigil by Nick's bedside. He'd sleep on the floor of that sterile hospital room if he had to. Each time Nick woke he caught a glimpse of the boy he'd once known still present in those big, soft eyes. Nicholas was in there. He'd never left. He'd just been buried underneath a couple decades of heartache and baggage. Perhaps Dale could change that, perhaps he couldn't. Perhaps it didn't matter. He would love his son regardless, and this time make sure he knew it. He'd show him just how strong a father's love really was.

23

REALITY

*N*ick was unconscious for five days after his motorcycle crash, in and out of deep sleep for three days, and restless, ready to leave the ICU for another four. His doctors were extra cautious, making sure the swelling on his brain had gone down before moving him to a regular room.

His speech, though slurred at times, was almost normal. His reflexes and response times were slower than usual, but his comprehension was excellent, astounding every physician attending his case. Doctors don't believe in miracles, but they can admit when a patient defies scientific reason.

The door flung open.

"There you are." Morgan Hutch waltzed into Nick's room, hands on hips.

Nick rubbed his bruised and still swollen face with his right hand, his good hand. He blinked and stared as though seeing a ghost. She shoved the door closed behind her and sauntered to his bedside, slinging her heavy purse over one shoulder.

"I heard you were here," she said.

Nick said nothing.

"You just can't die, can you? I had to see it for myself. Made a deal with the devil? Maybe you should be buying lottery tickets, scumbag."

Nick frowned. He watched her every movement, analyzed her body language. He knew this look, this scorn-laced saunter she'd always approached him and Jack with, ridiculing them for practically everything. They'd never gotten along. Conflicting personalities and stubborn tempers were largely to blame, but when it came down to it, Nick and Jack had never liked her and she had never liked them. Her relationship with Drew had been a conflict within the band since the two of them had met, but Drew loved her, a short, sassy blond with a raging fire always brewing under the surface. Nick had always tried to be cordial, but mostly he just avoided her.

"Can you speak? Say something!" she demanded.

He cleared his throat. Strained vocal noises emerged as he formed the words. "What do you want me to say?"

"Are you going to walk again? 'Cause Drew won't. I hear you might make a full recovery. Does that seem fair to you? Can you honestly stand to be alive?"

"No," he muttered, closing his eyes.

"Good! I hope you wallow in self-pity for the rest of your life. You have no idea . . . I can't even . . . Ugh! You scumbag!"

"You said that already."

"What?" she asked, distracted in her moment of rage.

"Scumbag. You called me that already."

"Are you trying to be cute? Is life still a big game to you?"

"Do I look cute?" he asked.

"I'm dead serious, Nick."

"So am I. Look at me. Do I look cute?"

"Of course not. You look like you've been chewed up and spit back out. You deserve that, you know."

"My point. I'm being punished. Might not be the punishment

you would have chosen, but I'm suffering. That not good enough for you?"

She looked him over. He watched her facial expression turn from anger, to pity, and then to what he could only define as disgust.

"If you walk out of this hospital, if you ever walk again, there's no way in hell it can be good enough. And I mean hell in the literal sense, because I hope that's where you're going."

Morgan turned to leave, stomping toward the door.

"Morgan."

She turned around.

"I'm sorry."

"For what?" she replied.

"For not giving you the keys that night. For treating the world like my personal playground and causing you pain in the process. I love Drew and he knows it. I'd trade places if I could, but I can't, and you know that. All I can do is say I'm sorry."

"Sorry isn't good enough."

"It's all I've got."

She huffed. "Then you've got nothing."

Morgan stormed out of his room as quickly as she'd stormed in, leaving Nick alone, wishing he hadn't woken up in ICU, wondering if he should have stayed in that mind-numbingly boring apartment in Richland instead of coming home. Nothing but anguish had plagued him since he returned.

When the door opened again he cringed, waking from a faint sleep, hoping it wasn't someone else come to berate him. It wasn't. It was Jess.

"Did I wake you?"

He shook his head.

"I did. Don't lie. I knew your dad was still at work so I came by to keep you company for a while. Brought you a better pillow. Memory foam. Not this standard-grade, hospital fluff that isn't fit for a cat." She smiled, stuffing the new pillow gently behind his head and neck.

"Thank you," he said.

"Can I get you anything? Have you eaten? Probably don't have much appetite." She hesitated. "I'll be honest. I don't know what to do for you. I don't know what you need. I don't know if I'm bothering you when I come or if I should be doing something when I'm here. I feel kind of useless." Jess shrugged.

Nick smiled. Her warm face brightened his room. He noticed her red lipstick, something he'd never seen her wear before. She wore a flouncy dress with a bright flower print and a peach sweater with tiny buttons that shined like pearls. Her hair looked different too, bouncy and portions of it loosely pinned back. A comforting vision for his tired eyes. He liked it. He enjoyed seeing her happy, or what appeared to be happy. At least happier than he'd seen her since they met.

"I don't need anything," he replied.

"Do you want me to leave?"

"No. That's not what I meant."

"You want me to sit here and stare at you? I can do that, but it might make us both uncomfortable."

Nick laughed, painfully holding his chest, choking back each jarring chuckle.

"Try not to make me laugh too much, okay?"

"Want me to make you cry?"

"No."

"Well, I'm running out of things to do here then." She took his hand, reassuring him.

"There. That. Don't let go."

She smiled. "I'm not going anywhere."

"Good. If the wicked witch of the west comes back, you can take her down for me."

"Who?"

"Nothing. Never mind. Just a ghost from the past. Tell me something. Anything. Just talk."

Jess sat down in a chair near the bed. "I don't know much. Don't get out much, remember? I think all I have is sad news. Not exactly what someone in a hospital bed needs to hear, right?"

"Is it about you?" he asked.

"No. Mark and Elise. I don't want to bother you with it."

"If it's some big secret . . ."

"It's not, but . . ."

"Tell me."

"They got bad news last night. The paternal grandmother of the baby they were going to adopt has petitioned the court for guardianship after it's born. The adoption fell through."

"I'm sorry."

"Well, it's certainly not your fault."

"Finally, one thing that's not."

"I just feel really bad for them. They've tried so hard for so many years. I don't know what that's like. It was easy for me to get pregnant with Abby. I never had to think about it."

"They seem so grounded. He does at least. I don't really know her."

"They say it's their faith that keeps them strong. I had faith once. It didn't keep me strong."

Nick studied her eyes, definitely green. "Maybe *you* didn't keep *it*."

"Good grief, Nick. You sound like my brother. Since when did you become so insightful about religion?"

He smirked. "I'm not. Just looking at it from the other perspective. Devil's advocate maybe?"

"You would be the devil," she said.

"Hey. What's that's supposed to mean?"

"You getting hurt, causing us all to worry. Thought we were going to lose you. You really scared me."

"I'm sorry. I didn't know you cared so much." He smiled.

"Who else is going to serenade me on my front porch?"

He laughed. "I hear Keith Richards is available."

"Who's Keith Richards?"

Nick shook his head in disbelief. "If you have to ask, then never mind."

"Are you cold? Need more blankets?"

"No, I'm fine. Just keep talking. I'm going to rest my eyes."

He drifted back to sleep, lulled by the sound of Jess's voice. She didn't talk about much, whatever she could think of to fill the void. He just needed to know that someone was there, that he wasn't alone. He needed a friend, and Jess was happy to be that friend. She stayed until Dale arrived later that evening.

On her way home, Mark was silent. He'd been late picking Jess up and she could sense his tension.

"How much do I owe you for gas?"

"I'm not worried about that."

"I'm sure these daily drives to Richland are adding up."

"Jess, please."

"Want to talk about it?" she asked.

"No."

"Okay."

If he didn't want to talk, she wouldn't press. She understood that some things needed to be left alone.

He glanced in her direction. "Are you wearing makeup?"

"Should I not be?"

"Just haven't seen you wear any in a while," he said, taking note of her dress. "You look nice."

She sighed. "Go ahead and say it."

"Say what?"

"I look like the old me."

Mark was silent for a moment.

"You do resemble the old you a bit."

"A bit? What's missing?"

He smiled. "Bellowing laughter."

"Bellowing? When have I ever bellowed?"

Mark snickered. "That deep belly laugh you've always been known for. I miss that."

She smiled. "Give it time. It's still in there somewhere. It's just not ready to come out yet."

"Save the first one for me then, okay?"

"Deal," she said. "I'm hungry. Let's get something to eat."

Music to his ears. "We can stop by the house, raid the fridge. I don't think Elise is cooking tonight, but there's never a shortage of food."

When they walked inside Mark's house they heard a strange commotion coming from upstairs. Mark called out to Elise and Jess followed him up the stairs to see what was going on.

In the nursery, Elise was hurling bibs and blankets into boxes. The room was a mess, clothes and toys scattered everywhere as she stuffed them into containers with fists of fury. The crib had been dismantled and lay in pieces across the floor. Drawers were open, bookshelves emptied, and numerous piles of random items made the room an obstacle course of baby accessories.

"Elise, honey, what are you doing?" Mark stepped over a bouncy seat and around a bathing tub, approaching his wife with caution.

Jess stood in the doorway. She'd never seen Elise like this.

"What does it look like I'm doing? I'm packing everything up," Elise snapped.

"Why?" he asked.

"We don't need it anymore. Why let everything sit around collecting dust? We could be using this room for exercise, or office space."

"I have an office downstairs, and when was last time either of us exercised in the house?"

She scolded him with her eyes. "Okay, a craft room then, or a storage room for your gazillion books. We all know a preacher needs three copies of every commentary on the market." She cut daggers right through Mark and returned to dumping a stack of diapers from a decorative basket into a large cardboard box in the middle of the floor.

Elise had always tried to keep a civilized composure, to be respectful and loving, all the things that made her the worthy woman of Proverbs 31. The preacher's wife was held to a higher standard. She didn't get angry or upset or argue with her husband. She didn't speak out of turn or allow her emotions to claim the best of her. Except that wasn't true. Preacher's wife or not, she was human and she struggled with every painful emotion. She'd gotten so used to not showing that side of herself, keeping everything bottled up, that when she'd finally reached her limit, the lid blew off and the ugly came tumbling out. Suddenly she didn't care if she was the picture-perfect preacher's wife. She had lost another child and her heart was in pieces.

"Why not a nursery?" he asked.

Her grieving eyes warned him to tread carefully. "You know why. It's over, Mark. We lost. It's not happening."

"So we try again."

"I'm tired. Tired of going through the same motions over and over, only to fail. You should be relieved. Aren't you the one who said maybe it's not God's will for us to have a child? You've been the reluctant one this whole time. You don't want to try again.

One last time, remember?" She picked up a large teddy bear and cocked her arm back to hurl it across the room.

He reached for her, taking the bear out of her hand, and pulled her close to him. "I'm the pessimist in this relationship. You've always been my shining optimist. Don't let me down now." He held her against him and kissed her tear-smeared face.

"There's only so much rejection one person can take. I don't have any tries left in me."

He squeezed her in his arms and tilted his head down to meet her eyes with tenderness, "We can look into foster care, fertility treatments, a surrogate perhaps—"

She pushed his arms away from her. "Enough. At some point we have to throw in the towel and accept our life the way it is. Childless."

Jess scooted into the room. The last thing she wanted to do was intrude on such a private moment, but she couldn't help herself. Her heart grieved deeply for Elise, and she realized fully for the first time that she and Elise understood each other's pain. They were sisters, bonded by a pain only women who've experienced the loss of a child can understand. Jess stood before her, sorrowful for things she'd said when blinded by her own suffering, too selfish to grasp that other people were suffering too. Most of all she was sorry for not being there when Elise needed her most.

"I'm sorry." Jess wrapped her arms around her sister-in-law, who returned the embrace. They held each other, releasing heavy burdens as they cried on each other's shoulders.

Mark stood back, gripping his clenched jaw. He'd never been one to cry in front of people. He struggled in that moment to conceal the eruption brooding beneath the surface of his resolute nature. The need to occupy himself took over. He began packing boxes and cleaning up the tornadic path Elise had left in her wake, trying not to dwell on what could have been, but instead what *was* the wonderful life they were sharing.

"I'll help," Jess said, drying her eyes and picking up a stuffed bunny.

The three of them packed together, reflecting on harsh realities. There was no easy way to accept the hand they were dealt, but for Elise, the occasional slam dunk and toy fastball seemed to help her vent her frustration. Mark breathed a sigh of relief. He was pleased to see this side of his wife, a side she rarely showed. In her moment of fury and anguish, she helped him see it was okay to let go and let it all out. He struggled with his own need to be strong for everyone else. But strength is often perfected in weakness, and in great distress contentment is formed. Mark was content. He was married to the most remarkable woman in the world.

24

FRUSTRATION

*D*ays and weeks trapped in a hospital wore heavy on Nick's nerves. He'd been forced to do some real thinking, contemplating his situation, which only made him angry and restless. He needed a distraction, a change of scenery. *I need to get out of here.*

"They were out of coffee so I got tea." Dale walked in carrying two Styrofoam cups.

"What kind of hospital runs out of coffee?" Nick shook his head.

Dale ignored his snarky tone. "Sugar?"

"You'd think they would cater to people's needs better than that."

"I hate to break it to you, but this isn't a five-star hotel."

Nick rolled his eyes. "I'm so sick of this place. I can't do anything on my own or have a moment to myself. Just for one day I'd like to get my own coffee and fix my own food."

"How exactly do you plan to do that?"

Nick huffed. He knew where this was going. He hadn't

thought past getting out, he just knew he wanted to be anywhere but Richland Memorial.

"You can't walk, you only have one good arm, and I seem to recall an issue with fine motor skills preventing you from using utensils adequately when you eat. Need I go on?"

"Don't be smug," Nick snapped.

"I'm not trying to be smug, just stating a few important facts. You're not healed yet, Nicholas."

"And so everyone continues to remind me. I need to get out of here. I'm going stir-crazy."

"As soon as a room opens at North Haven they're going to transfer you." Dale sat down in a nearby chair and opened the morning's newspaper, turning to the world news section.

"There's nothing on this stinking TV either."

"Would it kill you to stop complaining every five minutes?"

"Yes, actually, it would. Not complaining makes my leg hurt worse." Nick smirked.

Dale arched one eyebrow much higher than the other, peering over the top of his newspaper.

Nick flipped past channel after boring channel, mashing his fist against the remote. He wanted to get out, but he wasn't sure he'd like North Haven any better. Supposedly it was a top-notch rehabilitation facility, closer to Bridgetown, with a reputation that rivaled many other facilities in the region. Hopefully they had more TV channels than this forsaken place.

Without warning Nick's remote control went flying across the room, crashing into a whiteboard on the wall. Dale gazed over his newspaper to find his son wrestling with an assortment of tangled cords, explicit words rupturing from his mouth.

"Problem?"

"Yes! That remote is useless, and this ridiculous pile of garbage is in my way!"

Dale came to his aid, untangling the mess of cords without

speaking a word. He wasn't about to add more logs to that raging bonfire.

The door opened and Dr. Whitley entered, coffee mug in hand. He was the latest in a long line of physicians overseeing Nick's care.

"He gets coffee?" Nick huffed again.

"How are you today, Nick?"

Dr. Whitley was the only doctor who called him by his first name. A very personable man with a bedside manner that almost made Nick forget he was lying in a cripple ward.

"How does it look?" Nick retorted.

"Been in this mood long?" Dr. Whitley glanced at Dale.

"All day," Dale replied.

"It's not a mood. It's a call to freedom."

Dr. Whitley laughed. "I'm glad to see your sense of humor hasn't been affected."

"Ha! That's not humor. It's his natural, charming cynicism," Dale corrected.

Nick rolled his eyes again.

Dr. Whitley cocked his head. "Your coloring looks much better today. Your vitals are great. We just need to do something about this mess of a body you have going on here."

Nick groaned. He tried to shift his weight to relieve a stabbing pain currently running the full length of his right leg.

"A room at North Haven just opened up, and I have your release papers ready to go. Feel like getting out of here tomorrow?"

"I feel like going home."

"The good people at North Haven will see to it you're able to return home as soon as possible. You still have some minimal swelling on your brain, which should subside in time. Occupational therapy will work with you on regaining the fine motor skills you've lost, specifically your hand and finger coordination.

And once we get you out of these casts you'll be able to start some pretty rigorous PT to get you walking and moving again."

"Joy of joys," Nick moaned.

"You're one lucky man. I'd be thanking mother universe if I were you."

"Lucky? What part of this is luck, Doc? How is any of this lucky?" The scowl on Nick's face grew more defined.

Dr. Whitley set his mug down on the bedside table. His smile faded.

"Let me explain something to you. I've practiced medicine for almost thirty years, and it's been my pleasure to be part of your medical team. I've been privileged to witness something not every physician gets to see. Do you have any idea how different your case is from many accident victims we see come through here?"

"No, but I'm sure you're going to tell me," Nick murmured.

"Yes, I am. I think you need to know what a tremendous gift you've been given."

"You call *this* a gift? I can't walk. I can barely move. I'm doped up just so I can get through the day without passing out from the pain. And don't go and tell me how this is my fault. I know that. I get it. What I don't get is why I'm still alive. Got an answer for that one, Doc?"

Dr. Whitley looked down and then back up at Nick. "No, I don't. The blunt fact is that you shouldn't be alive. There is no medical reason for you to be here right now. You can call that sheer luck, a higher power, a sign from the universe. There's no logic in you surviving a motorcycle crash with that impact and being able to talk to me about it."

"Is this a motivational speech?" Nick replied.

"Listen to him, Nicholas." Dale's calm command rose from the other side of the room.

Nick released a long sigh and shook his head, but he stopped talking and listened to what Dr. Whitley had to say. He liked Dr. Whitley. He didn't want to admit he liked anything about his current circumstances, but Dr. Whitley was a friendly face, someone he didn't mind barging in his room unannounced.

"I'm a man of science. But what we've all witnessed taking care of you these last few weeks has made us think twice about our own beliefs. People don't just live through accidents like that. Some, but not the majority. I've seen patients live in comas for months and then die. I've had patients who came out of comas but were unable to speak or comprehend what was being said to them, rendered useless by the trauma their brains sustained. The bigger picture, Nick, is that even those cases are rare. A large percentage of motorcycle accident victims are pronounced dead at the scene, and the ones who actually live through an ambulance ride die in the ER or on the operating table. They don't get another chance to crack wise remarks or complain about their hospital accommodations."

Silence filled the room.

"I'm not trying to lecture you, but I'm rather impressed that I'm able to sit here and have a conversation with you. You look good, Nick. Really good, all things considered. I'm not a psychologist, but I will tell you you've been offered a rare second shot at life, and I hope you can fully grasp the importance of that. I've got a coma patient on another floor right now who woke up yesterday, but she isn't responding to stimuli. Her family hasn't left her bedside since she's been here. Someone or something was looking out for you, Nick. Let that sink in for a while."

Nick gave a plaintive nod.

"I'd love to hear reports of your progress over at North Haven. We'll get that release started. Should be able to transport you by late morning. Sound good?"

"Sounds good. Thank you," Dale replied.

"All right. You guys let me know if you need anything. I'll

send in one of the nurses to change out that IV bag and check your meds."

Dr. Whitley left the room and silence resumed for several minutes.

"Third," Dale finally spoke.

Nick turned his head.

"He said you were given a second shot at life, but it's a third shot."

Nick didn't say anything. His dad was right, but he couldn't bring himself to say that out loud.

Nick had lived through three near misses: his mother's deadly wreck, the night he killed Jack, and this . . . this situation he now endured because of his own stupidity, his own inability to man up and face his mistakes.

"Want me to see if I can find you some coffee?" Dale asked.

"No. Don't bother."

Nick knew he should be grateful, but emotionally he was still as marred and beaten as he had been before he got on that bike, before he placed that gun to his head. He still blamed himself for Jack's death, still harbored baggage from his mother's. He still felt the nagging pain of things left unresolved with his father, things he wished more than anything could be mended. So much of what was wrong in his life was his own fault, he admitted that. He just didn't know where to begin to make it right.

As he lay in bed staring out the window, listening to sounds of newspaper pages turning, he dreamed of a fresh start, a new chapter where he could make big changes. Then he wondered if new chapters really existed, or if they were simply pipe dreams created by guilty consciences. Either way, he knew he wanted, a better life. He wanted to be a better person.

25

NORTH HAVEN

*T*urned out North Haven was nothing special, a step up from the hospital, but he'd rather be at home in his own bed. Nick was given a private room, and by all accounts it was homier than his sterile quarters at Richland Memorial, but he didn't want to be there.

They had rules at North Haven. Rules he had to follow. One of those rules was that every patient had to come out of their room for certain periods each day. It wasn't dictated how they spent that time, but they were encouraged to associate with others and participate in activities. Nick felt like an old man in a nursing home. Each day he had to choose where he wanted the nurse's aide to wheel him: one of two large recreation rooms or the courtyard surrounded by gardens and two big water fountains. He preferred the comfort of his bed with the covers pulled over his face and the shades tightly drawn, but according to his therapists he needed to get out and move around as much as possible. Nick thought it absurd considering he was stuck in a wheelchair. Celeste, his occupational therapist, said the sunlight and socialization were just as good. Nick disagreed, but apparently his opinion didn't matter.

Sitting idly in his wheelchair, in a room of patients with differing conditions, Nick stared out the closest window with a view. His thoughts drifted. Random melodies played inside his head, chords and notes of unwritten songs dying to be composed. His brain was full of music he wasn't sure he'd be able to play again.

"Hey there." The voice of an angel brought him back to reality.

Nick looked up. Jess stood beside him, wearing a warm smile and that cardinal-red lipstick she'd been wearing lately. He realized he was staring, but he didn't want to look away.

"Hey."

"This seat taken?" she asked, pointing to a chair nearby.

"Not yet." He grinned.

"Good." She plopped down.

The room buzzed with activity. Patients practiced exercises, family members played board games while children ate snacks and employees answered questions. Everyone was imbibed with life . . . except Nick.

"Penny for your thoughts," Jess said.

"I doubt they're worth a penny," he replied.

"Okay, nothing for your thoughts then. Just tell me."

"Demanding, aren't you?"

"I can be. But I really don't want to overpay if your thoughts aren't worth anything."

"I bet you can guess what I'm thinking." He tilted his head.

"Probably." She stared at him. "You want to go home."

"In a nutshell," he said.

"That's nothing new, but I bet there's more. I bet there's a lot more. Don't worry. I won't make you divulge all your secrets. Just tell me one thing."

"What?"

"How are you?"

He huffed. "You asked me that yesterday."

"Yeah."

Nick let out a long sigh. "Honesty?"

"Of course," she said.

"I'm tired of everyone asking if I'm okay."

"I didn't ask if you were okay. I asked how you are."

"There's a difference?"

"As someone who's been in that boat . . . yes."

Jess waited for him to give an answer.

"I'm tired of feeling the same way all the time," he finally spoke.

She nodded.

"Every day it's the same emotions, spinning around and around like a ticking bomb, and I can't shake them," he continued.

She nodded again.

"I want to get through this, get over it, get better . . . but I don't know how. It's like being stuck in the mud, tires spinning, engine turning, but no forward motion."

Jess understood every word he was saying.

"One question keeps popping up over and over."

"What?"

"Why is it so hard for me to forgive myself?"

That one she couldn't relate to. Sure, she'd felt guilt as a mother, wishing she'd been the one to drive Abby to ballet, but most of her anger and resentment had been directed at Patrick. She blamed him for everything. Forgiving him had been one of her biggest struggles. Even now, when she finally felt like she might somehow be able to move on with her life in some uncertain capacity, she struggled to put those events behind her.

"I'm sorry," he said.

"For what?"

"You came to visit and here I am sucking the life out of this conversation."

"I'm the one who asked the soul-searching question."

"True," he replied.

"I didn't come here to make small talk, unless that's what you need. I came here to be a friend, and friends ask important questions."

He nodded.

"I worry about you," she said.

He watched her face, the way her features softened when she looked at him, the way her eyes flickered varying shades of green and layers of her hair fell against her forehead and temples. He wanted to touch her face, run his fingers through her hair. If he hadn't been such a mess he would have wished he could hold her in his arms. But then he realized what a silly thought that was. He'd blown any chance he might have had with her.

"Why?" he asked.

She hadn't even asked herself that question.

"I care. You have so much going for you."

"It doesn't feel like it. Feels like fate messed things up."

"How?"

"So many reasons I should be dead, but I'm not. And maybe the world would be better off if I was."

She didn't know what to say.

"Look, Jess, I'm sorry. I'm not very good company. I know that. I'm glad you came, but—"

"You can't blame this on fate," she cut him off.

"Why not?"

"Because fate, or whatever you believe it is, didn't do this to you."

"Yeah, I know. I did it to myself. Everything is my fault. I ruined people's lives. Blah, blah, blah. So why am I still here?

Why do I get to breathe and live?" Nick's raised voice drew attention from others in the room.

"You're asking me questions I can't answer. The bigger question is what are you going to do with the life you've been given? You can sit around and feel sorry for yourself, or you can get up and do something."

"Isn't that the pot calling the kettle black? What have you been doing the last year or so? You gave up too."

He was right. She knew that. But she was trying, and that was more than she could say for him.

"I did give up. I'm not proud of who I let myself become, but I'm trying to change that. I'm trying to live my life again."

"Well, it's just not that easy for me. Maybe I don't want to live."

"Then don't."

"What?"

"No one is forcing you to be here. You want to quit? Go ahead, throw in the towel. Fate didn't make a mistake. It gave you something. But if you can't see that, it's wasted on you."

Her words pierced him like an icy dagger. He knew she was right. She was always right. He wished he could prove himself to her, show her that he wasn't a complete fool, but he hadn't proven it to himself yet.

"I'm going to go." Jess got up.

"Wait." He reached for her, clasping fingers around her wrist. He slid his hand over hers and pulled her toward him with what little strength he possessed.

She touched his arm and hesitated for a moment, wishing she had a reason to stay. "I've got some things I need to do. I wasn't planning to stay long anyway. I'll come back."

"I'm sorry." He could kick himself if he had full use of his legs.

"Don't be. Just promise me something. Try to think about the good things, not just the bad. If you can think of one really good thing in your life, maybe it's something worth living for."

She patted his shoulder and smiled, turning to leave. Her thin figure disappeared through double doors, and Nick mulled her words over in his head. He hated feeling like they'd quarreled, like he'd disappointed her. He hated himself for always making a mess of everything. *Why am I such a screw-up?*

The double doors opened again. Nick scowled at the sight of Mark sauntering into the room. He hoped he wouldn't see him, but how could he miss the idiot wearing a giant leg cast sitting in a wheelchair. He didn't. He saw Nick right away and made a beeline for him, wearing a confident grin on his face.

"You look great, Nick," Mark teased, taking Jess's seat.

"Thanks. I feel like a million bucks. You just missed your sister."

"Elise is giving her a ride home."

Nick couldn't help but notice his satisfactory demeanor.

"What's up with you, man? Is there something I should know?"

Mark chuckled. "Well, since you asked, I wanted to break the news to you myself."

"What news?"

"I'm afraid you're going to be stuck with me for a while."

"I feel like I'm playing charades. Seriously, what are you talking about?"

"I did something that I thought was in your best interest even though I knew you probably wouldn't like it." Mark's face turned serious. "You can't just break probation without consequences."

Nick's stomach plunged to his knees. He hadn't even thought about his probation officer and what this might mean for the terms of his probation. He hadn't expected to live.

"I took care of it," Mark said.

"What do you mean you took care of it?"

"I paid a visit to your probation officer while you were still in the ICU. It was only a matter of time before word traveled, and apparently it had because some guy named Alan had already paid him a visit."

"Alan Worthing?" Nick asked.

"I guess. You know him?"

"He's my manager . . . or was . . . is . . . I don't know."

"He seemed very concerned about publicity and PR. I guess you can thank him for the lack of media coverage surrounding this."

Nick eyed the floor below, wishing he had a way out of this conversation.

"It's easier to keep things low key in Bridgetown. Richland is a big city. More press."

Nick nodded, still staring at the white tiled floor.

"Here's the deal. There's no broken probation, not yet. No court date. No prison time."

Nick looked up. Mark's brown eyes showed compassion, yet their seriousness made his stomach turn.

"So what is it? What do I owe you?"

"You don't owe me, Nick. I made a bargain, that's all. I told your probation officer you'd be in counseling. He agreed it was a good idea, and that if you complied and followed through he'd keep this whole thing off the books."

"Counseling?" Nick moaned.

"Yep," Mark replied.

"What kind of counseling?"

"I guess the usual protocol would be geared toward substance abuse. I explained to him that I'm a preacher and a licensed counselor. Once he saw my credentials he didn't ask a whole lot of questions. It's up to me what we talk about."

Nick's jaw dropped. Mark waited for him to say something.

"You? For how long?"

"Until I feel like you've reached a desired level of recovery and completed the program," Mark replied.

"What program?"

"The Keep Nick Out of Jail program," Mark said with a sobering look.

"Great," Nick huffed.

"You're running out of options."

Nick knew that was true. He just didn't like it.

"When do we start? What do you want me to do?" Nick tossed his one good hand up in the air, cringing at the shooting pain it sent through his collarbone.

"Now's as good a time as any. You don't look very busy."

"I have therapy," Nick replied.

"That's not until one. I checked," Mark shot back.

Nick sighed. "Go ahead. Psychoanalyze me. Counsel me, oh great one."

Mark took his sarcasm in stride. He knew his attitude was merely a coping mechanism. When a man hits rock bottom he has nothing else to do but climb up, or lie down and wait for the avalanche to take him. Mark wanted him to climb.

"It's not going to work like that. I'll come here every day, or as often as I can, and we'll talk."

"That's it? We just talk?"

"Yep," Mark replied.

"So, what do we talk about?"

Mark smiled, settling into his chair. "What's your middle name?"

"Huh?"

"Do you have one?" Mark asked again.

"Yeah, I have one. Why are we talking about my middle name?"

"Are you telling me how to do my job?" Mark replied.

"No, just seems a little odd. Unless you're trying to get me to trust you, build some kind of friendship so I'll tell you my life story and you can tell me where I went wrong and how to fix it."

"Why does it have to be that complicated? I don't have an ulterior motive here. My job is to counsel you, so let's just talk." Mark arched his brow. "Unless that scares you."

Nick thought for a moment, studying Mark's face, then the floor again.

"Lane," Nick finally replied.

"Your middle name is Lane?" Mark asked.

"Yeah. Nicholas Lane Miller. Lane was my mother's maiden name."

Mark nodded. "Not bad. Mine's Antonius."

"Antonius?"

"Yeah, don't laugh. My dad was a history buff. Ever heard of Marcus Antonius? Better known as Mark Antony, of Mark Anthony and Cleopatra?"

Nick laughed. "Really?"

"I've had to live with that my whole life. Most people think I'm named after Mark in the Bible, being a preacher and all. Some days I wish that were true."

"I never would have pegged you for an Antonius." Nick laughed again.

"Well, just goes to show you never really know people."

"I'm scared to ask about Jess."

Mark laughed. "Katelyn. She has a pretty normal name. Mom read a book with a character named Katelyn and thought it was a perfect girl's name."

Nick smiled. "Where did Jess come from? I assumed Jessica, but she was quick to correct me."

"She would. Jess Palmer, a famous jazz musician in the sixties. Our dad was a big jazz fan, as well as blues. History and music. It was quite a childhood."

"I bet." Nick relaxed his posture. Mark wasn't such a bad guy.

He'd never thought he was. He just figured Mark had made his mind up about him. Maybe he had. Maybe he was willing to change his opinion. If only Nick could change his opinion about himself.

"They have good food in this place?" Mark asked.

Nick shrugged. "It's all right."

"You like fried chicken?"

"I guess."

"There's a place on Water Street. They serve the best fried chicken you'll ever eat. It's a little spicy, full of juicy flavor, and not too greasy. I could bring us some next time."

"Sure. Whatever is fine. I haven't had the biggest appetite lately. Besides, eating is often a chore." Nick shrugged.

"What about milkshakes? Mark asked.

"This isn't going to be like us sitting around, bonding over food, and telling our life stories, is it? I mean, isn't that what women do?" Nick grimaced.

"Okay, okay. How about, no food, but I bring a soda or something. Elise won't keep them in the house, so I have to sneak them when she's not around."

"I can handle that. I'm guessing beer is out of the question, under the circumstances." Nick wasn't joking.

Mark nodded. "It's frowned upon."

"I figured," Nick conceded.

"Root beer is allowed."

"Yeah, and that's almost exactly the same thing." Nick rolled his eyes.

Mark grinned. "Elise needs help taking some boxes to Goodwill. We cleaned out a room recently, and there was quite a bit more stuff than we realized. I'll be back though. Like I said, you're stuck with me for a while."

"I'll be beside myself with anticipation."

"Ha! I'll remember that one." Mark laughed as he got up,

turning to face Nick. "Call me if you need anything." He handed Nick a card. "My number is on the back."

Nick took the card, glancing at the handwritten digits. He nodded, relieved to see Mark walk back through the double doors, and out of sight. He needed time to process. So many things were changing. The world around him seemed to spin faster. He wasn't sure he was ready to brave life again, and all the new commitments that would come along with it, but he didn't have much of a choice.

26

DRIVING LESSONS

*J*ess gripped the steering wheel of her white Toyota Camry, breathing in and out, eyes closed, all her energy focused on not falling apart.

You can do this. You can do this.

Keys hung from the ignition. She pressed her foot against the brake pedal.

Do it! she goaded herself.

Mrs. Timmons stood a few yards away pruning bushes, watching Jess with an occasional stink-eye.

"Mind your own business, old bat," Jess said under her breath. The last thing she needed while attempting to drive a car for the first time since Abby's death was her cantankerous old neighbor eyeing her like a hawk.

Mark's car pulled into the driveway behind hers. What was he doing here? Never a moment's peace.

He walked toward the front porch.

He doesn't know I'm in the car. Maybe he'll think I'm not home and leave.

"She's sitting in her car," Mrs. Timmons called out to Mark.

Mark squinted between rays of sun, peering from a distance to see inside Jess's car.

"How long has she been in there, Mrs. Timmons?"

"About thirty-six minutes. Timed her on my watch. She's an odd bird, your sister."

Mark chuckled. "That she is, Mrs. Timmons. Thank you."

Great. Yeah, thanks, Mrs. Timmons. What kind of lunatic would watch a person for over thirty minutes and time it on their watch? The old bat had lost it.

Mark leaned against the passenger side, forcing Jess to turn the key one notch, enabling the power windows. He rested his arms against the frame.

"Should I even ask what you're doing?"

"Obviously *not* avoiding the ever-watchful eye of Mrs. Timmons." She was, however, avoiding Mark's question.

"Going somewhere?"

I give up. "I need to drive, Mark. It's been long enough. I can't keep expecting you and Elise to cart me around every time I need to go somewhere. I'm thirty-four years old. It's pathetic."

Mark opened the door and sat down. "It's not pathetic. You're traumatized. It's a completely normal reaction."

"I wasn't even in the car when they had the accident. I've never actually been in an accident, not even a fender bender."

"You're a good driver."

"Was," she corrected.

"Stop beating yourself up. You'll get there."

"When? By the time I'm as old as Mrs. Timmons and my eyesight has failed enough for them to revoke my license?"

Mark laughed. "How about now."

"Well, that's kind of what I was trying to do."

"So, what's the problem? Turn the key and start her up."

Jess tilted her head, glaring at him sideways. "For one thing, your car is parked behind mine. Unless you'd like me to move it for you."

He waved an index finger. "Hold on . . ."

Mark moved his car across the street and hopped back in the passenger seat of Jess's Camry.

"Okay. Go," he said.

"Mark, really? If it were that easy, don't you think I'd have already been out and back by now?"

"What's stopping you?"

He was deliberately acting like it was no big deal, trying to coax her into it, and she knew that. He couldn't fool her, and he couldn't make this any easier by pretending it was just any routine activity.

"I can't start the stupid thing."

"Sure you can. Turn the key all the way until you hear the motor." He nodded as though it were as easy as switching on a light.

"Gee, why did I not think of that?" She rolled her eyes.

"You have to do it yourself. I can't do it for you," he said.

"You are so *not* helpful."

He grinned. "Close your eyes."

"Mark . . ."

"Just do it."

Huffing in protest, she did as he asked.

"What do you see?"

Is he for real?

"Come on, Jess. what do you see?"

"Darkness. My eyes are closed. It's black."

"Keep looking. Put your fingers on the key, but don't open your eyes."

She followed his instructions, thinking she had a mental case for a brother. Then it came to her. Abby playing outside, happy, smiling. She could even picture her buckled tightly in her car seat, licking a green sucker from the bank, Abby's favorite.

"I get it. Happy memories, right?"

"What do you mean? What did you see?"

"Oh, come on, Mark," she said, opening her eyes. "You wanted me to close my eyes and think of happy, peaceful times with Abby, when everything was okay and I wasn't afraid to get behind the wheel of a car like some crazy lady."

He smiled. "Well, I'm not sure I can take credit for all that. It was meant to be an exercise in relaxation and focus. You focus on one thing, forgetting the thing that keeps you from doing the thing you're trying to do . . ."

"Have you been drinking? That makes no sense."

"Of course not, and yes, it does. Jess, start the car."

She did it. She started the car. Jess could feel the vibrations of a purring engine beneath her feet.

"Are you going to drive this thing or give Mrs. Timmons a second half to the show?"

Jess checked her seat belt and mirrors. Everything was in place and ready to go. Except her.

"I can't."

"Sure you can."

"No, Mark. I can't."

"What's stopping you?"

Her breath quickened. Her heart beat faster.

"When I try to drive I can see the crash. I see Patrick's face. The horror he must have experienced when he knew he was sending them both to their death. The look in his eyes. It's like I was there, Mark. I can hear the sounds . . ."

He placed a reassuring hand on her shoulder and took a deep breath. She had a look of defeat plastered across her face though he knew she wanted to do this more than anything.

"What happens if you crash?" Mark asked.

She shot him a puzzled look.

"What if you wreck, rip this car to pieces, roll it around in a ditch a few times? What then?"

"I go to the hospital . . . die . . . I don't know."

"The same could happen when you're riding in a car with someone else. You could get hit just walking down the street," he said.

"Yes, but I wouldn't be responsible for killing someone," she answered quickly.

"That's it," he said.

Jess pondered.

"You're not afraid of getting into an accident or harming yourself. You're afraid of harming other people. You blame Patrick for what happened, and rightfully so. He made a reckless decision. But, Jess, that isn't you. You can't use what happened that day as an excuse to let your fears take over and keep you from participating in your own life. I believe you can do this. I see that you're ready. You just need a push."

"How do you know I'm ready?"

"Because you're sitting in the driver's seat with the engine on."

"I want to."

"Then do it. Put the car in reverse and go. I'm right here with you."

She held her hand against the gear shift, steadying her composure, preparing herself for something she couldn't completely make up her mind about. She squeezed the button and began moving it to reverse.

"No, wait!" Mark yelled.

Jess thrust it back to park, removed her hand quickly, and leaned as far back against her seat as she could, near panic.

"What?" she asked.

"I don't have my seat belt on," he said, laughing.

She glared like a vulture circling its prey. "Mark Antonius Stuart! Don't you ever do that to me again!" She slapped his arm.

He laughed again. Soon she was chuckling too.

"What are you waiting for? Let's go." He smiled.

Drawing a deep breath and exhaling in one sharp gust, Jess reversed the little white car, backing out of the driveway and turning onto the road. She had no idea where they were going, but *she* was taking them there. One foot on the gas, both hands on the wheel, and a giant lump of fear in the pit of her stomach.

I can do this. I am doing this.

27

COURTYARD CONVERSATIONS

$\mathcal{N}$ick couldn't remember how long he'd been sitting in the courtyard at North Haven, watching water flow continuously from both fountains. Cherub statues hid between thick rows of flowers and leafy plants. He was surrounded by a jungle of natural beauty, yet he couldn't see past the water flowing right in front of him. He spent a lot of time in reflection each day, forced by sheer boredom to examine himself from the inside out.

Patients, therapists, and staff passed him by but he paid them little attention. An overcast sky allowed for softened light, and cooler temperatures as the dry summer heat faded into crisp fall air. Leaves had started to change, a bit early, but not too far from their scheduled appearance. He'd been stuck in North Haven for nearly four weeks.

"I wondered when I was going to see you," a familiar voice rose up behind him.

Nick stretched his neck, twisting as far as he could to see for himself. Seymour emerged in front of him, shaking his good hand and greeting him with his usual wide-mouth grin.

"How you doing, man?" Seymour asked.

"I've been better," Nick replied.

"You look like you've been hit by a truck."

Nick took notice of Seymour's North Haven T-shirt and Nike athletic pants. "I feel like I've been stuck in a recurring nightmare."

"Come on now. Our service isn't that bad."

"You work here?" Nick asked.

"Sure do. Would have seen you sooner, but they've had me covering the pediatric wing since August. Short staffed. I'm back over here now."

"What do you do?"

"I'm a PTA, physical therapist assistant. It's not as glamorous as working road crew for B. B. King, but it pays well and I get to meet some terrific people."

Nick was floored. He'd lived with Seymour briefly, had many conversations with him, yet there was so much he apparently didn't know. The man was full of surprises. Nick didn't take him for the kind of guy who would work in a place like this, much less be any kind of therapist. The rule always stands: you can't judge a book by its cover.

"You never told me what you do for a living," Nick replied.

"You never asked."

Nick smiled. He hadn't asked. He had been too self-absorbed to care what was happening with other people. He'd spent months throwing himself one shindig of a pity party, and all he had left to show for it was a broken soul and a half-broken body.

"How's your therapy going?" Seymour asked.

"Slow. They can't do anything big until my casts come off. I'm still at least two weeks away from that, maybe longer."

"Bored stiff in here, aren't you?"

"Every day," Nick replied.

"Hang in there. You'll be home before you know it."

"Then what?"

"You start living again. Make some music. Get back on your feet."

"Easier said than done."

"You know what B. B. King used to say to me? The beautiful thing about learning is that nobody can take that away from you."

"What's your point?"

Seymour smiled. "I'd bet my drum set you've learned a thing or two recently. Puts a perspective on life, doesn't it?"

Nick had gained several perspectives. He was still processing so much of it, but he knew he could never go back to being the man he'd been before.

"Everything that happens in life has a lesson attached to it. I reckon you of all people have learned a few things you could teach the rest of us."

Nick huffed. "What can I possibly teach anyone except what not to do? I'm more of a warning sign than a guidebook."

"There's a beautiful life in that broken soul of yours, just waiting to take flight. You'll find it. Don't give up."

"I'm just trying to figure out why I'm still here."

Seymour nodded. "You don't see it now, but you will. In due time, all things are revealed."

"You sure you're not a philosopher?" Nick asked.

Seymour laughed. "An observer. Look, if you aren't getting the answers you're looking for, maybe you've been asking the wrong questions. I've got to run, but I'll see you around. You ain't going nowhere."

"Yeah, thanks," Nick grumbled.

"Keep your chin up, Nick," Seymour said before walking off.

As if it were that easy. You keep your chin up. You aren't stuck in a wheelchair.

Nearby, a young boy was playing in one of the fountains,

visiting a wheelchair-bound resident. He splashed water until his mother stopped him, scolding the child harshly. The man in the wheelchair was somber, distant eyes against a bushy black beard and several old scars across his face. Nick couldn't tell if he was the child's father or an uncle, or perhaps his grandfather. He seemed much older than the young woman wrangling the spitfire kid, yet he'd seen her console the man in such a way that made him wonder if they were married. Regardless, the melancholy man didn't pay much attention to them. Instead, he stared with empty eyes into the same fountain the boy had played in, as though seeing right through it, lost in another world.

Nick had seen him a few times, once in the same therapy room. He wore leg braces. His right arm had been amputated at the elbow. Nick wondered about his story.

Then he heard a soft sound coming from the preoccupied man. Humming. Nick recognized his tune. "Make You Feel My Love" by Bob Dylan. He thought of Jess. She loved Bob Dylan.

This guy had a pretty good tone. As the man began quietly singing the words, Nick thought he sounded like a young Tom Petty, raw and passionate. He wondered if he had been a musician at any point in his life. He couldn't stop himself from humming right along with him. What was it about that song that spanned so many genres, covered by artists from all across the music universe?

The man looked up, right at Nick. He'd heard him. For a brief moment there was a small connection, two ships passing in the night, flying the same mast. Their eyes met, locked in understanding. That's when Nick noticed an intense sorrow behind his eyes. He knew that look well; perhaps he wore the same look. Perhaps what he saw when he looked at this man was the same thing others saw when they looked at him.

"I love that song," Jess said, sneaking up behind him.

Her voice caught him off guard and brought him back to reality.

"My dad sang it to my mom." She walked around to face him.

"Is that why you like Dylan so much?" he asked.

"One of the reasons."

She sat down on a stone bench, her body angled to face him better. He was getting attached to their meetings, each one a little rally for his recovery laced with town news and her undivided attention. He enjoyed watching her personality unfold before him and the way she would occasionally take his hand in hers. She meant it as a friendly gesture, but it calmed him, soothed him, gave him strength to face just a little more uncertainty.

"It was their song near the end, when my mom was really sick."

"You don't talk about them much."

"No."

"It's okay."

"It's not that I never talk about them, it's just a sore spot, you know?"

"I get it."

"I'm surrounded by their memories every day, it's comforting. Did I tell you I live in their house?"

"No."

"It's the house Mark and I grew up in. When they died Mark and I lived there until he married Elise. I couldn't bear to give it up so we kept it. Patrick and I renovated it after we got married."

"A lot of mixed memories in one house," he said.

"Yeah."

"You'll never leave?"

"The good memories tend to outweigh the bad. At least most days. It's hard to leave a house your daughter came home from the hospital to, spoke her first words in, the place where she took her first steps. It would be like leaving her behind. Probably sounds silly."

"Not silly. I still have Jack's first bass guitar. It needs a lot of TLC. The thing is practically falling apart. He wanted to chuck it, but I wouldn't let him. Too many memories. It's like a good luck charm. He got it in middle school. Had it when we first moved to Richland. He was still playing it when we signed our first record deal and toured as the opening act for some band no one even remembers now. It's at my home in LA."

"I didn't know you live in LA."

"Well . . . *did*, I guess."

"Will you go back?"

As Nick thought about his answer he watched the sleeves of her thin blouse flutter in the wind. A few months ago he would have said yes, as soon as his probation was up, but now he had a reason to stay, or to want to.

"I don't know. I can't see past the walls of this forsaken place at the moment."

She smiled. "Don't be so negative."

"Tell me that story," he said.

"What story?"

"The one about your parents and that song."

The black-bearded patient resumed his humming, mixed with intermittent singing. His eyes were lost, a million miles away. He didn't notice the boy splashing in the fountain again, soaking the front of his pants.

"They had a typical marriage, I guess. Ups and downs, highs and lows. They were devoted to each other until the end. My dad was a terrible singer. That's where I get it from, I suppose. He used to sing to my mom all the time, though, in the kitchen, in the bathroom, at night when they were lying in bed. He sounded like a dying cat, but Mom loved it. He'd sing her favorites and a few of his own, like they'd been written for her.

So when she got sick and really depressed, he wanted to find the perfect song."

"Bob Dylan."

"He had always been a big fan. Kind of like your dad and Eric Clapton. Dad heard that song in a movie and knew it was the one. He sang it to Mom one night when she was up late, struggling with the effects of chemo. It was the middle of the night and she was puking her guts up. We could hear her down the hall. Then we heard him crooning his heart out, this perfect song that summed up their life together. Mark and I listened outside their bedroom door. Somehow it made us feel better too."

"Then what?"

"Silence."

"He just stopped singing?"

"He finished the song, Mom finished throwing up, and there was this long silence. It probably seemed longer than it was. But then . . ." She chuckled under her breath.

"What?"

"Mom started laughing. She couldn't stop. Dad started laughing too. I have no idea why, but they must have laughed for at least twenty minutes. Soon, Mark and I were laughing quietly outside the door, hoping they didn't hear us."

Nick smiled.

"He sang it to her during chemo treatments, and when she came home after and would fall asleep on the couch. He was singing it when she took her final breaths. She left this world hearing the love of her life sing their favorite song, in the worst tenor you've ever heard, holding her hand and promising to love her for eternity."

"Wow."

They listened to the soulful humming of the bearded man in the wheelchair. Then Nick began humming again. Of all the Bob Dylan songs he knew, this one had the most depth. He thought about the lyrics, about going to the ends of the earth for the person you love, willing to do anything to show them how much you care. It was a powerful statement to make about another human being.

"Dad was the Dylan fan, but Mom preferred Sinatra."

"Ah, yes. Sinatra. I remember you saying something about that."

"Our house was a giant mix of music styles. Dad loved big band music from the thirties and forties. Mom loved blues and jazz. Dad even liked the Grateful Dead, if you can believe it."

"They did a live album with Bob Dylan. *Dylan & the Dead.* Heard of it?"

"Yes! We listened to it a lot. I was a kid when it came out. Dad loved that album."

"So you really *weren't* exposed to any contemporary stuff growing up. Not even at school?"

"That's what Walkmans were for."

"Walkmans? Wow, you're ol—"

"Don't say it! I'm not old. I'm, what, six . . ."

"Seven years older than me," he quickly corrected.

"That's not much."

"Enough to put us in two totally different music eras."

Jess looked away. She hadn't really thought about it. The difference between twenty-seven and thirty-four didn't seem that big.

"And you didn't even listen to the really great music of your own era. Such a shame."

"That's opinion," she said.

"In my world, that's fact."

She grinned.

"I like seeing you smile," Nick said.

"Oh?"

"Yeah. You didn't smile much when we first met. You didn't laugh much either. You should laugh more."

"I didn't have much to smile about."

"More than me," he said.

"You should be smiling more than the rest of us. You get a clean slate. You can start over, make a new life."

He shook his head. "This feels like a prison. I'm trapped in the same emotions that were choking me before this whole thing happened, and now I'm rotting in this wheelchair, in this hellhole . . ."

"Don't say that. Look at what you have. Look what you've been given—"

"I am so tired of everyone saying that to me! Life hasn't done me any favors, Jess. If this is such a good thing, if I have so much to smile about, then why do I feel like a piece of sh—"

"Because you're acting like one," Mark's deep voice bellowed from behind.

Nick hung his head. *Great. Just who I wanted to see.*

"It will get better," Jess said.

"Easy for you to say. You get to walk out of here."

"Could be worse. You could go to jail," Mark said, walking around him, taking a seat next to Jess.

"I'm going to let you two talk. I'll come by tomorrow."

"Wait, Jess. Don't go. I'm just restless and impatient, and I get triggered easily."

"It's okay. You guys have official business to take care of. I'll see you later." She smiled to reassure him.

Jess said goodbye to Mark and walked away, leaving Nick feeling empty and foolish.

"Why is it that every time she's here things seem to end on a bad note? I'm not trying to start an argument."

Mark opened his mouth to speak.

"Don't answer that. It's a rhetorical question. I don't need advice from her big brother."

Mark closed his mouth.

"She probably thinks I'm a jerk. You probably think I'm an idiot. Why is this so hard? Why can't I just pick up the pieces and go on with my life?" Nick looked straight at Mark, waiting for a response.

"Are you actually asking me now, or this another rhetorical question?"

Nick debated. "Maybe I'm asking."

"You're standing in your own way. You've been busy putting up roadblocks around yourself."

"Why would I do that?"

"You tell me. Maybe you like wallowing in pity and feeling sorry for yourself. Maybe you're afraid to move on without your friend. Maybe you don't know what life holds for you now and that scares you. It's a question *you* have to find the answer to."

"This is counseling? Find your own answers?"

"No, this is guidance. Do your own soul searching," Mark replied.

Nick watched the bearded man being wheeled away by the young woman. The little boy skipped and hopped behind them, kicking stray pebbles and leaves on the concrete as he went.

"I don't want to be that guy."

"What guy?" Mark asked.

"The sad guy humming by the fountain."

Mark looked around.

"Never mind. I'm thinking out loud I guess." He paused. "I want things to change, but I've been sad longer than I can remember."

"Why?"

"Just stuff."

Mark leaned forward. "You're either ready to talk about it or you're not. I won't force you, but I will give you advice. You have to leave the past where it lies and move forward. You can't change anything that's already happened, but you can learn from it and affect the future. We don't know how long our future will be. You want to live? Live. Or keep on the path you were headed down before this accident, and I promise you won't live for very long."

Sobering words. Drops of water pooled in the corners of Nick's eyes. He looked away, blinking to be rid of them. His emotions were still raw, brimming at the surface, scouring his ego on a daily basis. Mark's words were logical. They were obvious. But knowledge and application are two different things. Nick struggled with the latter.

"It's pretty cool out here. Why don't we get you inside?" Mark said, getting up to take hold of Nick's chair.

Nick didn't say a word. He didn't care where he sat. His mind was spinning with multiple thoughts, analysis of the day's events, afraid that if he spoke, emotion would have the upper hand.

Mark wheeled him toward the courtyard entrance and into the east wing of North Haven.

Nick recalled the time Jack had broken his foot on tour. It was a hairline fracture, but the doctor ordered him to wear a big boot, which of course Jack hated. He'd complained incessantly for weeks about the boot, finally kicking the hotel wall in frustration, making the fracture worse and having to wear the boot even longer. They were a lot alike, Jack and Nick.

Nick had teased him about the injury so much that Jack finally mentioned it on stage at a show in Berlin. "How many of you think *he* could play five shows a week with a broken foot?" Jack asked their audience. Roaring cheers and laughter filled the arena, and both Nick and Jack continued their playful banter, enjoying the audience reactions.

Nick couldn't erase the image from his mind, Jack thrashing his head, hair flying about, as he plucked the strings of his bass. He moved around on stage as though he had no impediment at all. Broken foot or not, Jack never allowed anything to come between him and his music, his passion for performing.

Nick may have been the voice, the symbol of Votive, but Jack was the fire. He was the energy behind their band, the one who'd always kept the laughter going.

I need that laughter now.

28
─────
CAST OFF

*T*he removal of Nick's casts revealed weak and atrophied muscles. He struggled with the use of his fingers and injured limbs, discovering quickly that he needed to learn basic skills all over again. His brain knew what to do, but his body refused to cooperate. Simple tasks and routine movements were foreign to his extremities. He pushed until he couldn't anymore, giving in to exhaustion.

Jess cheered him through rigorous therapy. He liked it when she stood beside him, helping the therapists guide him, reassuring him with her gentle touch. It was only a pat on the arm or back, a squeeze of his hand, but her tender care, the warmth of her skin against his, reminded Nick the hardest most painful parts were worth it.

On a rainy afternoon, she had walked in on him changing his shirt with the help of a nurse and saw the teddy bear tattoo on his left shoulder blade. She'd teased him for a few days until he finally told her the stories of Jack nicknaming him "Big Teddy Bear" because Nick preferred playing acoustic rock ballads over Jack's metalcore thrashers. Jack had dared him to get the tattoo after a show in St. Louis. He'd even picked out the bear, a brown, fluffy thing with a black bowtie.

After that she started bringing gummy bears to his therapy sessions as motivational treats. He hated gummy bears, but each bag gave them something to joke about instead of argue.

Late at night, when moonbeams ran across his wall like waking dreams, his mind navigated dozens of thoughts and images. He couldn't steer his imagination away from Jess. Why did she care so much? The most beautiful woman he'd ever known, and not because she had the face of an angel, but because she was full of unwavering kindness, selfless devotion, and an ability to see good in him when all he could see was corruption. She inspired him to push away the roadblocks he'd planted and imagine a life where he could succeed as a person, not just a musician.

The door opened and Seymour scooted inside. "Look what I snagged from the kitchen. Last two pieces of cherry pie." He put a plate beside Nick and sat down at the foot of the bed.

"Right on time." Nick had gotten used to Seymour's late-night visits after hours, when the halls were quiet and he lay prisoner to his overactive mind. "I'm not a big fan of cherry, though."

"More for me then." Seymour grinned.

"Jess brought another pack of gummy bears. You can pick out all the green ones."

"When are you going to tell her you don't like those things?" Seymour scooped a big chunk of pie in his mouth.

"I can't tell her that. She'll stop bringing them." He smiled.

"How's it going with Layla? She driving you nuts yet?"

"Sometimes. She's hardcore." Nick tried to sit up. He rummaged in the drawer of the side table next to him and tossed a bag of gummy bears at Seymour. Nick pictured his last therapy session with Layla, the no-frills, no-nonsense physical therapist he'd been stuck with.

"She's good at her job. Not bad on the eyes either." Seymour opened the package of gummy bears and dug around for green, lime-flavored ones, his favorite.

"She's incredible." He paused, choosing his words carefully. "She's gorgeous, spunky, knows her stuff, and she doesn't let me sit and wallow. I like her." Nick pulled a cherry out of the pie and stuffed it in his mouth.

"Yeah, you like her all right," Seymour teased.

"Shut up, man." He couldn't help admire Layla Matik's sun-kissed Asian skin and long dark hair. She was exotic and militant. If his heart wasn't drawn in a different direction, he might be inclined to give her his undivided attention. His dad certainly had, and hadn't stopped talking about her name and his favorite Eric Clapton song since he'd met her.

"Your dad has been here every day. How are you guys getting along?"

"Okay, I guess. He's here every morning, on his lunch breaks, after work. I'm not sure when he catches a meal."

"He cares about you. He's trying to make sure you know that."

"I don't know how to talk to him."

"You'll find the words."

"Your confidence is annoying."

"Your disdain for cherry pie is annoying."

Nick shook his head. He hated dwelling on Jack and Jess, his dad, his condition. Seymour was much-needed respite from insomnia-induced overthinking.

"How's the *other* therapy?" Seymour eyed him curiously.

Nick pulled off a messy hunk of pie and chomped down.

"You don't like cherry?" Seymour teased.

Nick forced it down, wishing he had a cup of water. He'd rather have a beer, maybe a shot, but water would do.

"Mark is this bear I can't get off my back."

"How so?"

"He's Jess's brother, for one. I care about her. He comes with the package. He's got me in this corner where I have to sit and talk with him. I resent him for it, but I'm learning how to face my problems instead of running from them. It's not all bad, I guess."

"So?" Seymour waited for more.

"So, it's a rock and a hard place."

"He's speaking truth and that's hard to hear," Seymour corrected.

Nick shrugged. "I have a long way to go."

Seymour finished his pie and the last of the green gummy bears. "But you're on the path, and that's what matters."

"I just don't want to end up like my mom. I don't want to be that person who doesn't have control, who hurts their family." He took a sharp breath, thinking about who his mom really was and how close he'd come to ending up just like her. "I guess it's too late for that."

"You're not her yet. Who do you think she would want you to be?"

Nick thought for a moment, finishing his own piece of pie even though he really did hate cherry. "Honest with myself." He met Seymour's understanding gaze.

"And are you?"

Question of the hour. Had he ever been truly honest with himself?

"I'm trying to be."

"Keep at it. Renovations take time. You can't rebuild a damaged house overnight."

Nick grinned. "I'm a house?"

Seymour smiled back. "You're human. That makes you complicated, intricate, detailed. That kind of work takes skill and patience. You'll make it, but not without toil and tears."

Nick pondered his words. *He's right.*

"Toil and Tears . . .," Nick started. "That would make a good band name."

"There you go, my man. Thinking ahead. You need a drummer? I know a guy."

They both laughed.

"Can I pay him in gummy bears?"

"Cash only, my friend."

"I'll talk to my manager."

They laughed and bantered until Nick finally felt like dozing off and Seymour decided it was time to get some shut-eye of his own. For the first night since he'd been at North Haven, Nick rested well, no nightmares or ghosts haunting his subconscious.

"Come on, Nick, a few more steps," Layla demanded, during PT the following day.

Nick struggled to move his right leg forward, placing just enough weight on the feeble limb to propel his body into motion. Learning to walk on crutches was not his idea of progress, but he had to learn to walk with assistance before he could walk on his own again.

"I'm done," he moaned, releasing his right foot as he pushed more weight against the crutches, ready to collapse. His left shoulder burned. Every muscle ached, withdrawing in protest.

"You got this, Nick. One more step," Seymour encouraged him.

Panting heavy, air forcing in and out of his lungs, he summoned all his strength just to remain in a standing position.

"It hurts."

"One more, Nick. You have one more in you," Layla commanded.

He struggled through one more step, barely an inch, but it was enough to count and he collapsed into Seymour, who helped him to his wheelchair.

"Okay, take a break. You've made progress today." Layla patted his good shoulder.

"Keep it up, my man. You'll be turning somersaults in no time," Seymour checked the brakes on Nick's chair, making sure they were locked in place.

"Yeah, right. I'm barely standing on my own with the stupid crutches." Nick groaned and strained, stretching his sore muscles.

Layla handed him a cup of water.

"At least I can hold my own cup."

Dale stood behind him, rubbing his shoulders. Nick had been so focused on his therapy, he'd almost forgotten his dad was there. Jess was there too. So was Mark. He had a room full of supporters, *real* fans, yet he couldn't shake the desire to be left alone.

Jess took the cup when he finished and placed it on the table next to him. Mark echoed supportive words. The back-and-forth game of encouragement circled Nick like a ring of vultures, battering his nerves. *There are too many people in this room*, Nick thought. *A little space. I just need a little space.*

A moment's rest and Layla had him back up taking steps again. She worked with him on coming to a standing position, over and over, sit and stand, then right back to walking with the crutches. He dreaded the day he'd have to do that without assistance. Sometimes it was easier to accept the disability than try to overcome it. He had days of determination and days of sheer laziness. Today was a lazy day. Layla didn't tolerate lazy days. She was tough, tougher than most therapists at North Haven, but she was also one of the best.

"I'm tired," Nick groaned.

"I know you are, but you need to give me four more steps. Four more. Come on, Nick. You can do this."

"No, I can't.

"Yes, you can. *Can't* is not in your vocabulary," Layla persisted.

"I'm telling you I can't," he snapped back, wobbling.

Seymour stood next to him, ready to stabilize him if necessary.

"Come on, son. You've got this," Dale's voice chanted behind him.

Nick gave up, falling into Seymour, who quickly guided him back to his wheelchair.

"Good try, Nick," Seymour patted his back.

He gritted his teeth and slammed a fist into the arm of his chair. "Not good enough."

"You're getting there, but you're going to have to push yourself. You give up too soon," Layla scolded him in her drill sergeant way.

"I am pushing myself. I push myself every day!"

Layla bent down at eye level. Her dark eyes pierced his frustration "I know you want this. Now show me, show yourself, how much. You want to walk? It's going to hurt. You're going to get tired. You're going to hate everyone. But you're going to walk out those doors, and that's why we're here."

Shooting pain attacked his body like an explosion. He was exhausted. Feet numb, muscles cramping, if he didn't get to his room soon he feared he might pass out in front of everyone. He couldn't even think straight, senses dulled by raging fatigue. *I just need a break. Enough for today. I'm done.*

Nick woke up, lying stiff on his side with a drool coated mouth. *How attractive.* He sensed someone in the room with him, but hoped he was wrong. He hoped it wasn't Jess, sitting there waiting for him to wake up. He was only wearing a pair of sweatpants and a mess of twisted covers wrapped around his body like a storm-torn hammock. At least he was moving more.

The coarse sound of a throat clearing echoed next to him. It was definitely a male voice. He hoped. Otherwise the scariest-sounding woman he'd ever heard was stalking him. Not exactly what a guy wants to be confronted with when he first wakes up.

Turning over just enough to peek at the figure slumped in the chair beside his bed, he recognized his father and breathed a sigh of relief.

"Thank goodness," Nick whispered under his breath.

"Happy to see me?" Dale arched an eyebrow.

"I thought you were Jess."

"My looks must have improved significantly since the last time I was here."

"Don't joke. The last thing I need is her seeing me like this. I've made a big enough idiot of myself in front of her already."

"Son, I think your current situation excuses any embarrassment."

"The sooner I get out of here, the better. I'm ready to . . ." His voice disappeared as his thoughts took over. *What am I ready for?*

Dale stared attentively, waiting for Nick to finish.

"Dad?"

"Yes."

Nick hesitated. "What's next? Where do I go from here?"

Dale straightened his posture, shifting his weight to one side as he faced the bed. "You go home. You start over."

"Yeah, but what does that mean? How do I start over? What am I supposed to do with my life?"

Heavy questions.

"You're a musician. I suppose you go back to playing music."

"I'm not even sure I can play anymore. My fingers and hands don't work like they used to. My whole body feels foreign. It doesn't do what I want it to."

"That will get better."

"Will it? I don't know that. Even if it does, I don't know how to play without Jack and Drew. I mean, what kind of career would I have on my own? Votive is gone. I'm not even sure that's what I want anymore."

"You don't have to have everything figured out."

"Well, it helps. *You* always seem to have it all together."

Dale sighed. "No. No, I don't. I wing it every day. I wake up every morning, take a deep breath, and find enough courage to face it all."

Nick had never heard his father talk like that before. The strong guy who could fix anything, create something from nothing, was friends with pretty much everyone in town; he'd always had life figured out.

"Nicholas . . . Nick, when your mother died I was lost. Not only did I have you to take care of, but my daily purpose . . . my whole world changed. I was so used to taking care of *her*, picking up the pieces of *her* broken life. I was completely unprepared to handle my own when it fell apart. You'd think things would have gotten easier, less to worry about, but it was the opposite. I didn't know what to do with myself without her. Suddenly I was alone, feeling helpless and weak. Those aren't easy feelings for me. I fine-tune things, mold them, fashion them. Suddenly I was the one who needed help. I looked at you and, heaven help me, I didn't know what to do with you . . ."

A tear appeared on Dale's cheek. Nick looked away. *Why is it so hard to say all the things that need to be said?*

"I didn't know how to help you, a grieving eight-year-old boy. I didn't know how to help myself."

"Dad, you don't have to—"

"I want you to know. I want you to understand that you're not the only person suffering. We get through it the best we can. One day at a time."

"When I was sitting there with the barrel of your gun against my head, I couldn't do it. I couldn't pull the trigger. I had to get drunk just to work up the nerve. I remember that. I don't remember the wreck, but I remember crying. I remember taking your bike, wishing I'd crash so I wouldn't have to pull the trigger myself."

Dale froze. Shock creased his resolve. He reached over and placed a hand on Nick's, relishing the warmth of his son's dry skin as he realized the alternative. Dale studied his son's grown hands, larger versions of the hands he'd held many years ago, watching his little boy sleep. His little boy now a grown man, learning how to navigate murky waters and heavy decisions.

A minute or two passed. Nick looked down at his father. Dale's head was bent. Nick couldn't see his eyes. He started to speak, but waited. He always hesitated to say what needed to be said. How could he tell his father he was sorry for every harsh word, every rash moment of anger? How do you apologize to the one person who's been constant in your life when you've treated them like they don't deserve to exist? He said nothing, waiting for Dale to speak instead. Being a coward was his biggest regret.

A light tap on the door brought Jess tiptoeing into the room.

"I'm sorry. Am I interrupting? I can come back."

"No, no, stay. I need to get to the bank before they close. I'll see you later, son." Dale squeezed Nick's hand.

Nick tugged at the mess of blankets, making sure he was fully covered as she approached. He couldn't take his eyes off her. *Why is she here? Why is she wasting her time on a lowlife like me?*

"Sleep well?" she asked.

"I guess. I feel like a loser. I should be up doing exercises, getting stronger. I know I need to push myself harder, but sometimes I don't want to."

"I brought you something."

Nick perked up, noticing the small package she held in her left hand, wrapped neatly in brown and gold paper and tied with red satin ribbon.

"What's this?" he asked.

"Open it."

Nick eyed the flat package. "Easier said than done."

"Think of it as occupational therapy." Jess held it closer, encouraging him to take it.

"So you bring me a gift, but you make me work for it."

"Yep." She smiled.

He moved his arm slowly forward, ignoring its painful lag, grasping and pulling the present to his lap. It took concentration for his fingers to rip into the thin paper. Fumbling excessively, he managed to push the paper aside, revealing a plastic-covered DVD case.

"'*Pearl Jam Twenty*,'" he read the title.

"It's a documentary of the band."

"Yeah, I know. Cameron Crowe directed it. It's supposed to have a ton of rare footage."

"Oh good, you haven't seen it yet. I was afraid you already owned it," she said.

"No, we were on tour when it was released and our schedule was always so crazy between studio and promo stuff, writing new songs. I never had much free time."

"I found it at a bookstore in Richland. Thought you might like it. I know they're your favorite band."

"Thank you. I love it. They are. Vedder has been my biggest musical inspiration since I first discovered them by accident on the radio . . . after my mom died."

"I'm glad you like it."

"What were you doing in Richland?" he asked.

"Exploring. I haven't been there by myself in so long, I thought I'd take a day to go shopping and venture around some of the trendy areas that everyone always talks about. I found a great little coffee shop in the downtown area."

"You drove?"

"I didn't tell you?"

"Uh, no. Wow. That's great. What brought that on?"

"It was time. I've let too much pass by. Time doesn't stop when we lose someone, it keeps going whether we choose to accept it or not."

"You miss her," Nick said.

Jess nodded. "Every day. For the rest of my life."

Nick understood.

"You aren't the only one who feels remorse. I know your situation is different from mine, but we share so much. I'm learning how to let go of all the things I couldn't change. You have to let go of all the things you could."

He turned away. He didn't want to get emotional in front her. Not like this, not in this place.

Jess didn't care. She didn't need him to put on a brave face. She didn't care about the façade. She cared about him. "You don't have to go through this alone," she said, walking around his bed to face him.

She took his hand in hers, sitting down next to him on the soft mattress. Nick couldn't face her. Tears rolled steadily down his cheeks, but he didn't flinch or turn away when her fingers wiped the salty stains.

"I'll cry with you. Hold your hand. Stand beside you. Whatever you need. You are worth so much more than you've allowed yourself to believe," she said.

He looked at her glistening eyes, glossy with tears she cried for him . . . with him.

"How do you know?" he asked.

She squeezed harder, holding his hand between both of hers. "Because you're still here."

"I may never be the same again. I might not fit in this world like I used to."

She smiled, wiping stray tears from her own face. "Who says you need to?"

"I don't know how to start over."

"Neither do I," she said.

Words weren't necessary. The touch of this beautiful woman who seemed to care more than he deserved, silent stares, and understanding expressions were all he needed.

Jess traced the lines and wrinkles along Nick's fingers, holding his hands as he held hers. He began drifting in and out, and she thought he might fall asleep.

Sunlight waned, its golden light dimming to a soft yellow glow from the window. It was time to leave. She slipped away from the bed, slinking toward the door as quietly as she could.

"Jess," Nick whispered.

She stopped, turning slowly to face him. "Yes."

"I've made a mess of my life. I'm not sure I know where to begin to make it right."

She walked back to his bedside.

"I want to be someone my dad can be proud of. I want to look in the mirror and actually like what I see."

"Stop beating yourself up. Forgiveness means letting go. You keep clenching your fists when what you should be doing is opening your arms. There's a large group of people ready to let you in and love you, but you have to let us in, and you have to start loving yourself. I'm still struggling to forgive my husband for all the things he did wrong, but I've learned that true healing only comes with forgiveness. If you can't let it go, you can't move forward."

"I think I was moving backward. Now I'm just standing still."

She bent over and kissed his forehead. "We'll move forward together. Just don't give up."

He reached for her hand. "Don't go."

She smiled. "I have to, but I'll be back tomorrow. My grandmother used to tell me that every tomorrow is another opportunity. It's one of my favorite sayings."

He squeezed her hand and she turned to go, slipping away from him, leaving him with all the spinning thoughts inside his head.

"Jess . . ."

She turned back, one hand on the door.

"Thank you," he said.

Jess smiled. The kind of smile that could light up a dark room, draw people in, disarm them, make them forget there was anything wrong. An infectious smile that anchored him to a new way of life, one he wanted to live.

"I'll see you tomorrow," she said.

He watched the door close behind her.

True healing comes with forgiveness. If you can't let it go, you can't move forward. He couldn't forget her words. He didn't want to. *Every tomorrow is another opportunity.* He hoped he had several tomorrows to get it all right.

29

COFFEE AND DOUGHNUTS

*U*p, down, and up again. He sat in a chair. He stood up. He sat back down. He did it all over again. Piece of cake. Except it wasn't. If an activity required strength, Nick struggled. Making strides didn't boost his ego. It reminded him how far he'd fallen and how much further he had left to go.

"Again," Layla's sharp voice rang out.

Nick squeezed and tensed every working muscle in his body. Gripping his cane, squeezing its cold aluminum handle, he pushed all his weight into his right arm and left leg, bringing himself to a standing position. *Okay, I'm up.*

"Again." Layla commanded him as though she were his drill sergeant, and most of the time he felt like she was.

Down. I'm sitting. Now I'll stand again. Way to go, Nick. You've mastered the art of modified squats for idiots. You'll have a firm butt in two weeks or your money back.

"Again," she persisted.

He was beginning to think she only knew one word. Layla wasn't married, but if she had any kids, Nick envisioned them doing chores around the house with Layla following behind shouting, "Again!" He chuckled under his breath.

"One more, Nick. You're getting stronger. It shows."

He wondered if physical therapists could handle their own treatment if situations were reversed. *You can dish it, lady, but can you take it?*

Nick released all the wind from his lungs, relaxing into a softer, more comfortable chair than the rock-hard, folding contraption he'd been forced to do his therapy on.

Layla sat down next to him on a weight lifting bench, her long dark hair pulled into a sleek ponytail that hung halfway down her back. She was probably in her forties or fifties, judging from previous conversations they'd had, but she could easily pass for thirty-five on a bad day, thirty on a good one. They'd become friends since working together. He appreciated her brutal honesty.

"They'll discharge you soon. Ready for that?" she asked.

"You tell me."

"You're using your arm more, picking things up, putting them down. The doctor decreased your pain meds. Your leg is healing beautifully, and you've gained enough strength and mobility to move about safely in your home, with your cane, of course. You still need assistance. Don't go getting all heroic and macho on me, okay?"

He grinned. "I'll try to refrain from acrobatics. Can't promise I won't join any triathlons though."

"Hey, if you can compete in a triathlon, I want to see it. And believe me, I'll be the loudest one cheering you on."

"I'm pretty confident you don't have to worry about that."

"Keep your chin up, Nick. Of all my patients with traumatic brain injury, cases like yours, you're the fastest one to graduate from crutches to a cane. That says something about your prognosis."

"I guess."

"You're not getting all mopey and depressed on me, are you? That's not allowed. Look at what you've accomplished. You don't gain success without struggle. Suck it up and walk the rest of the mile."

Sometimes she scared him a little. Her brutal resistance to failure made her a grizzly bear in a dainty woman's frame, but she was no dainty woman.

"Yes, ma'am." Nick nodded.

"All right, let's get you off that cane and onto the parallel bars. I want you walking on your own before Easter."

Easter? Could it really take that long? It wasn't even December yet. The realization was a slap in the face, but he was thankful he'd soon be rid of the wheelchair.

Layla marched him back and forth on the bars, not allowing him to give in when he found himself out of breath. Layla took tough love to new levels, but she knew when to stop. Her skills and methods amazed him.

After therapy, Nick found Mark waiting for him in a corner of the room with a box of assorted doughnuts and two cups of coffee.

"And thus, the bearer of many doughnuts has arrived. Do you like your coffee black . . . or black?" Mark held them both out for Nick to make his choice.

"So, we're going to eat doughnuts and watch people do therapy?" He chose a cup of coffee and reached inside the open box, pulling out a chocolate-glazed ring of sugary perfection.

"Why not? They work. We eat all the calories. I'm thinking we get the better end of the deal."

"If you say so." Nick arched an eyebrow.

"I spoke to your probation officer today."

Nick almost choked on a large piece of the fried confection.

"Don't panic. He's checking up on you. He spoke to your

father too. Said he's paid you a few visits since you've been here. I guess you forgot to include that in our conversations. He seemed pretty nonchalant, real laidback guy. How much money did that record label of yours throw at him?" Mark said, only half joking.

"Yeah. He came by."

"I told him you were making great progress."

"Thanks."

"I meant it. No need to thank me."

"I do need to thank you. You stepped out on a limb for me. You picked me up when I was down . . . literally. You might be the craziest person on earth, but I think you believed in me."

"Still do. The great thing about my job is that I get to show people hope. We live in a dark world, and I can show people where to find the light. You may not be a spiritual man, Nick, but you possess something many church going people don't."

"What's that?"

"Humility."

Nick pondered. "I've been called a lot of things, Mark. Humble isn't one of them."

"I'm not talking about Nick the performer, the rock star. I'm talking about the down-to-earth guy you really are when you peel back all those layers and don't have a reason to pretend. You're not a bad guy. You just wandered off the road a little. You're growing. I am too."

Nick's ears perked.

"Don't look so surprised. I've learned a few things. Realized I don't always have the right answers. Sometimes I'm pushy when I shouldn't be. Other times I should probably push harder but don't."

"Is there a moral to this story?" Nick smiled.

"You aren't the only one with flaws to work on." Mark guzzled his coffee.

Nick leaned back, adjusting himself to get as comfortable as possible. "Remember when I told you I've been sad longer than I could remember?"

"Yes."

"I told you I wanted to change. You said I was getting in my own way."

"Yes."

"When I was younger I blamed myself for what happened to my mom."

"Why?"

"I watched her die. I couldn't stop it. I was a scared kid who didn't understand what was happening or whether or not it was my fault. For years after, I had nightmares about what happened. I spent a lot of time reliving it without any real direction or insight on how to handle something like that."

"How did your dad handle it?"

"I never talked to him about it, and he never asked. I don't think he knew what to do with me."

"It was a devastating thing for both of you."

"I was confused, and then as I got older I got angrier. I took out that anger on my dad, blamed him for everything even though I knew it wasn't his fault. Then I moved out. I punished him by disappearing from his life, treated him like he didn't exist."

"Have you talked to him about this?"

"I can't find the words."

"I know three you can start with," Mark said.

Nick met Mark's eyes.

"I love you. Every parent needs to hear that. I'm sorry works too, but I love you is better."

"I'm guessing you've never wished you could redo about half your life."

Mark laughed. "You see me as the preacher, man of God, Mr.

Upright. I wasn't born a preacher, Nick. I went down a rocky path after my parents died."

"You?"

"Yes, me. All have fallen short of the glory of God. No man is without sin."

"What happened?"

"Same old story. I was young, headstrong, trying to find my way. Hung around the wrong people, drinking, partying, typical college stuff."

"I have a hard time picturing that."

"Well, don't. It wasn't a pretty sight." Mark covered his face.

"What made you change?"

"Elise." Mark smiled. "She waltzed into my life, held a mirror to my face, and showed me who I really wanted to be. I believe God sends certain people into our lives. We just have to be wise enough to realize who they are."

"I still don't know if I believe in God." Nick studied the floor.

"I know, and I can't make you. But I believe in him, and I have dedicated my life to telling other people why."

"That's commendable," Nick replied.

"It's conviction."

The doughnuts were disappearing.

"How many have we eaten?" Nick asked, eyeing empty spaces still crusted with sugar.

"I lost count, but don't tell Elise. She's got me watching my blood pressure and cholesterol and all that midlife stuff. You're still young, but you'll get there."

"You can outrun me," Nick said.

"A turtle could outrun you right now."

"Way to boost morale," Nick said.

"Just keeping it real, my friend." Mark grinned.

Two more doughnuts disappeared.

"Do you think it's possible to start over? Really start over?" Nick asked.

"Yes. As long as we're living and breathing."

"I've come across so many people in my career, people who want to be important, who want the world to know them. They want power and praise. I achieved some of that, but all I really want now is to be the kind of person who doesn't have to wish they were someone else. I want to be comfortable in my own skin."

"No man should be placed on a pedestal. We're all fallible human beings. Our lives are fleeting." Mark watched a therapist across the room helping an elderly woman squeeze a bright orange ball in the palm of her hand. "'Surely every man at his best is a mere breath.'"

"Is that Shakespeare?" Nick asked.

"Psalms."

"As in the Bible?"

"Yep," Mark replied. "Psalm 39, verse five."

"Sounds like Shakespeare." Nick took a sip of coffee.

"'LORD, make me to know my end and what is the extent of my days; let me know how transient I am. Behold, You have made my days as handbreadths, and my lifetime as nothing in Your sight. Surely every man at his best is a mere breath. Surely every man walks about as a phantom. Surely they make an uproar for nothing; He amasses riches and does not know who will gather them.' That's Psalm 39, verses four through six."

"Wow, do you just sit around and memorize scripture? You don't have half the Bible memorized, do you?" Nick smirked.

"It's one of my favorite passages. Helps me when I'm stressed. Our lives here on earth are trivial compared to the bigger picture. No matter what I do, or how much I think I have control over, everything still rests in God's hands."

Nick shifted. "What if you don't believe in God? What then?"

"Well, you've got to believe in something. Everyone has a standard they live by. Everyone places their hope in something."

"How do you know if it's right?"

Mark smiled. "How do you know if it's wrong?"

"You can't answer a question with a question."

"You can't answer a question like that with one answer either. Common ground. That's where I start. In your case, though, I'd have to ask why you think you're still alive after so many close calls. Are you invincible? Is it coincidence? Or could it be providence? You just defied all the odds. That's no small thing."

Nick thought about it. "Everyone keeps saying that like I have some predestined purpose to fulfill."

"Ask yourself what you believe. Then question why. I can't give you faith. I can only show you why I hold on to mine."

"At least you're not going to hit me over the head with your Bible and say I'm healed or some crazy stuff like that," Nick joked.

"Nope, no Bible thumping. Not by me. I prefer to read mine; it's easier on the pages," Mark said.

Nick laughed.

"What?" Mark asked.

"I always imagined preachers as these stuffy old men in suits who wore glasses and yelled from a pulpit that everyone is going to hell."

Mark grinned. "That's not exactly how it goes."

"I hope not." Nick chuckled.

"I don't always wear suits, I'm in my early forties, and my glasses are generally for reading."

"So you're stuffy and condemn people to hell?" Nick teased.

"You'll have to get the congregation's opinion on that one. I'd like to think of myself as a humble servant, but then, humility has never been my strongest suit."

"Imperfect like the rest of us?"

"Yep. Every day. I just have a better track record than some."
He winked.

"Ah, I see what you mean about humility."

They laughed over another couple of doughnuts or so until
there was only one left in the box.

"Split it?" Mark asked.

"Flip a coin?"

Mark fumbled for a quarter. "I'd concede and give it to you
out of sympathy, but then it would just be a pity doughnut, and
those never taste as good. Call it."

"Heads," Nick said without hesitation.

Mark flung the shiny coin into the air, dodging sideways to
catch it. He barely grasped the quarter, slapping it down onto
his lap.

"Coordination isn't one of your strong points either," Nick
teased again. "What's the verdict?"

Mark lifted his hand, revealing George Washington's iconic
profile. "Heads." He frowned. "Elise will thank you. I'll be going
home to veggies and lean protein tonight."

"I'm so sorry to hear that." Nick spoke while chewing large
bites of gooey perfection. He exaggerated satisfied noises as he
swallowed each piece.

"You're an evil man."

"I know, and it's so good."

Mark stretched his back as he stood up from his chair.

"Leaving?" Nick asked, mouth still full.

"Alas, I have been charged with picking up bread, butter, and
cheese from the grocery store. I doubt any of those items will be
on the menu tonight. And she hasn't made a pie for us in over
two weeks. I'm starting to worry about my well-being."

"Married life . . ."

"Yep. But I wouldn't trade it. I'll see you soon. I know where
to find you."

"Yeah," Nick agreed.

Mark adjusted his jacket and turned to leave.

"Hey, Mark."

"Yeah?"

"Thank you."

"For the doughnuts? Sure, no problem. Got to put some meat on those skinny ribs of yours."

Nick grinned. "Yeah, for the doughnuts, but also for all the other stuff . . . for everything."

Mark nodded. "I'd do it all again. Hope I don't have to, but I would."

Nick nodded in return. A half smile graced his face, and he was left holding an empty box in an empty therapy room, evaluating his future. He'd be going home soon. He wasn't sure he was ready. Things would be different. A new normal was in order. The daily struggle to abstain from bad habits would plague him. It was easier in rehab, in a controlled environment. Home would be familiar, but Nick worried it might be too familiar.

30

BROKEN FINGERS

The first snowfall dusted Bridgetown before Christmas. Cold days and even colder nights put a damper on Nick's spirits. It didn't stop Dale from playing his Eric Clapton albums louder than ever. "Walkin' Blues" blasted from the living room stereo, a song Nick had once played. Now his fingers hung like foreign objects, broken instruments attached to useless hands.

Winter scenes unfolding outside his bedroom window beckoned creative juices, a longing to write new songs. He held his Gibson propped against an aching leg, seated on the edge of his bed, desperate to make something happen. He'd attempted a few strums awkwardly with his thumb, but he couldn't form the chords, couldn't make his magic.

His brain knew what to do. He could close his eyes and see every string, every pattern with perfection, but his fingers wouldn't form the necessary shapes. *If I can't play, then what am I supposed to do?*

Occupational therapy had worked with him longer than PT. The best therapists at North Haven had taught him how to eat, grasp with his hands, and brush his teeth and hair. He'd regained the ability to dress and shower. He'd even learned to play chess with Seymour, but some things would take longer. Nick had never imagined a moment when he wouldn't be able to play his guitar. He could belt out every note in perfect pitch, but he couldn't make his J-45 sing like she was made to do.

He heard his dad humming in the kitchen. *What would Clapton do if he found himself unable to play? What would Vedder do? They'll probably never know this agony.* He remembered the DVD Jess had given him. He'd been so busy with outpatient therapy and readjusting to life at home, he hadn't taken the time to watch it.

It took considerable effort to peel himself from the bed, grab his cane and the DVD, and shuffle down the narrow hallway like a ninety-year-old man. In the living room he turned off his dad's stereo, now blaring loud enough to irritate a teenager. *Enough with this music. How many times can one person listen to the same Eric Clapton album before their head explodes? No offense, Mr. Clapton, I still appreciate you, but I think we all need a break.*

Nick slid the disc into the only DVD player in the house. Dale wasn't much for technology. He owned two televisions, and one of them was a tragic flashback to the eighties. Thankfully he'd graduated to a rather nice LED model in their tiny living room.

Easing his tense body onto the couch, Nick realized he'd failed to grab the remote. *Great.* He weighed the value of actually getting back up to retrieve it versus staring at a blank screen. The latter felt like the better option. He knew all he needed to know about Pearl Jam anyway.

Dale interrupted Nick's big decision making to see why his beloved Clapton was no longer piercing eardrums. He scanned from Nick to the unpowered television, assessing the scene with curiosity.

"Good show?" he asked.

"Better than the workout it would take to go back for the remote."

"What is it with you and remotes?" Dale grinned, fetching the controller for his son. "What are we watching?" He sat down next to Nick.

"Aren't you cooking something?"

"Baking. Apple bread is in the oven and won't be ready for forty-five minutes."

Nick's double take was fast enough to cause whiplash. "*You are baking apple bread? Seriously?*"

"I make it every year at Christmas. I'm not Martha Stewart, but it tastes pretty good."

"You've taken bachelorhood to new levels, Dad."

"The office lady at the plant gave me this recipe a few years ago. She brought a loaf in one day for everyone to try. I figured, why not make it myself."

"You may need to get out more," Nick teased.

"Nothing wrong with a man in the kitchen. I actually enjoy it."

"Just doesn't seem like you."

"You were away for a long time. People change, but it gives us more to talk about."

"As long as you don't have a dress and high heels hiding in the back of your closet."

Dale laughed. "Not to my knowledge. If you find one it's not mine, I promise."

"I'll keep an eye out." Nick started the DVD.

It took a moment for the menu to load.

"Dad . . ."

"Yeah."

"I'm sorry about your bike."

Silence.

"I know how much work you put into it over the years and

how much you loved that thing." Nick picked at buttons on the remote.

"I can buy another bike. I only have one son."

Nick faced his dad. His eyes spoke a thousand words he couldn't form with his lips. He nodded. Dale placed a firm hand on Nick's leg, gripping his knee cap.

"I love you, son . . . Nick."

Nick released a deep sigh. "You can call me Nicholas."

Those were the best words Dale had heard in a long time. He started to say more, but nerves and a volcano of happiness and fear held him back. He didn't want to ruin an important moment with more words than needed to be said. He worried he'd say the wrong thing and screw it all up. He savored that moment, wishing time would stand still for just a little while. *Nicholas . . . I have my son back.*

Nick resisted saying anything else. He wasn't sure where to start. He figured he would take it one day at a time and get to know his father again. He'd taken him for granted, assumed more than he'd actually understood. There was much he could learn from the man who'd shown him how to throw the meanest curveball in his second-grade class.

"So, what are we watching?" Dale asked.

"*Pearl Jam Twenty*, a documentary of my favorite band."

"Sounds interesting. Have you played with them?"

"I wish!" Nick's voice nearly cracked. He pressed the pause button. "That would be a dream come true. Just to be in the same room with Eddie Vedder, Stone Gossard, Mike McCready, and Jeff Ament would be an honor. Even just have a conversation with them, especially Vedder. He's been a huge inspiration to my music. He's my Eric Clapton."

"Wow, I get it then." Dale smiled. "Maybe you'll meet them one day, play a set with them, record an album with them."

"Here's to hoping," Nick said.

"Let's watch it."

"You sure you want to watch this with me? I wouldn't want your apple bread to burn."

"I set a timer. Press play, son. I'm not getting any younger."

Nick started the disc, remembering the beautiful friend who had so thoughtfully given it to him. *I wonder what she's doing right now. I miss her.* He hadn't seen Jess in over a week.

Opening credits appeared on the screen. A documentary, filled with decades-old footage of one of Seattle's most prolific rock bands, flashed across the television, reminding Nick of his original purpose for making music. It wasn't about fame and fortune; it had never been about the name they made for themselves. They only wanted to play the music they loved and entertain others in the process. Somewhere along the way their dream for Votive had slowly faded into money, women, media blitz, and chart-topping hits.

Nick remembered one of their last conversations, when Drew had finally said what was on his mind.

"I moved to Richland to play hole-in-the-wall shows with my best friends. Sucking up to big-shot industry execs who wouldn't know real music if it punched them in the gut never crossed my mind," Drew had snapped in an argument with Jack after a show in Chicago, the last show they played before returning to Richland.

"There's nothing wrong with making money and playing sold-out arenas. What's the point of making music if you're only in a club with fifty people? Might as well have the ears of the world tuned in," Jack replied.

"It's not worth it if you can't make the music you really want to make. I'm not a sellout, and you didn't used to be either," Drew shot back.

"Cheap shot from a guy who takes the interview every time

the magazines call. I don't see you turning down royalties or giving Break Voice a piece of your mind."

Jack detested being called a sellout. He loved the fame, the money was great, and having an endless line of women throwing themselves at him, the guy who'd been ignored in high school by most of the girls he'd asked out, was a dream come true.

Their heated conversation that night almost became physical, alcohol fueling their tension. They needed to stay together, needed to keep making music. Nick never imagined he would be the one who broke them up.

That night Nick had taken Drew's side, and Jack didn't speak to him for two days. When the three of them finally sat down over coffee and cigarettes a day before the last show, they reevaluated everything, their friendship, their music, the future. Three hands coming together in the center of the table, clasped into a united fist, sitting in an old café in a rundown part of Richland made a pact to do things right, to play their music their way.

Memories of Votive ran through Nick's head as he watched the film with his dad. He thought about the heart and soul Vedder and his bandmates put into everything they did, the reason Pearl Jam had been so successful in the first place. Pearl Jam had never set out to copy a trend, they merely expressed their deepest feelings through melody and lyrics, and that's what Votive had been about until they allowed themselves to get caught up in all the glitz. Three young guys from Bridgetown had become the old cliché . . . "sex, drugs, and rock and roll." They had traded the music for the lifestyle.

Time passed quicker than Nick realized. They were halfway through the film when Dale's kitchen timer went off, and he got up to check on the bread now filling their house with a spicy, sweet scent.

They stuffed warm slices of moist apple bread in their mouths while finishing the film. The most peaceful moment the two of them had shared since Nick came back into his dad's life.

Nick spent the rest of the evening and the following week striking at his guitar, picking and plucking, fumbling at the strings, begging his fingers to relearn what they'd forgotten. He spent weeks and then months practicing chords and chord changes, even taking his guitar to every occupational therapy appointment. He worked on his instrument night and day until his fingers bled and his back hurt in places he didn't know existed. He consumed himself with rebuilding his life through music and appreciating the gift he'd been given.

"Not everyone can play like you," a musician once told Nick backstage at a benefit concert. Nick didn't think much about it until now, when playing was such a struggle.

Christmas passed. Winter froze. As spring became a reality, so did Nick's drive to return to his craft and make better use of it. He understood drive and determination, focus and passion in ways he never had before. He was amazed at how many songs a man could write, and write well, when he wasn't falling down drunk, or hanging out in clubs and bars until three o'clock in the morning.

He'd slowed down on the drinking. No more liquor, though beer was another story. He loved an ice-cold bottle in his hand, but getting drunk, losing control, those were no longer options. He'd promised himself and Jack he would make better choices.

Dale enjoyed listening to his son, even singing along terribly with any tune he knew. They sang duets, and Dale butchered each one. Nick didn't mind. They usually ended up laughing hysterically, reminiscing about something neither had thought about in years.

Even though they were getting along, Nick still hadn't found the right words to convey what his heart wanted to say to his father. He cowered, that little boy afraid of all the unresolved emotions and distance between them. He knew it would take more than a few humor-filled conversations to repair the rift it had taken years to create, but he enjoyed getting to know this softer, calmer side of his father, the compassionate man who'd been at his bedside every day since his recent accident.

31

SURPRISE VISIT

*W*inter months gone and passed hadn't been as kind to Mark and Elise. Holidays were difficult. They'd lost their first biological child near Christmas. They'd lost their second biological child a year later after New Year's. A few years after that they'd lost a baby girl on Valentine's Day. Holidays were wrought with mixed emotions, more grieving than celebrating.

Mark kept himself busy preparing sermons, holding Bible studies with young couples, and visiting Nick at every opportunity. He'd learned a few riffs on Nick's guitar, prompting him to shop around for a guitar of his own, and even sang a few songs with Nick and Dale. It was easy for Mark to stay distracted.

Elise, on the other hand, had always been a preacher's wife. She'd never held an outside job. Her days were spent cooking and cleaning, visiting nursing homes, making phone calls to check on church members. She was a walking stereotype, and it wasn't as easy to stay distracted when everything seem to run on autopilot.

Elise spent a quiet March morning scrubbing the fire out of

their clawfoot master bathtub, determined to clean her way to a better mood. *Where is Mark when the ceiling fans are caked with dust and I'm too short to reach them safely? Where is he when every trash can in this house is brimming and it's his job to empty them? Certainly not in this bathroom cleaning the toilet he spends hours on or the sink full of stray hairs left over from his shaving escapades.*

The doorbell rang abruptly, relieving her from further frustration against her husband. Of course, it would have been better if she hadn't smacked her head on the faucet as she jumped up. She rubbed the rising bump at her crown with rubber glove–covered hands.

Scurrying downstairs to the front door, wearing old jeans and one of Mark's university sweatshirts, she nearly tripped over his jogging shoes piled at the bottom of the stairs. *Mark Stuart! Ugh!* she growled under heavy breath.

Elise flung open the door.

"Tabitha?" She recognized the slender woman with choppy orange hair.

"I hope I'm not catching you at a bad time, Mrs. Stuart."

She swallowed, regretting her frazzled demeanor. "It's been a long day. What can I do for you?"

"Are you and Mark still looking to adopt a child?"

Elise tried to remain steady, her heart now thumping rapidly.

Tabitha had conducted their original home study during their first adoption attempt. The thought of going down this road again tied Elise's stomach in knots. She'd run out of strength. A sudden sinking feeling in the pit of her stomach heightened her anxiety and she thought she might be sick.

"Why do you ask?" Elise braced herself against the door frame.

"I have a little girl for you, if you're willing to take her."

The shock and disbelief must have shown on Elise's face.

"I'm quite serious. She's in the car." Tabitha pointed down the walkway where her car was parked in front of the house.

"I'm sorry, what? You're not making any sense." Elise's breathing quickened to a speed of near hyperventilating.

"May we come inside? I'll explain," Tabitha asked.

Elise nodded, watching her retrieve a little girl from a car seat in the back of a Honda Civic. A man she didn't recognize sat in the passenger seat tapping on the screen of his phone.

They sat in the living room, Tabitha and a bright-eyed toddler on the couch, Elise in a high-back, Victorian chair, trying to keep her legs from shaking.

"This is Sadie, Sadie Elizabeth. She's two. Her birthday was March second," Tabitha explained.

Elise remained silent, listening to Tabitha's report on the surprisingly well-behaved little girl. Sadie sat next to her companion playing with a small toy from Tabitha's purse that lit up when she shook it.

"Her mother died from a drug overdose. As far as we can tell, her mother didn't know who the father was. She hadn't had any long-term relationships. Sadie's grandmother legally adopted her after her daughter's death and has been raising her since she was almost a year old." Tabitha paused to look at Sadie. "Recently her grandmother's health has declined to a point that she is no longer able to care for Sadie. She had to move out of state for treatment and came to us for a private adoption. All the necessary paperwork has been signed, and we actually had a family that was supposed to take her, but they backed out at the last minute due to an unexpected pregnancy. Now Sadie has no official home, and if we don't find her one she will have to go into foster care until we can place her."

Elise watched Sadie, staring curiously at the tiny, beautiful child.

"Mrs. Stuart?"

"Yes," Elise answered, eyes still glued on Sadie.

"You haven't said anything. Do you have any questions? I understand you might need time to think about it, but we are considering this an emergency situation. Sadie needs a home now. You and your husband have already completed the necessary home study and paperwork. There will still be some legal matters to attend to, but we are authorized to turn her over to you tonight if you're willing to take her."

Elise suddenly realized she was still wearing her rubber gloves, caked in cleaner from the bathtub. Sadie eyed her with fascination as she slipped them off, dropping them onto her lap.

"Mrs. Stuart? Elise . . ."

"I need to call my husband."

"Of course." Tabitha smiled with an understanding nod.

Rising slowly from her chair, Elise struggled to make sense of the jumbled thoughts and conversation fragments running through her mind. She couldn't believe this was actually happening. Was she hallucinating? Had she inhaled too many cleaning fumes? *This cannot be real.*

The phone rang several times before Mark answered.

"Hey, babe." His deep, reassuring voice echoed through the phone and into her ear.

"You need to come home."

"Is everything okay?"

"Just come home, Mark. Now. Please." Her voice trembled.

"Elise, you're scaring me. Are you okay? Is Jess okay? What's going on?"

"You need to come home." She couldn't find the words to explain.

"I'm on my way. I'll be there in ten minutes." He hung up.

Elise returned to the living room and the lovely child, sitting so perfectly, so quietly on her couch, eating from a small box of raisins. She felt as though she were having an out-of-body experience. Something she'd hoped for and dreamed about nearly half her life, had resolved to never have, was sitting right in front of her. They were the longest ten minutes Elise had ever experienced.

When Mark entered the room he braced himself for something horrible, no clue what he was walking into. His eyes took special note of the tiny person standing on his couch, brown hair, brown eyes, jean dress, shaking an empty raisin box while making odd consonant sounds.

He recognized Tabitha, and his heart began to race. He remained standing, firmly planted like a tree growing from hardwood floors.

"Mark, Tabitha has a little girl for us." That was all Elise could say.

Tabitha took over, filling Mark in on everything she had told Elise. She went into even further detail with both of them, describing the exact process and how everything would go if they agreed. It was extraordinary how simple it all was. They were actually being handed a child after years of heartache and struggle.

"Things like this don't happen," Mark said.

"Not often, but these are unusual circumstances and I think the two of you would make a wonderful home for Sadie." Tabitha smiled.

Mark looked at his wife, then back at Tabitha. "There's no question here. If everything is certain as you say, we'll take her."

"I knew you would." Tabitha sounded relieved. "There will be an adjustment period, of course. It won't be easy. You will need time to get used to each other, but then you already know that. You've sat through many adoption classes. You're probably one of the most thorough couples we've had. Definitely one of the most experienced."

They *were* experienced. Every experience had left them with one more hole in their hearts. And a heart can only withstand so many holes before it begins to fall apart. Watching Sadie, they suddenly felt their brokenness begin to mend. There was no doubt they would love her. They already did.

Tabitha had stayed long enough to introduce Sadie to her new family, helping her warm to them as much as possible. Long after Tabitha left and the sun had gone down, the three of them sat quietly around their kitchen table, Mark and Elise feeding Sadie anything and everything they could find that a two-year-old might like. The realization was still sinking in. They couldn't shake the disbelief.

"We'll have to go shopping first thing tomorrow. We don't have anything for a two-year-old," Elise remarked.

"We don't have anything for an anything-old," Mark replied.

"She's so beautiful. Her hair feels like silk." Elise ran her fingers across the back of Sadie's head.

Sadie had responded to the news that they were going to be her new mommy and daddy better than they'd expected, but sitting at the table stuffing small pieces of banana muffin into her mouth, she eyed these new adults closely, taking in her new surroundings eagerly with big, chocolate-brown eyes.

"I'll call Jess and tell her," Mark said.

"Okay," Elise replied, never taking her eyes from Sadie.

Elise had finally accepted that she would never be a mother and now she was sitting next to a living, breathing child she could call her own. It didn't seem real, like a dream, and she hoped she wouldn't wake up. She already loved Sadie as though she'd been her mother since birth. Her heart overflowed with joy and thankfulness. It was the strangest, most wonderful day of her life.

Later that night, Elise held the sleeping child in the rocking chair she'd purchased so many years ago for their first child, a biological child who came too early. Rocking back and forth, stroking Sadie's skin and hair, Elise breathed in the delicate aroma of children's shampoo wafting from Sadie's head. A warm lump of happiness in her arms, limp and quietly snoring, she *was* real.

Elise made a space in the middle of their king-sized bed. Neither of them could stop looking at Sadie, holding her, smelling her. Elise found the smallest T-shirt she owned for Sadie to sleep in, wrapping her in blankets to ensure she stayed warm. Tabitha had left several training diapers to tide them over. Sadie needed so many things, the list already forming in Elise's mind. Suddenly she was charged with all the responsibilities of a mother and it thrilled her.

They spent the rest of the night thanking the God they served for the unexpected gift. They would have gone the rest of their lives without, made the best of it, and tried their hardest to see the positive through all the sadness and disappointment, but they didn't have to anymore. The one thing missing from their life together was sleeping between them, curled into an adorable little ball, mouth open, drool oozing. Her eyelids fluttered. *What is she dreaming about?* they wondered.

Ten fingers. Ten toes. Two big brown eyes. Two perfectly placed dimples. *Sadie Elizabeth Stuart. Our daughter.*

32

FORWARD MOTION

*J*ess stood outside the closed door to Abby's room, dreading what waited for her on the other side. She almost chickened out, but the need to keep moving forward nagged her to push through. She peered inside just enough to prepare her heart for the soul-wrenching task at hand. It was time to pack up Abby's things.

Abby wasn't coming back. Jess had kept everything as it had been the day Patrick left with Abby for ballet class. Her room had become a museum, haunted by memories, ghosts that lingered in each article of clothing and every toy and storybook. Her dolls were still having a tea party at their doll-sized table. Her favorite teddy bear still lay face down next to her bed where she'd dropped him in a hurry to meet Daddy at the door.

Boxing up Patrick's belongings had been easy. Three months after the tragedy she'd ransacked every possession of his, throwing away each one with violent anger. Blaming him had been the hardest thing to let go of. She didn't want to let go of anything that belonged to her precious child.

Jess knew it was time. She'd recently found herself picking up and cleaning the house, dusting and organizing neglected spaces. Without thinking she'd tidied toys and books, socks and hairbrushes that had been lying around, cluttering each room for those two years. She hadn't fallen apart or panicked as she put things back in their rightful places. For the first time since she'd lost her family they were just items, things to be used or put away. Once she realized what was happening it shocked her. Jess nearly cried thinking she'd forgotten her child in some careless moment.

But she hadn't forgotten. Abby was the center of her heart. She wasn't forgetting Abby; her heart was healing. She was learning how to survive with the pain and the memories. Jess was ready to move on, not away, not without, but looking forward to new memories and new experiences. Life, after all, is a forward journey.

Just do it. Jess wasted no time. A rainy Wednesday gave her perfect opportunity to go through Abby's room one drawer and shelf at a time. On a whim, during her impromptu trip to Richland, the same day she'd bought Nick's present, she'd purchased a CD. Colbie Caillat. The young guy working the music store had assured her it was good, that everyone loved this woman's music, so Jess took a chance. Nick was always saying she needed to branch out and listen to newer stuff. Jess listened to her new Colbie Caillat CD, hoping it would provide a pleasant distraction while she went through Abby's belongings.

Sorting clothing and shoes by size, books, games, toys, unused sticker books, dolls, and a handful of completely random miscellaneous items, assigning each to their own box and compartment, allowed Jess's slightly compulsive organizing skills to run wild. *If you're going to do something, you might as well do it right.*

It was easier than she'd thought it would be. Perhaps the hazy day, comfy pants, and steaming cup of hot tea eased her through it. Or maybe it was knowing she was becoming herself again. She planned to donate most of it. The sheer volume of toys and clothes surprised her. *How does one kid accumulate this much stuff?* She prepared a special stack for Mark and Elise. It was even more comforting to know Abby's memory would in some way be carried on by Sadie. She wasn't sure how she would feel the first time she saw Sadie wearing one of Abby's outfits. That thought scared her, but not enough to keep her from sharing a little of Abby with her new niece.

Watching drizzle through rain-coated windows, swallowing gulps of her second cup of tea, Jess took a break on the plush window seat Patrick had installed in the alcove of a large picture window in Abby's room. He'd been good for some things. Allowing her mind to drift away from boxes and begrudging chores, Jess focused on happier times she'd spent in that room, on that window seat with her family. It hadn't been all bad with Patrick. If she closed her eyes she could almost see Abby sitting across from her, picture book in hand, smiling as she flipped to her favorite pages. Jess could almost hear her breathing, whispering to herself as she tried to read the story. *Part of you is still here. I feel you.*

"Mommy, why do birds have feathers?" Jess remembered Abby asking her on a rainy, Saturday morning.

"That's a very good question."

"You don't know?" Abby asked.

"I do not. I've never thought about it. Should I know?" Jess smiled.

"Yes. Birds are important." Abby stared at her book.

"I suppose they are. I didn't realize you liked birds so much."

"Birds fly, and one day I want to fly. I think I might need feathers." Abby turned the page.

How insightful her little girl was.

"You might be right. Maybe we should go feather shopping."

"Mommy, you don't buy feathers at the store," Abby corrected.

"Where do you get them?" Jess asked, watching loose brown curls slide across Abby's cheek.

"You pick them up in the grass."

"Oh. What if you don't find enough?"

"You wait until you do," Abby replied.

"Then what?"

"You have to glue them or they fall off."

"Ah." Jess nodded with dramatic understanding.

"Mommy . . ." Abby turned the page again.

"Yes."

"You don't know very much." The child's eyes never looked up, engrossed in her book about caterpillars and ladybugs.

Jess had laughed, unable to conceal her amusement. "Thank you for your honesty, little bit. I'll try to learn a few more things before our next conversation." She covered a large grin stretching across her face.

"You're welcome, Mommy. It's not your fault," Abby replied.

"Oh, it's not?"

"No. You don't have as good of books as I do. You can read this one when I'm done."

Jess rubbed Abby's leg with a sock-covered foot. "Thank you, little bit. I can always count on you."

Patrick sauntered into the room, large coffee mug held firmly in one hand.

"What are you two lovely ladies up to?"

"Abby was just educating me on my lack of knowledge."

He grinned. "In general, or of certain subjects?"

"It began with birds, but I think general knowledge was implied," Jess said.

"Are you giving your mother a hard time, princess?" He slid onto the window seat next to Jess.

"Mommy doesn't know about birds," Abby said, glancing up long enough to meet her father's hazel eyes.

"Well, you'll have to teach her then," Patrick said.

"I tried. It didn't end well."

Is this kid for real? Patrick and Jess looked at each other with bewilderment. Abby never ceased to amaze them. She'd been the thread holding their failed marriage together. Her tiny smile and bright eyes often made Patrick wish he could take back every indiscretion. Jess wasn't the only one he was hurting, and he knew it.

"I happen to think your mom is super smart. She did marry me after all." Patrick grinned, arching his eyebrows at Jess, who immediately rolled her eyes.

"Daddy, Mommy only married you because she fell in love. You don't have to be smart to fall in love."

We are raising an Einstein.

"I suppose that's true," Patrick replied.

"But Mommy is smart. She taught me how to make pancakes. Only smart people can make pancakes." Abby looked up from her book, flashing a huge smile, melting Jess's already conquered heart.

"I can definitely see the logic in that one. Pancakes are important," Patrick said.

"Thank you, little bit. It's good to know my pancakes are appreciated," Jess said.

"Yes, but mine are better, Mommy," Abby added.

Patrick roared with laughter. "You can't win with this one, Jess."

"I guess not," Jess conceded, tickling Abby's toes.

"Mommy, stop! That tickles."

"That's the point." Jess tickled her again.

"Speaking of pancakes, any chance we can get some of those this morning?" Patrick eyed his wife with puppy eyes, offering her a sip of his coffee as incentive.

Jess smiled, a half smile full of mixed emotions. She treasured every family moment they shared no matter how short or few they were, but underneath the pleasant surface, her heart was broken into a thousand pieces knowing she wasn't the center of Patrick's heart and probably never had been. He loved her. She knew that. He just didn't love her enough.

Patrick leaned in, and Jess could feel his warm breath on her cheek. He pressed his nose against her temple, lightly kissing her cheekbone. Strands of her hair stuck to his lips.

"How about those pancakes, Mrs. Neill?"

Jess closed her eyes. She relished his warm body against hers, but not without picturing the other women who'd been that close to her husband. It was hard to be intimate with a man she was forced to share.

"What flavor?" she asked.

Patrick placed his hand against her other cheek, pulling her face toward his, his breath now brushing her mouth as his nose pressed against hers.

"Blueberry is nice, but I'm not picky." He brought her lips to meet his.

Jess returned his kiss reluctantly, but not without desire. Her heart raced like it had when they first got married, when he held her like she was the only woman on earth. Those moments had been so few and so fleeting since their first year of marriage.

His breathing quickened. His hold tightened. For a moment Jess thought he'd forgotten their five-year-old was seated directly across from them.

"I think we have some blueberries in the freezer," Jess replied, growing breathless herself.

Patrick pulled her closer, gently kissing her neck, inhaling the lavender scent of her lotion.

"Yucky, Daddy. Kisses are gross," Abby interrupted, plopping the book down in her lap.

He chuckled under heavy breath, pulling away from Jess but staring into her eyes. He mouthed three small words, inaudible but clear. *I love you.* Then he turned to face Abby.

"Oh, really? Well, I kiss you all the time, princess. I've never heard you complain." He picked her up, smothering Abby's cheek with kisses.

"Daddies are supposed to kiss their daughters." She wrapped her small arms around his neck.

"Husbands can't kiss their wives?" he asked.

"No, only on Sundays."

He laughed. "Why Sundays?"

"That's when Uncle Mark kisses Aunt Elise and says she makes the best pie in the world." Their weekly tradition of Sunday lunch at Mark's house was one of Abby's favorite things to do.

"Ah, I see. Well, if daddies didn't kiss the mommies, there'd be no babies."

"Patrick!" Jess eyed him. "Too young."

Abby grinned. "Daddy, you're silly."

He looked back at Jess. "See, she didn't understand."

"She understands more than you think."

He carried Abby toward the door. "Ask Mommy when she's going to start making those pancakes."

"I'm coming. Right behind you." Jess watched them bounce out of the room, a perfect father-daughter moment.

Jess remembered that morning as though it had happened yesterday. Sitting on the same window seat, watching beads of water fall in sequence down foggy glass, she could almost feel

Patrick's breath against her skin and Abby's skinny leg against her foot. She glanced at all the tubs and boxes stacked around the room, bringing her back to reality, away from the comfort of memories.

That perfect Saturday morning had taken place three months before the wreck. It was the last pancake breakfast they ate together, the last passionate moment experienced in her marriage. After that Saturday, Patrick started working more hours, coming home late and tired. He'd also started spending more time with the other woman in his life.

As the rain picked up and water droplets began to fall faster, showering the window beside her, a cold chill sent a shiver through her arms and she remembered the last words they'd spoken to each other.

"Just stop it, Jess. You're being ridiculous." Patrick grabbed his gym bag and headed down the porch steps.

"Oh, I'm being ridiculous? You were video chatting with *her* in the middle of the night while I was lying right next to you!" Jess stood on the porch, adjusting Abby's costume. She hated arguing in front of her daughter, but sometimes she couldn't help it.

"I already apologized for that. It has nothing to do with whether or not I take Abby to ballet."

"Mommy, don't yell at Daddy," Abby pleaded.

"I'm always left picking up the pieces you leave behind!" Jess held Abby's hand to keep her on the porch.

Patrick shook his head. "I'm not having this fight with you right now. You always do this."

"Why am I the one at fault?"

"Mommy, stop it." Abby pulled away, running down the steps to her father.

"I'm not the monster you're making me out to be." He tossed his gym bag in the car.

Jess stood on the porch, arms folded in front of her, blinking back tears.

Patrick rubbed Abby's head. "You ready, princess?"

Abby nodded.

"Go give your mom a hug."

She ran back up the porch steps to where Jess was standing, bear-hugging her mother around the hips. "Bye, Mommy."

Jess bent down and kissed her on the forehead. "Have fun, little bit."

"I will, Mommy. Bye." Abby pranced and bounced all the way to Patrick's car.

Patrick looked back at her one last time. His irritation was clear. In that moment she hadn't cared if Patrick ever came back, but she never imagined Abby wouldn't come back either.

Tears rolled down her cheeks, slow at first, then faster streams that turned into sobs as she relived that last kiss on Abby's forehead over and over, wishing she'd held on tighter. She would never forget, never fully heal. Losing Abby was like losing a part of her soul, but it wasn't the end. She leaned against the cold glass window crying not only for what she'd lost and for all the things she missed but for the life she was putting behind her. The future seemed so vast and unknown, a scary blank page. *You can't go back. You can only move forward.*

She packed a large container full of Abby's prettiest outfits, socks, and shoes. A smaller box of hair bows and tiny jewelry sat on top, just under the lid. Then she slipped Abby's favorite dolls and a few toys into a department store bag, wrapping each with a big red bow, Abby's favorite color.

Driving to Mark's house was easier than walking up the steps to their front porch. She nearly tripped. Her hands were shaking, her legs wobbly. Her heart beat like it had when Mark broke the news to her after the accident. She rang the bell.

Elise answered the door.

"Jess, my goodness. Here, let me help you." Elise took the large storage tub, placing it just inside the front door.

Jess held out the paper bag, blinking away tears.

"What is all this?" Elise asked.

Jess swallowed what seemed the largest lump she'd ever had in her throat. "My gift to you. Some of Abby's things. I thought you might want them for Sadie."

Elise put a hand to her mouth. "Oh, Jess. Thank you. I don't know what to say."

"You don't have to say anything."

"Please come in. I was just cooking dinner."

"No, thank you. I'd love to. I really would. But I think I need to go home. I still have some more things to box up. I'm kind of emotional right now." Jess let out a loud sigh, wiping at stray tears.

"I understand. Are you okay? Do you want Mark to come over?"

"No. I'm okay. Just processing. It's hard letting go. It's finally real." She couldn't fight the tears any longer.

"We love you. I love you," Elise said with a quivering voice.

Jess moved closer, hugging Elise tightly, then quickly turning to leave. "I love you too. I hope Sadie will know how wonderful her cousin was."

"Of course she will. None of us will ever forget Abby. She's still a part of our lives. Always will be."

Jess nodded, walking toward her car. She sat inside for several moments after Elise had gone back into the house. She watched the glow of light coming from the front room and pictured them sitting down to dinner, a happy family, full of joy. She wondered if she would ever have that much joy again. She hoped she would. She wanted it. Needed it. In some ways she was ready to embrace it, but she was also scared to death of it.

Jess pulled away slowly and made the short drive back to her house, wondering what the future might hold and hoping she was brave enough to embrace it.

33

MUSIC

*W*hen his fingers finally began cooperating, Nick felt whole again. He could even screw the toothpaste cap on by himself, no small feat since the accident. The cane took an extended stay to the attic, and he'd never been so happy to be rid of something. He still carried a slight limp in his right leg, but it was manageable, getting better each week. His left arm now glided over the frets of his Gibson with greater ease. He practiced several hours each day, still determined to regain and improve his skill.

Falling farther away, Climbing closer to you. Seeking waves I cannot ride, Crashing into you. Nick scribbled lyrics on scraps of paper, unedited thoughts as he composed music on his guitar. The melody always came first. He could hear the rise and fall of notes in his head, chord changes and harmony. Then he'd quickly strum it all out on one of his guitars, making notes as he went along. Once the music was solid he'd start writing lyrics to go with it. He'd always written this way. It awed some people and annoyed others. He'd told his former boss in Richland about it, the owner of a music store he worked at before Votive signed their first record deal, and his boss told him the story of how Paul McCartney wrote the song "Yesterday," waking up with the tune in his head. He'd never forgotten that. Nick had met McCartney when he was twenty-four at a world hunger event, and he'd never forgotten that either.

Sitting on his bed, Nick composed two songs simultaneously, one for Jack and one for Jess. He'd woken up thinking of melodies for Jack, tributary lyrics making repetitive rounds in his thoughts, but every time he started writing he couldn't get Jess out of his mind. Her smile haunted him. He strummed the chords, finding all the right notes. He just couldn't find the right words. Words for Jack were easier. He knew what he would say if his best friend were standing in front of him. What would he say to Jess? Were there even words to express all the feelings he held inside?

Mark would be there soon to pick him up. He needed to get this all out while it was still fresh. He wrote until every word flowed from his mouth in harmony to every chord he strummed. He couldn't stop playing, even when Dale peeked in to listen, even when Mark showed up early. Nick played until the moment his musical instinct told him to stop.

"You ready?" Mark asked from the half open door to Nick's room.

"Yeah. Let's go." Nick gathered his belongings.

Mark waited for him outside as Nick tossed a few guitar picks into his case. He heard a buzzing sound from under a blanket on his bed. It was his phone going off for the umpteenth time. He looked at the screen. A text from Alan. He'd been leaving texts and voicemails for several days and Nick had dodged each one. He opened the text and read it.

"Nick. Are you going to call me back? My patience is thin."

Nick tossed his phone back on the bed. He didn't have time to deal with this. He knew why Alan was calling.

The phone buzzed again.

"Nick. Break Voice is hounding me. You need to make a decision. Are you in or out?"

Nick opened the text and typed a hasty reply. "Out."

Alan's response came faster than Nick could close the window. "Can we talk? Call me."

Nick shook his head. He stuffed the phone in his back pocket and headed outside to Mark's car.

Mark drove them to Jake Langston's house. His basement spanned the entire bottom portion of his home, opening into a garage at the driveway. Nick was astonished to see his setup, high-dollar music equipment and his own studio. Some of the best speakers, amps, monitors, mixers, mics, and instruments were placed strategically around a large open room, ideal for rehearsing. Nick hadn't seen equipment this nice since his last tour.

"Sweet setup, man," Nick said, eyeing a vintage Fender Stratocaster in the corner.

"Thanks. I've put a lot of work into this," Jake replied.

"When you said you played gigs on the weekends I didn't realize you were so serious. This is awesome."

Jake laughed. "I'm not a pro like you, but to say it's a passion would be putting it lightly."

"I can see."

"Check out the studio." Jake led Nick into a locked room.

Nick's jaw dropped. They stood in a homemade recording studio as nice as many Nick had worked in.

"New York and LA have nothing on you, man," Nick said.

"I doubt that. It's an expensive hobby, but a man's got to spend his money on something, right?"

"Yeah."

They rejoined Monty and Seymour, who were setting up to play.

"Nick! What's up, my man?" Seymour embraced Nick with a near fatal hug.

"Hey! You playing drums today?" Nick asked.

"Always." Seymour grinned. "Good to see you looking so strong."

"All thanks to you . . . and Layla, drill sergeant that she is."

"Don't give me that credit. You worked hard. Still working hard. I'm just one man doing my job."

"Couldn't have done it without you," Nick said.

"We're in this together, my man."

Nick nodded.

"You slackers going to stand around all day or get this show on the road?" Greg Oppman entered the room sporting a newly groomed beard.

"Check out the new look. You trying to impress someone with that rat's nest on your face?" Monty joked.

"Nah, thought I'd show you how to grow one properly. Tired of seeing that pathetic excuse for a goatee on your chin," Greg retorted.

"Ouch!" Nick roared.

"We'll see who's pathetic when the music starts."

"My money's on Jake. He'll play you both under the table."

Nick smiled, laughing to himself as he listened to their chiding banter. Only true friends could tease each other like that. It reminded him of so many insults and sarcastic jabs he, Drew, and Jack had made to each other over the years. Perhaps it was the way guys expressed their feelings for each other, but it meant a lot to be in a room full of comrades who threw punches and hugs at the same time.

"Let's break this down. The festival is in a few weeks and we need to get our set list in stone," Jake announced.

"Yeah, if we can all agree," Greg laughed.

"What do you think, Mark?" Monty asked.

"I'm just here to watch, maybe sing along. I don't have a say."

Seymour chuckled. "Mark without an opinion? That's a first."

The other men laughed.

"Never said I didn't have an opinion. Just not my place to dictate what songs you guys play," Mark corrected.

"Never stopped you before," Greg laughed.

"Come on. Quit being stubborn. You know we want your input," Monty said.

"Nothing by Styx. I put my foot down on that one," Mark said.

"I second that," Seymour chimed in.

The set list discussion continued. What to play. What not to play. Nick took it all in. He was about to perform in a group for the first time in over a year. His heart raced just thinking about it. Anxious thoughts about his abilities, about Votive and his future as a musician ran circles through his mind, but he brushed them off and kept going.

The Bridgetown Dogwood Festival was approaching, and the guys had asked Nick to play with them. They were a yearly staple at the festival. They didn't even have a name, but Bridgetown natives loved them and they looked forward to hearing the group every year.

Rehearsal began. Nick and Jake on guitar, Greg on bass, Seymour on drums, and Monty switching back and forth from keyboard to harmonica or mandolin, depending on what was needed. They made great harmony together. Nick learned some new songs, got refreshed on some old ones, and taught the others a few of Votive's favorites. Monty, Jake, and Nick took turns singing. Greg and Seymour provided backup vocals when needed.

Nick had almost forgotten how it felt to be part of something like this, a close-knit group, expressing art and emotion through song. Making music with others had always been better than playing alone. That's what scared him about a solo career. The bonds of brotherhood were what made his music so meaningful. He enjoyed sharing success with Jack and Drew, and his music had been better because of them, one united harmony on stage and off. He missed it, but he also couldn't imagine starting a band without them. It wouldn't be the same. He worried that maybe he wasn't the same.

Nick warmed up his J-45. Then he picked up that gorgeous Fender Strat with Jake's approval and showed those oldies what a guitar could really do. He let loose, soaring high in his element, finally in touch with himself, who he'd always been under the rubble of self-sabotage. Not a victim, not a villain, but a man standing on two feet learning life from a new perspective.

They played and rehearsed for several hours, finally breaking for dinner and Seymour's famous smoked ribs.

Back home, Nick couldn't get the new compositions from that morning out of his head. He recorded Jack's song on his phone, raw and unedited, but more soulful than any track with studio swagger. He saved the audio file and before he could give himself a chance to reconsider, texted it to Ben O'Malley with a message that read: *For Jack. My closest brother and friend.*

His phone vibrated and Nick's heart skipped a beat thinking Ben had replied. But it was Alan. Again.

"Call me," the text read.

Nick stared at his phone, a thousand memories and thoughts swirling in his head. He needed more time. He was finally getting to know himself. He still wanted the career. He wanted to try again, but he needed to figure out who he was in that world now, without Votive. He opened his phone and texted back.

"Soon."

For several minutes there was no response, then a bubble popped up on Nick's phone.

"Ok."

Pillowing his head that night, Nick recalled Jack's performance on stage during their last show. Risk-takers that they were, they'd switched a few things up, rearranged some songs on the spot, added a couple extra verses, and hoped Drew wouldn't kill them later. They lived in the moment. Jack's beaming face, exuberant and deliriously happy, was the only way Nick wanted to remember him. They'd never played harder, never had more fun, and though that night was wrought with mistakes and regrets that would last a lifetime, he took solace in knowing they'd played the best show of their career and gone out on top.

Sleep came sooner than usual, but not without Jess's lovely face lulling him under, those beautiful eyes that often shined so green he was captive under their spell, and that red lipstick so vivid against her light complexion. He drifted into slumber with the comfort of her smile and the warmth of her touch soothing his tired mind. *Teach me how to be a better man. Show me how to deserve someone like you. Sweet Jess, how did you end up in my life?*

34

LEGACY

*N*ick hadn't visited his mother's grave since high school. His heart couldn't handle it. He stood there now with his father, against strong wind battering their skin. Gray clouds predicted rain as spring storms became more frequent. They stood side by side, quietly reading the words on her headstone, remembering her in their own ways.

Nick placed a solid hand on Dale's shoulder, avoiding eye contact as he looked straight ahead. Words between them had never been easy. Some things may never change, but words weren't always necessary.

"It wasn't all bad," Dale said.

"No," Nick replied.

"There were good times. She had some good moments."

"The best memory I have is of her laughter," Nick recalled.

Dale smiled. "She could steal an entire room when she laughed."

"And sang," Nick added.

"Do you remember her singing Beatles songs to you?"

"No. Did she?" Nick asked.

"Yeah. She used to sing her favorites to you at night when she tucked you in. You were very young, though. When her drinking got worse she was usually passed out somewhere by the time you went to bed. Or dancing naked in the backyard."

"I'm really glad I don't remember that."

"She was sick, Nicholas. She needed more help than I could give her."

"Some people don't want help. Mom made her choices just like I made mine. You can't blame yourself for what happened to her. You shouldn't blame yourself for me either."

Dale glanced at his son, a new man before him. "That's the first time you've said that."

"Yeah, well, I've been a jerk. And that's putting it lightly. It's going to take a long time to repair the rift between us, but I want you to know that I don't blame you. I blame myself."

Dale touched his son's hand, still on his shoulder. "There's a lot of things we both could have done differently. Living in the past won't change that. I don't need a perfect son. I hope you don't expect a perfect father."

"I lived nine years without a father. Which was my choice. I'm just glad you took me back. I don't need a perfect father, just one who's willing to forgive me."

"You have that, son. I hope you'll forgive me too."

Nick looked him in the eyes, teary but composed. "Nothing to forgive. You stuck by me. I should be thanking you."

Dale embraced his son. He'd waited years for a moment like this. When it came, he didn't want it to end. He didn't want to let go for fear it would all slip away. Nicholas was all he had left in the world, and he realized more than ever how much he needed him.

"What would Mom say if she were here?" Nick asked when they pulled away.

"She'd tell us enough is enough, stop standing around and get back to work. Or something to that effect." He smiled.

"I miss her."

"I know, son. Me too. She wouldn't want us dwelling on it. She'd own her part. She was a beautiful woman. So kind and vivacious before she hit bottom."

"Oatmeal cookies," Nick added.

"What?"

"She used to make oatmeal cookies, but not like the ones other people make. They were big and thick and smelled like cinnamon and vanilla. I remember her baking them on weekends. Oatmeal cookies and chocolate milk."

"I'm impressed. You were five when she stopped making those. She nearly burned the house down the last time she made a batch, so drunk she left oven mitts on a hot eye."

"They were good cookies." Nick could almost taste them, smell the aroma coming from a kitchen now fading in his memory.

"Cardamom."

"Cardamom?" Nick asked.

"Her secret ingredient. She used cardamom." Dale smiled.

"You should be baking those instead of that apple bread."

They both chuckled.

"All right. I think the recipe is still around somewhere. We'll bake them together, in honor of her."

"The two of us in the kitchen?"

"Why not?" Dale replied.

Nick grinned. "I'll try anything once."

Dale put an arm around his son. "That's how you got in trouble in the first place."

Nick huffed. "Good point."

They stood against the wind keeping silent company. If the

whole water under the bridge saying was true, a host of past sins and painful memories floated downstream that day.

Evening grew dim, and Dale went home to scavenge for supper. Nick chose to stay behind, wandering the cemetery collecting his thoughts. So much had changed since his last visit. His heart still hurt, but it no longer seemed unbearable. *I think I'm going to be okay.*

Inevitably he ended up near Jack's grave. He wasn't the only one there. Hovering several yards away, Nick watched Jack's father kneel in front of the headstone. Ben O'Malley held his hand against the cold granite, head bent low. His lips were mouthing words, but Nick couldn't hear them. He wanted to walk away, but his feet were frozen in place.

Ben rose to his feet, hands shaking, tears glazing his eyes. His countenance hung like a willow tree, drooping with the sorrow of a father who never got to say goodbye. With a rocky step backward, his gaze caught sight of Nick. For several seconds they stared at each other. The anguish expressed in Ben's eyes brought tears to Nick's. *I'm sorry.* Nick repeated the words over and over in his head.

Nick waited, anticipating Ben's face might fill with rage, that he might lunge forward, barreling toward him in heartsick retaliation, but he didn't. His expression softened. His arms hung heavy at his side. Ben turned to walk away, down the hill toward the cemetery entrance. He looked back at Nick, meeting Nick's gaze, man to man, eye to eye. Nick's heart beat faster.

Ben O'Malley looked back at his son's grave. Then he faced Nick again, nodding. It was a difficult nod to read, but it seemed like one of subtle understanding. Not forgiveness . . . not yet. But perhaps a kind of letting go. Maybe his song had conveyed the

things Nick wanted to say but hadn't been able to without
music. Or maybe Ben was tired of hating him. Either way, Nick
chose to take it as a positive sign.

He waited until Ben was out of sight before approaching
Jack's grave. His closest ally buried beneath soft spring grass. *Hey
there, old friend. I've missed you.*

Nick sat down, holding his hands to the ground as though
somehow it put him in touch with the man below. He longed for
some connection, anything to bring his friend back to him in
some way. The smell of honeysuckle grazed his nostrils as he
closed his eyes. He soaked up the peaceful moment. *I wish you
were.*

"Hey," Nick whispered. "Things got crazy around here.
Should have been here to smack me around a few times. You
always said I acted on impulse . . . or maybe that was Drew. I
think we both acted on impulse. We're kindred that way."

It took several deep breaths for Nick to continue, still barely a
whisper, hoping Jack could hear him somehow.

"I saw your dad. Your parents really miss you. Who wouldn't?
If you were here you'd call me a big baby." He laughed, wiping
tears. "I guess I am. Always the big teddy bear, right? Isn't that
what you called me? Big softy? We can't all be Mr. Macho like
you, you crazy, short brute."

Nick smiled, rubbing his hands along dew-dampened grass.

"Should have brought my guitar. I wrote a song for you. I
don't know if it's for you, about you . . . I guess it doesn't matter.
It's your song. Feels weird not singing it with you." He paused.
"I'm sorry. I wish I could take it back. I'd trade places with you if
I could. So many times I've wished I could." He breathed slow,
deep breaths.

It took several moments for Nick to compose his emotions.
He decided to sing Jack's song. It didn't have a title yet. He'd

tried to come up with one, but nothing seemed to be good enough. For now it would simply be "Jack's Song."

He sang the words, but he felt every note more deeply than his voice could convey. He pictured Jack standing among the graves playing bass, no amp, just Jack, his five-string Ibanez, the birds, and Nick. The sun set in deep orange tones, unusual for that time of year. It was a glorious show, the best concert he'd ever been a part of.

Jack had been the true entertainer, not shy like Nick, never inhibited. He was the life force of every room he entered. Sometimes that wasn't such a good thing, but all men leave a legacy. Jack left his smiling, laughing loudly, and playing his bass like a man ready for anything.

Play on, wild man. Play on.

He wanted to tell his friend about Jess. Jack would understand. But that would have to wait. It was time to go. Another day. Another conversation.

"I'll be back, old friend. I'm not going anywhere . . . not yet."

35

PROMISES

*B*utterflies in the stomach. Nick hadn't felt that sensation before a gig since high school. He'd been nervous many times since, mouth dry, limbs shaky, palms sweating, but not butterflies. Butterflies gave rise to a feeling of dread, a worry that things wouldn't go well, and performing had been the one thing Nick had always done well. Things were different now. He was different. This wasn't Votive, he wasn't playing his songs, and he most certainly was not drunk. He hadn't had any alcohol in a week, not even a beer. He hadn't been drunk since the last accident, and he was the first to admit he felt better.

He'd never been on stage without Jack and Drew. These new guys were great, but they were different, and the music they played was different. Nick wasn't sure what to expect or how he would feel once they got up there.

Bridgetown residents showed up early on a clear, brisk Saturday morning. The Dogwood Festival was hopping as Nick arrived to help set up. Apparently Greg was infamous for being late, and Seymour had accidentally slept in, so Nick and Jake were stuck unloading by themselves until Mark and Monty arrived to help.

"You act like you've never done this before," Jake noted.

"I haven't . . . not much."

"Not even before you hit it big?"

Nick laughed. "Nah, we mostly played at venues that furnished the equipment. We made Drew do most of the work while Jack and I goofed off. Most of our gear was crap anyway. We had no money back then, and what little we made went to rent."

"Then you got big and they gave you a road crew," Jake said.

"Yeah, those guys work harder than anyone I've ever seen. They don't stop."

"You should hear some of Seymour's stories," Jake added.

Seymour and Greg wandered slowly in their direction.

"Oh, look, it's the stragglers. We should make them finish all this and go watch the parade," Jake said within earshot of Seymour.

"My alarm clock took a nosedive," Seymour explained.

"We've heard that one before," Monty called out from several yards away.

"You can set an alarm on your phone," Nick chimed in.

"Hey now, whose side are you on, Nick?" Seymour frowned.

Greg waltzed up, tossing a gear bag on the stage and a pair of sunglasses on top.

"Whoa, you're in a mood," Jake said.

"Don't start. The wife was onto me about everything this morning. It was nag city." Greg shook his head and looked around to see how much they had already done.

"What'd you do this time?" Seymour asked.

"It's more like what I didn't do . . . the dishes, pick my laundry off the floor, wipe the toilet seat, take out the trash, you know the list."

"Man, you're a slob," Monty teased.

"Leave me alone," Greg huffed.

"Are we going to stand around and chitchat all day, or are we gonna play some music for these people?" Seymour asked.

Sound check went well. Getting everyone together, organized, and ready was a chore, but once they took the stage all evidence of a shaky start disappeared, and they were musicians doing what they did best, entertaining a crowd.

Butterflies faded and Nick regained his momentum, a magnetizing performer, lighting the stage on fire. As people gathered to watch the show, Nick could feel the buzz his presence was generating, igniting the atmosphere around them. He was drawing quite a crowd of curious and excited onlookers and his nerves began to shake again, but not for long. He was back in his element and it felt good. He and Jake took turns on vocals, and Nick provided backup vocals on some of Jake's songs. His fingers glided effortlessly across the frets of his blue Les Paul electric guitar, forming each chord with ease, his right-hand strumming and picking at strings the way he always had. It was the best feeling in the world. Making music meant more than it ever had. His reasons for playing, his purpose for writing songs, had all changed . . . for the better.

Crowds gathered around, some standing in open spaces, others sitting in chairs provided by the festival's organizers. They stood in the midst of families, couples, and tourists enjoying all the food, merchant booths, games, and activities the festival had to offer. *It feels good to be back on stage. It feels good to be alive.*

Jess tagged along with Elise as she pushed Sadie around in a stroller, peering inside local artisans' booths.

"Look, Sadie!" Elise pointed to a colorful clown making balloon animals for gathering children.

Sadie screamed, kicking and averting her eyes.

Jess bent down, stroking Sadie's head. "I don't think she likes clowns."

Elise turned the stroller, heading in the opposite direction. "It would appear so."

Once in the clear, Elise picked her up, holding her close, offering a soft shoulder for Sadie to dry her tears. The wind picked up, brushing wisps of Sadie's hair across her mother's face.

"It's okay." Elise patted her gently, holding her trembling child close.

Jess pushed the empty stroller as they walked past Irish dancers and caricature artists, vendors selling homemade baked goods and street performers breaking into random theatrical entertainment. A mixed aroma from over fifty different food vendors filled the cool spring air with savory, fried sweetness.

The Piedmont River flowed past a cozy residential area of Bridgetown, near wide-open spaces along the river's bank, where the festival was held each April. Festival goers strolled beside the river, watching boats as children and adults alike flew kites and skipped pebbles across murky water.

"She's asleep," Jess said, checking Sadie's eyes behind Elise's shoulder.

They rested on a bench near the water.

"Good. She didn't rest well last night. I think she's having nightmares."

"That's understandable." Jess touched Sadie's little hand, careful not to wake her. "How's everything going?"

Elise was quiet. "I've waited years to be a mother. Cried myself to sleep during some of the darkest times when it seemed it might never actually happen. We finally have everything we ever wanted . . ."

"But?" Jess asked.

"I didn't realize it would be this hard," she replied, rocking sideways as she cradled Sadie. "Don't misunderstand, I'm happier than I've ever been. I don't regret it for a moment, but being a mother is the most difficult thing I've ever tried to do."

Jess nodded. "You've only just begun. I hate to tell you, but it gets harder."

"I worry about her all the time. I still can't believe she's ours. Sometimes I go in her room at night to check on her and make sure she's breathing. Does that sound crazy?"

Jess smiled. "No. Not at all."

"She scares easily. Sometimes I think she still isn't sure about us, probably missing her grandmother. That's normal, right? These things take time. I just wish I could make it through one day without questioning every decision I make."

"Welcome to motherhood." Jess nudged her sister-in-law.

"Thanks. Just the encouragement I wanted to hear."

"Hang in there. You're still getting used to it all, learning the ropes," Jess said.

"Yes, but most people get their feet wet with a newborn. Sadie speaks coherent phrases, eats with plastic utensils . . . well, somewhat. She prefers her fingers most of all."

"So you skipped ahead a little bit. At least you're nearly out of the diaper-changing phase."

"That's a plus. I never needed a newborn to make me happy. I just wanted a child, any child, to love, nurture, teach, and experience the world with." Elise thought for a moment. "I've often wondered why I needed that so badly. Now I look at her and I know that being a mother is who I am, who I always was, even before I had a child."

Jess looked at Sadie, then back at Elise. "You were born to be a mother. I think there's a need inside all of us to nurture and grow. Your faith teaches you that."

"*My* faith?"

Jess turned away, watching crystal gleams across the sun-kissed water. Speed boats raced past lazy sailboats and busy river barges. The pungent smell of fish and drowning earth lingered at the shore.

"I'm trying, Elise. Don't push it. I still have a lot to work through. I wake up every day determined to start fresh, find the person I used to be, but the truth is that person is gone. She died with Abby and Patrick. It's not altogether a bad thing. I just can't go back. I'll never be the same, and now I have to figure out who I am and what it is I'm going to do for the rest of my life."

"I hear what you're saying, Jess. But please remember that life is full of change. It's the things that remain the same that often become our anchor in times of distress. Don't turn your back on what you know to be true."

Jess didn't answer. She didn't have a reply, not one she chose to give. Instead, she listened to cawing birds overhead and rippling water glide across soggy land. Some moments were better left in silence.

Nick and the guys had played three sets, taking water and snack breaks in between. The gathering crowds seemed to love what they were doing. He'd missed this. He'd missed it a lot.

Nick found himself glancing around the crowd, searching for Jess's face, always landing on Mark's exuberant grin, their biggest fan of the day, cheering them on during each song. Mark sat alone, two spaces reserved beside him. Nick kept playing, trying to avoid the distraction, but he couldn't get her out of his mind.

He'd never had more fun than he was having in that moment. Jake owned the stage, some truly worthy competition. Nick wondered why Jake never tried to make it in the biz. The guy had spunk, not to mention a terrific voice. He had a harmony going with Nick. They worked seamlessly on stage together, catching each other's cues, timing things just right . . . a great team.

Bending to the rhythm and lost in the beat, Nick closed his eyes, feeling every note and chord from the inside out. He poured himself into the moment, playing as if his life depended on it. He opened his eyes to a swaying crowd, moved by the same feeling. Then he saw her. *Jess.*

Mark rose, allowing his wife and sister to take the seats next to him. Jess smiled when her eyes met Nick's. He smiled back.

She's watching. Don't mess up. Just keep playing and try not to stare. Snap out of it, man. Keep your head in the game.

Nick glanced at his dad, who'd been listening faithfully through two sets. The butterflies returned. Sweat dripped down the back of his neck, gliding across his shoulder blades, underneath his gray T-shirt. *Just don't get shaky. You can't play when you're shaky.* He breathed steady breaths, diverting his eyes away from her. He cleared a lump in his throat. As the song neared its end, a heavy weight sunk in the pit of his stomach.

"You're up, man." Jake patted Nick's shoulder.

Nick whispered in his ear, a change in song order. He reached for his J-45, returning his Les Paul to its stand.

Jake informed the others of Nick's song choice, giving them a moment to prepare, then picked up an acoustic of his own.

Nick cleared his throat, strapping on his good luck charm, his favorite guitar, and walked toward the mic. He fumbled with his pick, dropping it. He grabbed another. His nerves were taking over. If this moment was any indication of how the next song would go, perhaps he should back out now and run away. He eyed the nearest exit through the crowd whose eyes were locked on him, waiting for more.

Standing at the mic, Nick watched people passing by, stopping to have a listen. It was time. *You can do this. You may only ever get one shot at this. Just do it. Tell her how you feel.*

Cheers and screams rang out from many of the onlookers. Nick's fans were gathering from all corners of the festival and teenaged girls were pushing to get a better view.

"Thank you," he buzzed into the mic. "This next song is for Jess." He looked right at her, smiling, hoping she'd appreciate what he was about to do.

When he started playing, plucking single strings between intermittent strums, the melodic beauty of an old classic filled the spaces around them.

His mouth opened and the words poured out. He'd never been a huge Bob Dylan fan, but it was a gorgeous song, and he'd heard some pretty sharp covers of it over the years. Now, as he met her eyes from several yards away, he understood the words of this beloved tune—"To Make You Feel My Love"—in a way he never had before. The same song her father had sung for her mother, Nick now sang for her.

As he sang the words, he pictured himself saying them to Jess, alone on her porch, in a heartfelt plea for her to see him the way he saw her. A song about life's difficult moments, the loneliness we often feel, and needing to have someone by your side. Nick wanted to be that someone for Jess. He didn't know how she felt about him, and he had so much regret, but he was ready to do just about anything to prove himself, to prove his love.

Mark looked at Jess, trying to read her expression. She sat still as a board as the crowd clapped and cheered, whooping and hollering at the song's end. Teenage girls screamed with delight, still pushing, trying to move closer to see Votive's lead singer. But Jess didn't move.

"Thank you! We're taking a break. We'll be back in a bit," Jake told the audience.

Nick removed his acoustic and Jess got up, disappearing into the crowd. He couldn't tell which way she was going, and then she was gone. He hopped off the stage, grabbing a bottle of water from Monty, who was about to make a food run.

"You guys want anything," he asked.

"Nah, I'm good," Nick said.

"We'll come with you," Jake and Seymour replied.

Nick chugged his water, eyeing Mark's approach toward the stage.

"Bold move," Mark said.

Nick nodded.

"Did she tell you that story? About our parents?"

"Yeah. I wanted it to mean something. And the words . . . they fit."

"Were you going for epic love story or most romantic gesture?" Mark asked.

Nick grinned. "I was trying not to throw up on stage. It's the only thing I could think of to show her how I feel. Make her believe me. I've done a lot of stupid things where she's concerned."

"She's a forgiving person."

"Yeah . . . but."

"But?"

"Does she feel the same way?"

"You won't know until you ask her," Mark said.

"Kind of hard to do that when she walked away."

"I guess you could stand here talking to me about it all day, or you could take a chance and go find her."

Nick hated it when Mark was right, which was most of the time.

"Before you go charging off into the sunset, Romeo, answer one question for me," Mark said.

"Okay."

"Why?"

"Why what?" Nick asked.

"Why do you love her?"

What kind of question was that? *Why does anyone love someone? Because they just do. You can't help falling in love. Even Elvis sang a song about that one.*

"It's a simple question, Nick. You know you love her. You just proclaimed it to a crowd full of strangers. My question is why?"

Nick took only a moment to think about it. He didn't know what answer Mark was looking for or what kind of a test this was, but he knew he had to answer the question honestly.

"I don't care what people think about me. They're going to form opinions and spread gossip. I do care what Jess thinks. I don't want to let her down. Her opinion is the only one that matters. I'd spend the rest of my life trying to make her happy, trying to prove my sincerity. She's worth waiting for, and she's worth walking away from if I'm not the one who can make her happy or keep her safe. I don't care what happens to me. I just want to know that she's okay."

Mark nodded, grabbing Nick's shoulder with a firm hand. "Then why are you still here talking to me? Go find her."

This guy is exhausting. He makes you want to hug him and push him off a cliff at the same time.

"At this rate she'll be old and gray by the time you get to her," Mark added.

Nick took the hint. He searched through festival crowds, hordes of people in every direction, some noticing him and others oblivious as they participated in the activities. He finally found her near a bagpipe player and a mime juggling fruit.

"Jess."

She turned around.

"Hey."

"Hey." She had one foot pointed in the opposite direction, ready to walk away. He stood there with no idea what to say next.

"You left." It was all he could think of.

"Nick—"

"Wait. Don't say anything. Look, Jess, I know I've made a big mess of a lot of things, but I'm trying to make it right. There's one thing I'm sure of in all of this, and that's how I feel about you. At least give me the chance to prove myself."

She relaxed her stance. "Nick, I appreciate the gesture. It was a little indiscreet in front of so many people, but I appreciate the sentiment behind it—"

"Jess," he interrupted.

"No, Nick. Listen. I'm not ready for all this. I'm still trying to figure out my own life. I'm not good for anyone right now. You don't want me. You think you love me because I'm the one person you trusted through all this, but we haven't even known each other that long."

"Nine months and four days."

"What?"

"I've known you nine months and four days. That's when we met, on your front porch, in the rain."

"You're keeping track?" she asked.

"A man has a lot of time to ponder when he's stuck in a wheelchair. I'm not so bad at math"

She didn't know what to say.

"Jess, I put myself out on a limb, and that's okay. I was prepared for rejection, but I know how I feel. This isn't some school-boy crush. I've never cared about anyone the way I care about you."

She breathed in deeply. "I'm just not ready. I don't know if I'll ever be ready. Don't waste your time on me. You could be happy with someone else, but not me."

"Jess . . ."

"I'm sorry, Nick." She walked away, winding through the crowd as quickly as she could.

That's just it. I don't want to be happy with anyone else. Nick stood alone until people began to recognize him, crowding around him for autographs and questions. He pushed past them and found a quieter place to sit down and reflect on the day's events.

"There you are." Dale slipped in beside him on the makeshift bench.

"Hey."

"More people than usual this year. Thought I'd never find you."

"Well, you found me."

"What's wrong?" Dale asked.

"I bet you could guess if you really wanted to."

"Does it have anything to do with your recent declaration of love?"

"Ding! You win. Congratulations."

"I take it that it didn't go well."

"If that's the politically correct term for rejection, then yeah, not so well."

"Not a whole lot I can say to help then. I'd probably just make things worse talking about it."

"It's not your fault. I'm not even sure it's mine. I guess she doesn't feel the same way."

"I didn't realize your feelings for her were that strong. I guess I never asked," Dale said.

Nick kicked at the ground, making shapes in the dirt with his shoes. "I'm not really sure when it happened. It just did."

"Am I allowed to ask if she's the first woman you've ever loved?" Dale asked.

"There's been a couple I really cared about. But comparing them to Jess, there's no contest. I didn't understand what it really meant until now, until her. All for nothing, though, right?"

"Love is never for nothing. I wouldn't say that loving your mother was all for nothing. I got my heart ripped out on a daily basis, but I wouldn't trade my life with her for anything. I got you out of it. I learned how precious life is. Don't ever say it's for nothing."

"Yeah, but you had a life with Mom. She gave you the opportunity to love her."

"Are you sure there's no hope with Jess?"

"It sure seemed that way."

Dale opened his mouth to speak when Patti O'Malley walked over. Nick and Dale both looked up at the same time.

Patti stared right at Nick. "I don't mean to interrupt, but I'd like to speak with you if I may."

Dale offered his seat, taking a walk into the crowd.

"I hope you didn't come here to add insult to injury," Nick said.

Her eyes revealed she was in no mood to joke. "No, that would be my husband's job."

"Fair enough. What can I do for you? Because I know you didn't come over here to chat."

"No, I didn't." She held out a small box, the size a bracelet or pendant might come in from a jewelry store.

"What's this?" he asked.

"Open it."

Nick hesitated. He wasn't sure he really wanted to open it, but he did. Inside the square box was a bronze-looking medal, a round medallion on a blue ribbon. The inscription read *Jackson O'Malley, First place music competition, ninth grade division, Bridgetown High School.*

"He was very proud of that award. It was the only time he ever won, but he kept it near his bed, and sometimes I would see him take it out and look at it. It kept him going when he had doubts about his life. Perhaps he *had* found what he was really meant to do after all."

Nick rubbed the medal between his fingers, staring at Jack's name on the inscription.

"Why are you giving it to me?"

"Because I think he would want you to have it. Because you were a big inspiration to him and to his music. And because I listened to the song you sent my husband. I know you loved Jack. I never doubted that. I also know you didn't intend to harm him. But you did. I'm not so ignorant to think that Jack didn't play a part in his own demise. But please don't fault us if we struggle with emotions we find very difficult to control. Forgiveness isn't easy, Nick."

He nodded his agreement with glossy eyes.

"I'm not as strong-willed as my husband. Jack was a lot like him in many ways. I just wanted you to know that we don't hate you. I don't hate you. We're just not ready to make amends. I am proud of you, though, the changes you're making. Jack would be proud too."

Nick had a hard time holding back brimming emotions. She'd said everything he needed to hear.

She got up to leave, patting one hand to his leg.

"Mrs. O'Malley."

She faced him. "Yes?"

"He had your gentle spirit. He never would have admitted it, but he was more like you than maybe you realized."

She put a hand to her chest. "Thank you."

He nodded. "Thank *you.*"

She walked away from him, and as she stepped through a passing line of people, he could see Ben waiting for her in the distance. His penetrating stare sent chills through Nick's bones. Their eyes met once again, just like they had at the cemetery. He wondered what Mr. O'Malley was thinking. Their eyes were glued for only a moment, and for a brief second Nick thought he almost saw a half smile on Ben's face. Not a happy smile, but one of agreement and understanding. He could have been wrong, but there was something there, something different in that look from every grimace they'd exchanged since Nick returned.

Ben nodded, lingering for a moment as he made eye contact with Nick, and then he led Patti away with his hand on her back.

"You just walked away?" Mark asked Jess as he scarfed down a greasy hunk of fried chicken under a red-and-white-striped food vendor tent.

"Technically, yes. What was I supposed to do? Okay, don't answer that."

"Talk to him about it, tell him how you feel, listen to—"

"Okay, okay. I said don't answer that."

"Jess, he's sincere. I think he really cares about you."

"And that obligates me to cater to his feelings regardless of mine?" she snapped.

Mark dipped his chicken breast into a vat of honey mustard, shoving half of it in his mouth.

"What are your feelings?" he asked, still chewing.

"About what?"

"About Nick."

She pondered. How was she supposed to answer that?

Mark grew impatient. "So you just like him as a friend?"

"I didn't say that."

"Okay, more than a friend then."

"I didn't say that either."

"You aren't saying much of anything. It's kind of annoying."

"I'm annoying? That's rich coming from the caveman eating chicken."

"It's a simple question, Jess. Do you feel the same way he does or not?"

She let out a deep sigh. "It doesn't matter if I do or don't. The problem is that I don't know if I'm ready to move on in that way. I don't know if I can ever have that kind of relationship with a man again. When I met Patrick, my whole world changed. I gave him everything I had, devoted myself to him. When things got bad I lost a piece of who I was. I can't go through that again."

Mark sucked the grease from his fingers. "Patrick was a scoundrel. He was arrogant and selfish, with no thought for your feelings. Who says Nick would put you through that?"

"I'm not saying he would. I'm just saying it's a huge step. It's a big deal. I won't go into it lightly."

"No, you're evading the whole subject and you're making excuses. Come on, Jess, let's get real. You know how you feel. You just aren't ready to admit it out loud to yourself yet."

"Oh, you claim to know how I feel?"

"Are you even listening to me? I said *you* know how you feel. You have to be willing to take a leap. If you're not, then things will stay as they are."

"Is that so bad?" she asked.

"I don't know. Is it?"

She hated her brother's smug demeanor, his know-it-all comebacks. He'd always been quick-witted and impossibly perceptive. Mark had a true knack for seeing the bigger picture and guiding others down less turbulent paths.

"It scares me," she said. "A lot."

Mark wiped his face, placed his elbows on the table, and folded his hands in front of his chin. "Sometimes the best things in life come from the scariest decisions we ever had to make."

"Sometimes isn't always," she shot back.

"No, but you'll never know for sure unless you take a chance. He didn't propose marriage. He just told you he loved you, and in a very romantic way, I might add. There's no pressure, Jess. It costs you nothing to get a little closer and see where that path might lead. If you think you might feel the same way too."

"Maybe," she said.

"The flipside is letting him walk away and realizing too late he's someone you don't want to live without."

Dang it. There he goes again.

"I see what you're saying," she said.

"And?"

"And I'll think about it."

Mark nodded. He knew she would, and she did. She thought about it the rest of the afternoon, walking around the festival alone, finding quiet areas near the river, clearing her head and searching her heart. She needed space, time away from people, time to really think.

Music chimed up, away from the river, in the direction of the festival stage. Jess pictured Nick playing his guitar, how natural and at ease he looked, how happy he seemed when he played. She thought about walking back to watch him, but she couldn't. His declaration still hung fresh in her mind, making her question so many things she thought she'd already figured out.

Jess heard footsteps behind her as she watched birds flying low above the Piedmont River. When she turned, she was greeted by Nick's half-cocked smile.

"Mind if I join you?" he asked.

"I thought you were playing."

"Told the guys I needed a break. They can handle it without me."

"I was going for a walk."

"I don't want to intrude," he said.

"You're not."

He came closer. "I hoped I'd have another chance to talk to you."

She looked away.

"I don't want to scare you off, but I'd be an idiot if I didn't tell you how I feel. Maybe that's selfish, but I can't just be your friend anymore. I don't want to just be your friend."

"Why the sudden change?"

He shook his head. "Jess, if you think this is sudden . . . I don't know how to put it into words, but this has been taking shape for a while. I'm a different person because of you. You're the first person who's ever come into my life and made me question who I want to be and how I can be better. I think about you all the time. You're the first thing on my mind when I wake up and the last image I see in my head before I fall asleep. I'm happy when I'm with you. I smile when I think of you. How many superlatives do I need to give to show you that you're the most amazing thing that's ever happened to me?"

Jess didn't have a response, but not for lack of trying. "I don't know what to say."

"You have to say something. I feel like I'm hanging off a cliff here."

"I don't know if I'm ready for this," she said, averting her eyes.

He stepped closer. "Does that mean there's hope? Do you care about me even a little?"

"I care about you a lot. Nick . . . I . . . this is too hard. You're asking me to take a leap."

"I'm not asking you to do anything. I've got all the time in the world, the rest of my life."

"Don't put your life on hold for me."

He took one step closer, close enough to see the changing flecks of color in her eyes. "You *are* my life. I can't imagine it without you. I don't want to imagine it without you."

Jess swallowed a growing lump in her throat. Fighting nerves, her hands began to tremble. She could feel her chest rising and falling faster.

"You deserve more," she said.

Nick could feel her trembling when he touched her hand, holding it ever so lightly in his own.

"If I lived a thousand lifetimes and righted a million wrongs, I still wouldn't deserve you. I will never deserve you no matter what I do. I can never be the man who belongs in your arms, but I'd get on my knees to beg you for a chance, just one moment to show you how much I love you."

She'd only been this close to him once before, when he'd tried to kiss her on the porch. She was glad they didn't kiss that day. It would have been for the wrong reasons, bad timing, a different Nick. She'd regretted hurting him, but she didn't feel then what she knew she felt now. Jess didn't know if it was love or the deepest, most meaningful friendship she'd ever had in her life, but she found herself drawn to him. She felt safe with him. She felt more comfortable with Nick Miller than any other man she'd ever known, including Patrick.

"I've been hurt, Nick. I have all these unresolved issues. I'm still a mess. It might not work. What if we end up hating each other?"

He laughed, grinning from ear to ear. "If you think there's any chance on this earth I could ever hate you, dislike you even, then you have so much to learn about how I feel about you and what you mean to me. Sweet Jess. I love you more than my own life.

And I just got another chance at it. I'm not going to waste a single moment. I know what I want, but I'll wait forever from afar if I have to."

"I can't promise you anything. I don't want to hurt you."

"I don't need promises. There are a lot of promises we can't make. I can't promise I'll never hurt you. I can't promise you a perfect life. I don't even know what that is. I can promise to love you with all that I am, with all that I have to offer, no matter what happens, for the rest of my life . . . if you'll let me."

Patrick had never spoken to her like that. Jess had never been cared for as though she were a gift to be treasured. Nick opened his heart to her, his whole heart. She'd only claimed a very small portion of Patrick's.

"Nick."

"Yes?"

"I'm not good at this."

He smiled, taking a final step closer, as close as could be in front of her.

"Neither am I."

Jess released a tense sigh, looking down, a soft smile gracing her face. Nick tilted his head toward hers, lifting her chin to face him. A moment passed, meaningful stares in each other's eyes. There really *are* looks that can speak a thousand words.

"I'd like to kiss you," he said.

"You're asking my permission?"

"Yeah. I don't want to mess this up."

She smiled. Then nodded. She closed her eyes, and for a brief moment she thought she might actually stop breathing.

Nick started to close his eyes, but he couldn't help watching her as he leaned in, taking her head in his hands, pulling her mouth to his. He kissed her softly at first, then deeper as the warmth and smell of her skin, the softness of her lips, stirred his love and passion for her. This amazing woman he held in his arms had helped him realize how precious his own life was. He'd hold her all day, for all eternity if he could. Just having her close, he felt whole again, his heart healed quicker. She filled a void he didn't know he had.

"I love you, Jess. And you don't have to say it back." Nick hugged her close.

She turned her face toward his cheek and kissed it. "I do love you," she whispered in his ear. "I'm just not ready to say it yet."

"You just did," he whispered back.

They walked by the river, hand in hand, talking. They talked about everything as though they had never really spoken before. Nick told her more about Votive, about Jack. He shared memories of his mother and recent conversations with his father. Jess told him more about Patrick and their life together, and about Abby. They would have walked until dark, but a chilled air had Jess shivering, so Nick walked her to her car.

"Pretty lame that I can't drive," he said.

"You'll get there. I'll help you."

"Why do you have so much faith in me?"

"Because I see you for who you really are, not the guy you put on for the world. You're a pretty great guy when you get out of your own way."

"Ha! You make a valid point."

"Thank you."

"So, just pretty great?" he asked.

"Well, you know, you do have a habit of trespassing on stranger's porches." Jess winked.

Nick leaned in and kissed her forehead. "That was the best day of my life."

"No, it wasn't. The best is yet to come."

"Promise?" he asked.

"Promise." This time Jess kissed him before getting into her car and driving home.

She left Nick in the festival parking lot, knowing he'd see her the next day on that fateful front porch with his rather lucky acoustic guitar. He wondered if it had brought Eric Clapton as much good fortune as it had him. Probably not. Clapton made his own good fortune. He must have known someone out there needed it more.

By the time Nick found his dad, fireworks were about to start. He wished Jess had stayed, but if all went well, perhaps they'd have many years of fireworks, river walks, and music playing together.

36

SONGS ON THE PORCH

A perfect Sunday afternoon. Warm spring breeze. Sun shining. The five of them sat on Jess's porch, Mark, Elise, Sadie, Nick, and Jess. Conversation mostly, but Nick couldn't resist breaking out his guitar. He sat on the porch rail, perfectly content as he strummed his six-string, glancing at Jess every so often. He was at peace. He finally had a reason to push forward. He had someone in his life who completed the best parts of him and was willing to help him manage the worst parts. He'd found a hope and a purpose on that porch.

Nick continued playing and Mark started guessing the song titles. After three correct answers Nick decided to play one he didn't think Mark would know. He struggled at first, but Nick could tell he recognized it. It was on the tip of his tongue.

"Okay, don't tell me. I have to guess this one." Mark listened intently.

"Sing it," Elise said to Nick.

"No, I want to get this. No help."

"Well, you know I'll never get it," Jess said.

Nick strummed harder. His head bobbed up and down, back and forth. He couldn't resist singing. It was such a catchy tune.

"Ed Sheeran! 'I'm a Mess,'" Mark blurted out.

Nick nodded his head and kept playing.

"Ha-ha! Yes! I really feel like I should have gotten that sooner."

"Are we playing *Name That Tune*? Because I want out if we are." Jess shot Mark a sarcastic look.

"Sore loser." Mark winked back.

Sadie slept peacefully in Elise's arms, snuggled against her mother's gray sweater. Elise swayed, gently rocking her while Mark stroked Sadie's face, watching her sleep.

So many things had changed. Jess watched her handsome stranger play his guitar, making beautiful melodies. He wasn't a stranger anymore. He was the best chance meeting she'd ever had. Nick had helped her realize how distant from herself she had become. He'd given her a reason to leave her porch and live again. She blushed when he looked up and grinned at her, his eyes revealing how much he cared. This mysterious trespasser in the rain had helped her find her way and opened her heart to love again.

"I've got one." Mark raised a finger. "What's that song? It's on the radio all the time." He walked over to Nick.

Nick stopped playing. "That narrows it down," he teased.

"It's by a woman. I think she has dark hair. Beautiful singing voice."

"You're going to need to be a little more specific." Nick grinned, stealing another obvious glance over at Jess.

"Got it! Sara Bareilles. 'Love Song.'"

"Not exactly a macho song. You a closet chick music fanatic?" Nick grinned, tuning his guitar.

"Heard it driving into work one day. It's a catchy tune."

"Yeah, I bet you have some Taylor Swift CDs hidden at the house," Nick said.

"I like all kinds of music," Mark asserted.

"Is this it?" Nick started playing "Love Song."

"Yep, that's the one."

Nick strummed the first verse, and when he got to the chorus, Mark started singing. Nick joined in, and they sang together, joking as though they were singing to each other.

Jess rolled her eyes, glancing toward Elise, who shook her head.

Their little duet continued and they sang louder with each verse, making silly faces and eventually involving the women in their antics.

"You do realize that song is written to a man by a woman," Jess said.

"Where's your sense of humor?" Mark threw a cushion at her.

"It left when you got here." She tossed the cushion back at him.

Nick couldn't help but laugh.

"She thinks she's quippy." Mark pretended to throw the cushion at her again.

"I know I'm quippy." Jess shot him a sassy look.

"You get it from me."

"Oh, whatever." She rolled her eyes.

"This is what I have to put up with, Nick," Elise warned him.

They laughed and joked, relaxing on the porch. The simplest of days. Nick didn't need complicated. He'd had plenty of that. He'd written the book on complicated. Everything he needed was right there in front of him, and he would do whatever it took to hold on to it. He listened to them tell family stories and reminisce about the past. He felt like he was becoming part of their family. He hoped he would be. Then Nick thought about Alan, who was still waiting for an answer. He decided he would call Alan when he got back to his dad's house and tell him he planned to stay in Bridgetown. He would decline the record deal, but not because he wouldn't consider going solo. He refused to go back to a life where he was forced to live for other people and lose himself in the process. If Nick was going to continue performing, he was going to do it on his terms. He'd earned that much.

Nick could take his time. There was no rush. He still had so much to work on, things he wanted to do. He thought about visiting Drew once his probation was over. Maybe he would take Jess. Drew would like her. If Morgan liked her, maybe she wouldn't hate Nick so much. The thought of seeing Drew after so long and in his condition scared Nick a little, but he owed it to him to face it, to face him after everything that happened. If Jess was with him, he could face anything.

He propped his guitar against the porch rail, in the same spot he had when he and Jess first met, and sat down in the Adirondack chair next to hers, scooting it closer. He reached for her hand, lacing his fingers between hers. He met her eyes, stroking her index finger with his thumb. They both smiled and looked away, but they couldn't help looking back at each other again, smiling, Jess blushing and Nick's heart beating a little bit faster. Mark was talking in the background, something about a new restaurant and an old building the city tore down, but Nick's attention was focused on the beautiful angel sitting next to him who gave him a reason to try harder, be better.

"Are you two even listening?" Mark called out from across the porch.

Nick and Jess grinned at each other and looked over at Mark.

"Were you talking?" Nick smirked.

Mark squinted his eyes at Nick, then softened and gave him an approving nod. "As long as you keep her happy," he said.

Nick looked back at Jess, squeezing her hand, his heart now pounding inside his chest. "I hope I can. For as long as she'll have me."

She smiled, holding his hand a little tighter. He watched the flecks in her eyes change colors, a little more blue than green, and wished Mark and Elise weren't there so he could hold her in his arms, touch her face, kiss her lips. But holding her hand was good enough for now. He still had so much to learn, and he hoped a lifetime with her to get it right.

ACKNOWLEDGMENTS

It would be impossible to thank everyone who helped make this dream a reality. My deepest gratitude to the following people for their contributions to this book:

My dear friend and editor, Blake Leyers, for her insight, dedication, and moral support. I appreciate you more than you know.

My editor, Julie Breihan, for her wit, wisdom, and the incredible gift she has for putting my brain on the right track and helping me see the bigger picture. We make a great team!

Jacque for allowing me to pick her brain about physical and occupational therapy. You are a wealth of information.

To my dearest friends who read what I write in the early stages of each manuscript and urge me forward. Lynnda, you kept me going when I wanted to give up. Audrey, you answered every text I sent you with random medical questions and cheered me on through countless sentences and word changes. I can always count on you both at midnight when I'm still up and need advice. You are my champions.

Laura Hill, who encouraged me to keep going and guided me along the way. You are my hero.

Angela Redden at Reading Rock Books for her unwavering support.

Karen and Zera for their artistic expertise, inspiration, and for doing what they do best. You create beautiful things.

Sharon for her proofreading and beta reading skills. Your phone calls were the highlight of the process.

Elijah for inspiring Jack and giving him a life on the page like no one else could.

And the biggest thanks and many hugs to my family and friends who keep me strong, keep me sane, and love me far more than I deserve.

My sons, Connor and Sean. You make me a better person.

Ashley, you are the sister I never had. Your strength amazes me.

And my husband, Brian, for everything. You are truly the better part of me.

ABOUT THE AUTHOR

Sarah Jenkins is the former director of Players of Light Theater Troop, a non-profit community theater program benefitting Vanderbilt Children's Hospital.

She has been a high school tutor and youth mentor for over a decade.

Sarah lives on a small farm near Nashville, Tennessee with her husband, two sons, and their dog, Charlie.

Every Beaten Path is her debut novel.